If Not Us
Life Goes On 4

Surviving the Evacuation

Frank Tayell

If not now, when? If not us, who?

Surviving the Evacuation: If Not Us
Life Goes On, Book 4

Published by Frank Tayell

ISBN: 9798 749 756 821
All people, places, and (most) events are fictional.

Post-Apocalyptic Detective Novels
Strike a Match 1. Serious Crimes 2. Counterfeit Conspiracy
Strike a Match 3. Endangered Nation & Work. Rest. Repeat.

Surviving The Evacuation / Here We Stand / Life Goes On
Book 1: London, Book 2: Wasteland
Zombies vs The Living Dead
Book 3: Family, Book 4: Unsafe Haven
Book 5: Reunion, Book 6: Harvest
Book 7: Home
Here We Stand 1: Infected & 2: Divided
Book 8: Anglesey, Book 9: Ireland
Book 10: The Last Candidate
Book 11: Search and Rescue
Book 12: Britain's End, Book 13: Future's Beginning
Book 14: Mort Vivant, Book 15: Where There's Hope
Book 16: Unwanted Visitors, Unwelcome Guests
Life Goes On 1: Outback Outbreak
Life Goes On 2: No More News
Life Goes On 3: While the Lights Are On
Book 17: There We Stood
Life Goes On 4: If Not Us

For more information, visit:
http://www.FrankTayell.com
www.facebook.com/TheEvacuation
http://twitter.com/FrankTayell

Part 1

Evacuation

Australia and Africa

The Investigation So Far

Canberra International Airport, Australia

Canberra's first-class lounge echoed with a metallic, and occasionally wooden, clatter as four Australian conscripts opened travel-worn crates of AKM assault rifles: Clyde Brook, a soldier turned aid-worker; Teegan Toppley, a retired gunrunner still technically serving a four-year sentence; Bianca Clague, a former socialite who still wore her jewels; and Elaina Slater, a primary school teacher who'd volunteered as a soldier to keep her pupils safe.

"Even I know you shouldn't store guns in sand," Bianca said.

"These weren't stored," Teegan Toppley said. "They were hidden. Probably on a beach, with the location recorded on an X-marks-the-spot treasure map."

"Oh, c'mon, Teegan," Elaina said. "There's only one time in history where X ever *really* marked the spot, and it wasn't even in this hemisphere."

Clyde picked up a rifle. "These should work after a quick clean, but if you're keeping a tally of how many we've found, Elaina, wait until we've given them a test-fire."

"Oh, no. I wasn't writing that," Elaina said. "I was making notes on everything that happened."

"To whom?" Bianca asked.

"To everyone," Elaina said. "We're conscript-cops, aren't we? Cops solve crimes. The zombies, the coup, the nuclear war, that's the crime to end all crimes."

"In my experience of human nature, there will never be an end to crime," Toppley said. "It is an immutable law, and almost certainly one of Dr Dodson's rules."

"Fair dinkum," Elaina said. "Let's call this a war crime, and hope history will record it as the last in our lifetimes. I was never a big of a fan of mysteries, and this one is only half solved."

"You've landed in the wrong job," Bianca said.

"Better than being one of those conscripts sent by ship to America," Elaina said. "The pilots on the plane which just landed said those ships lost power due to the EMP and are dead in the water out in the Pacific."

"Not all of them, surely," Bianca said.

"We'll know soon enough," Clyde said. "We're here because we've all got to help each other, and the government decided conscription was the best way to get it done."

"Not me," Toppley said. "I'm here because Commissioner Qwong saved me from a short drop and a shallow grave. To think it took *two* weeks for society to collapse to the point where an oil refinery administrator decided to play Madame Guillotine."

"I know," Elaina said. "I can't believe everything fell apart so quickly."

"Oh, no, don't misunderstand me," Toppley said. "I'm shocked it took a *whole* two weeks. I should have been serving my sentence in Darwin, but a wrong turn by the wrong bus driver, and I was nearly hanged. The commissioner, and Dr Dodson, flew us to Brisbane just as it was hit by a tsunami. An hour earlier, we'd have drowned. Instead, we landed here, met you, and we all stopped the coup."

"As much as that's a cautionary lesson I'll teach as soon as I get back in the classroom," Elaina said, "your story can be summed up as a bureaucratic mix-up. Sorry, Teegan."

"Ah, how the once-mighty have fallen," Toppley said.

"We're no different," Elaina said. "There but for the slip of a pen, we could be aboard one of those conscript-ships. The satellites went down soon after the outbreak in Manhattan, and the internet didn't last much longer. For three weeks, everyone's been cut off from each other. Very little information is coming in, but I still want to know how it began, and how we know it's over, and how was it linked to the zoms?"

"Before the outbreak, a plane landed in Broken Hill," Bianca said. "Commissioner Qwong was a police inspector. Mick Dodson worked for the Flying Doctors, and Anna Dodson taught there, before she was elected to parliament. The plane is the key. It was a business jet, belonging to Lisa Kempton. Aboard was… oh, who was it? Ms Qwong said he was a carpet salesman, but he must have been a spy."

"He sold carpets," Clyde said. "The bloke's name was Guinn. Don't think the boss ever told me what his first name was. But he did just sell carpets. He was a trick, a trap, a feint, a dupe. Unimportant, except that his sister worked in the outback up by the dingo-fence. From what the sister told our boss, and what she told me, the point of sending this Guinn bloke down to Oz was to get the plane, and pilots, out of America."

"But the cartel were waiting for the plane," Bianca said.

"Exactly," Elaina said. "They kidnapped the pilots, and tortured them. Do you think it was like in the bunker? Skinned alive?"

"That's what the boss says," Clyde said. "But she's certain that it was the work of a different torturer."

"So there's more than one skin-peeler in Oz?" Elaina asked. "Well, that's a piece of news that'll keep me up at night! The Guinns flew north, on that plane, yes? All the way to Canada, and that's how we knew a fight-back was underway up there. It's how those scientists, Smilovitz and Avalon, ended up in Canberra. But what happened to the siblings next?"

"They're still stuck in the frozen never-never," Clyde said. "Word is, it wasn't them who were supposed to be on the plane, but a squad of Special Forces."

"Like you?" Bianca asked.

"I'm just an aid worker," Clyde said.

"And I'm just a jewel thief," Toppley said.

"I wish I *was* still a teacher," Elaina said. "The plane went north, the commissioner and Dr Dodson came to Canberra to report in, and then… well, then we met Ms Qwong, and we found Senator Aaron Bryce's body in the burbs a few hours later. Do you think Senator Bryce really committed suicide?"

"Probably, but maybe not," Clyde said.

"Probably not, but maybe," Toppley said.

"Surely he wouldn't have," Bianca said.

"That's that cleared up then," Elaina said. "He is, or he was, Sir Malcolm Baker's son-in-law, right? And as a senator he worked with Anna Dodson in the cabinet."

"After most of the politicians had been sent to Tasmania," Bianca said. "Those who weren't killed. The commissioner is sure some were murdered."

"Right, making it easier for Erin Vaughn and Ian Lignatiev to seize power."

"Those two's families had been kidnapped," Bianca said.

"Which is no excuse," Elaina said. "Not for mass-murder and complicity in a nuclear war."

"Oh, they can't have known about that," Bianca said.

"You *hope* they didn't," Elaina said. "But someone did. Vaughn and Lignatiev sent most of the politicians away from Canberra and killed the rest. They sent away most of the soldiers and police, too. Which is why it was Commissioner Qwong, and us, who were clearing the ruins."

"Under orders of their lead mercenary, Kelly," Clyde said. "I reckon Vaughn gave her a rank in the army so she could do what she wanted, go where she needed, deploy people how best it suited her. She gave the boss a particular assignment, a particular street to clear. But we got lost. If we hadn't, I reckon we'd have walked into a trap."

"So it was good luck we got lost and found Bryce's body," Bianca said.

"No, it was sheer chance we *didn't* walk into an ambush," Clyde said. "But if we hadn't found that body, someone else would. Bryce was famous enough to be recognised. Either his death was staged to look like suicide so there'd be no investigation, or he killed himself there, knowing his body would be discovered by someone who wouldn't cover it up. But my money is on him being murdered, and on Kelly being uncertain how much he'd told Ms Dodson. That's why they decided to kill her next."

"By locking Ms Dodson in with some zoms?" Bianca said.

"I think it was the cartel-killer, Kelly, who did that," Clyde said.

"But Vaughn and Lignatiev share responsibility," Elaina said. "We rescued Ms Dodson."

"And Oswald Owen," Bianca said.

"Well, I don't trust him," Elaina said, "even if he *is* the prime minister now. We tracked down Lignatiev, and then Kelly, and finally Vaughn. But not Sir Malcolm."

"He's a despicable man, always printing his lies and hate," Clyde said. "He's a grub who'll have crawled into a deep, dark hole to hide. Let's hope he died there."

"Even if he didn't, the coup's over, isn't it?" Bianca said.

"Is it?" Elaina asked. "I hope it is. I hope that the last bomb has been dropped and now we can rebuild, but I still don't understand why it all happened. I suppose that's what I'm trying to figure out." She put the notepad down. "An outbreak in Manhattan. Planes spread the infection all over the world. Europe and North America collapsed in days, and few places last much longer. Australia nearly collapsed. Then came the bombs, and the tsunami which wiped out the east coast and most of the Pacific Islands. New Zealand, Australia, Papua, and a few other islands, we're all that's left with however many refugees made it here before the collapse. Sixty million? Eighty? Even if it's a hundred million, there were seven billion three weeks ago."

"Some of them will still be alive," Clyde said, picking up the crowbar. "And so are we, so open the rest of the crates and let's see what we can salvage."

14th March

Chapter 1 - While the Lights Are On
Australia National University, Canberra, Australia

"You have a week to find Sir Malcolm Baker, Tess," Anna Dodson said. "If you can't, someone else will take over the investigation while you accompany the scientists to Britain and New York. We must stop the cartel. I hate to think what kind of new world people like that would create. But if we don't stop the undead, none of us will have any kind of future."

"The parliamentary session will be broadcast at six p.m.? Then I've time to grab some sleep first," Tess Qwong said. She stood, stiffly, wincing from the exertion of the night's hunt for last of the traitorous conspirators and the previous day's battle to stop the attempted coup. As she rested a hand on the back of the chair, the room dimmed. The lights had gone out. The fan had stopped humming. Outside, Anna's RSAS bodyguards had both raised their weapons, while in the corridor, people had stopped, turning to one another in baffled confusion.

Her weary limbs, bruised muscles, and cut skin forgotten, Tess quick-stepped to the light switch on the wall. She flicked it once, twice, and a third time in desperate hope, but the lights wouldn't turn on.

"Stay here, Anna," she said, opening the door. "You two, protect the —"

But before she could finish, the lights flickered back to life.

"Just a power surge, Tess," Anna said, her words edged with desperate relief. "We'll be jumping at shadows next."

"These days, the shadows jump back," Tess said. "I'll see you this evening." She nodded to the two soldiers, and hurried past the academics and conscripts busily converting the School of Medical Sciences into a fortified pharmaceutical lab, but paused when she saw the Canadian scientist, Leo Smilovitz. He'd donned a lab coat, though beneath it he wore a tool belt with a handgun in a holster designed for a power drill, a dosimeter dangling next to a flashlight, and a rock-hammer looped between the screwdrivers.

"Do you know what's going wrong with the electricity?" Tess asked, keeping her voice low. "The lights are on, but the fans aren't."

"There's been a power cut," Leo said. "The generators have kicked in, but the lights are on a different circuit to the air-con. The lights come on to aid an evacuation of the building. The fans don't, in case the reason for a power cut is a fire."

"A power cut? And you don't know why the electricity's down?" she asked. "Could it be an EMP?"

He tapped his lethally loaded tool-belt. "I'm on my way to find out."

"Don't leave the building," she said, and hurried outside.

Zach, the teenage conscript she'd drafted as her driver, snapped to a rigid attempt at attention, giving her an equally rigid salute so as not to be shown up by the second pair of RSAS soldiers standing guard by Anna's car. But those two soldiers weren't looking at him, or at Tess. Both had their hands close to their triggers, while their eyes scanned opposite halves of the horizon.

"Zach, try the radio," Tess said, opening the passenger door. "Quick."

"What's wrong, boss?" he asked.

"Just turn on the radio," she said, looking up at the streetlights, the neighbouring buildings, and the square of grass where the agricultural academics oversaw the conscripts who were converting lawns to fields.

An up-tempo song about love and betrayal warbled from the speakers.

Tess sighed. "Back in the car, Zach, and back to the airport." She raised her voice, pitching it to the two soldiers. "The radio station is still transmitting!"

One gave a nod, but neither relaxed.

Aided by exhaustion, Tess's fears swirled together as Zach sped the car, far too fast, through the growing barricades of the increasingly militarised city.

"Slow down, Zach, this isn't a street race!" she said, as he overshot a handbrake turn. "You do have a licence, right?"

"No worries, Commish," he said, which wasn't an answer to anything.

A week ago, Zach had been another civilian conscript, allocated to help clear Canberra's suburbs. He'd lied about his name, and she was increasingly convinced he'd lied about his age, too, assuming anyone had bothered to ask. In body-armour and camouflage he looked more like a kid playing dress-up than a soldier in training. But he'd proven himself loyal during the attempted coup, and that was worth a few frayed nerves as he zigzagged across the lanes.

Theirs was the only car on the road, not counting the vehicles co-opted into the junction-barricades of the city's new internal defences. As they approached the airport, a 747 overtook them overhead.

"Don't you dare try to race the plane!" she said as Zach's hand dropped to the gears.

"Wasn't even thinking of it, boss," he said, reluctantly slowing instead.

The gates to the international airport were open, but guarded. The sentries waved them through.

"Mick's by that twin-prop," Tess said. "Drive me there."

Mick Dodson was the most experienced pilot and medic in the Royal Flying Doctor Service, and stood a chance of holding the title for the whole of Australia. He was also Anna's father, and, despite the age gap, one of Tess's dearest friends. Appointed as Surgeon Emeritus of the flying doctors in the hope he'd take the hint and retire, Mick had instead taken it to mean he couldn't be fired.

Zach braked, and Tess jumped out, while Mick stepped away from the partially dismantled plane, wiping his oil-stained hands on an already oil-stained jumpsuit.

"Speeding like that, you're either trying to get away from trouble, or you're trying to catch it," Mick said.

"The power's out at the university," Tess said.

"Yep, a fire spread to a transformer up in Aranda," Mick said. "The rest of the network wasn't properly balanced to compensate. Rolling blackouts will be a nuisance for a day or two."

"How much of that is a guess, Mick?" Tess asked.

"Less than half," he said. "I stuck two private-jet pilots up in PC-12 to fly P.A.P. over the city. They spotted the smoke."

"What's P.A.P.?" Zach asked.

"Penance Air Patrol," Mick said. "It's like C.A.P., but without the combat. They thought they knew better than me how to run an airport."

Tess looked skyward. "They're radioing back what they see?" she asked.

"Our eyes in the sky," Mick said.

Tess nodded, relaxing, but only for a heartbeat. "Mick, who's going to put out the fire?"

They stared at one another in silence.

"I've still got the airport fire engines here," Mick said. "A couple of the fire-crew, too."

"Zach, drive Mick to the fire engines," Tess said. "Mick, you're not to try putting the fire out yourself. Zach, you make sure he doesn't. No arguments, Mick. Not today. Go on."

As Zach and Mick climbed back in the car, Tess turned to the now-landed 747. She didn't recognise the logo on the plane's tail, nor the uniform worn by the armed soldiers. Two were aboard the tug-truck approaching the front of the plane, while two more soldiers were aboard the set of mobile-stairs trundling towards the closed door near the tail.

The power-cut wasn't caused by a nuclear bomb. Not here. Not yet. The fire was just another in the increasingly long string of minor disasters that were occurring too frequently to be remembered, let alone be counted.

The mobile-stairs stopped four metres from the cabin door. One soldier ran to the top, the other to the tarmac, but both aimed their weapons on the cabin door. Slowly, it opened. After a seemingly interminable pause, the guns were lowered, and the stairs reversed the last few metres. The exhausted passengers were finally allowed to disembark and make their way to the quarantine-hangar. Tess headed for the terminal.

After the outbreak, an alliance of Pacific nations had emerged almost by accident. As much of the world was consumed by chaos, some local leaders packed ships with refugees as the simplest way to reduce potential infection. Those ships headed south, making landfall in Australia, New Zealand, or whichever Pacific island they had the fuel to reach. Most of the world's behemothic cruise ships had already been taking advantage of the southern-hemisphere summer. Cargo freighters had been hauling minerals from Australia, Indonesia, and the Philippines to the ever-hungry factories in the northern Pacific. Over ten thousand vessels, varying in size from large to gargantuan, with refugees crammed ten to a cabin, twenty to a corridor, with hundreds more on deck. Ports had a limited number of piers, and Australia had a limited capacity for refugees. As soon as the vessels arrived, they were refuelled and re-filled, this time with tourist-soldiers, A.D.F. retirees, refugee-recruits, and unlucky conscripts. Armed with rumours the Americans and Japanese would supply weapons at the northern fronts, the ships were sent back to sea.

Then came the nuclear exchange. But most of the missiles in the first wave were detonated in the ocean. In turn, this triggered a tsunami. Ships caught in the EMP were left dead in the water. Those in port were swamped by the sky-scraping waves. Military vessels had been gathered together into massive fleets centred around U.S. nuclear-powered aircraft carriers. Those had been destroyed in the second wave of nuclear missiles, fired by the nuclear-armed submarines which had obeyed their last suicidal orders for mutually assured destruction.

Though neither she, nor even Anna, knew the full extent of the damage, not all shipping would have been lost. Not all ports would have been submerged. Only a fraction of a percent of global sea capability now remained, but planes still arrived. Fewer than a week ago, and each with only a few hundred refugees aboard. Where the group aboard this 747 came from was a mystery. They traipsed towards quarantine in the repurposed hangar. After twenty-four hours, they would be transferred to a work detail in the city. But not the unaccompanied children.

Tess followed the sound of a guitar to the now-dormant baggage-claim hall, where a terrifyingly sinister man was singing a song about a kangaroo-sled team.

"And the 'roo bounced," he sang. "And the sled bounced, and the driver went… Everyone?"

"Flying!" about half of the children chorused.

With a flourish, Dan Blaze strummed a finish. A young woman in a matronly pink cardigan stepped forward. "Thank *you*, Mr Blaze," she said with pedagogical professionalism. "Line up, children. In pairs, please. We'll take you to the boarding school where breakfast awaits. I think you'll find the bus a smidge more comfortable than a sled pulled by kangaroos."

Blaze strummed a quick chord, gave a bow, and made his way over to Tess.

When they'd first met, he'd been a convict ten minutes short of a long drop. Withdrawn. Watchful. Wary. The very definition of bad news walking. But in reality, he was a Canadian children's entertainer, universally recognised across the English-singing world, at least among his core audience of under-tens and their parents. Blaze had found himself playing nurse aboard a medical mercy-flight from Vancouver, and then miscategorised as a convict in Darwin. Tess had saved him from a last dance, and he'd saved her, and helped save Anna and civilisation, during the attempted coup.

"G'day, Dan," she said. "Where are the kids from?"

"Lombok," he said. "Should have landed in Darwin, but the runway was full. They were redirected here. Arrived in the middle of the night. Came in on the plane before that one," he added, gesturing outside. "That's two planes since midnight."

"What happened to their parents?" she asked.

"They knew this could be the last plane out," Blaze said. "They stayed behind so more kids could board."

She nodded. "Who's the teacher?"

"She said she'd been sent by Ms Nguyen," Blaze said. "They're going to a refugee camp at a race course we're now calling a school. We're storing up problems for later."

"For at least a generation," Tess said. "So let's hope we have many future years in which to regret what we did today. Where's Sophia?"

"In the main quarantine centre keeping watch with the soldiers," he said, tapping his holster. "I said I'd go help after these kids were collected."

"Leave that to the soldiers," Tess said. "I've a job for you both. Grab Sophia, and meet me up in the lounge."

She paused a moment to watch the last of the refugee children heading away. Civilisation had fallen, but they might just have caught enough pieces to patch it back together.

In the early days of the outbreak, while she was still in Broken Hill, most of Canberra's police officers, along with the military units including Parliament's ceremonial ADF guards, had been dispatched to the outback and the coast, to deal with rising numbers of the undead. Yes, in part they had been sent where calm minds, steady hands, and familiarity with a firearm could assist the most. But their deployment was also a deliberate policy of Erin Vaughn and Ian Lignatiev's to remove loyal obstacles before their attempted coup.

Now, with few personnel, a patchy electricity supply, and with the data-centres powered down, there was little purpose in operating out of the AFP headquarters. Even so, she'd rather the sign on the first-class lounge read something more professional than *Team Stonefish*. But that was the name Zach had picked for their original crew of conscripts, and it had stuck.

She opened the door, and entered an armourer's workshop.

"G'day, Commish," Elaina Slater said. "Is there more trouble?"

"No more than usual," Tess said. "Where did these rifles come from?"

"They were aboard the plane which came in from Lombok with all those kids," Clyde Brook said. "Should have been left with the defenders, but must have been overlooked. Twelve crates of AKMs dragged out of storage."

"Stored in a sandy pit below ground," Teegan Toppley added. "It's a disgrace keeping weapons like this."

"We're triaging them," Clyde said. "Stripping and rebuilding, but we'll leave the cleaning to whomever is issued with them. Reckon we can salvage seventy percent."

"I thought I told you lot to get some sleep," Tess said.

"Day-time sleep is notoriously bad for one's mental well-being," Bianca Clague said.

Bianca claimed to be a pastry chef from Adelaide, but her accent and jewellery, worn in addition to her new uniform, said she'd been more likely to own the patisserie than work there. In her late forties, she still wore a wedding ring, though she never spoke of her husband.

Clyde Brook *did* speak of his husband, and his son, but never his more distant past. From his easy familiarity with a rifle, he'd spent it in uniform. Tess guessed he'd been Special Forces, but Clyde would only ever say he was now a charity worker.

Teegan Toppley's own reinvention put those two to shame. The one genuine convict in their group, her sentence for tax evasion was part of a complex plea-deal where she'd been allowed to return to Australia for cancer treatment. The press report during her trial described her as being a forty-six-year-old jewel-thief, but the police report listed her as a fifty-nine-year-old arms-dealer. That report had been sealed, and the deal agreed, because it also contained details of best-forgotten negotiations on behalf of the Australian government with groups diplomatically described as rebels.

Elaina Slater, by contrast, wasn't trying to be anyone other than herself: a twenty-five-year-old primary-school-teacher from Wagga Wagga whose gaze was alternating between a firing pin and the rifle which was otherwise reassembled.

Add in Zach, Dan Blaze, and Sophia Peresta, the former yoga teacher, who'd taken a bullet to the arm during the coup, and only one word could adequately describe her team: conscripts.

But they were loyal. Not just to Tess and the government in which Anna was now deputy prime minister, but to the notion of restoring a civilisation built on democracy, justice, and equality. Another descriptor could be given to them, and to her, and Anna, Mick, and even Oswald Owen: stubbornly over-optimistic.

"Did any ammo get shipped with these guns?" Tess asked.

"That's in those crates by the bar," Clyde said, gesturing to the corner of the room.

"Ammunition is like alibis," Toppley said. "One can never have enough."

"A dollar in the crim-jar," Elaina said. "I think you mean that ammunition is like *evidence*. D'you know if any of the new factories are making more?"

"I know they're prioritising canning, so we don't waste any food," Tess said. "And I know they hoped the conscripts would be equipped by the U.S. when they were dumped ashore in Mexico, but those were Lignatiev and Vaughn's plans."

"I'll add ammo to the list," Elaina said. "Clyde, happy Christmas." She pushed the incorrectly assembled rifle towards him, and placed the pin on top, before taking out a notepad and pen.

"What list?" Tess asked.

"For Ms Nguyen," Elaina said. "We're writing down everything which might be forgotten, in case everyone else assumes someone is dealing with it."

"Add a city-wide fire-crew," Tess said. "And finish up because I've got a job for us all."

The door opened, and Zach slouched in. "Wow. That's a lot of guns."

"Which aren't toys," Elaina said, her tone reflexively switching to teacherly-stern.

"Yeah, I know," Zach said, just as reflexively subdued.

"What did you do with Mick?" Tess asked.

"He's gone to quarantine to inspect the new arrivals," Zach said. "They came from Mozambique. Perth sent them."

"Perth's ferrying people here?" Elaina asked.

Zach shrugged. "I guess."

"What about the fire?" Tess asked.

"Oh, no worries. Mick sent the fire engine, and a couple of vans," Zach said.

"*Doctor* Dodson," Elaina corrected, and Tess couldn't help but smile.

"What adventure did you have planned for us, Commissioner?" Toppley asked.

"Ms Dodson has given me a week to wrap up the investigation into the coup," Tess said. "After that, I'm playing escort for those Canadian scientists."

The door opened again. Sophia Peresta and Dan Blaze entered. Like the other conscripts, Sophia wore the requisitioned grey and black clothes-shop-camouflage they were calling a uniform. Unlike them, her arm was in a sling.

"Any trouble in quarantine?" Tess asked.

"Any zombies?" Zach added.

"Not yet, and they've been on that plane for twenty hours already," Sophia said.

"From Mozambique?" Tess asked.

"Flew into Perth, and barely landed," Sophia said. "They weren't allowed off the plane, but were refuelled, and sent here."

"Elaina, can I borrow that pen and notepad, thanks. Sophia, I'm allocating you as personal assistant to Anna Dodson. As long as she needs that wheelchair, there might be some very *personal* assistance for which I don't think her SAS bodyguards were trained."

"Like what?" Zach asked, puzzled. "Clyde said the diggers train for everything."

"Dan, you're on chair-pushing duty," Tess added, raising her voice over Clyde's snort of laughter. "Keep your rifle close, but your guitar closer. Over the next week, Anna's doing a tour of the refugee camps. She'll have soldiers for a bodyguard, but a bloke carrying a guitar will make her look less like a warlord. Everyone you meet will be desperate, hungry, and terrified. Singing a few songs to the kids might give people pause before they fling a brick."

"How long will we be away?" Sophia asked. "I only saw my daughter for five minutes this entire last week."

"She's at the university?" Tess asked.

"At the crèche," Sophia said. "My husband's digging fields there. So is my mother, unless they've dug graves for one another by now. I know Alice is being looked after, but it's just not the same, not when I know she's so close."

"Anna's not leaving until tomorrow," Tess said. "So you'll have time to visit after you report in. There's supposed to be a broadcasted session of parliament tonight where some state representatives and politicians returning from Hobart will be sworn in as a new parliament. They'll give a speech blaming Sir Malcolm Baker, Erin Vaughn, and Ian Lignatiev for the coup, and acknowledge Oswald Owen as prime minister. You don't need to be there for that. Anna will probably be away for a week, but when she gets back, things should be returning to normal."

"Things are okay in Tasmania, then?" Clyde asked.

"Your husband's there, yes?" Tess asked.

"And my son," Clyde said.

"I've heard no bad things," Tess said.

"Clyde could go there, couldn't he?" Zach asked. "I mean, we just saved the world, didn't we? He deserves a reward. Fair's fair, right?"

"That's not how the army works," Clyde said. "Or the police. Or a society. We've got to help those nearby, and hope those near our dearest do the same."

Tess held out the pen. "Write a letter, Clyde. I'll ask Mick to make sure it's on the next plane heading south. Maybe in a day or two, we can fly you down to pick them up. But first, we've got to close the chapter on the coup."

“And find Sir Malcolm Baker, right?” Elaina asked.

“In a perfect world, yes,” Tess said. “Baker is our only lead. We know he was backing the coup in a bid to get his son-in-law, Aaron Bryce, into the number-one job. A month ago, we’d identify every property Baker owned, and send a strike-team to each, followed by analysts to comb through every digital file and scrap of paper, locate every contact, and lean on them until the truth popped loose. That’s not an option now.”

“But this inconvenience cuts both ways,” Toppley said. “He’ll have just as much difficulty putting together a second attack, or even an escape.”

“Exactly,” Tess said. “He’s probably in some shack in the bush, dreading his Ned Kelly moment. We’ve got a week to ensure he’s not an active threat. Our best bet is to dig up a generator, find a hacker, and see if any tax records can be recovered here in Canberra. We’ll find his registered businesses, and start there. We won’t find him, but maybe the address of the shack is cached in a computer.”

“His charity was on the waterfront in Brisbane,” Clyde said. “Massive place. Huge ballroom. Beautiful views from the sky-terrace. If the press were attending, particularly the rival press, he’d rent the space to genuine charities on condition he got a positive mention or twelve.”

“What kind of charity did he run?” Elaina asked.

“Mono-directional vertical income redistribution,” Clyde said. “It was a tax dodge. Just like his warehouse. I forget the name of the suburb. Place to the east of the city.”

“Crestmead,” Elaina said. “He was going to open a factory to make slot machines. Got the land for a song, and then had the pokies made overseas and just used the warehouse for storage. It was supposed to be a hundred jobs, but ended up being ten. I’d an aunt who used to make the push-plates and frames. Baker bought them out and shut them down.”

“A warehouse doesn’t sound a likely place for a millionaire’s bunker,” Tess said. “And the old waterfront is now a swamp.”

"I might know where he could be," Bianca said. "It'd be somewhere remote, but not too remote, right? Away from desperate refugees, but close enough to an airport he could reach it if he had to fly in. Do you remember Denis Bergoff?"

"The spin-bowler?" Clyde said. "Made a fortune in sponsorship, and even more in match fixing."

"When he was caught, he had to sell his house," Bianca said. "It's a mansion west of Brissie. A compound, really. It has a wall and its own aquifer, and is surrounded by grazing land. Three swimming pools, two of which are outside, and a kitchen worthy of a hotel, but it's not a very big house. Only twelve bedrooms."

"*Only*?" Elaina said. "How *did* he manage?"

"Inside, there's this long hall he used for indoor cricket, and for balls," Bianca said.

"You mean bowling?" Zach asked.

"Yes, but also for dancing," Bianca said. "Every year, Bergoff held a party in the city on December first. One thousand would be invited. From them, two hundred would be selected for a special New Year's Eve event in his mansion."

"Oh, and you did the catering?" Zach asked.

"Something like that," Bianca said. "Looking back at the extravagance, and the arrogance of a function with a selection process, it's no surprise he was involved in some nefarious activity."

"Bloke was always batting above his ability," Clyde said.

"What's the link with Baker?" Tess asked.

"Sir Malcolm was never invited to the parties," Bianca said. "It was the most exclusive event of the year and he was deliberately snubbed. So when Bergoff was arrested and the house was put up for auction, Baker bought it."

"It's close to Brisbane?" Tess asked.

"About an hour's limo-ride from the airport," Bianca said. "I've got the address on my phone."

"They sent a limo for the caterers?" Zach asked.

"Did they have security?" Tess asked.

“Bergoff did,” Bianca said. “I don’t know about Sir Malcolm. I only met him twice. On both occasions, I kept my distance. Everyone knows the stories about him, right?”

“I don’t,” Zach said. “What stories?”

“I’ll tell you later,” Clyde said.

“A security team would have the contact details for the other teams in other properties,” Tess said. “Maybe including the outback rock he’s slithered under. Bianca, find a map that shows us where this place is. Sophia, Dan, you better report to Anna. Clyde, gear everyone else up. We’ll assume they have security, so I want everyone in body-armour. I’ll offer a pardon to any guard who’ll talk. But after the flooding, Brisbane’s on the brink. We’re as likely to find armed refugees there as rent-a-cops. I’ll see if Mick can find us a plane.”

Chapter 2 - No Ball Games in the Garage
Mount Forbes, Queensland, Australia

"Of course Dr Dodson's flying," Clyde said, as their plane soared skyward. "That bloke's done so many road-landings, if you put him in an ambulance, he'd try to take off."

Which was, more or less, what Mick had said when Tess had asked for a pilot and a plane. Mick had also told them that Brisbane Airport was underwater. So was Jacob's Well. An A380 had failed to land in Archerfield and had left a crater where the runway had been. A helicopter-based rescue of those stranded in the city was being run out of Caboulture, but she couldn't pinpoint that with a compass, let alone on a map. She'd bowed to the inevitable, and stopped arguing with the stubborn old pilot.

Bianca was in the co-pilot's seat, ready to play spotter when they came within range. According to the address Bianca had dug out of her phone, their destination was Hedricks Road, which wasn't on their map. The second line of the address, Mount Forbes, was. The mansion was eighty kilometres west of Brisbane's coastal airport, and thirty kilometres southwest of the satellite-city of Ipswich, which put it well within range of the millions of flooded-out refugees.

The Beechcraft was a civilian aircraft rather than one modified for the military or for outback service, but she assumed it had similar specifications to the planes in Broken Hill upon which Mick had lavished his attention. It was an eleven-hundred-kilometre flight. At a speed of five hundred and seventy kilometres per hour, they'd be above their target in two hours. They'd have half an hour to find the place from above, and another half hour to find somewhere to land, unless they wanted to refuel locally.

She'd allocated, and prepared for, up to twenty-four hours to search the crook's mansion. But if they found a security guard willing to trade information for a pardon, they could be back in Canberra for the start of

Oswald Owen's political showdown. She didn't need to be there for that; Bruce Hawker's soldiers would stop a coup. No one could stop a vote being called and O.O. being dethroned. But that was democracy, and what they were sweating to defend.

She turned her gaze to the window. She loved Australia from the air. Except for the giant mines, occasionally larger cities, and black-thread roads connecting each, it had barely been touched in two centuries of immigration. Mick completely, and vocally, disagreed, but that debate had kept them distracted on their way to many remote accidents and too many return flights to the morgue. Now, it was truly changing. Fast.

Grey plumes rose from the pastureland surrounding a sprawling farm. A controlled burn of undead corpses? Perhaps, but this *was* bushfire season. Puffs of cooking smoke rose from a fortified town outside of which sat a long column of stationary vehicles. Beyond the town, dust trails marked vehicles speeding north. Could it be Goulburn? Probably not, though that name had stuck in her brain from the route Mick had picked. Follow the main roads to the coast, and follow the coast north, that was how they'd find Brisbane. From there, turn west, overfly Ipswich, and then do a handbrake turn to find the mansion.

Whether or not that town was Goulburn, there were ghouls beneath the plane now. A slow-moving column, at least a hundred strong, lumbered between two low, grassy hills. Gravity kept them to the lowland, and so kept them together. One hundred wasn't so many if they attacked a settlement guarded by rifle-carrying soldiers. If the defenders were civilian-refugees armed only with tools, it would be a massacre.

She pulled the shade down, closed her eyes, and tried to banish the thought with sleep.

She was roused from an inadequately shallow slumber by Bianca's voice over the cabin-address system. "We've arrived. Our destination can be viewed on the left— sorry, the port side."

"Can't miss it," Mick added.

"Did I sleep through Brisbane?" Tess asked, raising her blind.

"And the refugee camps," Topppley said. "I'd say Brisbane jumped into a ute and moved in with Ipswich. The camps are extensive, but fortified."

Below, now, lay grassland, occasionally sloping, occasionally sunken, and just as occasionally broken by a neatly ploughed rectangle. It was mostly grazing land, though she could see no livestock. A smattering of tracks led between a sprinkling of farmhouses, but the mansion stood out, ringed by a near-gleaming white wall. Inside, straight lines and ninety-degree angles marked the alternating raised and sunken lawns, now turned brown. The late summer heat had boiled the swimming pools green, but the house glistened white, like the outer wall.

Two storeys high, with a balcony at the rear, and a large driveway in the east leading to a solid gate. In the north was an extended rooftop terrace, while the southern side was dotted with solar panels. It was an odd feature for a house of Sir Malcolm's, whose newspapers devoted more ink to astrology than climate science. Odd unless you were worried about a failure of the grid. Behind the house, and running to the compound's rear wall, was a garage almost the length of a hangar, covered in wilting brown grass. Behind that, a jet-black road sliced through the pastureland, about ten kilometres in length.

"I'm going to set us down on that road," Mick announced. "I'll give her one low pass to check for obstacles, a sharp turn, then a quick landing, so buckle-up and hold onto your lunch."

"What was the name of that mining company who were running the outback opal mine?" Toppley asked.

"Harris Global," Tess said. "I just had the same thought. It looks like a runway, doesn't it?"

"There are bodies by the house," Clyde said. "Near the rear. By the garage."

"It looks more like a plane hangar," Toppley said.

It was a disconcertingly smooth and quiet landing, which spoke of how much money had gone into the surface. A fact confirmed by a visual inspection when Tess followed Clyde out of the plane. The roadside trees had been removed, and the pasture on either side had no drainage ditch.

"Clear," Clyde said, letting his rifle drop to the low-ready with the barrel aimed at the road. "No movement from the compound."

"No smoke, either," Elaina said, as the rest of the team climbed out of the plane. "But I saw solar panels, so maybe that's why."

"This surface isn't wide enough for a runway," Mick said. "It's just a road. But a good one. Too good for out here. A heavy tractor would churn it to shreds."

"So why build it?" Zach asked.

Clyde whistled, and pointed away from the compound, across the gently rising pasture to where a figure lumbered out of the shadows of a slumping tuckeroo tree.

"Zom," Zach said.

"Hold fire," Clyde said, raising his rifle, a suppressed HK416 which had originally belonged to the RSAS, but which Bruce Hawker had given Tess in Broken Hill. She'd given it to Clyde, as he'd proved himself the best shot in their team, and swapped it for a shotgun, but hoped she'd need nothing more than the Taser counterbalancing the pistol on her other hip. Everyone else was similarly armed with what they'd scrounged, largely from the mercenaries who'd attempted the coup.

The bullet whispered from the suppressed assault rifle. The shape tumbled into the wilted grass, and Tess stepped away from the plane. "Mick, how long would you need to take off?"

"Less time than it'll take for you lot to climb aboard," he said.

"Fine. Wait here with Zach and Elaina. I'll take Clyde, Teegan, and Bianca, and be back in twenty."

"Not on your life," Mick said. "Not on *my* life. Rule-one from every horror movie ever made: the pilot dies first. Besides, since I can't leave without you, there's no point me kicking my heels here."

Tess knew him too well to argue. "Clyde, take point. Bianca, you're with Clyde. I've got the rear."

"Stick to the road. Watch the long grass," Clyde said. "Listen for noise. A lot of noise. Zoms aren't going to sneak up on us."

"Not the best spot," Mick said, falling into step next to Tess. "No, it's not where I'd build an apocalyptic retreat. It's too close to Ipswich."

"About thirty kilometres, isn't it?" Tess asked, scanning the grassland.

"Thereabouts. Couldn't tell you how far to the coast because I'm not sure where that is now. Picked up a bit of radio chatter before we turned west. Very officious."

"From the refugee camps?" Tess asked.

"I was told to keep the airspace clear," Mick said.

"You should have told them who you were."

"I did. They were unmoved, which shows things are getting back to normal. It sounded organised. Or getting that way. Local government, local governance, that's the answer, not top down from Canberra."

"Oh, so you agree with O.O.?" Tess said. "That's what he wants, isn't it?"

"Don't you dare tell him I approve," Mick said.

"No power lines near the road," Tess said, "but there is a transmission line over there, leading to the compound. Wonder if they've got a back-up generator, too."

"A sheep station in Western Australia," Mick said. "Somewhere in the north. The sheep would be a walking pantry."

"What are you talking about?" Tess asked.

"Where I'd pick if I'd known this was all going to happen."

"Nah, you'd have stayed in Broken Hill."

"Could be, but I wouldn't have come to a place like this."

A short strip of tarmac led from the road to the compound, widening as it drew near the white-clad walls. The hangar-garage doors were three metres tall, and thirty long, painted white rather than clad in the odd panelling coating the walls. To the right was a pedestrian door, and outside it, and the garage, was an open graveyard.

Clyde whistled, raising his rifle, but aiming the barrel low, into the high grass. "Crawler," he said, and fired. "Hold. Clear."

"They're all dead, but are they undead?" Tess said, picking a path through the bodies, noting the discarded bullet casings. A body-armoured corpse didn't have a head wound. He didn't have any legs, either. They'd been torn off, leaving ragged lumps of flesh behind and one booted foot a metre away. A second guard lay two metres closer to the wall, but he'd been shot in the face. Even before his corpse began to bloat in the late summer heat, he'd been bursting out of his body-armour.

"MP5 submachine gun," Clyde said, pointing his barrel at the corpse's still-strapped weapon. "Not a common weapon in the ADF except with Special Forces, and that bloke's one burger short of a coronary."

"No one looted the gun," Toppley said, gingerly pulling a magazine from the corpse's vest-pouch. "Or the ammunition. This magazine is fully loaded."

The bodies lay thickest next to the pedestrian door, with a third body-armoured corpse lying in the doorway itself, and atop a foundry of spent brass.

"It was a rear-guard action," Clyde said. "They were overrun as they fell back."

"Those garage doors are wide enough for a small plane," Mick said. "Tall enough, too. But I swear that road's wrong for a runway."

"This wasn't clad white when I came here," Bianca said, her voice shaking as she looked up, away from the litter of bodies. Zach was equally pale, while Elaina was turning green.

"What did it look like before?" Tess asked, stepping closer to the door.

"Grey stone, I think," Bianca said. "It wasn't white."

"This is plastic," Tess said, eyeing the hole in the facade made by a stray round. "About a centimetre thick. Weird thing to stick on your home. No lights inside. Flashlights on."

"I don't have one," Elaina said.

"It's attached to your rifle," Clyde said.

Tess slung her shotgun, drew her sidearm, slotted in her own tactical light, and switched it on. "Me and Clyde first. Everyone else, wait for the word."

"The word better not be *run*," Mick said.

The door led into a windowless waiting room with three other doors, four leather armchairs, a broken glass table, and a body atop the fractured shards. The cleaver in her skull *definitely* wasn't military issue, while the tactical gear and body-armour spoke of another private mercenary. On the wall opposite the entrance, near the door leading into the compound's gardens, was a control box which had been broken open, revealing wires and switches inside.

"Try that door," Tess said, turning to the door to the right.

"Locked," Clyde said.

"This one's not," Tess said. "In here's a security station. CCTV monitors. Coffee pot. A couple of other doors. Probably staff quarters. Yep," she added, opening a door. "Bunk room. Four bunks. Curtains pulled back. Beds made. The other door is… it's a bathroom."

"This door's unlocked," Clyde said, having crossed to the final door, nearest to the hangar-garage. "Oh, this is very definitely a garage. Was there a weapons locker in the office?"

"Nope," Tess said. "Everyone inside!" she called. "Teegan, look for some tape in that office-room. The locks are electric and the power is out. I don't want us trapped in here."

"Here," Clyde said, pulling a roll from a pouch. "Far more versatile than zip-ties."

"What kind of charity work did you say you did again?" Elaina asked, as she used the tape to cover the lock-mechanism.

"Restoration," Clyde said. "We'll go through the garage. If there's a door at the far end, it'll be close to the house."

"Hang about," Tess said, bending over the corpse. "I want to check… no. No tattoos on the arm. Which doesn't mean anything. Four bunks in that place, but it's not their permanent quarters. Four guards on duty, so call it a minimum of eight on-site. One here, one in the doorway, and two dead outside. We might find another four inside."

"Four hostiles?" Zach asked.

"Four witnesses," Tess said. "Or four zombies."

It *was* a garage, not a hangar, and it contained twelve cars, each on its own raised stand, six on either side of the long chamber, parked diagonally as if they were ready to be driven away.

"Now that's a beaut," Zach said.

"She's a Ferrari," Bianca said.

"It's hideous," Clyde said, moving light and rifle from one vehicle to the next.

"What's that yellow one?" Zach asked, walking over to it.

"A waste of steel and rubber," Clyde said.

"And polymers and rare metals," Tess said. "Must cost more than my house."

"More than my school," Elaina said as their team fanned out, moving along the rows of vehicles, and towards the far end. "You don't approve, Clyde?"

"They're built to reach maximum efficiency at a velocity higher than the speed-limit," Clyde said. "How are you supposed to enjoy the countryside when you're driving at two hundred kilometres an hour with a police helicopter buzzing overhead?"

"Yeah, but *that's* not why, is it?" Elaina said. "Didn't you go to a race track for your honeymoon?"

"I *had* to," he said. "I didn't want to, but that's the sacrifice you pay for love."

"Strewth, mate, I'd love a turn in one of these," Mick said, angling around an olive-green Bugatti.

"Where are you going, Mick?" Tess asked.

"The fuel tanks," he said, aiming his light ahead.

A clatter echoed around the room. Tess spun.

"Hostile!" Clyde barked. "Watch your six."

They'd spread out as they entered the garage. Unintentionally. Unconsciously. Unprofessionally, like the amateurs they were.

Tess was still trying to identify where the sound had come from when Elaina yelled. Her light dropped, spinning and turning, flashing in every direction.

"Hold fire!" Clyde yelled. "Hold fire!"

Tess's light found Elaina. The teacher had been knocked from her feet. Now weaponless, on the ground, she rolled from her front to her back, kicking at the curled, cold, lifeless hands coiling around her leg.

Bianca grabbed Elaina's arm, pulling. Toppley stamped on the zombie's wrist before firing her shotgun, point-blank, into its skull.

"You okay?" Tess asked as the echo of shot and scream died away.

"Fine," Elaina said as Bianca helped her up. "Wait, is that my blood?"

"Nah, that's its brains," Zach said.

"Oh, don't, Zach," Elaina said.

Tess shone her light on the corpse. "Green overalls, not body-armour. Could have been a mechanic, a gardener, or an infected refugee. We'll assume he brought friends. Stay close together from now on."

At the far end of the garage, they found another door, and another corpse in body-armour.

"It's locked with a mechanical keypad," Mick said. "But they got through using a Kalgoorlie bump-key."

"What's that mean?" Zach asked.

"An acetylene torch," Mick said, shining his light on the burn marks around the door where the lock-plate had been burned through.

It was a relief to step through the door, and back outside into the warm summer's air, but that relief only lasted long enough for a trio of flies to land on her neck. On the road, she'd been aware of the insects, but her focus had been on the bodies. Here, the flies swarmed in an infestation two hatchings away from becoming a plague.

"Ah, gerroff!" Zach snapped, ineffectually swatting at the haze.

"Insects aren't too interested in zombie corpses," Tess said. "Expect to see a lot of bodies ahead of us. Clyde, take point. We're going to the house."

A square of courtyard narrowed into a path. To either side, the plots of lawns were raised by a metre, bordered by a wilting hedge. All together it created the effect of a sunken walkway, which felt increasingly like a death trap with every step she took. Through the withered hedge she saw a trio of bodies, and a winged cloud slowly recycling the dead.

Through a white-panelled gate, just beyond a white-panelled shed from which white-painted pipes rooted into the ground, a buzzing cloud hovered above what had been a swimming pool. Four decomposed skeletons lay in the bloody soup of the mostly evaporated pool. A fifth, in a shimmering purple suit and with a knife through its eye, lay poolside, almost ignored by the buzzing swarm.

No order had to be given for everyone to hurry on to the relative calm of another sunken walkway, which abruptly became a raised path through lowered squares of lawn, then a patio outside the house itself. The slabs, made of marble rather than anything so common as granite, occupied a plot big enough for a manageable house. The furniture, again all white, was piled outside the wall-sized sliding-glass doors. That glass was dented rather than cracked, and nearly as thick as a brick. Inside the room, more furniture, this mostly old wood, had been haphazardly stacked, blocking the view.

"You'd need a miner to hack through that lot," Mick said.

"Do you see that bookshelf on top of this table?" Tess said. "That was used as a ladder up to the balcony. We can try to get in up there."

The table was white, except where insect effluvia lay field-thick, and made of wood-effect plastic. The bookcase, however, was hand-carved mahogany.

"Me first, Commish," Clyde said, jumping onto the table. Placing one foot on the bookcase, he jumped up, testing his weight. "Balcony. Door's open. Think it's a bedroom." As he was about to leap up again, shards of white plastic erupted from the stone-effect balustrade as, from inside, someone opened fire.

"Police!" Tess yelled, while Clyde ducked down, and got another burst of automatic fire in response.

"I could have told you that wasn't going to work," Mick said calmly.

"Tell me what *would* work?" Tess hissed back.

"Get ready to follow me!" Clyde hissed, before pulling a spare magazine from his belt. "Someone give me a grenade!" he yelled, at the top of his lungs before flinging the magazine over the balcony. "Fire in the hole!" he yelled, flinging himself up the bookcase and over the balcony.

As Tess clambered up onto the table, she heard glass shatter, and plaster erupt as Clyde fired a suppressed burst into the house.

"Clear!" Clyde called, even as Tess rolled over the rail.

The man lay inside the room beyond the glass doors, by a pushed-aside bed with crumpled, blood-stained sheets.

"Jeans. Bullet-proof vest," Tess said, taking in the corpse, while keeping her finger close to her trigger.

"Carrying a B&T APC submachine gun," Clyde said. "Swiss. It's not military. Not our military, anyway."

"Get everyone else up here," Tess said, crossing to the door. It was polished wood with a wooden frame rather than the white plastic panels covering everything outside. She tried the handle. The door was closed, but not locked.

"An APC9," Topplev said, making a beeline for the gun.

"What can you tell me about it?" Tess asked.

"That this man had a rich benefactor," Topplev said. "It's the kind of weapon you pick from a catalogue. Showy rather than tried-and-tested."

"But still deadly," Clyde said. "What do you want to do, Commish?"

"Wrong question, mate," Mick said. "Why aren't we running back to the plane?"

"I'm giving them a chance to steal it," Tess said. "Elaina, Bianca, watch the windows, but stay out of sight."

"You'll let them nick my plane?" Mick asked.

"Yes, because we know what it looks like, and exactly how much fuel it has in the tanks," Tess said. "We'll borrow a couple of those cars, drive to the refugee camp, commandeer another plane, and then start scouting the outback for that Beechcraft. Mick, you and Teegan watch the gardens. Elaina, Bianca, Zach, watch this door. Clyde and me will flush them out. We don't want a gunfight, understand? Let them run."

"You know what happens when people split up in movies," Mick said.

"That's why I'm glad I'm not wearing a red shirt today," Zach said. "What's the call sign so we know it's you?"

"Remember rule-one," Mick said. "Rule-two is the counter sign."

Reflexively, Tess looked down at her boots before she reached for the handle, and pulled the door open. Silently, Clyde pivoted outside, ducking into a crouch. Tess followed, keeping her back to him, her gun raised. They were in a wide and long corridor with walls covered in minimalist monochrome abstracts set in ostentatious gilt frames. Four doors were on the garden-side of the property, with a fifth at the far end of the corridor.

"On me," Clyde said.

Tess pivoted around, taking up position behind and above Clyde as he ran in a crouch towards a set of glass doors. Beyond, the corridor opened, became lighter, brighter, airier. Just before the glass-fronted doors was an open doorway. Clyde slowed as they neared.

Tess kept her aim on the glass doors at the far end. Beyond them, she could make out a gold-coated bannister, a wraparound staircase mirrored on both sides of a large hall.

"Clear," Clyde whispered, moving on, and beyond the open doorway.

Tess glanced inside. A sitting room, judging by the green-leather sofa and five matching chairs.

Without warning, Clyde pushed her sideways, into the room, even as he fired, and someone else fired back.

Bullets shattered the glass doors, slamming into the corridor's wall, splintering the gold picture frames, shredding the artwork.

Clyde eased his gun-barrel around the door, firing a pair of shots which she heard thud into a wall. Half a magazine tore down the corridor in reply.

They had taken refuge in a large room, sparsely furnished. The chairs were arranged in a circle in the middle. In the near corner stood a bar dotted with glasses and bottles. An ill-hidden projector faced the other, blank wall. On the far side were tinted glass windows, all closed. There was no other door.

Outside, the second half of that magazine shredded plaster and paintings.

"Hope you're a good shot," Tess whispered. "I've got an idea, but it'll only work once. Be ready." She holstered her gun, and stepped closer to the door. "Hold your fire! We're friendly! Hold your fire!"

No shots came in return, which she took as a step in the right direction, but she didn't take one of her own out into the corridor, not yet.

"We're friendly," she called again. "We've come from Canberra."

"Why are you here?" the man called back.

Tess nodded. Pick a name, and she had a fifty-fifty of it being the right one. Pick the wrong one, and she'd never know. "Kelly sent us," she said. "I'm coming out. Unarmed."

Empty hands first, she stepped around the door and out into the corridor, but stayed close to the wall as she took a step, then another towards the now-shattered glass doors.

She saw the gun, the man's eye close to the barrel, the top of his head, and the spray of blood as Clyde's bullet smashed bone and scrambled brain.

Even as she breathed out in relief, he overtook her, dashed past, and to the doors, pushing them open.

"Clear," he said. "Don't do that again, Commish."

"Here's hoping," she said.

"Main doors are barricaded," he said. "That's the front entrance. Looks like more rooms on the other side of the hallway. Down or along?"

"Along," Tess said. "Quick, though."

The other end of the hall was marked by another set of glass doors. Unlike the first set, these weren't broken, though they were dented, marred, scratched by heavy blows from the sledgehammer lying next to them. In the centre, scorched and burned, a handprint-lock dangled loose.

With his boot, Clyde pushed the door open.

"Found it," he said, pointing with his rifle's barrel into the first room on the other side.

"Found what?" she asked.

"The panic room," he said.

It was a library of leather-bound tomes, shelved according to colour. Not a single spine was cracked, not a single cover was creased. In the room's centre, far more worn than any of the books, was a snooker table. Against the far wall, one bank of shelves had been pulled out. Built on a hinge, it had concealed the vault-like door, at the base of which, along with an acetylene torch, were chisels, drills, and another sledgehammer. Despite the scars, char, dents, and abrasions, the vault-door remained firmly closed.

"Considering who owned this house, and how he got rich, I'm going to say jackpot," Clyde said. "But we'll need a professional to get into this. Is it Toppley's area?"

"She was more into fencing what was inside a safe than cracking into it," Tess said. "We'll send Mick, Zach, and Elaina up to the refugee camp, and get them to come down here by road with an engineering team."

"Worth checking whether there's some diesel in the garage," Clyde said. "Maybe bring down a few earth-movers to clear those bodies. This place was supposed to have its own well, wasn't it? It'd make for a decent fortified farm after it's had a bit of a clean-up."

"Good plan," Tess said. "First, we better check there's no one else here. So we'll clear downstairs, then—"

She was interrupted by an off-key buzz coming from the door itself.

"Who are ya?" a man asked. Through the small speaker, his voice was spidery, but it oozed a malicious superiority familiar to anyone who kept abreast of taunting courthouse-step press conferences.

"My name is Tess Qwong, Australian Federal Police, and you, Sir Malcolm Baker, are under arrest."

"Press the button!" Baker said. "You've got to press the button to speak. Who are ya!"

Tess sighed.

"Kinda loses the effect when you've got to take a do-over," Clyde said. He pressed the button.

"Police," Tess said. "The coup's over, Baker. You lost. You're under arrest. Open up, or—" Before she could finish the threat, the door clicked, and a malignant miasma wafted out.

"Strewth," Clyde said, stepping back.

The door opened further, the stench grew worse, and was followed by a sewer-scarecrow spotted with effluent.

"One more hour!" Sir Malcolm Baker said. "One more hour and I'd have given up. Didn't plumb it in!"

"Who didn't plumb what in?" Clyde asked.

"The dunny!" Baker said. "Half a mil, I paid for that panic room, and they didn't plumb the bloody toilet in. It's just a pipe in the wall!"

"Sir Malcolm Baker," Tess began, "you're under arrest for insurrection and treason, and for—"

"Yeah, I know all that," he said. "I might have been locked in the syphilitic circle of Hell, but I know what's going on. That's why those bastards turned on me. What happened to Aaron?"

"He's dead," Tess said.

"Ah, pity," Baker said, with just a hint of emotion in his voice, enough to show that, beneath seven decades of ruining other people's lives, there was a memory of humanity. It was gone in a flash. "Well," he snapped. "What are you waiting for? Aren't you taking me in? Prisoners get clothes and a shower, right?"

"How many hostiles are here in the house?" Tess asked.

"Two. But you got 'em both," Baker said. "Watched you plug them. Better than front row seats, that was. Still got my cameras. Every room. Every angle. They run on battery in case thieves cut the power. Smart, right?"

"Clyde, get the others," Tess said. "Baker, sit on the floor."

"I won't," he growled.

"You misunderstand your value," Tess said, "and you overestimate my desire to bother with a trial."

"I don't," Baker said. "On either count. I know *everything*, and you want to know it, too."

"You mean about the coup?" Tess asked.

"Nah, that's old news," Baker said. "Aaron's dead. Vaughn's dead. Lignatiev's dead. Is Kelly dead?"

"She is."

"Good. Then the coup's finished. I can give you bank accounts, but that's not going to do you much good. Nah, it's over except for the history books and no one ever made a profit out of them. O.O.'s not a bad sort, though, so it's not worked out too badly."

"What is it you think you know?" Tess said.

"I know who started the outbreak," Baker said. "I know who created the zombies. I know *where* they did it, and where they are now." His slime-coated face cracked into a grin. "I bet that's worth a bit of deference, right?"

"At six tonight, parliament is meeting in a televised session," Tess said. "There'll be a lot of speeches, but I bet they could squeeze in a quick vote to reintroduce capital punishment. Particularly if they can also announce your capture and trial. A quick trial, and a quick death. That's your future unless you start talking right now, and don't leave anything out."

Baker raised a finger to his mouth, picking at a molar before screwing his face and spitting. "At least give me some soap."

Clyde returned, the rest of the team behind.

"This is the police, is it?" Baker said. "Talk about scraping beneath the barrel. If this is the best you've got left, I must have been close to winning."

"Clyde, keep him covered, while I search him," Tess said, then paused. "Actually, no. Baker, where's your bedroom?"

"Upstairs," he said. "But we could *both* do with a shower first."

"Clyde, Teegan, find him some clothes, and some water for washing, and some bags in which we can stick the evidence. Air-tight bags," she added. "He said there were only two mercenaries here, but I don't trust him further than I can kick him."

"Charming," Baker said.

"On it, Commish," Clyde said, and left the room, Toppley in tow.

"Elaina, Mick, watch the door. Baker, put your hands on the snooker table," Tess said, drawing the Taser. "You were going to tell us how the outbreak started."

"See, you don't even know what questions to ask. You want to know about the sisters."

"Your sister started the outbreak?" Zach asked.

"Not *my* sister, *the* sisters," Baker said. "In my firm, a kid like you moves his jaw without permission, I'd fly you out to the Gibson, and tell you to walk home."

Zach took a reflexive step backward, then smiled. "Except I'm the kid with the gun, and you're covered in your own—"

"Tell me about these sisters," Tess cut in.

"They're Colombian," Baker said. "Spent some time in India. Some in Russia. I heard enough stories about them to know most of them are myths. But Colombia is where I met them. Horrid little place. Right on the Caribbean. Spitting distance of Aruba, and they kept their house next to a coal mine. You've heard of designer drugs?"

"Which ones?" Tess said.

"All of 'em," Baker said. "Those synthetic amphetamines which started appearing a decade ago? They invented them. In their labs. Are you starting to get the picture?"

"Keep drawing," Tess said.

"The story is probably a myth, but it goes that their father was one of those big cocaine bosses. The bloke had a private army, hippos, the works. He was another Cold War narco-baron who took money from the Yanks and then from the Commies, and then got murdered by a lieutenant. His daughters, the sisters, fled. Either to India or Russia, depending on whom you believe, and found a chemist who could make them something as good as cocaine but which didn't require the farmland. Paid off the local judges, police, and coast guard, set up some international franchises, moved back to Colombia, and got their revenge. Killed thousands if you can believe it, which I didn't, until I met them."

"What's this to do with the outbreak?" Tess asked.

"The labs!" Baker said. "Strewth, no wonder they nearly won, with cops like you. The chemists! Don't you see? Their business model was to own the competition. To own the monopoly for every narcotic. They wanted an empire. But there was no way for them to be legitimate emperors— sorry, ladies, I mean emp*resses*, under the existing framework of international judiciary. They needed a planetary reset. Hence the apocalypse."

"The zombies," Tess said.

"I didn't know anything about that," Baker said. "I'll take a chance, any chance, but what they created was sheer insanity. All they said was there'd be a limited nuclear war. Couple of hundred nukes, taking out the military bases in the Northern Hemisphere. They had agents in the governments of all nine nuclear powers."

"I thought there were five," Zach said.

"Plus India, Pakistan, Israel, and North Korea," Elaina said.

"You know what you want to ask next?" Baker said. "How did they get someone *inside* North Korea? Rumour goes they ran the pill-factories Kim used back in the day, back when he had his diplomats flogging a high to make hard cash."

"Get to the point or I'll start looking for rope," Tess said.

"You're not one for small talk, are ya? The nuclear war was supposed to destroy the armies. But it wasn't *their* plan. A bunch of politicos in the north cooked it up. The sisters were just taking advantage of it. Oz was supposed to be their backup, their fall-back in case something went wrong, which it obviously did, because as crazy as those sheilas were, they'd not have unleashed zombies onto the world."

"What do you mean Australia was their backup?" Tess said.

"What, you need me to spell it out?" Baker said. "They wanted a friendly government here after the Northern Hemisphere became a radioactive swamp. They wanted a friendly leader. I said Aaron, obviously. The kid was soft, but he'd have done. They preferred Lignatiev. Had something on him. Never knew what. Vaughn was supposed to be deputy. But I reckoned I'd have got Aaron to the top spot in a year or three. He was a good kid, in his way."

"What did the sisters have on you?" Tess asked.

"Nothing I couldn't fight in court," Baker said. "That's why they took me to Colombia. They skinned my secretary alive in front of me. She didn't travel with me. They kidnapped her. Drugged her. Smuggled her out on my *own* plane! Then skinned her alive in front of me. Not them personally. They had a bloke do it for them. Australian, he was."

"On the strength of that, you planned a coup rather than went to the police?" Elaina asked.

"No. Of course not," Baker said. "They provided other lessons. Demonstrations. They had it all planned. They gave the summary of seven court cases going on in seven different countries. Told me to pick one. So I did. They made a call, and the judge threw out the case. Bloke who beat his wife to death, right when she was making a video call to her sister. The evidence was indisputable."

"You can't be serious," Elaina said.

"Just a second," Tess said. "All of this makes a wonderful campfire yarn. None of it saves you from a firing squad."

"The names will," Baker said. "You're not going to execute me until you've got them all. All the judges, the lawyers, in every country. It'll be like Nuremberg again, won't it?"

"Nope," Tess said. "Because it's just a story that won't save a single other life. Especially not your own."

"How about the address?" Baker said, this time with a hint of desperation. "The location in Colombia where they'll be now, and where they made the virus that caused this mess. They had the front to fly me there in my own bloody jet, so I've got the co-ordinates. Wrote them down on the back of my daughter's wedding photo. It's in there."

"I'll get it," Bianca said. She paused in the doorway to the panic room, took a shallow breath, and darted inside.

The photo she returned with showed a young woman in a white dress, her smile barely making it past her lips. There was no groom in the picture. Tess took the picture out of the frame. On the back of the photograph was a set of co-ordinates.

"You want someone to put on trial, that's where you go," Baker said. "I bet *that* buys me a nice safe cell."

Clyde and Teegan returned with a crate of bottled water, and a bottle of bleach. Leaving the team to gather evidence, and Clyde to douse the prisoner, Tess stepped back out into the hallway.

"It's smoke and mirrors," Mick said. "If I were creating a biological super-weapon, I wouldn't bring a newspaper magnate to the lab. Not even one as corrupt as him. Especially *not* him, since he might run the story just so he could write himself up as the hero."

"Yes, sure," Tess said. "Except… except Dr Avalon was adamant it was created somewhere."

"Are you saying you believe him?" Mick asked.

"I don't *dis*believe him," Tess said. "I reckon he'll still get the death penalty. But he's correct. We're not going to execute him while we still think he's got some useful information. There's one thing he certainly could help with: the identity of the Australian torturer. I think it's the same killer who was in Broken Hill."

"What about Colombia?" Mick said. "The coordinates seem about right, though I'd like to check them on a map."

"Not my jurisdiction," Tess said. She checked her watch. "If we get in the air now, can you radio Brisbane, tell them to send a team here? It'd make a good farmstead."

"You're not looking to collect evidence?"

"Oh, I am. But it'd take a week just to box this place up. We'll have to leave that to Brisbane, because we should get Baker back to Canberra so O.O. can announce his arrest. That should stop any vote of no-confidence."

"You're a supporter of his now?" Mick asked.

"No, but I'm a supporter of Anna's. If Owen goes, so does she."

Chapter 3 - A New Parliament
Parliament House, Canberra, Australia

It was an uneventful, if noisome, flight back. Until more permanent accommodation could be arranged, Baker was installed in the detention cells at Canberra's airport.

"Zach, find a car. We better inform Mr Owen we caught our suspect," Tess said. "Clyde, you stay on guard here until an official replacement can be found."

"Commissioner, can I have a word?" Toppley asked. "Bianca filled me in on what Baker said about the sisters while Clyde and I were impersonating personal shoppers. I didn't want to say anything while Baker was listening."

"That door's soundproof," Tess said. "But let's move down the corridor. Bianca, take notes."

Toppley looked at the socialite, but shrugged. "What purpose do secrets ever have?" she asked.

"You tell me," Tess said. "You know about these sisters?"

"I know they had a base in Colombia," Toppley said. "They're real, and a presence to be avoided. If they were active in a region, you backed away, and stayed away."

"Did *you* back away?" Tess asked.

"As grotty as it might seem, I was just in facilitation," Toppley said. "Some people had guns. Some people had raw materials. Some people had the kind of tourist-facing businesses where gems could become jewellery, and so be a catalyst to create cash. High-end tourists, high-end jewellery, but still the kind of business where you stay under the radar."

"How does this connect to these sisters?" Tess asked.

"They bought weapons in bulk, and sold them to those who'd swear fealty. Their competitors were armed with regionally produced old-model Kalashnikovs, but the sisters provided hardware from the U.S.

and Britain. Hardware which came with export certificates signed and stamped to prove they weren't being shipped to the very places where they ended up."

"They had connections with customs officials?" Tess said. "That's not unheard of."

"Consistent connections lasting many years," Toppley said. "They owned more than just customs officers. If you operated on their territory, you got a warning. Second time, they made an example. Warnings were polite. The examples were brutal. I really was just a facilitator. Though I was a participant in enough midnight escapes to make for a profitable biography, most of my work was in daylight, in towns, and over a drink or a meal. A few years ago, I had an assistant who went his own way. He wanted to take a few more risks in exchange for a life-changing payday. He took a shipment of MDMA as payment instead of cash, and sailed it into the Philippines. He was found in a cemetery, burned alive."

"So they live up to their reputation," Tess said. "What else? Specifically."

"They *were* from Colombia. They are, probably, sisters. Must be at least sixty by now. That's all I *know*, but I heard that one of them is a chemist. Russia offered them sanctuary for a while when they were younger, but they were thrown out. You must know how the North Korean government was involved in the drug trade as a way of generating hard currency? The sisters were the facilitators. In turn, that gave them a source for weaponry. That's how they began."

"Other than they're about sixty years old, it sounds like more rumours," Bianca said.

"They were said to have a small house on the Caribbean Sea. Not a palace," Toppley said.

"Which matches what Baker told us," Tess said. "Okay, so that's confirmation he wasn't lying about everything."

"I have a name, too, for whatever that's worth," Toppley said. "Herrera."

"The Herrera sisters?" Tess said. "It might be worth powering up a few databases, see what we can dig up."

"How about visiting a bookshop, or a library?" Bianca said. "If their father was a powerful narco-baron, won't the name appear in some of the more lurid crime-histories?"

"They could have assumed that name," Toppley said. "But if they didn't, would it—"

But she was interrupted by a shout.

"Commish! Ms Qwong!" Zach called as he sprinted down the corridor.

"What is it?" Tess asked.

"There's been another bomb!" Zach said. "In Bass Strait. You know all those politicians who were supposed to be coming back from Hobart? Their planes were blown up. They're all dead."

The sound of someone clearing their throat woke Tess from her uncomfortable chair-based doze in a meeting room in Parliament House. She opened her eyes and saw Dr Leo Smilovitz.

The Canadian scientist held out a cup. "Coffee?" he said.

"You're a lifesaver. What time is it?" she asked, taking a sip.

"Half nine," Leo said, pulling out the chair next to her. "Parliament's over. Ms Dodson and Mr Owen are just speaking with the state reps who made it here."

"Did I miss any fireworks?" she asked.

"Thankfully, no," Leo said. "After Mr Owen began his speech by announcing the death of the old politicians, the state reps responded with a unanimous vote of support for the new government. You've got ten new senators, and twenty MPs. There's a new U.N., too, formed of the ambassadors who were stuck in Canberra. They endorsed Ms Dodson."

"And O.O.?"

"And him," Leo said. "He gave a good speech. Promised new elections as soon as possible. He said our focus, now we've lost all the planet's shipping, should be to rebuild Australia, rebuild the fleets, and rescue those nearby."

"Which is what people within range of the radio broadcast would need to hear," Tess said. "Any more information from Tasmania?"

"A little," Leo said.

The swing doors opened. Dan Blaze pushed Anna Dodson's wheelchair through. Bruce Hawker, of the RSAS, followed behind. He'd found a dress-uniform somewhere, but not a pair of dress-shoes to replace his dusty battle-boots.

"G'day, Tess," Anna said, "and *what* a day. Thank you, Dan. Can you wait outside?"

"A soldier with a guitar, another with a gun," Leo said. "That makes for an interesting escort."

"Both of whom were in shot for the press photographs," Anna said. "I don't know when anyone will see them, or how many will have seen the television broadcast. But, yes, imagery is important if for no other reason than gossip. But we must discuss Tasmania. Are there any more updates, Leo?"

"A nuclear warhead detonated either just before, or just as it was leaving, the silo aboard a Jin-class Chinese submarine," Leo said. "The planes were affected by the EMP. Total losses are four 777s and three fighter-aircraft escorts."

"And, of course, the politicians and their staff and families who were aboard," Anna said. "How do you know any of this?"

"The shielding aboard one fighter jet functioned correctly," Leo said. "They were able to land. That's who brought us the initial report. A follow-up has been gathered from the surviving shipping. We lost twelve fishing boats, a freighter, and the HMAS…" He paused to check his notes. "The HMAS *Brisbane*."

"She's a Hobart-class destroyer," Hawker said. "Brand-new. Barely out of the box."

"It was caught in the detonation," Leo said. "It picked up the sub, and it's from them we know the type. But it also picked up a U.S. submarine which was also destroyed in the blast, and which we had no idea was down there. Just before the warhead was detonated, the U.S. sub launched a torpedo and sent a warning. Said they were the *Guam*, but before anything else they said could be relayed from the *Brisbane* to anyone out of range, the warhead was detonated. The *Guam* is, or was, a Virginia-class attack sub."

"What damage was done on shore?" Anna asked.

"Minimal, according to the initial reports," Leo said. "The wreckage, and the radiation, will impact fishing for six to nine months, minimum."

"A U.S. boat was chasing a Chinese sub?" Tess asked. "But the bomb detonated at the surface? Was this a suicide mission?"

Leo shrugged. "I'm just reading a collated version of the radio reports," he said. "I set up the listening post, but I'm not running it. Naval warfare was never my area. My knowledge is tangential, while these reports are still incomplete. As only one warhead detonated, the most statistically probable explanation is that the warhead malfunctioned. Less likely, but still plausible, is that it was their sole warhead left. They had no torpedoes, and they were determined to sink that U.S. submarine. Those suggestions were given by Admiral Shikubu."

"Who's that?" Tess asked.

"A Japanese admiral who was attached to their embassy," Anna said. "He was a spy. Now he's running military intelligence."

"He was spying on us?" Tess asked.

"He described it as spying along a parallel stream to us, whatever that means," Anna said. "Part of the fragile deal which gives Oswald, Canberra, parliament, *us*, final say in the day-to-day running of… well, of everything, is that we make this a global relief effort with a global command. There is a United Nations, and an international leadership. With most of our navy, most of our shipping, sunk, and our people dispersed or dead, we have little choice but to fill our top ranks with anyone who's qualified."

"I guess old flags don't matter," Tess said. "But the timing is coincidental, isn't it? That this bomb goes off just as the planes containing most of parliament are flying overhead?"

"More than just coincidental," Anna said. "But if this was a political mass murder, suspicion should fall on Oswald and myself. That's why it's imperative we avoid suspicion among our allies. Individually, they are a minority. Collectively, the number of refugees here is... well, we're not sure, but we think the population has doubled in a month."

"It *is* a coincidence," Hawker said. "If the target was those politicians, they would have attacked Hobart before the planes took off, or Canberra after they'd landed."

"Your voice of experience would be more comforting if we'd not just survived an internationally funded coup," Tess said.

"Which brings us to Baker," Anna said. "Congratulations on his capture. Have you learned anything from him?"

"The sisters provided him with a mercenary bodyguard," Tess said. "The soldiers were from the same group who were watching over Lignatiev and Vaughn. They had orders to kill Baker if the coup failed, but he made it to his panic room. So far, he's confessed to everything. He facilitated, and funded, the coup. He's confirmed that it was partly organised by a pair of narco-barons, two sisters called Herrera. We believe one is a chemist. They operated out of northern Colombia on the Caribbean Sea. Baker gave us the co-ordinates. It's close to Punta Gallinas, the most northerly cape in South America, and not that far from the resort-island of Aruba. These sisters had influence in local, and regional, governments across the world. I don't know how extensive, and how much was rumour, or how far to believe Baker, but it sounds like they were working with people in the U.K, the U.S., and had connections in Russia, India, and North Korea."

"Not countries you usually hear mentioned together," Anna said.

"Except when listing nuclear-armed powers," Hawker said.

"North Korea doesn't count, does it?" Leo said. "Not in the kind of exchange we've just experienced."

“It might,” Tess said. “I know from the investigation before the outbreak that the cartel had been making a major push into France. That was at street-level, but safe to assume they’d set their aim higher, too. It could be they had agents in every nuclear power.”

“Did you say you have co-ordinates?” Leo asked, taking out a tablet.

“Sure.” Tess pushed her notebook across to him. “Baker has a lot more to tell, but he’s deliberately taking his time so as to push off the date of his trial. If we want to speed him up, he’ll need to be given a deal.”

“My vote’s for telling him whatever he needs to hear to get him to talk,” Hawker said.

“You mean—” Anna began. “Actually, no. There are some things best not even said aloud.” She closed her eyes. “What a week. Between the outbreak and the atomic genocide, every ship in the world became a refugee vessel. Over three-quarters of the world’s shipping made it into the Pacific or the Indian Ocean. The military ships had been gathered into giant fleets centred around U.S. nuclear-powered carriers, and those were deliberately targeted. Ships in harbour were sunk by the tsunami. Ships at sea lost power due to the electromagnetic pulse. Others were overwhelmed, or sunk, during the naval battles. Unless a ship sails into a harbour, we must assume it is lost.”

“Do we have any ships?” Tess asked.

“A small fleet was ferrying refugees and supplies between Papua and the smaller Indonesian islands,” Anna said. “Forty-seven vessels, all small cargo freighters. They appear to be intact. Or they were, as of fourteen hours ago. Otherwise, it’s a bare handful. A few submarines, a few military vessels, a few small cruise ships which were being repaired in Perth. Under two hundred in total.”

“More will have survived,” Hawker said. “Plenty will be able to repair their systems and get underway.”

“I hope so,” Anna said. “But we have no way of assisting them, or refuelling them. If they don’t sail into harbour, we must assume they are gone.”

"What about planes?" Tess asked. "One arrived from Mozambique this morning, and one from Lombok yesterday."

"We can't refuel overseas runways," Anna said. "We have only two tanker-ships in the entire ocean. New Zealand lost its major refinery to a plane crash and fire. There were zombies on the plane, and they survived the crash. This created a delay in the fire-fighting efforts. While we have been assured the outbreak was eliminated, there are ten million people in New Zealand now. Until they can build a replacement refinery, we need those tanker-ships to maintain a rudimentary sea-bridge. It'll be at least a month before the vessels can be deployed elsewhere."

"Does that mean Oswald wasn't lying?" Tess asked. "The war, the relief effort, whatever we were calling the attempt to retake the world, is over?"

"Effectively, yes," Anna said. "We had reservists, retirees, and conscripts crammed ten to a cabin and twenty to a corridor sailing for Hawaii and then Baja California, where we hoped the U.S. would be providing military support. The ships are gone. The conscripts are lost. We don't know where that military equipment is, and we have no way of retrieving it. We will have to replace it. This will require new factories, and shipyards, but the people must be fed, and protected, first. We will focus our efforts on assisting Papua, Indonesia, and New Zealand, and together we shall assist recovery nearby before we dream of setting foot in the Americas."

"You're right," Tess said. "It has been quite a day."

"Leo, do you think this lab in Colombia could really be where the virus was made?" Anna asked.

"It *was* made somewhere," Leo said. "Without more information, that's all I could say."

"Leo, you and Dr Avalon wanted to go to Manhattan to collect samples from patient zero, and to Britain to pick up their vaccine, because you need those to make this weapon, yes?"

"They would help," Leo said.

"It's possible without them?" Hawker asked.

"Yes, but it will take us longer," Leo said. "It's the difference between weeks and years."

"So you really can make a weapon that will kill the zombies?" Hawker asked.

"Sure. Or Flo can," Leo said. "But developing something which'll kill a zombie when you inject it, isn't the same as creating something we can use on a battlefield."

"But it's a start," Hawker said.

"If you went to the actual lab where it was developed, wouldn't that be even more useful than going to New York?" Anna asked.

"You want me to go to Colombia?" Leo asked.

"Obviously not on your own," Anna said. "But if you found the lab there, you wouldn't need to go to New York or England, no?"

"That really depends on what we find," Leo said.

"We've received conflicting reports on how badly the Panama Canal was damaged," Anna said. "But if we're to one day restore a naval link with the Atlantic, it will have to be through the canal."

"You want to send a ship north, to the canal, and see if we can force a passage?" Hawker asked.

"No, because if it is impassable, the journey will have been wasted," Anna said. "The report I have from Mozambique says three warships are anchored off the coast of…" She paused, reaching into her pocket to pull out a small notebook. "Inhambane. Two U.S. frigates, and the HMAS *Adelaide*, a Canberra-class ship which has a range of seventeen thousand kilometres, yes?" She looked to Hawker.

"I'm more familiar with planes, and mostly how to jump out of them," he said. "But that sounds about right."

"The ships were there to assist in the evacuation of Africa to Madagascar," Anna said. "That evacuation failed over a week ago. The island was overrun. The remaining refugees have been evacuated. No purpose is served having three warships off that coast. You'll take the *Adelaide* around Africa, across the Atlantic to Colombia, and then to the canal. Hopefully, you can sail through it and home. Or, if Leo and Dr Avalon decide, you can continue to New York. Even Britain."

"Fuel allowing," Leo said.

"Agreed," Anna said. "And food and radiation, but there is a limit to how much planning we can do here."

"If the Herrera sisters really did make the virus in a lab there, they could have an army with them," Tess said.

"You'll have one, too," Anna said. "There are a hundred U.S. Rangers in Perth. Technically, only sixty are Army Rangers. The others are really C.I.A., evacuated from their postings in South East Asia. Bruce, will that be enough?"

Hawker slowly undid his tie. "Saying no won't get me more, so it'll have to be. The Canberra-class is a landing platform, not a frigate. Do you know which U.S. ships are there?"

"Sorry, no."

"Then we don't know what their range is," Hawker said. "And we don't know where this lab is? Whether it's underground, even?"

"No," Tess said.

"We've no satellite coverage, no recon photos," Hawker said. "We don't how well they're defended. There will be casualties."

"I know," Anna said. "But my hands are tied. This information will have to be taken to the U.N. They will demand action. They will demand justice against those responsible for this horror. So would the people, if they were asked. They would demand to know why action hasn't already been taken. Better to send a ship now, because if we don't, they'll install a different leadership who will, but the last thing we need now is the instability that would bring."

"Let me take all three ships," Hawker said. "With two U.S. frigates, I can guarantee the destruction of this facility. I can't promise the lab will survive. Understood?"

"I'll put it in writing that the priority is the neutralisation of the threat," Anna said.

"Thank you," Hawker said. "Then there are two issues I'd like to address. You're the politician, ma'am. I'm your soldier and I'll follow your orders, but I'm duty-bound to offer my counsel. First, fuel. The

Adelaide does have the range to reach the canal from Mozambique if her tanks are full. I can't speak for the frigates."

"And I can't help you," Anna said. "But a ship's captain is more likely to know where to refuel."

"As long as you understand undertaking this mission is fraught with more complexity than it would have been a month ago," Hawker said. "Second, if we can refuel in Panama, and don't go north, it could be a month before we're home. If we go north, it could be two months." He turned to Leo. "If you're so certain this weapon is possible, can you afford that much time away from a lab?"

"Flo has some theoretical work to finish before we can unpack the test-tubes," Leo said. "I'd estimate that will take about a month."

"Sure, but do *you* need to come with us?" Hawker asked. "This *will* be dangerous."

"We don't need to go if you can find someone better qualified," Leo said. "I'm certain there's someone, somewhere, but after the last few weeks, you're as likely to find them digging a field as working in a lab."

"If this is to be done, I want it begun tonight," Anna said. "When we tell the new parliament, the new U.N., I want it to be too late for them to have an input. The last thing we need now is to have every soldier still alive put aboard every ship still left. Let's not forget what just happened off Tasmania."

"Sorry, this might seem obvious," Tess said, "but is there a reason we don't fly there?"

"No runways," Anna said. "Inhambane is the most westerly that we know of that is still open. As far as I understand, no planes have arrived there from the north, or the west, in over a week. I suppose you could fly over this compound in a long-range jet and parachute, but I don't know how we'd get you home."

"Jumping out of a plane is where I draw the line," Leo said.

"Then ship it is," Anna said. "If I could send anyone else, I would, but I don't know whom else I can trust, and we can't afford to waste any more time. Gentlemen, thank you. I'll give Tess the orders, and I'd like you to be in Perth by dawn."

Hawker stood, and saluted. "Ma'am. Commissioner."

"Do you really think those two can make a weapon?" Tess asked when she and Anna were alone.

"I don't know, Tess, and I'm in two minds whether I want them to," Anna said. "What if it works, but mutates the undead into something worse?"

"Fast zombies," Tess said. "I really have to stop watching movies with your dad. Is that why you're sending the scientists away?"

"No. Politics is returning, Tess. I've told Oswald not to tell anyone anything about the weapon, but you know how O.O. likes to brag. He'll tell people that it's being developed, so word will spread, and everyone will want progress updates and demonstrations. It will still take months before we've something ready to deploy. We can't be so distracted we take our attention away from everything else we need to do to survive. Do you know Clive Oakes?"

"He ran my unit in Sydney. Didn't he run for office?"

"He was a state senator until a few hours ago. He's now in charge of policing for all of Australia. The New South Wales delegation insisted. I wanted to give the post to you, but it wasn't my choice."

"He's a better candidate," Tess said. "He was always more of an administrator than an investigator. A bit too fond of long sentences, both in his speeches and from the judges, but he's a good bloke. Visited me a few times in the hospital before I moved back home."

"Good," Anna said. "Yes, politics is returning. We should be grateful. I *will* be grateful when I've had more sleep, but it means we have to consider what the public needs as much as what they want. They want a victory. I'm sending the hero who stopped the coup on a mission to hunt down the people responsible for the outbreak. That's the headline we'll broadcast in a couple of days. On your return, we'll broadcast how you destroyed the cartel's base in Colombia."

"So this is purely propaganda," Tess said.

"Not entirely," Anna said. "These sisters committed a true crime against humanity. We should attempt to serve justice. Honestly, what other use do we have for warships and Special Forces now? We're in retreat. We've diagnosed malaria in Broome and cholera in Darwin. Radiation is rising everywhere we can record it, and we still don't know if the last bomb has been dropped. Things are difficult and will get a lot worse before they get better."

"Are you still going on your goodwill tour of the refugee camps?" Tess asked.

"Starting tomorrow," Anna said.

"Take my team with you," Tess said.

"I already have bodyguards," Anna said.

"My people are your management team. They're loyal to *you*, Anna. Have Mick fly you."

"Don't you think that'll give the impression of me as the girl being taxied around by her dad?"

"Not if Dan Blaze is the bloke pushing your chair," Tess said. "His voice is famous, even if his face isn't. Not a bad-looking bloke, either, when he's not scowling. And his voice is something to—" She stopped, and coughed.

"What?" Anna asked, leaning forward. "Go on, say it."

"I'm just describing how others would see him," Tess said quickly. "Who knows how they'd interpret him pushing your chair, but it'd be a good photo for them to gossip over. Distractions can be healthy."

"I *completely* agree, Tess," Anna said.

"Yeah, well, I'll tell my team to find some suits. It'll look like a political delegation rather than a paramilitary enforcement squad."

"You don't want to take them with you to the Atlantic?"

"I'll have Bruce for company, Leo for entertainment, and Avalon to infuriate me," Tess said. "The ships will be crowded with all those Rangers. My lot would only get in the way."

"I'm promoting Bruce to colonel," Anna said. "That should be sufficient rank to impress the Navy captains and the C.I.A. spooks, but you're the government representative. You'll have letters from Oswald, and from the U.N. Bruce will decide on the strategy, but there'll be no contact until you return. I don't know what decisions will have to be made, but they should be made by a civilian, not the military, or by the spies."

"The C.I.A. can provide intel, Bruce will press the button, but I'll pick the target," Tess said. "I understand."

"I'm sending you into the unknown," Anna said "Look for ships, for people, for runways. Look for radiation and craters, too. Find out if we really are all that's left of the world. But if you can't come back with good news, just make sure you come back. Oh, and if I don't see you before you depart, don't worry, I'll keep an eye on Dan for you."

Chapter 4 - Family Loyalties
Red Hill, Canberra, Australia

Outside Parliament House, Tess found Mick and her team next to the police cars in which they'd arrived. They were eating cake and drinking… she sniffed. "Is that coffee?" she asked.

"A gift from Mr Owen," Mick said. "That bloke's growing on me."

"Where did you find cake?" Tess asked.

"That's from O.O., too," Mick said.

"For you?" Tess asked. "It's not that I expect it's poison, but if Oswald Owen wished you g'day, it's guaranteed the invoice is already in the post."

"Nah, it was a bulk order for all those politicos from Tassie," Mick said.

"Here you go, Commish," Elaina said. "There's no coconut, but it's not a bad way of ending a day."

"Not bad at all," Tess said, looking over her team. "Thank you all for your help in saving what's left of civilisation."

"*Australian* civilisation," Mick added.

"The best kind of civilisation," Clyde said.

"I'm serious," Tess said.

"So am I," Mick said.

"Yep, me too," Clyde said.

Tess gave up, and took a bite. "This is *good* cake. How come there's cake to spare? Is Owen snaffling food for his own use?"

"Probably," Bianca said. "But Ms Nguyen said there was an excess of eggs, and an insufficiency of packaging to distribute them to the refugee camps. A brewery over in Fyshwick has been converted to a drying facility to make powdered eggs."

"You can do that with a brewery?" Tess asked.

"The brewery is close to the railway line," Mick said. "The eggs are being rolled in, cracked open, and the empty cases stuck back on the train and returned to the farm. Trouble is, they've now got an excess of powdered egg and nowhere to store it. Since the trains are busy carting the eggs back and forth, they can't use them to ship out the flour or sugar that came in last week. Since there's a bakery next to the brewery, Oswald decreed everyone should have their cake and eat it."

"I bet he did," Tess said. "Sounds like we've a transportation problem. Are there no trucks?"

"Not enough fuel tankers," Mick said. "Lost a few with the flooding. The rest are running to the refinery in convoy in case of zoms, but someone didn't take into account that's slower than letting them travel individually. Give it a few days, and it'll all be ironed out. But until then, we've got cake."

"It's a good problem to have," Tess said. "And it's good news for all of you. The investigation is over. One day, you'll all get a medal. I'm serious. Thank you. Tomorrow, I'm heading to Perth with Bruce Hawker and the scientists. We're picking up some U.S. Rangers there for help in following up that lead Malcolm Baker gave us. You are being reassigned. Mick, to you falls the duty no father can escape. You'll be flying your daughter around for the next couple of weeks while she tours the refugee camps. The rest of you are going with Anna to help with the admin."

"We're not in the police anymore?" Zach asked.

"It'll be a while before justice is back on the agenda," Tess said. "Restoring order comes first. I don't want you lot in uniform. I want people to see the politician pushed around by the bloke with the guitar, surrounded by civilians with clipboards and pens rather than rifles and body-armour. You're public servants, or journalists, if you like. It'll look bureaucratic not dictatorial, implying the focus is on restoring normality, and so it's worth putting up with discomfort and long hours for a little while longer."

"We'll need new clothes," Bianca said. "We could get them from my house."

"I thought you lived in Adelaide," Tess said.

“We kept a house here in the city,” Bianca said. “Cameron, my husband, is a lobbyist. Or he was.”

“He’s passed?” Elaina asked.

“No, but I don’t think there’s much call for lobbying anymore,” Bianca said.

“Here’s hoping,” Tess said. “So you’ve got clothes there?”

“D’you mean ball gowns?” Elaina asked.

“Yes, but I have some more practical pieces, too,” Bianca said. “Some of my husband’s suits would fit Clyde and Dr Dodson. My son’s should fit Zach.”

“Your son has suits?” Zach asked, his face strained in puzzlement. “There’s a lot of money in baking, then?”

“Anna wants to leave first thing in the morning,” Tess said, finishing her cake. “This sounds like the best idea. I’ll go with you, Bianca. Elaina, you can help carry. Everyone else, back to the airport. Mick, I’ll need a pilot and plane to take us to Perth as soon as Leo, Dr Avalon, and Colonel Hawker turn up.”

“You better drive, Bianca,” Tess said, climbing into the passenger seat.

“Perfect,” Elaina said, getting into the back. “I could do with a rest.”

“How are you doing?” Tess asked as Bianca started the engine.

“Badly,” Elaina said bluntly. “But we all are. It’s too much trauma all in one go. But what can we do but pretend tomorrow won’t be as bad as today? Hey, maybe it will be.”

“Touring refugee camps is going to be a different kind of horror,” Tess said. “If you like, I can get you work at the airport.”

“No, we’ve all got to do our part,” Elaina said. “But it’s good to have a bit of a whinge. Do you know where you’re going, Bee?”

“Mugga Way in Red Hill,” Bianca said.

“But do you know the way?” Elaina asked. “Because you’re driving us back towards Parliament House.”

“Sorry. Should have turned left,” Bianca said, pulling a pi-point turn.

“Did you spend much time in Canberra?” Tess asked.

"Me? No," Bianca said. "We came here just after the outbreak. Cam reasoned the capital would be better defended than elsewhere, while his contacts would ensure a better quality of life. I… well, I disagreed, so he told me to stay behind. But Ron wanted to go with his father. He always does. When the conscription van arrived, Cam said we were exempt, so I volunteered."

"Not a happy marriage, then?" Tess asked.

"It was over sixteen years ago. Just after our son was born," she said. "But Cam said we were staying together for the look of it, then for our son."

"*He* said?" Elaina asked. "He told you?"

"There's a pre-nup," Bianca said. She touched the necklace around her throat. "But it doesn't include my personal jewellery."

"Smart girl," Elaina said.

"Fifteen million dollars in gems," Bianca said.

"*How* much?" Elaina said.

"But how much are they worth today?" Bianca said. "So I might as well wear them."

"Wear them and hope they're worth something again sometime soon," Elaina said. "They should be, shouldn't they, Commissioner? If things are getting back to normal."

"I never understood why colourful bits of rock were so valuable in the gone-before," Tess said, "so who knows what they'll be worth in the coming-soon?"

"This is it? Honestly, Bee, I was expecting something bigger," Elaina said, when Bianca rolled the car up onto the kerb.

"It's primarily for entertaining, not for living," Bianca said. "I won't say whom he was entertaining, but he was happy if I stayed away."

"What a ratbag," Elaina said.

"Oh, he's not all bad."

"Your husband is Cam, and the son's Ron, yes?" Tess asked as she got out of the car.

"Cameron Constantine Clague," Bianca said. "My husband is the fifth, and my son is the sixth. He made it clear what our child's name would be on our first date."

"Strewth, Bee, and you still went out on a second?" Elaina asked.

"I was young. He was rich," Bianca said wistfully. "I thought I was in love."

It was a small house on a large plot. Cubist in design, with a box hedge to provide privacy, but with a new, almost-complete, wood fence behind. Through the gaps, on what had been lawn, were a quartet of camper vans. On the roof of one was a night-time sentry.

"Police!" Tess called up to the guard. "We're looking for Cameron Clague." Deliberately ignoring the shouted query from the sentry, Tess inspected the neighbouring properties. It was a suburb of large gardens, thick hedges, and tall fences, but was already losing its air of affluence. Every garden, front, side, and back, had gained a vehicle or two. Not for transport, but overspill accommodation for the surge in refugees. But missing here, and common elsewhere, were community checkpoints and local roadblocks. Each of these houses had become an island unto itself.

"Lights," Bianca said.

They'd come on in the house, a bright searchlight glow, from which a separate beam detached itself and came over to the gate.

"Who's there?" a man growled.

"Cam, it's Bee."

"Bianca? What do you want?"

"To talk," Bianca said. "Can I speak to Ronnie?"

"It's all right, Diego," Cameron said. "It's only my *ex*-wife."

"Who's there with you?" Bianca asked.

"I hired some new staff," Cameron said. "You know my motto, expand or die."

"Can you open the gate?" Bianca asked.

"Wouldn't be safe, would it?" Cameron said. "Got to think of other people, don't we, Bianca?"

"Well, can you call Ronnie, ask him to come down?" Bianca asked.

“Not at this time of night,” Cameron said. “Why are you here?”

“To speak to my son, Cam!” Bianca said. “My unit’s leaving Canberra for a while. I don’t know when I’ll be back.”

“Your unit? So you still think you’re a soldier, do you? You picked your team, so you better play on until the whistle.” On the other side of the wall, the light went out.

“Cam?” Bianca said. “Cam!”

He didn’t reply, letting his feet do the talking as they squeaked across the driveway and back to the house.

“I’ve got some chains in the truck,” Elaina said. “We could pull down the gate.”

“That wouldn’t help,” Bianca said.

“It’d make you feel better,” Elaina said.

“No, I don’t think it would,” Bianca said.

“Well, tell him how you helped stop the coup,” Elaina said. “Tell him you’re working for the government.”

“Oh, he’d love to hear that,” Bianca said. “He’d switch to champagne and roses if he thought I could get him a meeting with Mr Owen. But that’s not what I want.”

“Window, upstairs,” Tess said.

In the upper corner of the house, a flashlight shone through a closed window of a dark room.

Bianca raised a hand. “Love you, Ronnie!” she called.

The torch blinked on, off, on off.

Bianca waved. “I love you,” she whispered. “Let’s go.”

Wordlessly, they got into the car, and drove back to the airport.

15th March

Chapter 5 - The Taste of a Dollar
Perth, Australia

"Good morning, Commissioner," Teegan Toppley said.

"Can't be," Tess said, reluctantly opening an eye. "It's still bat-dark outside."

"It's two a.m. Truly the best part of the morning, when the police are asleep," Teegan said. "Thus it grated against every grain of my soul to wake you, but our plane is almost ready to leave."

Tess pulled herself up. "Two whole hours of sleep? Luxury. You're still in uniform. Couldn't you find any civilian clothes?"

"Suits are being pieced together out of the emergency uniforms the air-stewards left behind. But I'm not joining the goodwill tour. I'm coming with you."

"You are? Why?" Tess asked.

"For the same reason Dan Blaze is pushing the deputy prime minister's wheelchair," Toppley said. "I *am* a recognisable figure, universally known to have been sentenced to a term in prison. I can't be seen to now be *in* government."

"Working *for* the government," Tess said. "But that's a fair point."

Anna Dodson, Leo Smilovitz, Bruce Hawker, and Mick Dodson were waiting downstairs.

"I feel like I'm late for a funeral," Tess said.

"A court martial," Colonel Hawker said. "Not yours," he added, handing her a mug of coffee.

"Your pilot's drunk, Tess," Mick said. "It'll be a day before he's sober enough to drive, but he'll never fly again if I have my way."

"Where are the other pilots?" Tess said. "There were dozens here a few days ago."

"Idle hands still need feeding," Mick said. "Rule-twelve, that is."

“It’s at least number fifty-three,” Tess said.

“Rule-nine-million-and-twelve by my count,” Anna said. “Ms Nguyen allocated the pilots to the driving pool. We thought that was a good way of ensuring we always knew where they were. Except, now, half are driving trucks and buses filled with buckets of flour, individually wrapped eggs, and beer-bottles of milk to the refugee camps in the east. The other half are ferrying generators and every empty tanker truck we could find to fill up at the refinery. But since yours is a one-way flight, I’m going to start my inspection in Perth, and we’ll all fly there together.”

“Don’t say one-way,” Tess said. “Where’s the rest of my team?”

“Swapping the cargo,” Hawker said. “We’ve got a supply of M4-carbines and ammunition for the Army Rangers, in case any are without, and we’re loading supplies Ms Dodson needs for her tour. She’s leaving her bodyguard behind.”

“Only the soldiers,” Anna said. “I’ll have your team, Tess. If any of us has to fire a shot, we’re in deeper trouble than a few soldiers could save us from.”

“I disagree,” Hawker said.

“So do I,” Mick said.

“But it’s *my* decision,” Anna said.

“We’ll have to leave some of the food behind,” Mick said. “The Gulfstream wasn’t designed to be a cargo plane.”

“Which is a perfect excuse to eat some now,” Anna said.

“There’s food?” Tess asked.

“Of a sort,” Hawker said. He held out a cereal bar.

“Ah, processed food, how I’ve missed you,” Tess said, tearing the wrapper off. She took a bite and began to chew. She stopped. “Why are you all staring at me?”

“What’s your gastronomic assessment?” Leo asked.

“It’s food and I’m hungry,” Tess said.

“To think you grew up in a restaurant,” Mick said. “What would your mum say?”

"That there's too much sugar, and not enough cinnamon. Why the quiz?"

"The bar was made *yesterday*," Anna said. "A group of mums had turned a school bake-sale idea into a kitchen-table biscuit-by-post business. Just before Christmas, they took over a large warehouse near the railway. They had the kitchens, and the packaging machines, all on-site. We don't have storage space for raw ingredients, so cooking them is essential, and this factory was ready to go. If it works, we'll expand their operation."

"Tastes good," Tess said, taking another bite. "I'd say expand away."

"Take another look at the packaging," Mick said.

"Plain and sensible," Tess said. "Oh, it says it costs a dollar. We're using the old currency again?"

"That *is* currency," Anna said. "The bars should last for a year, and so will be sold, and can be traded, at a nominal rate of a dollar."

"We're replacing bank notes with biscuit-bars?" Tess asked.

"They're a lot harder to forge," Mick said.

"If people are starving, they'll eat the bars," Anna said. "But if they're not, they'll trade them. This establishes a baseline for bartering. We can't use the old currency, and we can't waste the resources in printing new notes, or the electricity in running a digital currency. Not yet. Until then, a two-hundred-and-fifty-calorie oat-bar is worth a dollar. So your daily calorie requirement should cost ten dollars, but people can thrash out the specific costs and wages for themselves."

Tess nodded. "Money you can eat, but which truly won't last forever? The future is now. Where's Dr Avalon?"

"Working," Leo said. "Or sleeping. Probably both. I better find her."

"We best find everyone," Anna said.

"On it, ma'am," Hawker said. He and the scientist hurried away.

Tess took a final bite, finishing the oat-bar. "Does this mean we're okay for food, nationally?"

"The days of local surpluses will soon be over," Anna said. "The canning factories are running at full capacity, with the bottleneck now in steel. We have more bakeries than we can equip, so I think we'll begin canning pre-cooked meals and stick a price on those, too. It's what happens next month which is giving me a migraine. We should be approaching harvest-time, but there are zombies in the fields, and double the population in the cities. Over winter, Leo's worried the oceans might be too radioactive to fish. But there's an idea for hydroponics through the cold months if we can sort out the electricity supply."

"This country could do with a diet," Mick said. "Starting with our prime minister."

"Don't you dare say that to him," Anna said.

"Someone should," Mick said. "It's a three-hour time difference to Perth, and we'll be flying about a hundred kilometres an hour slower than the sunrise. We should land as the day's first light is shining on the wrong side of the right desert. Let's get you aboard Oz-Force-One, Anna."

"Dad, please don't call it that," Anna said.

A month ago, the Gulfstream V had been a USAF VIP transport, with space for fourteen passengers, each in their own bed-comfortable lounge-seat. From Dr Avalon's headphones came a muffled roar of drums and guitars as she drowned her ears in music while alternating between writing in a notebook and tapping away on a laptop. Bruce Hawker had brought one soldier with him, Sergeant Nick Oakes, who had a vaguely familiar face which was currently throwing curious looks towards Clyde, who sat by the door. Sophia and Bianca were catching each other up. Elaina was dictating the lyrics of Australian folk songs to Blaze. Zach was making a bid at hyperinflation by methodically chewing his way through a crate of the edible banknotes wedged next to his seat. Hawker was up front with Mick, Anna was reading, Toppley was writing, and Leo had closed his eyes.

This morning, *this* flight, felt different to yesterday's and to all the days prior to that. It was as if they had turned a corner. Tess didn't even dare hope the last bomb had now been dropped, and so the recovery could truly begin, but they were now talking in terms of weeks and months, not hours and days. They were planning convoys and bakeries, rather than walls and patrols. They were worried about steel for canning, not graves because of starvation. They worried about a political challenge, not a coup, and drunken pilots, not the undead. Yes, things were changing. Perhaps it was the uniforms, or the lack thereof.

Team Stonefish had lost their camouflage, and were now in shirts and blazers, slacks or skirts. Zach looked younger, as if he were on a school trip. Bianca, perhaps because of the jewellery, looked considerably older. Sophia looked more professional, while Clyde, somehow, looked less. Topple, by contrast, still wearing camo, looked even less like the infamous photos from the Christmas news bulletins.

"No gunshots," Tess said as she buckled her seatbelt. "There were no gunshots last night."

"Hmm, sorry?" Anna asked.

"Don't mind me," Tess said. "What are you reading?"

"Notes on water usage," Anna said, turning a densely annotated page. "These are suggestions of how we can reduce consumption. But you can't ration visits to the loo. We certainly can't tell people not to wash their hands afterwards. We have to plan for fifty million people who all need a home, water, and food."

"Fifty?"

"I'm being optimistic. A census is not a priority. The Murray-Darling basin just won't produce enough water, no matter what crops we grow. Desalination is one solution, as long as we can manufacture the new-style graphene filters. These pages explain how difficult they are to make. Want a try deciphering it?"

"Not on your life," Tess said.

"Then you better read this," Anna said, pulling a large bound document from the bottom of her pile. "It's everything we have on the collapse of the Madagascan evacuation." She picked up another, slightly thinner, bundle. "This is everything we know about the Atlantic. Leo has copies of all the videos uploaded to the internet before the power went down. Something for you to watch while you're at sea."

"Who put these together?" Tess asked.

"Admiral Shikubu and Chief Oakes," Anna said.

"Shikubu is the Japanese spy, yes? Oakes?" Tess said, half turning in her seat so she could look at *Sergeant* Oakes. Yes, he did share a resemblance with the old police officer Tess had known in Sydney. It was a question to ask when they landed. She flipped through the pages. "This is a list of impact sites. None of these are very specific locations," Tess said. "I'm starting to get a feel for the extent of the mission."

"This is a letter signed by Oswald, a warrant, if you like," Anna said, handing over an envelope. "And there's a letter signed by Edith Vasco."

"Who's that?"

"The new Secretary-General of our equally new United Nations."

"Was she an ambassador?" Tess asked.

"A Nobel Laureate from the Philippines, teaching at the university."

"A scientist?"

"A poet and philosopher. Considering what's happened, that's who the world needs."

Tess nodded, pocketing the letter, and then returned to the briefing packet. Inevitably, she fell asleep.

A hand on her arm woke her. "We're landing," Toppley said.

Even as she buckled her seatbelt, Bruce Hawker entered the cabin from the cockpit.

"We're not expected, ma'am," he said, addressing Anna as much as Tess. "The U.S. Rangers, and the C-5 Galaxy, were sent north. They're aiding in the evacuation of the Andaman Islands."

"That's still on-going?" Anna said. "That's good. We might retain control of the islands."

"But it's not so great if we want to fly west," Tess said.

"They're not expecting you, either, ma'am," Hawker added.

"Good," Anna said. "They won't have had time to brush the crumbs under the sofa. I'm sure we'll find you another plane, Tess."

As soon as the wheels touched the ground, and the plane began braking, Tess stood. "Blaze, the Deputy Prime Minister comes off the plane next, everyone else waits."

Hawker met her by the door, opening it for her. Outside, a Hawkei PMV was speeding towards them. On the parallel runway, an F-35 screeched skyward, nearly scraping the tops of the cranes. Hundreds of cranes, towers, and platforms filling every corner of the horizon.

"What are they building?" Tess asked.

"Walls," Hawker said. "We saw them from the air. They have walls everywhere. The city is growing bigger by the hour."

By the time Tess had both feet on the tarmac, the military patrol vehicle had stopped, five metres from their wing.

A uniformed officer jumped out of the passenger-side. "You're from Canberra?" she asked. It sounded like an accusation.

"Commissioner Tess Qwong. This is Colonel Bruce Hawker. Aboard is Deputy Prime Minister Dodson. She's here on an inspection tour, and we're here to catch a C-5 Galaxy with a hundred U.S. Rangers."

"The C-5 flew north last night," the officer said. "Only sixty of the passengers were U.S. Army Rangers. The other forty were civilians."

"There's no ramp, no lift," Hawker said. "Wing Commander, yes?" he said, reading the woman's rank. "Where's the elevator?"

"What elevator?" the wing commander replied.

"Commissioner, I can rig a hoist, but it won't be graceful," Hawker said.

Tess, still more than half asleep, caught up. "It'll be quickest," she said. "Though the deputy prime minister will not be pleased." She turned her gaze on the wing commander who simply ignored it.

"You need to get your plane off my runway," she said.

"It's the—" Tess began, but stopped as a second fighter jet tore into the sky. "It's the deputy prime minister's plane," she said.

"I don't care," the wing commander said. "The fighter wing will need to land in forty minutes, with refugee flights expected from Broome in two hours. Who does your pilot think he is that he can set down without permission? I told you not to land, but you did anyway, endangering the entire city." The words were laden with anger, but the officer's eyes were sagging with exhaustion.

"What's your name?" Tess asked.

"Wing Commander O'Bryan." She turned back to the Hawkei. "Fetch the tug. Get this plane moved. Is that a wheelchair?"

Tess turned to look at the plane. The wheelchair, and half the team, were on the ground. Clyde had secured a rope somewhere inside the cabin. Tess turned back to the wing commander. "The wheelchair is for the deputy prime minister who was shot during the attempted coup. She's here with a press team to see how the relief effort is going, find out what's needed, and to make sure it gets delivered. The colonel and myself are here to link up with those American soldiers, and then head west, initially to Mozambique, in pursuit of the people responsible for the outbreak and the nuclear war. We intend to bring them to justice. Did you hear Prime Minister Owen's address last night?"

"I was too busy," the wing commander said, now staring at the plane. "The deputy prime minister was shot?"

"The world's spinning fast, these days," Tess said.

"You said you're going to Mozambique? I don't know if the runway is still open. It's been a day since a plane arrived from there. We re-directed it to Canberra."

"Yes, it arrived. Do you know if there are ships in Mozambique?"

"Three, I think," O'Bryan said. "An African Union regiment is guarding the port. After the refugees were evacuated, we were told the priority was the northern Indian Ocean."

"Told by whom?" Tess asked.

The wing commander just threw up her hands. "Look, we're doing all we can. There are eight million people here now. Eight! That's nearly six million refugees. The governor— sorry, I mean the mayor. That's what you wanted, wasn't it? A local council led by a mayor. So the governor of Western Australia is now a mayor, but it's not magically reduced our overcrowding. We're already running a rescue of all shipping that lost power after those bombs, and then you tell us you need an evacuation of the Andaman Islands, so we send our planes north. Now you want to go west."

"Everything needs to be done yesterday, doesn't it?" Tess said.

"G'day!" Anna said, as the colonel wheeled her over, Mick a step behind. "Deputy Prime Minister Anna Dodson."

"We weren't expecting you," the wing commander said, adding only a moment too late "ma'am."

"No worries. I'd like to meet some people," Anna said. "Enough people that word will spread that I'm here. Then I'd like you to show me the problems, and tell me what you'd like me to do to fix them. But I also need to get Commissioner Qwong on her way to Africa."

"Of course, ma'am," O'Bryan said, switching to military formality. "You'll need to speak to the governor, I mean the mayor. I'll take you there now. But there are no planes here that can reach Africa. The passenger planes have gone north, except those we sent east. We're stretched to breaking just rescuing the passengers from the stranded shipping."

"Of course," Anna said. "I'll need to visit the docks, and the shipyard. But the commissioner *does* need to get to Africa."

O'Bryan pointed at the USAF Gulfstream. "Your plane has the range."

"They require military support as well," Anna said. "Where are the U.S. Rangers?"

"By now? In Port Blair," O'Bryan said. "Refugees arrived from across the Andaman Islands, and from across the coastal regions of the Indian Ocean. Port Blair is in danger of being overrun. Too many infected. Troops were requested, and those Rangers were already stood next to a plane. Over three hundred thousand civilians, ma'am. Broome won't be able to cope. We'll have to bring the refugees south, unless you can relocate them elsewhere."

"We'll find them a home," Anna said. "And I think we can relieve some of the pressure on you here. Now, *how* will you help the commissioner get to Africa?"

"You want a hundred soldiers?" the wing commander asked, looking to the high walls under construction beyond the runway. "I can get them here in an hour. But a plane will take longer."

"You've got a C-17 over there," Mick said.

"It doesn't have the range to reach Africa, when carrying a full complement of troops," O'Bryan said.

"But it could refuel in Diego Garcia," Mick said.

"Diego Garcia is underwater," O'Bryan said.

"There's been a tsunami?" Anna asked. "Here?"

"Not here," O'Bryan said. "Localised flooding was reported among the islands to the west. We've had reports of mushroom clouds at sea. Twelve, so far, spread throughout the ocean, but nothing to indicate as severe an attack as in the Pacific. Our information is incomplete, but we're not wrong about that island runway."

"What about Mauritius?" Mick asked.

"Similarly unusable," O'Bryan said. "The runways in Madagascar have been overrun. Inhambane is the only operational runway we know of."

"We'll take the Gulfstream," Hawker said.

"What of the soldiers?" Anna asked.

"A cohesive unit of Army Rangers afford a number of tactical options," Hawker said. "Conscripts are an entirely different proposition. Sailors will suffice for a shore-party. The ships will have a limited quantity of supplies, so better we don't put a strain on them. I would ask if Major Brook can join us. He's a force multiplier all on his own."

"Do you mean Clyde?" Tess asked.

"According to the blokes who brought that refugee plane to Canberra, there's fuel in Inhambane," Mick said. "Were they right?"

"Frustratingly, there is an abundance in Mozambique," O'Bryan said, unbending now it appeared none of her own people or resources would be requisitioned. "Supplies were sent to Inhambane to aid in the evacuation of Madagascar, but the island fell before the supplies were used."

"But you said a regiment is guarding the port, and three warships are still anchored offshore," Tess said.

"For all the good they'll do there," O'Bryan said.

"Oh, they will do us some good, indeed," Tess said.

"Refuel my plane, and we'll be out of here in an hour," Mick said.

"No, Dad. You're not flying to Africa," Anna said.

"There's no one better qualified," Mick said. "Unless you fancy a trip west, Wing Commander?"

"I have plenty of commercial pilots here in Perth," O'Bryan said. "Many from Africa."

"But by the time we find one who's flown a Gulfstream, and who's flown to Inhambane, another day will have gone by," Mick said. "I'm here now. There's a job to be done, Anna, for which I'm best qualified. Our own interests have to be put aside."

"You can fly to Africa, but no further. That's an order," Anna said. "Tess, you better take your team with you."

"You still need a bodyguard," Tess said.

"I've got Dan and Sophia," Anna said, "and I have the wing commander and her air force. I want your team to make sure my father returns." Another fighter took off. "Where are those going?"

"To the edge of the desert," O'Bryan said. "They'll lure the undead to bastions we've built far from the city. There, we'll destroy them."

"I'd like to see more of that," Anna said. "Dad, you drop Tess off, and then you come back. Don't make me have to come pick you up. Tess, stay safe."

"You, too," Tess said.

Blaze pushed Anna off the runway. Sophia followed behind, leaving the wing commander momentarily uncertain whether to drive after them, or walk alongside. Tess turned to her team. They were one short.

"Where's Dr Avalon?" she asked.

"Still on the plane," Leo said.

"Still? Fine. Listen up. Change of plans. We're going on, alone and together, to Mozambique. Clyde, you're now with me. Elaina, Zach,

Bianca, you'll make sure Mick comes home. The refugees have been evacuated. There are African Union soldiers holding the runway, and three warships in the harbour. But it's an ocean away. Anyone who wants to volunteer to stay with Anna can, no judgement. Otherwise you've got until Mick's got the plane prepped to find clothing suited for war."

"Where we want to be isn't always where we *need* to be," Clyde said. "What about the ammunition and carbines in the hold?"

"We'll take them with us," Tess said. "I don't know where the front line is these days, but we're travelling far behind it."

Chapter 6 - Out of the Fire, Into the Firing Line
Inhambane, Mozambique

When Mick announced they'd reached cruising altitude, belt-buckles clunked, cloth rustled, laces shuffled, and zips whizzed as her team changed clothes. Almost as loud was the hum of embarrassment generated by maintaining the polite pretence of privacy. Tess watched the view beyond the small window. Perth truly was a construction site. Walls were rising everywhere, but if the city had acquired six million refugees, floors and windows would surely be added soon.

The sea was speckled with white sails from yachts repurposed into fishing boats, but there were no larger vessels. She'd misunderstood the wing commander: the authorities in Perth were still engaged in the search part of their rescue attempt.

Her ears pricked as they picked up the end of a conversation two seats behind her.

"If you give me your clothes, sir, I'll stow them overhead," Sergeant Oakes said.

"Just call me Clyde, mate. I'm a long time retired."

Tess stood. "Okay, listen up. I've got some briefing notes here about Mozambique which will be of interest, but before we go any further, there's one big question I reckon we *all* want cleared up." She turned to Clyde. "*Major* Clyde Brook?"

"I'm just a charity worker," he said.

"The Raging Brook?" Oakes said. "You're a force of nature."

"Want to elaborate?" Tess asked.

"Not especially," Clyde said.

"Fair enough," Tess said. "Sergeant Nick Oakes."

"Yes, ma'am."

"Was your father a superintendent in Sydney a few years back?"

"My uncle, ma'am. He told me about you. The copper who flew across the rooftops."

"Would you like to elaborate on *that*?" Leo asked.

"Not especially," Tess said. "All right, here's the situation. We're going to land in Inhambane, Mozambique, and pick up a ship. Either a U.S. frigate or the HMAS *Adelaide*, which will take us to Colombia. We might continue east with three ships, but that'll depend on what level of on-going support the African Union soldiers require. Elaina, Bianca, Zach, you're Mick's ground crew, and will make sure he returns to Perth. The rest of us will sail around Africa, across the Atlantic, and to the Panama Canal, via Colombia. We're going to the property owned by the cartel bosses who were linked to the coup and had some hand in the outbreak."

"That's the lead we got from Sir Malcolm?" Bianca asked.

"The very same," Tess said. "Colombia could be where they created the virus. Ideally, Dr Avalon will get to rummage around inside the lab, but we thought we'd be bringing a hundred U.S. Rangers with us for onshore support. We'll make a new plan when we're at sea, when we know what ships we're sailing with, and what kind of crew they have. Throughout the voyage we're tasked with finding out what's become of the world. That makes this a scientific expedition, so we'll listen to Dr Smilovitz."

"And he listens to me," Avalon said, without removing her headphones, or even pausing the music.

Her back to the scientist, Tess gave a theatrical shrug.

"Did you say we had some intel on Mozambique?" Clyde asked.

Tess held out the binder Anna had given her. "It's mostly about the evacuation to Madagascar. An evacuation which failed. Embarkation was at Beira in the north, and at the capital, Maputo, in the south. Inhambane, where we're landing, is halfway between."

"While it's halfway between Maputo and Beira, it's still in the south of the country," Clyde said. "Beira is a port in the middle of Mozambique, and roughly contiguous with the mid-point of Madagascar. We'll be about ten degrees farther north than Canberra."

"You mean it's ten degrees warmer?" Zach asked.

"The latitude," Clyde said. "It'll be about five degrees warmer."

"Have you been to Mozambique before, Clyde?" Elaina asked.

"I spent some time waiting there," Clyde said. "When you've finished your book, you read whatever you can get your hands on, and that was usually government brochures upselling the investment opportunities in the country. Why weren't they using Nacala? That's contiguous with the northern coast of Madagascar, and it's one of the deepest harbours in Africa."

"Fuel tanker blew up," Tess said, pointing at the briefing book. "It's assumed to be deliberate."

"What went wrong in Madagascar?" Elaina asked. "Something did, didn't it? I assume so or we'd be flying there."

"Take a read and find out," Tess said. "But all I know is that it was overrun by the infected. But we've still got a foothold at Inhambane. It's possible someone might retake Madagascar, though it won't be us. Get some rest, because when we land, I don't expect we'll linger long. Within an hour or two of arrival, I want to be underway."

She returned to her seat, pulled down the blind, and closed her eyes, trying to remember whether or not the RSAS used the rank of major.

Catching up on a month's sleep, one snatched hour at a time, she dozed fitfully until finally woken by a tap on her shoulder.

"Mick wants you up front, Tess," Colonel Hawker whispered.

She followed him back to the cockpit where, below, the ocean's surface was slick with wreckage and oil, and an occasional floating hulk. Ahead, smoke rose from a forested shore.

"Where are we?" Tess asked.

"About fifty miles due east of Madagascar," Mick said.

"*That's* Madagascar?" she asked. "I… I had an image in my head. Lush trees. Wide beaches. Sweeping rivers. Bright-coloured animals. Not carnage."

"There's nothing on the radio," Hawker said, retaking the co-pilot's seat.

"But people must be down there," Tess said, trying to pick out details between the smoke. Smouldering shipwrecks dotted the beach.

The fires had spread to the buildings ashore, creating a giant plume which merged with that rising from the blazing inland forests.

"Zoms," Hawker said. "Down there. Has to be zoms. Nothing on the radio yet."

"It's worse than I was expecting," Mick said.

"It's worse than Brisbane," Tess said.

"Twice over," Mick said. "But I was thinking about alternate runways. We're about an hour from Inhambane. We've enough fuel to hunt up and down the coast, but not to return home."

"No worries," Tess said, since the time to worry was before they'd taken off. "I'll get everyone up and ready."

In the cabin, only one blind was up. Leo was looking outside, but his hand still wrote. Avalon typed in time with the fast music leaking around the edge of her headphones. Clyde and Zach played cards. Elaina and Bianca were engrossed in a hushed, smiling debate. Oakes was reading a thick paperback whose cover was mostly an explosion.

"Everything okay?" Toppley asked.

"We're above Madagascar," Tess said. "We're about an hour out from the airport. Take a look out the window. Get your gear packed. Get ready to leave the plane."

A few more blinds went up.

"Strewth," Elaina said.

"Vile," Zach said.

"Dante's Inferno," Bianca said. "It truly is."

"Get up," Clyde called. "Eat up. Wash up. Pack up."

Tess sat, bent, and tightened her laces, doing her best not to look outside. After Sydney, when she'd been recovering, she'd binged the *ooh-pretty-animal* nature shows. Madagascar had been a favourite since it could give Australia a run for most bizarre ecosystem in the world. Now, realistically, the aye-aye was extinct. The ring-tailed lemur was gone. The fossa had been wiped out. TV shows about faraway places were nothing but memories.

Korea was gone, and she'd never been. Persimmons were grown in Australia, but her mother always said they never tasted better than fresh from the tree in the safe-house north of Busan where she'd been debriefed after her defection. The world she'd known was past history, and the future of which she'd daydreamed was less real than the smoke clouds now buffeting the plane.

"Are you okay, Commissioner?" Toppley asked.

"First time out of the country for a while," Tess said. "Couldn't remember if I'd packed my towel."

The intercom clicked. "We've picked up the beacon for Inhambane," Mick said.

A muted susurrus of relief shot around the cabin.

"That's an Anzac-class frigate down there," Oakes said, looking out the window. "She's firing her gun."

Tess turned to the window and caught the glimpse of a freighter-ship, but she couldn't see the warships.

"That frigate must be our ride," Tess said. "I thought it was a Canberra-class ship. Someone must have got them mixed up."

"Who were they shooting?" Elaina asked, as the plane shook.

"Buckle up," Tess said, following her own advice. Her trepidation grew faster than the smoke below. Oily, dark, thick, swirled by the wind to obscure what looked more like a refugee camp than a war zone, but certainly wasn't a secure military outpost.

A hard landing was followed by an equally hard deceleration, but before it was over, Hawker came from the cockpit into the cabin. "Perth was wrong," he said. "There are refugees still here, and they were expecting an airlift. They're engaged with the zoms."

"Ah, hell," Tess said, pulling herself up. "Clyde, Oakes, get ready to help refuel, or fight, and probably both. Bruce, did they say how many refugees?" she added, following the colonel to the door.

"They asked where the *big* planes were," Hawker said. "So I'm guessing lots." Just before he opened the door, the colonel raised his voice. "If they want to take the plane, we'll let them," he said. "We do not have sufficient fuel to return home, so we are not killing for the chance to drown in the Indian Ocean. We'll retreat to a ship, or retreat inland. Bring weapons, food, water. Expect to never come back aboard."

"You think it'll be that bad?" Tess asked.

"Let's find out," Hawker said, threw the door open, and jumped down. Tess followed.

Smoke, oil, and oceanic salt seasoned a swirling miasma of blood, sewage, and burned flesh. The air reverberated with a thunderclap roar as the distant warship fired her gun. From the south came a muted applause of small-arms fire. Amid the smoke, she saw hints of barricades ringing the runway, but no other planes, and no tall buildings.

An open-top bus sped towards their plane. Duct tape held the cracked windscreen together. Muddy sand covered the pearl-pink bodywork. The sky-blue cloth sunshade above the passenger cabin had been reduced to loose rags, flapping and streaming as the bus sped to a hard halt just shy of the wing.

Oakes was at Hawker's side, and Clyde was at hers before she'd taken another step.

"Friendly!" Hawker called. "Hold your fire!"

Tess didn't know if he was talking to her team, or to the passengers on the bus. The figure who jumped out wore dark blue naval fatigues, a stained bandage on her forehead, and a *Ta Moka* tattoo on her chin.

"*Kia ora*," Tess said, exhausting one quarter of her Maori vocabulary.

"When do the other planes arrive?" the New Zealand sailor replied.

"We flew out of Perth," Tess said, approaching the woman. "They said the refugees were gone. Only five thousand soldiers and three ships remained."

"I've five thousand ready to go, right now," the sailor said.

"You've got five thousand refugees still here?" Tess asked, as the ship fired its cannon.

"I've five thousand kids expecting an airlift which should have begun at dawn," the sailor said. "There's another thousand wounded, waiting in the cathedral, and twenty thousand volunteers who said they'd fight but only as long as the kids, the sick, and the old were taken to safety."

"Damn," Tess muttered. "Canberra doesn't know. Clyde, get Mick."

"I'm here," Mick Dodson said from right behind her, with the rest of her team right behind him. "I heard. I've seen," he added, pointing at the bus.

Tess followed his finger and saw the terrified faces of the children who were no longer crouched low in the seats, but were staring at her, and their far-too-small plane, with forlorn disappointment.

"Have you got fuel?" Tess asked. "Can you refuel this plane?"

"Of course," the sailor said.

"Mick?"

"Ditch the cargo," Mick said. "I'll need webbing, ropes, straps, anything you've got to keep the kids in place."

"Sergeant, unload the carbines. Get our gear off the plane. Elaina, Bianca, get those kids lined up and ready to board as soon as the pilot gives the go-ahead." She turned back to the sailor. "When the plane arrives in Perth, Mick will organise the airlift. But it'll take sixteen, maybe twenty, hours before the next plane arrives."

"I was told the same thing by a pilot yesterday," the sailor said.

"Perth thought the civilians were gone, so redirected the rescue-planes to the Andaman Islands," Tess said. "Once Mick brings them this news, they'll send help."

The sailor nodded. "Our orders are to protect the refugees. We'll hold until relieved," she said.

"I guess we're staying, too," Tess said. "I'm Commissioner Tess Qwong, Australian Federal Police. We're in pursuit of the people responsible for the outbreak, the nuclear war, and an attempted coup in Australia. We're supposed to pick up a Canberra-class warship here."

"Commander Kuara Tusitala, executive officer of the *Te Taiki.* We're the only warship here."

"There are no U.S. frigates?" Tess asked.

"One was sunk a week ago. The other set off in pursuit of the pirates," Commander Tusitala said, just as a distant cannon-thunderclap echoed from the ocean. "We've two fuel-freighters, a lot of dhows, but we're the only combat vessel."

"You said pirates, is that with whom you're engaged?" Tess asked.

"Zombies," Tusitala said. "They're approaching from the south."

Tess turned to look. Having expected to rush from the runway to the ship, she'd only taken the briefest of glances at the map. She recalled Inhambane was on a curving, bulbous peninsula. Immediately to the north, and twenty kilometres to the east, was the sea. To the west was a wide river-estuary. To the south, the headland narrowed, but then joined the African mainland.

"Where's your fuel supply?" Mick asked, coming over to the pair.

"Mick, when you get back to Perth, you need to organise an airlift," Tess said.

"No worries," Mick said. "I need this runway extended. Double its length. Knock down those buildings. Level the ground. Flatten it if you can. You've got sixteen hours. Plan-A is I find more planes which can land on this runway as it is. Plan-B is flying in with every 777 I can find in Oz. We'll pick up the kids and fly them on to Diego Garcia."

"The runway was submerged, Mick," Tess said.

"But waters recede," Mick said. "We'll land, and push the planes into the lagoon. Or maybe it'll be Mauritius. Depends on what and where we can secure. We'll use as little of the fuel here as we can, because there's no way there'll be enough. I'll get the kids out. Get the injured out. We'll get a ship underway. Those two freighter ships I saw at sea, are those fuel tankers?"

"Diesel-transports," the commander said.

"We need those ships, and that's how we guarantee Perth listens," Mick said. "So I better get back there before Anna leaves."

"Who?"

"The deputy prime minister," Tess said, relaxing an inch. "I'll explain later, but I can guarantee this *will* get done. We've got M4-

carbines, ammunition, and some Special Forces soldiers in our team. Where would they be most use?"

"The bridge in the south," Tusitala said. "Luis can take you. I'll get your fuel."

"Check your boots, Tess," Mick said. "I'll see you tomorrow."

Tess took a deep breath, and turned around. Bianca and Elaina were each now carrying a bandage-wrapped child off the bus. By the driver's door, the olive-green-clad driver stood, watching, his brow furrowed, his left arm rubbing his right which was held tight across his chest in a splint and sling.

"G'day, I'm Tess, are you Luis?" she asked.

"Luis Magaia," he said.

"Bianca, Elaina, get the kids to the plane," Tess said. "Everyone else, get those crates of ammo and carbines aboard the bus. We're going to the front. Luis, can you show us the way?"

"I can drive," he said.

"With your arm in a splint?" she asked.

"Perhaps I could drive, sir, and you could navigate," Clyde said with practiced diplomacy.

Tess was the last to board the bus, entering at the back, and found them two passengers too many. "Leo, I don't think you and Dr Avalon should come with us," she said.

"We're no strangers to war zones," Leo said, opening a crate of M4-carbines. "We're where we need to be."

"Ugh," Avalon said, opening a crate. "You know I hate it when you talk like that. You're implying some omnipotent hand has written our destiny." She held up a bullet. "When it's patently obvious to any student of recent history that fate holds a gun in *both* hands while loudly dictating her terms. Zachary, strip the magazines from those carbines. Leo, load."

"It's Zach, not Zachary," he said.

"Zach has to be short for something," Avalon said. "Since Zachariah has an absurd number of syllables, it must be Zachary. Why are we not moving?"

“Clyde?” Tess called, and moved to the bench row behind the driver. Oakes was stationed at the rear-right, standing upright and sheathing his bayonet having cut away most of the already shredded roof. Toppley was in the mid-left, with Hawker sat next to Zach, whistling the outback waltz as his hands patiently loaded a magazine.

“Are you a soldier, sir?” Tess asked of Luis Magaia as the bus began to move.

“A teacher,” Luis said. “These clothes were all that were available.”

“You were a school teacher here in Inhambane?” Tess asked.

“No one here is *from* here,” Luis said. “We are all refugees, and those who lived here became refugees elsewhere during the evacuation to Madagascar.”

“A lot of those children were injured,” Clyde said. “How’d it happen?”

“A stray shell from one of the pirate ships hit a van of cooking oil,” Luis said. “They are the survivors. Turn left here at the end of the runway. There is only one road.”

As they drove south, through the hastily fortified city, Tess developed a mental picture of how it must have been a month ago. A sleepy tourist town of pastel-painted cafes and small hotels, none more than three storeys high. Colonnades supported balconies overhanging the narrow road. It wasn’t so much a city in decline as an ancient one in retirement, enjoying the tranquil calm of the near-ocean life.

Their navigator was correct: there truly was only one road through the city. Not because it was so impoverished it couldn’t afford more, but because every alley and side road was barricaded. Every ground-floor window, of store, cafe, or home, was blocked. Every rooftop was linked to the next with a new, rickety walkway built with whatever could be salvaged from inside. On those roofs were people. Civilians. Refugees. Passengers for an airlift yet to arrive. Some were armed with machetes and improvised spears, but only a handful held long-arms. Almost all of them watched the sky, looking for the rest of the planes they’d been promised were coming.

“What happened here?” Tess asked.

"Where does that story begin?" Luis replied.

"Start with the end," Clyde said. "Who's attacking us?"

"*Morto-viva,*" Luis said. "From Pretoria. From Johannesburg."

"Jo'burg's about a thousand kilometres southwest," Clyde said.

"They follow the refugees," Luis said. "We lost Maxixe yesterday. The town due west, across the river from Inhambane."

"What's our destination?" Clyde asked.

"The bridge over Rio Mutamba," Luis said. "The river creates this peninsula. The bridge is the defensive line. Captain Adams wants to hold the bridge. It is thirty-five kilometres away."

"E.T.A, thirty minutes," Clyde said. "Hold the bridge, hold the peninsula. Keep the zoms from the town."

"Until the planes come," Luis said. "They *are* coming, yes?"

"Yes," Tess said. The properties grew less numerous as they reached the edge of the small city. "It's just going to take a little longer than you hoped. Is Captain Adams from the warship?"

"She is in charge today," Luis said. "So many have been in charge. So many went to Madagascar. It is why I came here. Why we all came here."

"Where did you come from, sir?" Clyde asked.

"Myself? Maputo," Luis said. "A student told me of the evacuation to Madagascar. I told others. But the harbour was full of so many. The entire city expected to leave. We waited until refugees arrived from South Africa. They said Durban had been overrun. We decided to copy the South Africans and drive north. Myself, my students, their parents. We came here and found it empty. Sailors had taken to their dhows, while everyone else had been taken to Toliara."

"In Madagascar," Clyde said.

"Yes," Luis said. "And here, at sea, east of Tofo Beach, there were ships. Freighters under the protection of warships. Those were the refugee ships. They were waiting here, but the refugees were waiting in Maputo. The ships went south. It was not a noble deed," he added, with weary admission. "If ships arrived in Maputo, the refugees would wait there for a ship rather than copying us and coming north, bringing the infected with them. *Colhes o que semeias*."

"Eventually, we *all* reap what we sow, mate," Clyde said in partial translation and complete agreement. "Madagascar was a refuge for Mozambique and South Africa, too?"

"So everyone thought," Luis said. "But everyone in Tanzania, Kenya, and Somalia thought the same. Word spread over the radio, and must have been heard in Zambia and Zimbabwe, Namibia and even Niger, because planes arrived. The infected arrived. So did the pirates. Chinese. Americans. South Africans. Somali. Madagascan. Some wanted to steal food and fuel so they could remain at sea, aboard their ships. Others, the warships, they desired only to sink one another. It was madness. The large ships, the cruise ships and freighters which had carried the refugees, remained in Madagascar, in harbour, while the sea ran red with more blood than has been spilled in these waters for five hundred years. But *os mortos* had arrived by air."

"The zombies arrived here on planes?" Tess asked.

"In Madagascar," Luis said. "Earlier groups of refugees had moved inland. They were attacked. Infected. The island was lost from the inside. The refugees re-boarded the ships. *Mortos* were among them. The ships pulled anchor, and now they float at sea, ships of the dead, while the lost souls march on us from South Africa."

"Inhambane is in the northwest of the peninsula, yes?" Tess said. "Tofo Beach is thirty kilometres east, on the northeast of this peninsula. To the east of Tofo Beach is the sea, and a hundred kilometres of ocean filled with zombie-ships?"

"Yes."

"To the west of Inhambane, there's the river, and then another shore-facing town, that's also been overrun?" Tess asked.

"Maxixe, yes," Luis said.

"And to the south, there's a few bridges separating us from all the zombies from the capital of Mozambique, and from South Africa?"

"Oh no," Luis said. "There is also a ford."

Chapter 7 - Warriors
Rio Mutamba, Mozambique

They left the city, and its smouldering cooking fires, behind, but the estuary-river kept them company as they followed the dusty road south. After a kilometre of burned and abandoned cars, licensed to five different countries, they reached an under-defended barricade. A military-green truck was parked next to a single-storey L-shaped home. On the roof of the truck's cab stood a woman with a rifle, while a man stood on the flat roof of the house. Perhaps they were the property's owners, perhaps they were looters, but they ignored the bus as it sped south.

To the east lay barren summer-parched and mining-ruined scrub. Here, the horizon was broken with an occasional palm instead of an acacia; otherwise it was achingly similar to Broken Hill. Zombies had been right at home in the outback and the same would be true here.

"Bridge ahead, Commish," Clyde said.

"No, not *this* bridge," Luis said. "Keep going until the mines. You will see the mines. Then you will see the bridge."

The two-lane, hundred-metre-long, beam-bridge crossed a muddily sleeping estuarial bite the river had chewed from the peninsula. A tank was parked on the northern bank, with a self-propelled howitzer stopped at the bridge's midpoint. Except the cannons were aimed north, not south. Their treads were snapped. They hadn't been parked, they'd been abandoned.

"What type are they? I think I recognise them," Tess said.

"From a history book," Clyde said. "The tank's a T-54."

"Soviet?" Tess asked.

"Originally," Clyde said. "The howitzer is a Gvodzika. That's still in production but I didn't think anyone south of Ethiopia operated them. From the direction of their guns, they broke down during a retreat."

The drivers were gone, and no one was now left to guard this bridge. Nor the next. But someone still fought on the peninsula. As the wind changed, from ahead, she caught the sound of gunfire.

Scrub turned to scree, and then to slag as they drove south, and into terrain torn asunder by strip mining. Those machines had been re-purposed, driven onto the hundred-metre-long bridge. There, they had joined ancient tanks to become steel barricades at either end of the bridge, with a third barricade halfway along. The bridge ran nearly north to south. Below, the river had shrunk to a meandering twenty-metre-wide path, surrounded either side by a semi-lush, flood-plain forest. To the northwest, she could make out a patch of semi-cleared land that would have been farmed in any other year. But now, the people were gone, except from on the bridge itself. The sound of gunfire marked a last desperate defence against the undead.

Even as they braked, a woman jumped from the giant crane which mostly blocked this end of the bridge, and ran towards them. She wore jeans, a sweat-stained shirt, and a blood stained hijab, and carried an old rifle with a very short magazine.

"*As-salamu alaykum*," she said. "You have guns? *Proper* guns?"

"I guess we do," Tess said. "How many do you need?"

"All of them," the woman said.

Tess, Clyde, Hawker, and Oakes followed the woman back onto the bridge, leaving the scientists, Toppley, and Zach to continue loading magazines.

Next to another stalled history-book tank was an achingly modern crane. Her closest friend, Liu Higson, had a husband whose job was to fly such machines between the mineral deposits of the world. From him, and those occasional investigations which led her to outback mines, she recognised it as being used to haul even larger pieces of mining equipment into place. But here, it reminded her of more recent stories of the Canadian army using earth-movers as tanks with which to crush the undead.

With caterpillar treads as tall as her head, its height certainly offered safety from the undead for the people on top. Women. All bandaged, blood-stained, and battle-weary. That crane must be an impromptu aid-station. But their young guide was running too fast for Tess to ask questions. Too fast for her to keep up.

She fell behind the men, angling across the roadway, slowing her pace, taking in the bridge, the bodies, the bullet casings, and the open grassland below.

The undead must, previously, have reached the far end of the bridge, but been driven back. No, not driven. Because the undead would never retreat. They arrived in waves. One wave had been obliterated, but at the cost of tens of thousands of rounds of ammunition. Another wave was being held halfway along the bridge, at the second barricade, this one made of four bulldozers parked abreast. On top were more civilian-clad defenders. Eighteen, perhaps twenty. It was both their number, and their age. About half wore a hijab, none wore uniforms, while every single one of them was a woman.

"Come. Up. Go. Fight," their guide said, pausing at the ladder at the rear of the right-most caterpillar.

"Oakes, take the left. Major, on the right," Hawker said. "Commissioner, with me," he added, crossing to the next bulldozer along.

Hawker was already firing when she reached the top. Tess took one look at the bridge, and the irregular ranks of the hellish legion beyond. "Here," she handed her carbine to their guide. "And take these." She pulled out her magazines. "Hold the line, Colonel!"

She jumped back down and ran, pushing through the pain from her hip, sprinting back to the bus.

"Keep loading!" she yelled at Teegan and Zach as she put the bus into gear.

"How bad is it?" Avalon asked.

"Five hundred zombies," Tess said. "More coming. About three minutes from over-running this bridge." She drove, foot to the floor, around the crane. "They're at the base of the dozers. About twenty women with rifles as old as those tanks are just about holding them at bay."

The bus bounced over corpses. Metal shook. The bus juddered even after she'd braked, barely a metre from the rear of a bulldozer.

"Load the carbines, and get them passed out to the defenders," Tess said, grabbing a carbine and slotting a loaded magazine into place.

"No," Avalon said. "That's too inefficient. We will load weapons for those in these two central bulldozers. Injured people are atop that rear-most crane. We need to get them aboard, and get them loading magazines, too. Mr Magaia, Zachary, fetch them. If required, we'll use this bus to retreat at least as far as the end of the bridge. Well?" she added. "Why are you waiting? Leo, grab those magazines. Tess, the guns. Zachary, drive back and fetch the wounded."

"Do it," Tess said, loading another carbine, jumping off, and then climbing up to the dozer on which their guide, Hawker, and two other women shot the undead.

"Loaded guns," Tess said, placing a carbine next to each of the local women, before raising one of her own. She lowered it without firing a shot, but not for the lack of a target. Four hundred metres lay between this central barricade and the barrier at the bridge's western shore, and each square metre contained at least one of the undead. Pushing. Shoving. Scrumming towards the thick-steeled construction machines. Some in rags, some in uniform, some already mutilated from a previous fight.

With the locals now armed with fast-firing carbines, and with her soldiers firing precise single shots at an almost fully automatic pace, a wall of aimed lead was being flung into the slow-moving horde. But not all shots were kills. The sound of gunfire was too great to call out targets. Gore sprayed from shoulders, arced from backs, pulsed from chests, but nothing other than a headshot would stop these living demons.

The bulldozers, if they had fuel, could advance, but only if each advanced at the exact same speed. Anything else would open a gap through which the undead would squirm, slither, and slide behind their lines, trapping them, and dooming the children still trapped in Inhambane. But the corpses were beginning to form an uneven mound in front of the dozer's giant blades. While the giant mining machines shook under the pressure of the surging death-wave, they weren't moving, but they would soon be swamped, overwhelmed.

"Magazine!" Hawker called.

"Loaded rifle!" Tess replied, holding out her carbine.

"Good on ya, but we need mags!"

"On it," she said, and jumped back down.

Over the sound of flesh beating steel, of lead smashing skull, and the whisper of air concertinaing from dead lungs, came the bus's struggling growl. Zach was behind the wheel, and spun the bus in a brake-squealing, rubber-burning, dust-flinging, one-hundred-degree turn. Aboard were four women, and Luis Magaia.

"There's two more ladies up on the crane," Zach said. "But they're unconscious. I need Clyde and Nicko to help get them down."

"They're safe where they are for now," Tess said. "Zach, Luis, take the loaded rifles to dozers. Bring back the empties. Mags and guns. Ladies, hi. We're loading," she said, ripping the lid from an ammo crate.

Each M4-carbine was shipped with a magazine, but unloaded. Magazine-less carbines now littered the floor, while only one crate of guns had yet to be opened. She grabbed a carbine, and ejected the magazine.

"We know what to do," a woman said. "The bullets go in… this way around."

It wasn't a question, and was followed by instructions in Portuguese, directed at the two women with bandaged legs, then in Arabic for the woman whose head and neck were covered in gauze.

Tess followed those same instructions, and began stripping the remaining carbines of their magazines.

"Are you New Zealanders from the battleship?" the woman asked, not taking her eyes from the magazine.

"Australians from the plane," Tess said. "My name's Tess Qwong."

"Laila Tembe," the woman said. Her accent was learned-from-a-tutor British that Tess associated with the old black and white English movies her mother had loved though never understood. Laila wore a brown hijab and a white shirt, both splattered with blood. The left sleeve had been cut away so that a bandage could be affixed to her arm. "I was bitten an hour ago," Laila added. "Please be ready."

Tess undid the flap of her holster. "Understood."

"Thank you," Laila said. "The planes have arrived for the children?"

"I'm sorry, no, not yet. We thought all the refugees had already been evacuated. My pilot's fetching more planes, but it'll be another day before they arrive."

"A whole day?" Her face tightened, but her hands didn't stop moving. "Then we must fight for one more day. Just one more."

The magazines now removed, Tess began loading. "What happened here? Where are the tank drivers?"

"Gone," Laila said. "All the others left."

"They crossed the bridge?

"They went south," Laila said. "Across other bridges."

"More please!" Zach said, jumping aboard.

"Help yourself," Tess said.

"This is something, isn't it?" Zach said, and sounded genuinely enthused. But he was gone before Tess could formulate a reply.

"Better to be excited than terrified," Laila said, as if reading Tess's thoughts. "My brother was the same."

"Did he make it this far?" Tess asked.

"He's alive. Waiting for a plane," Laila said. "But he was caught in the fire. The explosion, as was Saleema." She nodded to the woman whose head and shoulders were bandaged.

"Explosion?" Tess asked. "What happened here?"

"We fought. We fight. Some gave up," Laila said. "More were here. A rear guard. They left when this defensive line was breached. We remained because we must keep the dead souls away from the children."

"Those are your kids at the airport?" Tess asked.

Laila laughed, and when she translated Tess's question into Portuguese and then Arabic, so did two of the other women, while Saleema gave a wetly guttural grunt. "We're not married," Laila said. "We're *nurses*. We brought the children here from the hospital. We wanted to put them on a boat to Madagascar where they would be safe. So we were told."

"Ah, got it," Tess said.

"G'day, ladies," Oakes said, appearing in the door. "The name's Nicko. I'm told one of you knows which of those tanks was fired this morning."

"At the end of the bridge, next to the crane," Laila said.

"Bonzer," Oakes said. "Mind your ears, there's gonna be a bang."

"Wait, Oakes!" Tess began, but the sergeant was already sprinting back along the bridge.

"Any more?" Leo asked, taking Oakes's place a second later.

"Take what you can," Tess said, her fingers twitching as she kept on reloading.

The bandaged woman, Saleema, hissed a pained question in Arabic.

"Is she all right?" Tess asked.

"Second-degree burns," Laila said. "She would like to know if you're a soldier."

"I'm a police officer," Tess said.

"Police?" Laila translated. Saleema gave a rasping reply. Laila laughed, then spoke in Portuguese. The other two women laughed in turn. "She asked if you've come to arrest the zombies for loitering or for littering," Laila said.

Tess forced a chuckle. "Hey, at this point, I'm willing to try anything."

A loud pop came from the north, a sound Tess didn't have time to interpret before a massive explosion erupted in the south, drowning the irregular drumroll of rifle fire. The bus shook. The windows rattled. Tess's heart skipped a beat.

"We had three tank shells left when the tank drivers ran," Laila said calmly.

And the second was fired a moment later. The third so swiftly afterward that the bus didn't have time to settle between each mini-quake.

Tess picked up a carbine, slotting a magazine into place, but placed the M4 next to her leg.

Laila did the same. "My sisters and I will ensure you can retreat," she said.

"We'll all retreat together," Tess said. "Get ready for the rush," she added, seeing Zach jump down from the dozer.

"Yeah, it's over," Zach said. "You should have seen the explosion. It was awesome!"

Gunfire crackled from the barricade.

"If it's over, why are they still shooting?" Tess said. "Take over. Finish loading the magazines." She paused in the doorway. "Zach, this woman was bitten. She might turn."

"Oh," he said, suddenly deflating. "I… What do I do?"

"Kill me, if you have to," Laila said calmly. "Sit down. There is work to be done before then."

Chapter 8 - A Bridge Too Far
Rio Mutamba, Mozambique

Tess held tight to the edge of the dozer's cab as she leaned forward, but she couldn't lean far enough. "I see what you mean," she said. "You can't see the zombies lying right up against the blade."

Below, the living ghouls banged and clawed, slithered and crawled over each other, only occasionally managing to stand and present their heads as a target for Clyde or Toppley. Everyone else held their fire. For now.

The bridge-way had become an open graveyard of occasionally moving corpses. Hundreds of dead had created a thick mat close to the dozer, thinning towards the barricade at the bridge's far end. Beyond, and below, more milled and gathered around the large craters the tank's shells had left at the edge of the flood plain. They came from inland, and from east and west, and from among the long grasses of the lush river basin immediately below the bridge.

"How many zoms are still down there, close to the dozers?" Tess asked.

"Assume fifty for the purposes of planning," Hawker said. "We can't move the dozers without opening a point of entry. It's a solid defensive line. We can hold against two more similar assaults. The trouble will come from below. That river isn't wide enough to stop them."

"That's why you fired the shells?" Tess asked.

"It was a case of use 'em or lose 'em," Hawker said. "Because if the zoms get across that river, we'll lose this position. They follow each other, don't they? The gunfire will lure them in, but the clock's ticking on how long before we have to retreat."

"We're far further from Inhambane than the New Zealand commander implied," Tess said. "I think this is the wrong bridge. We're not where the New Zealanders think the front is, and it's less well defended than it should be. But you saw them off." A louder than usual bang came from dozer-blades, followed by a sharp rifle crack. "I mean you've stopped the advance. No, that's wrong too."

"We destroyed that wave," Hawker said. "But they're approaching from the southeast and southwest. Southwest isn't an immediate problem. They'll follow the lowland and the river basin until it becomes the estuary. It's the southeast we've got to watch. If they knew what they were doing, they could ford that river, and get behind us. That they *don't* know what they're doing, that they *can't* think, that's what'll allow us to hold this position for a few more hours."

Sergeant Oakes bounded across the bridge-way and leaped up the ladder. "Did I hit the wicket, sir?" he asked.

"Close enough," Hawker said. "Help the major snipe any targets within range. Commissioner, we need to get word to town that we're under-equipped, and overextended. We need people and material to create a secondary barricade. Build a defensive line ten metres back that way, fuel up these dozers and drive them forward to crush the zoms. That'll preserve a good portion of ammunition, and kill enough of the enemy to reduce the threat to the city up north."

"We've already used about a third of the bullets we brought with us," Tess said.

"Only a third?" Hawker said. "That's good. Send Toppley back to Inhambane with Zendaya." He pointed to the guide who'd met them at the end of the bridge. "Send Zach with them, and any of the injured nurses who can't run."

"Ah," she said, understanding. "What about the scientists?"

"They're competent shots, and calm in a crisis," Hawker said. "They can stay. We'll send the nurses to the rear to rest. Take on the next wave ourselves. The third wave is when things will get tight." He pointed to the dozer on the extreme right. "That machine moved five centimetres in the last attack. It'll move more in the next."

Tess turned to look, but was distracted by a shout.

"Inbound!" Clyde called.

Tess turned towards the far end of the bridge. Three zoms had made it around the furthest barricade. But Clyde was pointing north.

A helicopter, approaching at a height of fifty metres, was following the road. The copter banked east, crossing the river.

"Must be the Kiwis," Tess said.

"That's a U.S. Coastguard Seahawk," Hawker said, just before a machine gun opened fire. "An up-gunned Seahawk," he added. "Sounds like a fifty-cal."

Mounted in the open cabin door, the machine gun unleashed a hail of lead into the ranks of the undead massed beyond the bridge. Added to the burr of the rotors, the sound tore up the sky while the bullets tore through the dead souls tramping through the long grass, around the trees, and over one another in their attempt to reach this new and noisy foe.

Just as Tess thought *another five minutes and the zoms will all be dead*, the machine gun ceased fire, the helicopter turned, and buzzed back along the bridge.

"They're landing!" Hawker yelled, raising his voice over the rotor's sawing burr.

"Hostiles inbound!" Oakes called.

At the far end of the bridge, a pair of zombies walked abreast, another behind, and more behind it.

"We've got this, Tess," Hawker said. "Speak to the Kiwis. Arrange reinforcements."

Tess climbed back down, and jogged towards the landing helicopter. As she approached the bus, she slowed long enough to hear an odd mix of Australian, Arabic, and Portuguese topped with laughter. She might not understand the words, and the bantering tone was forced and fearful, yet it was proof to her, and to each other, that they were still alive. So far.

A co-pilot remained behind the stick while two figures had disembarked from the copter. One had a wrench with which she was attacking the machine-gun mount, while the other was Commander Tusitala who beckoned Tess a little way from the spinning blades.

"Where's the tank crew and radio-team?" Tusitala asked.

"We found twenty nurses here, armed with rifles," Tess said. "Everyone else had fled. What's wrong with your helicopter?"

Tusitala turned to look. "Impromptu machine-gun mount. Hurry it up, Sullivan!" she said, addressing the sailor-mechanic. "Almost lost the weapon. Our Seasprite was downed by—" She shook her head. "Another time. How long can you hold this bridge?"

"Until the ammo runs out," Tess said. "But we've already burned through a third. It all depends on how many more zoms come, and how soon. Those dozers could be used to crush the undead. We'll need more personnel for that."

"We must hold the bridges," Tusitala said. "They're our land-link to the continent, and our escape route from the city."

"If we lose the airport, there'll be no airlift," Tess said.

The commander shook her head. "There'll never be enough planes for everyone," she said. "Medical supplies have run out. Drinking water will last three days. Ammunition will last four, and food will be gone in five. It would take a week to airlift everyone from here, but your pilot is planning to return with commercial aircraft, landing on an improperly extended runway. A crash is all but inevitable. Your people are Special Forces, aren't they?"

"Three are," Tess said. "Two are scientists. The rest are civilian-support. What are you planning?"

"Captain Adams wants to seize control of a ship used for the Madagascan evacuation."

"Do you mean a drifting ship full of zombies?" Tess asked.

"One vessel, possibly two, should suffice as a temporary sea-bastion until a rescue fleet can arrive. We'll repair the engines and make for safer waters. Unless you can come up with an alternative, we'll take the first ship at dawn. Your pilot should return two hours afterwards, at which point, we'll assess casualties, and better assess the possibilities. Agreed?"

The carbine fire was increasing in volume.

"We'll need fuel and drivers for the dozers," Tess said. "And ammunition. A lot."

“I’ll arrange a relief,” the commander said. “When they arrive, you’re to return to Inhambane.” With a final nod, she jogged back to the helicopter. Tess didn’t wait to watch it take off, but returned to the dozer.

The second wave, already shredded by the helicopter-mounted heavy machine gun, was smaller than the first. After ten minutes, Hawker yelled “Cease fire! Cease fire! Only the snipers.”

Tess lowered her carbine, taking in the battered, body-littered bridge. The undead kept coming. Kept walking into death. Neither fear nor failure had any meaning to this foe. Objectively, she’d known it for weeks, but it was still hard to accept this counter-intuitive reality.

She jumped down from the dozer. In the bus, the bandaged nurse, Saleema, was repeating words in Arabic, which Zach was slowly repeating.

“You’re learning the alphabet?”

“Waltzing Matilda,” Zach said. “You’ll never guess what the Arabic for jumbuck is.”

Avalon had stopped loading, and had drawn a small revolver. Though it wasn’t pointing directly at Laila, her attention was. The nurse had her eyes closed, her head leaning back against the bus’s metal roof strut.

“Laila, how are feeling?” Tess asked.

“Tired,” the nurse said. “My sisters, at the rear, could you see how they are?”

“No worries,” Tess said. Outside, she saw Toppley walking back to the bus with a webbing bag full of spent magazines. “Fancy a stroll, Teegan?”

“I always do before lunch,” Toppley said, dropping the bag by the steps of the bus. “It’s about that time, isn’t it?”

“Give or take an hour,” Tess said, as the two women began walking towards the far end of the bridge. “How’s the bus?”

“They are an impressive group, those nurses,” Toppley said. “We’re running short of ammunition. Half is gone already. What news did the helicopter bring?”

"There should have been a radio team here. Soldiers, too. Relief is on its way. Should be here in twenty minutes or so, depending on how fast they drive. I'd never been to war before. I stood on the walls in Canberra, and fought in the outback. This is something different. You?"

"Not like this, no. I have been witness to violence, to murder, and, sadly, to massacres, but never have I seen so many come willingly to the slaughter."

"Massacres?" Tess asked.

"I did my best to stay on the right side of history," Toppley said. "In the middle of events, it is difficult to know which side is which, but why should revolutions be won by those who've won the favour of a super-power? But I digress, and so do you. What did the pilot say?"

"They don't come willingly," Tess said. "The zoms. There's no will involved. That's why this is different to war."

"You're still digressing."

Tess stepped around a long-dead corpse whose chest had more holes than a putting green, but which had finally been stopped by the machete still embedded in its skull.

"I'm not," Tess said. "I've read a lot about war. The Korean War, particularly. I was trying to make sense of the world my mum grew up in. I read about the atrocities, and the barbarity of the north. She'd never talk about it."

"Ah. She was a defector, yes?" Toppley said. "How she escaped is a story I'd truly like to hear, though not until after I know what the helicopter pilot said. I take it that it's not good news."

"What I learned about the frenetic chaos of war is that unit commanders often don't have a complete picture," Tess said. "It feels like we're winning, when the war has already been lost. Inhambane is a few days away from running out of food, water, and ammo. After Mick took off, Commander Tusitala must have returned to the ship, and spoken with the captain. The captain has assessed the situation, and determined that the last chance for a successful airlift was today, and our arrival confirms it won't happen in time. Tomorrow, at dawn, they're going to attempt to seize control of one of those floating freighters full of zombies, and turn that into an offshore refuge. Failing that, they want to keep this bridge open as a means of escape."

"Ah. Then things *are* bad. The Kiwis don't believe an airlift will happen. Do you?"

"Mick'll try," Tess said. "He's a legend in the outback, where he really was the difference between life and death. But after we landed, things happened too quickly for me to properly process it all. An airlift requires extending that runway, and flying to a semi-flooded runway in Diego Garcia. If we weren't under attack, or short of supplies, I'd say it was fifty-fifty we'd pull it off. But the ship has been here longer. The captain knows the odds of success, and thinks going cabin-to-cabin on a zombie-infested boat gives us a greater chance of survival."

"I hate to agree, seeing as what that means for our future," Toppley said, "but the truth can't be avoided. That river below is more of an obstacle than a barrier."

"We could hold off another two similar-sized attacks," Tess said. "So it comes down to how many zoms are out there, and how many are heading this way. But if we'd arrived an hour later, this bridge would already have fallen. No, this isn't a defence, it's a fighting retreat."

Atop the crane-platform at the eastern edge of the bridge, they found the teacher, Luis Magaia, clutching an M4-carbine with the safety still on.

"I was watching them," he said. "In case they turned."

"She's dead," Toppley said, closing the eyes of a now deceased nurse.

"But she's not," Tess said, checking the pulse of the other nurse, a woman with bandages on her face, and more on a stumpy wrist. "We'll transfer her to the bus. The other nurses can watch her until we can get her back to town. We'll need to create a hoist, lower her at shoulders, waist, and ankles. We need four people, Teegan, and the bus."

"Of course, Commissioner," Teegan said, wincing as she straightened, pressing her hand into the small of her back. "Ah, there are some moments I miss my prison cell. Not many, but with a frequency which increases with each of these grinding reminders of my advancing years."

"I thought you were still in your forties," Tess said.

"Ha! Look at me and see your future, young lady," Toppley said, as she bent to climb back down. She paused. "Tess, vehicles."

"It's the relief column," Tess said. "Get the bus, and get everyone aboard. We're heading back to the city."

"Relief indeed," Toppley said, continuing down to the ground.

Eight vehicles approached. Three up-armoured Landcruisers, two factory-armoured cars, and three battered open-topped trucks. They were full of people and supplies. The vehicles stopped in a cloud of tyre-thrown dust a hundred metres from the bridge. The lead Landcruiser continued alone.

Luis Magaia climbed down the ladder, but Tess stayed atop the crane-platform, looking, watching, and assessing these new arrivals. She turned to the unconscious woman. "Hold on just a bit longer, ma'am. We'll get you out of here." Finally, she climbed down the ladder.

A shot came from the centre of the bridge, then a second. The gunfire had become an ignorable background patter, but as her brain switched modes from proto-general back into suspicious-cop, she became aware of the shooting again. She counted the time between shots as she walked over to the Landcruiser where Luis was frantically addressing the soldiers who'd disembarked.

Three soldiers: a driver and a passenger, both armed with some variety of Kalashnikov, as was the third, standing in the back, weapon resting on a semi-circular steel shield.

"G'day," Tess said. "Glad to see you. Worst seems to be over. Police Commissioner Tess Qwong, out of Australia but here with the U.N."

"Captain De Silva," the driver said. "You will need secure transport to take the injured women to the city. We will give you one of our trucks."

"Our bus will do the job," Tess said, looking back at the remains of the convoy. They were full of people and supplies. But some of the people were children. Few of the supplies looked to be defensive. Yes, there were water containers, but there were also spare tyres, fuel cans, ropes, chains, shovels and picks. The suitcases were as likely to contain clothes as ammo, while she couldn't think of a single strategic purpose to the three chickens in the cage atop the rearmost Landcruiser.

Tess turned back to the bridge where the nurses were boarding the bus. A shot came from the dozer. The newly arrived captain made no move to reinforce the bulldozer-barricade. Tess looked up at the crane. Even if she immobilised the dozers, they could easily be hauled out of the way.

"Did you bring the radio?" Tess asked, turning back to the captain.

"There is a radio in the Landcruiser," he said, waving to one of vehicles behind, less heavily loaded than the others. "It is a *good* car. Better than your bus."

"I'm sure it is," Tess said, stalling for time. "Do you have anyone who knows how to drive a bulldozer?"

"Yes, but they need too much fuel," De Silva said. "So does a bus like yours. Take our Landcruiser. You need to get back to the city quickly, yes?"

"Not so quickly we'd leave our people behind," Tess said. Behind her, the engine purred, and the bus sped towards them. "You best get your people in position. Our ammo and rifles are up on the dozers."

"Ah. You left the guns? Then you will have room for these injured women," De Silva said. "You won't need our Landcruiser?"

"No worries, you're all right. Good luck." Tess gave a half smile, and turned to the bus, waving it down. "There's an injured woman on the roof. Double quick, get her inside."

"With me, Sergeant," Hawker said, throwing himself up the ladder.

With her and Clyde below, they had the nurse off the roof and into the back.

"Drive now, drive fast," Tess said, holding onto the doorway, even as Laila tended to the unconscious woman.

"Only speed I know," Zach said, from behind the wheel.

When they were beyond the parked convoy she began to relax.

"Don't slow," Tess said. "But don't race. I don't want to crash, but I don't want them to try to catch us."

"You mean the zoms?" Zach asked.

"No, those soldiers," Tess said. "Maybe I read the situation wrong, but they brought their kids. The commander sent them, but they brought their kids to the bridge. They must have come to Inhambane looking for an evacuation. An airlift was promised, but only one plane arrived. Now, they're looking to escape. They wanted our bus for the ammo and carbines."

"Oh. Were we supposed to leave them behind?" Zach asked.

"Nope," Tess said. "We'll need them to protect the city."

"We have to protect the bridges," Laila said.

"If we stayed, we'd have fought over the guns," Tess said.

"We'd have won," Oakes said.

"We'd have made those kids orphans, and we'd still be defending the bridge, but with even less ammo. We'd have had to retreat anyway. No, we can't start killing each other. Not now. The commander said she was sending reinforcements to hold that bridge. When we get to the city, we can ask her to send the helicopter to check they're still there. But those were the best people she could find, and I'm pretty certain they plan to run, not fight. Maybe they will hold the bridge for a while, but when they leave, it won't be to return to Inhambane."

Chapter 9 - Almost Paradise
Tofo Beach, Mozambique

The new walls of Inhambane were rising around the city's outskirts, but not fast enough.

"Where do we go?" Zach asked, slowing the bus as he drove around a pile of rubble over which a team were pouring cement. The labourers, like her driver, should still be in school.

"Good question," Tess said. "Laila, where's the hospital?"

"The old cathedral," she said.

"I will guide you," Zendaya said.

If Inhambane had known busier decades, the old cathedral had seen better centuries. The paint had skinned, the plaster had creviced, and the mortar had powdered while the three-storey tower was one amen away from collapse. A fresh red cross had been painted to the left of the doors, a red crescent to the right, while from inside came the soft moans of the dying.

As the nurses carried their injured sisters inside, and Dr Avalon went to assist, Tess leaned against the bus.

"Water," Hawker said, holding out a bottle.

"Good on ya," Tess said. "How long can we hold this city?"

"As long as we have to," Hawker said. "Mick'll need to bring in about a hundred and fifty flights. They achieved fifteen hundred a day during the Berlin airlift. Now, fair dinkum, their logistical system wasn't as ropey as ours, but we've got no shortage of planes back home. No shortage of pilots. We've just got to get them to Perth. Everyone here came from somewhere else, so there's no refuge within easy driving distance. There's no secondary position we can escape to, and no way we can surrender. No, we'll hold the line until everyone's safe. If it's not by air, it'll be aboard a ship. Either way, I'd say twenty-four to thirty-six hours, and we'll be out of here."

"I wish I had your certainty."

He shrugged. "I know how to take a ship. Confined corridors will work to our advantage against the zoms. We can go deck-by-deck, clearing and sealing them as we go."

"You've done that before?"

"Ship-work? Sure. Hostage situations. But zoms don't hide, and they don't shoot back. Won't say it'll be a cool breeze on a December day, but I'd prefer it to a battle in the open."

"You, me, Oakes, and Clyde," Tess said. "What about the nurses?"

"They're fierce enough, but this will be relentless. Metal bulkheads bring a risk of ricochets. Better to pick people who've been trained in when *not* to pull the trigger. We can ask the commander who on their crew could assist. This is the reason we're supposed to be here."

"You believe in destiny?" Tess asked.

"I wouldn't call it that," he said. "Every life has moments where the future of the many turns on the actions of a few. In jobs like yours and mine, those moments happen more often than most. Doesn't mean we're guaranteed success, but I'm confident in our ability to pull this off. We all end up where we're supposed to be. Speaking of which, I'll find out where we're supposed to be now."

He went inside, while Tess turned her gaze to the people sheltering on the nearby rooftops. The zoms at the bridge had pulped their hands to the bone against the dozers' steel blades. In the process, they'd pushed one back five centimetres. Once the ammo was gone, once the spears had been thrown, the masonry dropped, the defenders would be able to do nothing but watch the zoms beat and claw at the walls below. How sturdy were the houses in this sleepy backwater city? Not sturdy enough.

Hawker returned outside with Laila at his side, Elaina just behind.

"Look who I found," Hawker said.

"I thought you were with Mick," Tess said.

"We'd have taken a seat from a kid," Elaina said. "After Dr Dodson took off, Bianca and I came here to help."

"Bianca's inside?" Tess asked.

"Watching the wounded," Elaina said. "You know, the bitten people. We're not nurses, but we're doing what we can. We'll stay here, if that's okay, because we're not soldiers, either. The colonel told us about the battle on the bridge."

"If we're not together," Tess said, "I can't guarantee there's a way out for you."

"I don't think anyone can guarantee that, Commissioner," Elaina said.

"It's where they're supposed to be," Hawker said with a shrug and smile.

"We should go to Tofo Beach," Laila said. "It's under-defended."

"The beach needs defending?" Tess asked.

"Oh, yes," Laila said. "The beach is the front line."

According to Clyde, Tofo Beach was famous. Molten gold sands met azure seas so packed with mantas you could use them as stepping stones to reach Madagascar. Well, perhaps. *Once*. Before the war. Oil-black waves frothed greenish-red foam as they broke against the grounded hulks. Broken ships filled the shallows. A mix of single-masted dhows and metal-hulled freighters created a nearly solid wall of steel and wood for as far as she could see. Around them, waves surged, dragging rope, cloth, and plastic ashore. The sands were stained every hue of the chemical rainbow, covered in the bodies of fish and birds, people and the undead.

The smell of decay, as much as the vision of Armageddon, made them all grateful to get inside the restaurant which would be their base for the night.

"Never been in a grass-roofed restaurant before," Zach said.

"There should be sentries here," Laila said. "This is the front line."

"I thought that was the bridge," Zach said.

"The ships sailed to Madagascar from Mozambique and South Africa, from Tanzania and Kenya," Laila said. "But the island was overrun with infected arriving by plane. Refugees re-boarded the ships. Some were infected. When the ports were attacked, the ships put to sea.

Those who didn't succumb to the virus took the boats, leaving only the dead aboard, and the ships adrift. Now those ships drift with the tide, until they run aground."

"It's not a virus," Avalon muttered.

"The general should be here," Laila said, looking at the half-ruined restaurant.

"Which general?" Tess asked.

"I think that is now you," Laila said. "We shall go ask. Watch the water."

"Would you ladies like an escort?" Oakes asked.

Which was met with a string of Portuguese and then Arabic as Laila translated, and then elaborated. Tess didn't understand the words, but the nurse's exaggeratedly appraising gaze, stage bow, and stifled laughter was universal.

"No harm in asking," Oakes said.

Sand lay ankle-deep across the restaurant's floor, rising to a knee-height embankment by the bar. Some furniture lay beneath the partially collapsed roof, while the rest had joined a jumbled entanglement between this property and the next.

"I've seen worse kitchens," Toppley said. "But not many. It's a playground for bugs, and they'll form a plague-sized graduation class by dawn. Between what's in there and what's on the beach, I wouldn't want to dine here, so we're fortunate the cupboards have been completely emptied."

"Congratulations, Zach," Hawker said, as he picked up a broom. "You're promoted to sweeper, first-class. Shift some of the sand for us, mate."

"No worries, sir," Zach said. "Does the promotion mean I get extra pay?"

"If you do a good job, why not?" Hawker said, extracting an oat-bar from his pocket. "Let's say an extra dollar a day." He threw the bar to Zach who grabbed it, tore the wrapper open, and inhaled the bar before, carefully, folding the wrapper up and pocketing it.

"With us wading through muck, I don't think you need to worry about littering," Oakes said.

"Yeah, but this is money, isn't it?" Zach said. "It says so. One dollar."

"Not after you've eaten the contents," Oakes said.

"Everything's worth something to someone," Zach said. "That's what Ms Godwin said."

"Twenty minutes, people!" Hawker said. "Clear the room. This is the front line. Major, would you mind scoping the perimeter."

"Clyde, please," he said. "I've been a civilian for years."

"Clyde, you go north. Nicko, south," Hawker said. "But Nicko, disable the bus first. I want to make sure no one else drives it away from here."

Avalon tugged a table from beneath the fallen roof, righted it, picked up a fallen chair, and sat. She opened her bag, and withdrew her laptop.

"Aren't you helping, Doc?" Zach asked.

"This *is* helping, Zachary," she said.

"Zach," he muttered.

"What are you working on?" Tess asked quickly, in a bid to stop Zach engaging in an impossible-to-win battle.

"I'm eliminating the unfeasible alternatives," Avalon said.

"Alternatives for what?" Tess asked.

"The weapon," Avalon said.

"You really can make one?" Zach asked.

"Of course," Avalon said. "But lethality is less critical than subject-targeting, hence my current studies, which would be easier without distraction."

Tess tugged at the fallen mat of grass, but it was more tightly bound than it had first appeared.

"Try this," Leo said, opening his pack and pulling out his weapons-belt-tool-holster. "Hatchet?"

"Worth a try," Tess said.

"Someone lit a fire here," Zach said, shoving aside the large pile of sand close to the wood panel bar. "Shall we do the same?"

"It won't get cold enough tonight," Avalon said. "This close to the equator, it will *never* get cold enough."

"Are you missing Canada?" Tess asked. Beneath her feet, glass crunched. She bent down, and picked up a photo-frame showing happy tourists. A dozen similar photos still clung to the wall, and many more lay broken among the debris.

"Homesickness is merely a manifestation of regret and fear," Avalon said.

"Yep, that sounds about my current mix of emotions," Tess said.

"This place won lots of awards," Zach said, pointing his broom at one of the frames.

"They're fake," Tess said. "Two things give it away. I don't know if the *Seoul Star* is a real paper, but I'm reasonably confident they wouldn't print in Portuguese, and certainly wouldn't stick a restaurant review on the front page."

"Dunno," Zach said. "Ms Godwin said newspapers were getting so desperate they'd print a lie today just so they could print the apology tomorrow."

"Who's Ms Godwin?" Tess asked.

"Oh, a librarian," Zach said. "Those photos *must* be real. They're all of this restaurant. This place looked nice. Look at the crowds."

"The pictures all look pretty empty to me," Tess said. "A couple, or a small group, always by the bar. Drink in hand, sometimes coffee, sometimes not, but always smiling."

"Yeah, but look at this one, you can see beyond the restaurant, to the beach, and the sea. There's lots of people at tables and… ah, yeah." He sighed, and continued sweeping.

"You've got a good eye," Tess said. "We'll make a copper out of you yet."

The air shook with a cannon's roar. Everyone stopped working and moved towards the door.

"It's the frigate," Tess said.

"Shooting at infected ships," Hawker said.

“Teegan, take watch here,” Tess said. “Everyone else, back to work.” Tess went to join Hawker by the bar. “What do you think of this place?”

“For defence? It’s terrible,” the colonel said, pulling out his water bottle. “For sleep, it won’t be much better. Keeping people here simply avoids too much pressure in the city. More refugees will depart overnight.”

“I don’t think we can stop them,” Tess said. “Morally, or practically.”

“No, but that’s why I had Nicko disable the bus. It’ll slow our escape, but guarantee we’ll get back to the city.”

“The ship’s engineers are extending the runway,” Avalon said. “From the description, I would describe the activity as clearing, rather than extending. Suitable for twenty landings at most.”

“When did you hear that?” Tess asked.

“Laila was discussing it with her nurse-friends,” Avalon said.

“In Arabic?” Tess asked.

“And Portuguese,” Avalon said.

“What were they saying about Sergeant Nicko?” Zach asked.

“Just keep sweeping, Zach,” Tess said.

The job was half done when the nurse, Laila, returned.

“I bring you dinner,” Laila said, entering with one of her fellow warrior-nurses and with two large saucepans.

“Ace,” Zach said.

“Zachary, finish sweeping,” Avalon said.

“What’s the point, the wind only blows it back in,” Zach said, but continued his Canutian chore of brushing the sand toward the beach.

“Did I smell tucker?” Oakes asked, re-appearing absurdly fast.

“If only your eyes were as good as your nose—” Hawker began, but was interrupted by a shot. Not a cannon’s roar, but a rifle’s bark. Then another, followed by a short barrage.

“Rest time’s over,” Hawker said. “Oakes, up front. Zach, secure the saucepan. Avalon, secure your notes. Form up on Nicko, but hold your fire until we’re certain of the target.”

Chapter 10 - Waves of Death
Tofo Beach, Mozambique

The setting sun cast a prismatic sheen on the oil-drenched sands. Small wrecks filled the shallows, while the shoreline was dotted with metal and timber flotsam. Ragged sails and bright rags floated on the surface, while the surf continually dragged rotting corpses ashore. Those buzzing with insects had recently been the living, while those with crushed skulls were the recently living dead.

The rifle fire had now ceased. The target was as unclear as who had fired, though the man walking towards them carried his gun close to his shoulder, the barrel aimed at the sea. It was Clyde.

"It gets worse after dark," Laila said. "I shall return to my sisters. Dawn will come, and we will see you then."

"It's a date," Oakes said.

"No, it will be breakfast," Laila said.

"What were you shooting at, Major?" Hawker asked.

"Not me," Clyde said. "Target was a corpse, moving with the waves. Defenders are all civilians. Poorly trained and poorly armed. One always makes the other worse. Everyone who had a vehicle, or who could steal one, has already fled."

"What's the resolve of the people who remain?" Hawker asked. "Will they stand?"

"For as long as they have bullets," Clyde said. "So not for very long."

Minutes became hours, marked by the irregular roar of the ship's cannon. Driftwood was gathered and stacked outside their restaurant, ready to be lit when the undead came. Night came first. The stars followed. The only humanoid shadows belonged to skulking refugee-defenders who'd decided survival lay elsewhere. With spotlights and lamps rigged about its deck, the frigate became a new star, as deadly, as life-giving, and as impossibly far away.

Dinner was eaten in silence, hurriedly, and, despite the surrounding rot, left Tess wanting more.

"This darkness is absurd," Avalon said, standing up. "Leo, be useful and help me."

"Back in a bit," Leo said, handing his own half-finished bowl to Zach.

"Where are you going?" Tess asked.

"We will commune with Joseph Swan," Avalon said.

"Is that Canuck for painting the dunny?" Oakes asked.

But the scientists were already disappearing among the shadows. They weren't gone long.

"Mind your eyes," Leo said, raising his hands. A dull yellow beam stretched southward across the beach. "It's one of the bus's headlamps rigged to the laptop's spare battery pack."

"How long will it last?" Hawker asked.

"A couple of hours," Leo said.

"Zach, take it up to the restaurant's roof," Hawker said. "Nicko, give him a boost. Zach, stick to the central beams, they'll take your weight. Don't switch on the lamp until you get the order. When you do, aim it at the shallows, not at us."

"Don't forget your weapon," Nicko said.

"Take these," Avalon said, handing Zach a notebook, pen, and a small reading light.

"What is it?"

"Homework," Avalon said. "Education should never wait."

Zach turned the light on, and opened the notebook. "If a train is travelling at— You seriously want me to do equations?"

"We don't want you falling asleep," Avalon said.

"Bet I will now," Zach grumbled as he followed Sergeant Oakes back to the restaurant.

The ship's cannon roared. The sky briefly glowed orange as the shell impacted somewhere beyond the horizon. More lights sprang from the ship, followed by two flares, fired fore and aft, then a third, fired shoreward, creating ominously stretched shadows among the floating wreckage.

"Danger is still a long time away," Clyde said, his voice low and calm, but so close to her ear Tess jumped.

"Strewth, mate, you made me spring high enough to leave my boots behind," she said.

The warship fired again, followed by a sharper staccato burst from a machine gun. To their left and right, single shots joined the distant automatic fire. But those bullets, fired blind into a roiling sea, did no harm to the waves.

Two lights detached themselves from the warship.

"They're sending out a boat," Clyde said. "But they can't approach too close to shore, not while the civilians are shooting at shadows."

"But *what* are they shooting at?" Tess asked.

The warship's main gun ceased fire, while the machine gun had switched to short, irregular bursts. Another flare turned the sea crimson, though some patches appeared more red than others. From the ship came a put-put-put almost instantly followed by a triplet of at-surface explosions.

"Grenade launcher," Clyde said. "Part of a close-combat weapons system in case pirates, in fast boats, try to swarm the ship."

"You think there are pirates out there?" Tess asked.

"Nope," Clyde said. "It's all zoms."

Ship-plates and twisted hulls clanked and groaned as waves surged over the shore-side wreckage. But above that, distant and indistinct, she could hear the sound of gunfire from the warship.

"Are they using rifles?" she asked.

"Could be," Clyde said. "The small boat's stopped firing. It's heading north, towards the two diesel freighters, I guess."

"Running away?" Tess asked. "Or are they running towards a new danger?"

"Neither, they're getting clear of the crossfire," Clyde said.

Another flare rose from the ship, illuminating the sea, now scattered with reflective-red strips and dotted with small lights.

"Is it just me, or are there lights at sea? Lots of them?" she said.

"Yep," Clyde said.

"They're life jackets, aren't they?" she said. "People in life jackets, but the ship is firing. Zombies! Zombies in life jackets."

"Floaters inbound!" Clyde called. "Ten minutes."

"Ten minutes? That long?" Tess asked.

"With this tide? Ten minutes, and then for a couple of hours," Clyde said, still utterly calm. "Must have been a cruise ship for them to have so many life jackets to hand out. The frigate didn't sink the ship, she burst it."

"We're forming a line," the colonel called. "Us and the nurses, five metres apart. You deal with your section, and let your neighbour deal with theirs. I've got the north. Nicko, get Zach to turn on the spotlight, then you take the south. If I set fire to that pile of kindling, it's time to retreat to the bus, and back to Inhambane."

Tess knew enough to keep her rifle lowered as she watched the crimson shadows creep into the beam of the bus's removed headlamp. Flare light glinted from the life jacket's reflective strips, overwhelming the vest's weakly flashing light. This was worse than the bridge. There she'd been one part of an improvised killing machine, effective as long as the ammo lasted, and the dozers remained in position. It was worse than Broken Hill where the principal enemy had been familiarly human. It was worse than the coup, for then there had been no time for fear.

The floater's arm languidly rose. He had a beard, mostly grey. His head was close-shaved. Beneath the vest, his shirt was green and red. Not a uniform. Just a civilian. Just another person. The mouth opened. The arms thrashed. The shallows foamed as hands splashed. Just another zombie. She fired. The figure slumped. Finally, utterly, eternally motionless. She kept her light on the corpse, watching the body drift with the waves, forth, then back, then forth, until it snagged on a semi-submerged spar.

She scanned the waves for the next patch of reflected light, then lowered the carbine as she realised it would take another minute before it was in range.

At first, it was easy. Surprisingly so. The blinking lights and reflective strips grew more distinct as the floating bodies approached. As some became entangled with sunken wreckage, those same lights gave her a distance-marker by which to judge her aim. From beyond their section of beach, the gunfire rose to a frenzy, but more quickly slackened as ammunition was expended. But the neighbouring gunfire didn't entirely cease. As long as the other defenders held the line, as long as they had ammunition, as long as they didn't flee, they could control this beach. But for how long would that be?

When her trigger clicked on an empty chamber, it came as a surprise. She slotted a new magazine into place, forcing herself to pocket the empty before raising the carbine and firing her thirty-first shot at what had to be nearly the same number of dead. A quick glance up and down the beach, and she saw a star-field of lights decorating the wreckage, illuminating the carpet of reflective-red in the nearby shallows. Her confidence fled.

The ships which had arrived in Australia, and those which they had sent back to sea, had been crammed ten times beyond capacity. Here, the number of passengers was irrelevant. How many life jackets did a cruise ship carry? Hundreds of corpses had already washed onto an already toxic shore. By mid-day, this beach would be uninhabitable. No matter how hard they fought, this beach was lost. But they had no method of organising a retreat, and nowhere to escape to, so she fired on, until she heard a scream, then a burst of automatic fire from behind. The light from the dim headlamp vanished.

"Hold the line!" Tess yelled as she spun around.

The restaurant's grass roof had collapsed. Zach's belly was balanced on the roof beam, his legs on one side, his arms on the other. Beneath him, the fallen roof shuddered and broke as a zombie punched and kicked through the withered grass. Only its cumbersome red life jacket prevented the creature from reaching high enough to grab Zach's legs.

"Hold on, Zach!" she said.

"Yeah, you think?" Zach yelled back.

A second zombie rose like a volcano from under the collapsed grass roof. She fired, but it stumbled. Her shot missed. A second bullet blew the ghoul's skull apart, but that shot hadn't come from her weapon.

"Drop, Zachary!" Laila called.

"Get him out of here, I'll secure the street," Tess said.

"Of course," Laila said.

"No," Hawker said.

Tess half-turned. She'd not heard the soldier following her.

"The zombies are behind us," Tess said, as Laila hauled Zach through the collapsed branches.

"An unknown number of hostiles, in an unlit town, in unfamiliar terrain," Hawker said. "We'll form a square on the beach, where any stray bullets are unlikely to hit our transport. As long as our ammo lasts, we've nothing to fear."

"It won't last forever," Tess said. "I'm down to two magazines."

"When we're down to one, that's when we'll retreat," Hawker said.

16th March

Chapter 11 - Prayer for the Living
Inhambane, Mozambique

Never had dawn taken so long to arrive, though when it did, and Tess looked around, she found that no one had died. In fact, their numbers had grown. Either not understanding Colonel Hawker's orders, or pretending not to, the nurses had dashed into the darkness, returning with one or two survivors, again and again. While a running figure was the best indication in near-darkness that a person wasn't undead, it had still been nearly impossible not to shoot the figures charging in from every direction.

"We need a better way of telling zombies from the living," Tess said, as Laila jogged back to their beachfront square beside a rotund man struggling to keep up. "How's your arm?"

"Almost as alive as I am," Laila said. "I worry the wound has become infected. We must locate more antibiotics."

"The sun's rising," Tess said. "We'll find some this morning."

"There are none here," Laila said. "Before you arrived, we had searched for as far as the helicopter can reach. We must look elsewhere."

"The helicopter has been flying off in search of supplies?" Tess asked, getting another clue to the nightmare existence for these refugees hoping help would come with the new dawn. But this dawn had only brought clarity as to the extent of the destruction.

"Never understood why they called dawn a cold light," Clyde said. "Feels pretty warm to me."

"It's a massacre," Zach said.

The sand was covered in red-vested corpses. The life-vests' emergency lights still flashed, though they were barely visible against the rising sun. More bodies, some still moving, were snagged on the semi-sunken debris littering the shore. Even more dotted the now calm sea.

"The tide's going out, isn't it?" Tess asked.

"We've got a few hours respite," Hawker said. "My advice—"

But before he could give it, four-engined salvation lumbered through the sky, shredding the stillness twice over as a cheer erupted from among the refugee-defenders.

"That's a C-5 Galaxy," Clyde said. "She's the plane which should have brought us here."

"Better late than never," Tess said. "Bruce, what do we do?"

"I'll clear the beach," Hawker said. "Pick up survivors. Eliminate any hostiles. But this position won't hold. We'll fall back inland, and away from the shore. I need to know how many planes are inbound, and a timeframe for a complete evac."

"Laila, could you come with me to translate? C'mon, Zach."

"Me?" he asked.

"You're my driver, aren't you?" Tess said. "We'll take the injured with us, back to the airport."

It took a few minutes to translate the words, and a few more to get the injured, and one incredibly pregnant woman, aboard. She was glassy-eyed, barely out of her teens, and utterly exhausted.

"It's all right, ma'am," Zach said, almost lifting her aboard. "A bus, a plane, and you'll be in a hospital in Perth."

Even as Tess asked herself how true that was, she spotted two children moving through the bullet-flecked palm trees. Boys wearing shorts, t-shirts, and a bandolier, each carrying an old rifle almost as big as they were tall.

"Hey, kids, over here!" she called. "Get aboard."

They seemed to understand, in that one shook his head, and both continued through the trees towards the beach.

"Come, Tess," Laila said. "Please."

The notion of leaving the children behind grated against her years of service where the resources of an entire department, state, and sometimes country, would go into saving just one life. Now the scales had flipped, and the world was reduced to a handful of individuals, trying to save what remained of the entire world; they truly couldn't help everyone.

As Zach drove them inland, the road was already filling with pedestrian survivors who'd remained hidden during the long night. Clearly, the arrival of the plane, as much as the dawn, had been the signal that it was time to flee.

"Slow down," Laila said, jumping out of the bus's open door. Zach eased off the gas, though he was travelling barely faster than the crowd.

The nurse approached an old woman walking between two teenage girls, and spoke with them briefly, before the old woman turned around and resumed walking. Laila jogged back to the bus, and jumped aboard.

"Did you offer them a ride?" Tess asked.

"Yes, but she lost interest when I said we were going to Inhambane," Laila said.

"But that's where the plane's gone," Zach said, pivoting around to look back at the walking trio.

"Hands on the wheel," Tess said. "Eyes on the road."

"Yeah, sure," Zach said. "But why don't they want to come to the city?"

"Because it is only one plane," Laila said. "One plane yesterday. One plane this morning. The city is full of refugees. There will be no seats for them, and so they will leave now, before everyone else."

"Did they say where they're heading?" Tess asked.

"South," Laila said. "If the South Africans came here, then South Africa is empty, that is their thinking."

"It's a long way to the border," Tess said. "Did you tell them about the zombies on the bridge?"

"There are lost souls everywhere," Laila said. "They are the new universal truth."

Tess counted over two hundred refugees before the road branched and Zach drove them due west. With only a hundred now on the beach, and perhaps twice that many still hiding among the ruins, thousands must have fled during the night. Fled, died, or been infected. Not all the undead they'd killed had been wearing life jackets.

No one was fleeing from Inhambane. Nor did she see any undead on the road leading to the small city. Not until they reached the new walls. Three corpses lay splayed by the road. Two bore savage cuts on arms and chest, while their slowly decaying skin carried an increasingly familiar lifeless pallor. The third? Well, better to assume all three were zombies, though friendly fire was an unfortunate consequence of their new reality.

"Can we hurry, please," Laila asked, now standing next to the pregnant young woman. "Please!"

"Hoy! Let us in!" Zach called. "We're New Zealanders from the frigate!"

"I don't know if—" Tess began, but the truck blocking the road began to reverse as it was towed clear. "Neat trick, Zach," she said.

The road was empty as they drove to the airport, but the rooftops were more full than ever. So was the concourse close to the runway.

"Stop here, Zach," Tess said. "Wait with the bus."

Rows of children were lining up at the apron's edge, under the watchful eyes of Elaina, Bianca, and the bandaged Saleema. Something about that rang alarm bells. So did the sight of the plane. Scores of soldiers were slowly disembarking.

"Saleema! There's a woman about to give birth in the bus, can you help?"

The bandaged nurse frowned in partial comprehension, but jogged towards the bus.

Tess hurried over to the plane where Commander Tusitala was speaking with Mick Dodson, and two of the new arrivals, both wearing mottled-mud and bush-red camouflage.

"G'day, Tess," Mick said. "Back on time, just as promised."

"Mick, there's a woman giving birth in that bus," Tess said.

"No worries, I'll get my bag," Mick said, and dashed back to the plane.

"Commander," Tess said, taking in the two newcomers. "The plane was supposed to pick up refugees, not bring more people."

"You are Commissioner Qwong?" the woman with the tired eyes and worn smile said. "I am Ambassador Lebogang Gwala of South Africa." She indicated her companion. "This is General Mafika Mbuli of the African Union."

"Where are the Mozambique leaders?" the general asked.

"On the bus, bringing a new life into this world," Tess said. "Are more planes coming? Are more soldiers?"

"We will not abandon Africa," the ambassador said.

"I was explaining that this position is no longer tenable," Commander Tusitala said.

Mick jumped off the plane, a red med-kit hanging over his shoulder, and sprinted to the bus.

"Zombies don't swim," Tess said. "They float. They were wearing life jackets when they were infected. They fall from the relief ships which never disembarked in Madagascar. The floating zombies drift ashore. Last night, we fought, dusk till dawn, to hold Tofo Beach. This morning, the shore is covered in bodies. The shallows are full of wreckage. The sand is stained black with infected blood. Nothing will live there ever again. But the zoms will still come. They will still float ashore. Every day. Every night. The civilians are fleeing, and they're not coming here. They're going south. Taking their chances in the interior."

"This is what I was trying to explain," Tusitala said. "The waters are too polluted to fish. Thankfully, we've got a surplus of diesel aboard those two freighters, but we're low on food and ammunition, and almost out of water. We can hold this town if the planes bring in supplies, but not if they're full of people."

Tess spotted Mick, walking over with far less haste than he'd run from the plane, and without his red bag.

"Is the baby okay?"

"Just a bit shy," Mick said. "Give her another two hours. I got some of those soldiers to help the mum into the shade. We'll get her, and the baby, onto one of the next planes. Speaking of whom, they'll be here within the hour." He looked down at his watch. "Forty minutes unless they stopped to enjoy the view, so I've got to get this plane out of here. You lot sorted it out?"

"How many more planes are coming, Mick?" Tess asked.

"Four more of these," Mick said. "Each with a hundred or so troops aboard."

"We have four thousand more soldiers in Perth," the general said. "We were promised ships would bring us to Africa."

"But we know the ships are sunk," the ambassador said, her comment directed more at the general.

"How many kids can you get aboard?" Tess asked.

"About three hundred," Mick said. "Diego Garcia is underwater. Réunion has been wrecked, but the runway on the island of Rodrigues is open. We're going to fly the kids there."

"When you say open, do you mean defended?" Tess asked.

"More or less," Mick said. "A bunch of fighter pilots flew a long-range civilian jet over the islands. The runway is usable. We're going to relay the civilians there. There's enough fuel here for about forty hops. That'll get the kids and the injured out of here. There's a couple of Globemasters on their way to Rodrigues with some food, and if the fuel holds up, we'll add them to our ferry-fleet. Get some lights up on the runways, keep the beacon running, and we can fly through the night. We'll be done in twenty-four hours."

"But that's only the children," the ambassador said. "How long to remove all of the civilians?"

"A few days," Mick said. "Depends on fuel, planes, and the state of the runway after we get the kids safe, so ask me tomorrow. I better get these children aboard."

"The planes are already on their way," Tess said. "But Tofo Beach *has* been lost. With these new soldiers, we can defend the city, and put together a couple of strike teams. Commander, does the captain still think we can seize one of the floating ships?"

"Do you mean a ship full of the living dead?" the general asked.

"Yes, sir," Tusitala said. "If we can repair the engines, anchor offshore, it can be a floating castle, far safer than this city."

"Aren't these ships drifting towards the shore?" the ambassador asked. "Before securing the vessel, these commandos must secure the engine room, and then bring tools and machines aboard, and then transfer fuel, *and* complete the work before the ship runs aground? How many engineers do you have? How many can you lose?"

"Commissioner?" a timid and exhausted voice asked.

Tess turned, and saw Bianca standing a nearly respectful distance behind Mick.

"Give me a moment, Bee," Tess said.

"This is important," Bianca said.

Tess turned her back on the debate that was already morphing into an argument. "What's up?" she asked.

"Those children are being flown to a small island with virtually no one there," Bianca said. "Someone must take care of them, and there are two military pilots aboard the plane. As Doctor Dodson isn't flying, I'm worried it will be him. But I can go instead."

"You're volunteering to look after five thousand kids?" Tess asked.

"Dr Dodson has to return to Perth to keep the airlift running," Bianca said. "I'm not good with children, but I should have learned how sixteen years ago."

"Strewth, Bee, this isn't the time to hunt for repentance."

"Isn't it?" Bianca said. "If not now, when? I'm not a soldier. I'm not a doctor, or pilot, or sailor. I can help the children. Please, let me be useful."

Tess unslung her carbine, and held it out. "Take this. I wish I could give you more."

"We are not abandoning Africa!" the general roared, his words echoing across the runway.

"Who'd be a diplomat?" Tess muttered. "I'll see you in Perth, Bee. Good luck, and thank you. Get aboard, and tell the pilots to get ready to take off." She turned back to the argument.

"General," Tess said. "You don't want to abandon Africa. Nor do I."

"We will not leave," the general said.

"Good," Tess said. "Inhambane is lost. Because of those ships which went to Madagascar, because of the refugees who headed to the coast in hope of escaping by sea, there are too many zombies. In Canada, a general was using construction machines as tanks to lead a relief column into the United States. We've got two diesel-transport ships in the harbour, and a load of mining machines on the bridges to the south. Take the fuel, take those machines, and drive away from here."

"And go where?" the general asked.

"It's your continent, mate, you tell me," Tess said. "But it needs to be somewhere on the coast where a relief-fleet can pick up refugees. Somewhere far enough away from Madagascar we don't have to worry about ships filled with the dead. Somewhere which had a runway, and is within flying range of the island of Rodrigues."

"South Africa," the general said.

"Cape Town," the ambassador said. "It has to be Cape Town. We can drive there, but it is within range of a plane."

"Cape Town's a major hub, which would have made it a major target for a nuclear bomb," Tusitala said.

"No one knows if it was," the general said.

"The refugees might," Tusitala said. "We should canvass them."

"We've no time," Tess said. "We've got to pick a destination so I can tell Mick, and he can tell Perth, and they can tell the captains of the rescue ships."

"Cape Hangklip," the ambassador said. "On the east of False Bay. It is close to Cape Town, but still a safe distance from the city. We will find a refuge, but we will send scouts ahead of us to Cape Hangklip. Find them there, and they will tell you where to find the rest of us."

"Sounds good," Tess said. "General?"

He gave a slow nod. "Agreed."

"I'll speak to Captain Adams," Tusitala said.

"And I better tell Mick," Tess said.

“This plan breaks all my rules,” Mick said. He and Tess stood on the tarmac as the last of the children got aboard.

“There’s no alternative,” Tess said. “We can’t stay here. People are already leaving. But if we try to stay, you’d have to fly these planes in full of supplies, and we both know what a mess Australia’s logistics are in. One plane crashes, takes out the runway, and it’s over. Too many zoms come from the south, and there’s no escape. But there is an escape now.”

“Through two thousand kilometres of a potentially radioactive continent, to a potentially radioactive ruin of a city neither of us have heard a peep about since the sky fell on our heads,” Mick said. “Sounds like that ambassador isn’t any better informed. Are you going with them?”

“By ship or by road,” Tess said. “But I can’t leave by plane, and you can’t be on the next one. You’ve got to go back to Perth and make sure the rescue ships are coming.”

17th March

Chapter 12 - The Worst Workout
HMNZS *Te Taiki*, Mozambique

A weight dropped from her shoulders as fast as the helicopter soared upwards, taking her to the HMNZS *Te Taiki.*

The previous day, after Mick's plane had departed, Tess had driven back to the beach. The injured had been loaded into the bus, while the surviving defenders had been marshalled into a column and walked back to town. Clyde had set a gruelling pace. Frustratingly, Toppley had no difficulty keeping up, while Tess's hip had made itself known at the three-kilometre mark.

They'd sung bush songs to maintain their spirits, alternating between African and Australian, all of which Clyde knew. Dr Avalon attempted a quiz on the electrical conductivity of alloys, but Leo was the only one who might have understood the questions, and he was suffering the heat in silence. Oakes dealt with the undead, for a total of nineteen lost souls. Worryingly, all came from the south. All were recently turned. But their column walked into Inhambane alive. Exhausted, but alive.

As the sun hovered directly overhead, seemingly for hours, Tess had longed for sleep, but instead had walked the rooftops, being seen, offering what words of reassurance she could that departure was imminent. The fuel-freighters were brought inshore, their contents unloaded into the harbour-side tanks. The general went south to retrieve the mining machines, and came back with, among other vehicles, the four bulldozers which had been barricading the bridge.

After the dozers arrived, it was far too late to put them back. While their presence guaranteed the peninsula would fall sooner, it confirmed the general's intent to drive south.

All that time, and after, planes arrived. Soldiers disembarked. Children boarded. The sun burned. The sun set, and Tess sent the scientists and Zach to the warship. Night's arrival brought the return of fear and the release of grief. Tess, once more, paced the rooftops, offering what comfort and reassurance she could. The night was punctuated by rifle fire, and warning shouts. Whenever she reached that part of the city, she always found Clyde, Hawker, or Oakes already there, and the danger long dealt with.

When dawn arrived, over fifty hours since she'd properly slept, so did orders for her to report aboard the frigate.

As the helicopter set down, a deckhand threw open the door. Head bowed, Tess trudged from the helicopter, following the sailor to a bulkhead door. Inside, suddenly, she was enveloped in cool silence. The ship thrummed with engine vibrations, and it was barely cooler inside than out, but she was out of the sun, and away from the flies, a growing menace on the mainland. Laying her hand against the cool metal wall, she made the mistake of closing her eyes.

"Ma'am?" the sailor said. "Do you need to visit the doc?"

Tess forced her eyes open. "Sorry. It's been a busy month."

The sailor led her through cramped corridors and crowded landings, until they reached a nearly empty room near the stern: a gym. Well-equipped but as cramped as the corridors. It was reminiscent of the just-out-of-town hotels where equipment was purchased so it could be listed as a feature, with no consideration for how it would all fit into one room. Treadmills, recumbent bikes, weights, and a pair of rowing machines, though the last seemed distasteful aboard a ship. Between and atop the equipment, however, were crates. Plastic. Not military. Secured with rope and webbing to the room's walls and the bolted-down equipment.

One person was in the room, standing hands on hips, clearly having been sorting through the boxes.

"Captain Adams, this is Commissioner Qwong,"

"Thank you, Sullivan. Those three crates by the door are bandages. Send them ashore to travel with the convoy."

"Aye-aye, ma'am." The sailor grabbed a crate and hurried away.

"Captain Robyn Adams, g'day," the captain said, holding out a hand. She wore sweats and a short-sleeved t-shirt, though with combat-boots on her feet. About fifty years old, her clipped hair was salted at the temples, and peppered on the crown. Around one-point-eight metres tall, thin waisted, broad shouldered, well toned, and with a cobweb of shrapnel scar tissue running up her right arm.

"Tess Qwong. *Kia ora*. Didn't know warships had gyms."

"Gotta stay fit," Adams said. "I'm supposed to get ten minutes a day for rehab, but chucking crates is not the same as three rounds in the ring."

"You're a boxer?" Tess asked.

"I was. I started an inter-ship tournament when I took command. Do you know what happened the same day we had our first bout? Manhattan. I'm not as superstitious as some sailors, but my gloves will stay in my locker until we're back in home-port."

"Me, I'm a reluctant runner," Tess said. She tapped her hip. "Stab-wound, a few years back. I'm supposed to clock up a gentle five-k every other day. Now, it's too often a gruelling hike. What is all this gear?"

"Salvage from the ships which were here before us," Adams said. "As are thirty members of our crew. I've swapped some of mine onto the diesel freighters. Lost a few to suicide. Only one to action." She lifted the lid of the box. "Rope. More rope. Useful, but weight is fuel. Weight is speed. Weight is time." She put the lid back on the box and crossed to a triple-stack of crates piled on the treadmill. On the lid of the topmost box were a tablet, a flask, and two glasses. "We're three months out of a major refit, on a shakedown, and two weeks overdue for our return to home-port. Our orders were to protect the refugees. They have not been countermanded. Did you hear about the civil war?"

"No? Where?" Tess asked.

"At sea. Some are calling it piracy. Ships attacked one another. Understandable in the chaos. We saved who we could, and what supplies we could, but we're still figuring out what we picked up. We're over-stocked on munitions, but I've offloaded most of the medical supplies, and food, to the convoy. Tea? It's cold."

"Iced tea?" Tess said, taking a glass. "Good on ya."

"It's powdered," Adams said. "We're out of coffee. But we have this in abundance. Salvaged from a food-freighter. We unloaded four shipping containers before she went down. Sadly, we found no real tea, but this'll do in a squeeze. I spoke with your scientists when they came aboard. Dr Smilovitz gave me a general understanding of your mission. Dr Avalon just gave me a headache."

"She has that effect," Tess said.

"Can she really build a weapon to destroy the undead?" Adams asked. "It seems too good to be true."

"We've no reason to disbelieve her," Tess said. "We canvassed some of the staff at the university in Canberra, and they confirmed she is as good as she says she is. Those two worked for the U.N. eliminating bio-chemical threats to the world before the outbreak."

"And they want to go to Colombia in search of the lab where it was made, or to New York to find patient zero?" Adams asked.

"They say it would help reduce development time," Tess said.

"To think that this nightmare could end is simply too distracting. I want to believe it, but I don't dare let myself."

"Tell me about it," Tess said.

"I *do* want to assist you," Adams said. "However, it would be stretching our capabilities. As I say, we're three months out of an austerity-refit. The majority of our systems were downgraded. We run solely on diesel now. That's reduced our top speed, but increased our range. Even so, depending on weight and weather, our fuel tanks will run dry at seven thousand nautical miles."

"What's that in land-speak?" Tess asked.

"Thirteen thousand kilometres. From here to Cape Town is nearly three thousand kilometres. The Guajira Peninsula in Colombia is twelve thousand kilometres from Cape Town."

"And the Panama Canal is another two thousand kilometres from there," Tess said. "Hopefully, that'll be our way home, if the scientists could find what they need in Colombia."

"The canal was blocked," Adams said. "I've had three separate reports confirming it, though none were first-hand. It's unlikely we'll be able to force a passage through that water-route. If we can't refuel in Cape Town, we can't go any further."

"What about the two fuel-freighters here?" Tess asked.

"I'm sending them back to Australia. As I understand it, we've only got two other bulk fuel-transport ships in the entire Pacific. I'll risk my crew to save these tens of thousands in Africa, but those ships are needed to supply the hospital generators for every island in the Pacific. We're sailing alone to Cape Town. If we can refuel there, we'd only be able to travel westward for half our range. To continue on to Colombia, we'd first have to refuel on Ascension Island, and despite that island's scientific work, it was primarily a military base. Why should it have survived when so many others were targeted? There's no other circumstance you'd hear me say this about my command, but this is the wrong ship for the mission, Commissioner."

"It's the only ship we've got," Tess said. "We can't fly, because we don't know of any runways. We can't parachute out over the target because the whole point is to get any research we find back to Oz. I could put the scientists on a plane, but it would only take them to Rodrigues. It could be another two days before we get back to Perth, and who knows how long before we find another ship? At least you're travelling in the right direction."

"My orders are to protect the refugees," Adams said. "The refugees are now heading in convoy to Cape Town, and so will we. If I had the range to reach Colombia, I would strongly consider making the voyage, but running adrift off the coast of Brazil helps no one."

"Fair dinkum. We were supposed to pick up a hundred U.S. Rangers in Perth, and find two U.S. frigates here. Plans change," Tess said. "That's probably rule-three of living through the apocalypse."

"I'd say it was rule-one," Adams said. "There could be a ship anchored off Cape Town with the range you need. We could transfer fuel from one of the rescue ships. But that's something to discuss when we get there. I just didn't want to waste these scientists' time. Which brings me to point two. They said they're finishing off the theory for their weapon. If practical comes next, I'm hesitant to allow any experiments aboard my ship. We've been lucky so far, but I've sunk twenty-three ships overtaken by the infected. I appreciate the importance of this work, but I want to know in advance before they bring infected tissue samples aboard."

"Me too, so I'll keep an eye on them."

"Good. Point three. Your pilot, Mick Dodson, is the father of the new deputy prime minister, and she is a childhood friend of yours, is that correct?"

"I'd say I knew Mick better than Anna, but we all grew up in the same town. I've known them all my life."

"And you helped stop a coup that was organised by the same people who created the outbreak?"

"Broadly speaking," Tess said. "A couple of narco-barons were the muscle to some politicians who were behind all this. Two sisters, about sixty years old, called Herrera, and they're about as evil as a human can get. I'm not sure who all of the politicians were, or which countries they were from, but seeing what happened a week ago, I'm guessing they represented each of the major nuclear powers. Closer to home, they were working with Sir Malcolm Baker to organise the coup in Australia."

"Him? Why am I not surprised? Tell me he's dead."

"He's in custody and is our primary source," Tess said. "But we've had some secondary confirmation. Baker knows helping us is the only way he'll avoid execution for war crimes. We can trust him on this, if absolutely nothing else."

"This coup, was it restricted to Australia?" Adams asked.

"I believe so," Tess said. "We've had no word of trouble in New Zealand, if that's what you're asking."

"I am, because that is the one duty which could see me return east."

"The coup's over," Tess said. "I'm still waiting on the judges to give us our score, but we definitely won. Back home, we're worrying about industrial output and water shortages for farming, housing for refugees, and the long-term impacts of radiation. I'm sorry that I don't know more about New Zealand, but the biggest international concern was how long it would take your people to build a new mega-refinery."

An alarm buzzed. "Ah," Adams said. "My ten minutes are up." She secured the cap on her flask. "No, lifting boxes is not the same as a run, and that's not even close to a bout. You'll travel with us?"

"The general has made it clear he doesn't want the confusion of command my presence would bring," Tess said.

"Then I'll let you take the helicopter back ashore. Gather your people. Get ready to leave. I'll have the freighters pull anchor within the hour. As soon as the last plane departs, so will we. The convoy should have departed at first light, and if we've gone, there's no reason for the general to loiter."

Inhambane felt different on her return, though she'd only been away for an hour. The changes of the previous twenty-four hours were more obviously manifest from the empty rooftops. Either the refugees were at the airport waiting for the last set of flights, or aboard one of the mining vehicles where they guarded the best seat they'd found.

The vehicles had formed a refugee column, rather than a military front, bolstered by almost every civilian vehicle remaining on the peninsula. Now they were parked outside the city walls, silent, except for the occasional crack of a rifle marking the ever-present danger approaching from the south. She found Colonel Hawker, Sergeant Oakes, Clyde, and Toppley at the airport guarding the refuelling tanker, and the tourist bus.

"Trouble?" she asked after she'd jogged over from where the helicopter had set down.

"Only interest," Hawker said. "Road vehicles are in short supply. A group is aiming to take this tanker the second we leave."

"They're going to miss the convoy's departure," Tess said.

"I don't believe they intend to go south," Toppley said. "I had a word with them, making certain they understood the bus belonged to the nurses. They claim interest in the fuel truck for reasons they wouldn't entirely explain, but I think one of them is a pilot."

"They're hoping there's fuel left, and they can fly out of here?" Tess asked.

"Not from here," Toppley said. "But they wouldn't say where they thought they might find a plane."

"We'll be getting aboard the helicopter, and then the ship," Tess said. "We'll leave as soon as the plane takes off."

"Then the nurses should join the convoy now," Hawker said. "If they wait until we're gone, I don't like their odds if the truck-thieves decide to take their bus as well."

"Where are Laila and Elaina?" Tess asked.

"With the kids," Clyde said.

The handful of nurses remaining in the city were scattered through the crowd, while Elaina was at the front of the pack of waiting children. They sat on the ground while she stood, waving her arms around to the befuddlement of most of the young teens, but to the amusement of some others.

"Oh, hi Commish," Elaina said, suddenly freezing and blushing with embarrassment. That produced smiles from even more of the children.

"G'day," Tess said. "Should I ask what that was?"

"Language lessons," Elaina said. "I mime the animal, and they have to teach me the correct word for it."

"Ah. And that was a squid?"

"A giraffe," she said, which received a chuckle, but a louder laugh after the answer had been translated. "Is everything okay?"

"Absolutely," Tess said, speaking loud enough the children could hear. "The plane should be here soon. When the kids are aboard, the convoy will go south, and the ship will depart. We're sailing south down to Cape Town where we'll meet the convoy and we'll secure a safe harbour for the rescue fleet."

"Bianca went to Rodrigues, didn't she?" Elaina asked.

"Someone had to stay with the kids," Tess said. "She didn't want Mick to think it had to be him."

"There's a lot of children," Elaina said.

"Quite a few of Laila's nurses have gone to Rodrigues," Tess said.

"It's still a *lot* of children," Elaina said. "Right now, we should be calling those nurses patients, but they'll be stretched dealing with all the wounded. Bee's lovely, but last week she thought, to make an omelette, you shook the egg before cracking it."

"Really?" Tess said. "Well, now you've got me wanting to try it."

"Let me go help her," Elaina said. "Please. I'm not shirking, but I'm supposed to be looking after children. It's what I'm good at."

"It's where you're supposed to be," Tess said. "Good on ya, and good luck. I'll see you back in Perth."

Laila was at the other end of the line of children, changing a bandage on a young girl's arm.

Tess waited until she was finished, then motioned her out of earshot.

"We're sailing to Cape Town," Tess said. "You and your nurses should come with us."

"No, thank you," Laila said. "It is kind of you to make the offer, but we can't travel with you. Do you see the cathedral?"

Tess turned. From the edge of the airport's runway, it was just possible to make out the crumbling top of its spire. "I do."

"My aunt had a house just behind and to the left," Laila said. "When the zoo closed, she came here and set up a cab company for tourists and a shelter for women."

"She's why you came here?" Tess asked.

"When the infected reached us, we had to go somewhere. We gathered the children from the wards, and drove here. But she was dead before we arrived. Infected. Locked in her bedroom."

"I'm sorry," Tess said.

"We've all lost someone," Laila said. "We've all lost nearly everyone. Most of us don't realise it yet, but this is a new beginning. Everyone left belongs to everyone else. We are one people again, as we have not been since the very earliest days. My aunt had a saying. She was a zoologist. Trained in Cairo," she added with a hint of pride. "She said that there is a type of man who, when cleaning an elephant's tusks, will begin at the tail. The general is one such man."

"The kind of bloke who doesn't lock his car, then yells at the cops when it's stolen, right?" Tess asked. "I know what you mean, but you're in danger of having that bus stolen. If you are determined to travel with the convoy, go now. We'll stay with the kids until the plane comes. Go on. We'll see you in Cape Town."

Part 2

A Copper Log

The Personal Journal of Tess Qwong

18th March

Chapter 13 - A Commissioner's Diary

Journals are written by kids; I've read too many of them in my career. Last time I kept one, I was a teen. But Anna wanted a report on what the world was like beyond our home shores, so I'll make some notes. Besides, for once, there are no other calls on my time. The U.S. Army Rangers weren't in Perth, but Anna knows that. Only one warship was anchored off Mozambique, and the refugees were far from evacuated to safety. But Mick's carried that news back to Australia.

What can I say about the ship? It floats. Beyond that, I'll report back when I've seen more than the deck our cabins are on. What can I say about the crew? So far, I can name six, including the three whose names I learned before we left Inhambane yesterday.

After we came aboard, and after we'd pulled anchor, I spoke with the captain again, as did Bruce. Separately. The rest of our people were quizzed by members of the crew. Captain Adams is making sure our stories add up. Specifically, the story about the coup, Sir Malcolm Baker, and the conditions in Australia and the Pacific. I can't blame her for being suspicious, or concerned about her own island home.

We were introduced to the crew remotely, over the address-system, as police and scientists hunting those responsible for the outbreak and looking for their lab. But the captain also said we were catching a ride with the *Te Taiki* only as far as Cape Town. She wants a weapon more than revenge, but understands the value in both. She wants to help us, but her crew want to go home. My impression, so far, is that she's probing their feelings, testing whether they would accept an extension to their voyage. So it'll come down to them, and to whether we find fuel in Cape Town. If not, then I'll take one of the rescue ships, assuming there are enough to spare.

It's twenty-three hours since we departed Inhambane, most of which I've spent asleep. Oh, it's been glorious. Dr Avalon and Leo are sharing a cabin at the end of the corridor. I've assigned Zach to be their assistant. I didn't *tell* him he's spying on the scientists in case they run any practical experiments, but I'm certain he'll tell me if they are. I don't think the Canadians brought infected tissue samples aboard, but they're the kind of people who'll ask for forgiveness rather than permission.

Hawker, Oakes, Clyde, and Zach have been given a four-bunk room that had been a storage locker. I've been given a one-bunk cabin in which the table and a cabinet were removed, and an extra bunk installed. That's been given to Teegan Toppley.

"It's smaller than a cell," Toppley said, on seeing it, "but I appreciate having a view."

"A bed is all I need," I said.

"There are clean clothes in the locker, ma'am," the sailor detailed to show us to our quarters said. Her name's Sullivan, and her primary duty has something to do with the helicopter. I think she was the sailor operating the machine gun during the battle at the bridge. "If you bag what you're wearing, I'll take it to the laundry."

"There's a laundry?" I asked.

"Of course," Sullivan said, just about managing to conceal a smirk.

"*Far* better than a cell," Toppley said.

"A cell?" Sullivan said.

"Ah, young lady, I am the most notorious criminal in Australia."

"You are?" Sullivan asked.

"She's winding you up," I said. "Sullivan, yes?"

"Yes, ma'am. Able Rate, ma'am."

"Do you possess a first name to go along with your rank?" Toppley asked.

"Pippa, ma'am."

"I'm no one's ma'am," Toppley said. "Call me Teegan."

"Teegan *Toppley*?" Sullivan asked, realisation slowly dawning.

"Ah, so my reputation *has* ventured across the Tasman Sea," Toppley said. "Why don't you show me where this mystical laundry is, and I shall tell you the story of my life, including those details the papers weren't gracious enough to print."

If she'd asked, I'd have told Toppley to shelve her past because you can never overtake your reputation, but it was absolutely too late. After she'd gone, I barely managed to get my boots off before I fell asleep.

I'd forgotten the sheer pleasure of clean clothes. Back in Canberra, the hotel had its own laundry, but I rarely had the time to use it. Ms Hoa Nguyen, the elderly public servant who'd adopted Anna as her personal project, was insistent that a politician should look the part, and so found clothes for Anna. I stole a few of them, and took others from the airport or wherever, and whenever, I could. Dirties were dumped.

I didn't even have to do the laundry here. Toppley did. She's making herself useful. Making friends. If I get clean clothes out of it, who am I to argue?

So what else can I say about the ship? A laundry. Showers. Soap. Clean clothes. Food! Room service, in fact, brought to the cabin by Toppley and waiting for me when I woke. Sandwiches made with actual bread. Some of the instant tea, kept cold in a flask. I'd have preferred hot coffee, but only out of habit. In the day since we left Inhambane, I've eaten. I've slept. I've spoken briefly with the captain, and a little longer with my team. Mostly, I've slept, barely disturbed by Toppley's snores.

Cape Town is two thousand kilometres from Inhambane by air, two and a half thousand by road, and at least two thousand seven hundred for the ship, depending on how close we stay to the coast. The ship can make twenty-seven knots, but is most efficient at seventeen knots, or thirty kilometres an hour. We can travel at night, while Laila won't. She'll be delayed by obstacles in the road, and by the undead. We'll be slowed by tides and currents. Assuming one balances the other, we'll reach Cape Town around the same time. For us, it's the second full day aboard the ship, the third day of sailing, with around seventy-two hours to go.

19th March

Chapter 14 - Daily Exercise

With there being a limit to how much time anyone can spend in bed, *even* me, when Toppley got up to help with the sailors' chores, I finally dragged myself up. A long shower later, and I went hunting for the mess.

I've become lost in the never-never more times than I'd like Mick to know about, but you don't find many mazes in the outback. The heat, the thirst, the dry wind, and, of course, the spiders: it would take a particularly sick mind to add high walls and dead-ends to the experience. But Korea has, or had, the largest maze in the world, a visit to which was on my kick-list. Can't see I'll ever get to visit now. But I now know where maze builders learn their craft: designing the interior of ships.

I kept walking in what I was sure was the direction of daylight, and ended up back at my cabin, where I found Toppley, reading.

"Weren't you helping in the laundry?" I asked.

"Sadly, my reputation arrived before me," she said, raising her eyes from the page. "I hoped I could pre-emptively explain my past actions, but too many of these sailors worked anti-piracy routes in the Pacific."

"They were hunting you?" I asked.

"None are that old," she said with a weary sigh. "I do suddenly feel *so* old. It's inescapable, surrounded by so much youth, not to imagine how I might have lived a different life, and be looking forward to a different future. One with a little house near the sea, waiting for my grandchildren to visit."

"You're not *that* old," I said. "But I'd be lying if I said I don't have those same glimpses of an alternate future. They're a burden, a nightmare in their own way. Yet we are where we are. We are who we had to become in order to survive. You were framed, weren't you? And the cops were after you? If you'd not run, you'd have been caught, and without any chance of singing a few years off your sentence."

"Ah, no. Today's particular dollop of regret was served by wondering if I could have enlisted as an alternative to jail-time, before remembering the ADF didn't allow women to serve in combat back then."

"Then take solace in not being so old that military service was still being offered as an alternative to prison even when you were young," I said. "But it is a punishment in the here-and-now, so in a way, you got your wish."

"Yes, indeed, I've become victim of that ancient curse of my dreams coming true," she said. "Regret is a path I've walked so often I no longer need a map. But I made my choices. I lived my life. Unfortunately, it has caught up to me here, but maintaining a low profile is an easy price to pay. Dr Avalon was kind enough to loan me a book for entertainment."

"She doesn't strike me as a fan of fiction," I said.

"Look at the cover," Toppley said.

"*Survival on Titan*, by… by L. Smilovitz. Leo wrote it?"

"He did. Dr Avalon carries copies around with her. Yet when I asked how long they'd been a couple, she said they weren't."

"They're the definition of complicated," I said. "So Leo wrote a proper book?"

"A trilogy about the struggle for survival in a human settlement on Titan after Earth is destroyed."

"No fooling? How is it?"

"A little technical in places. But it works on multiple levels, one of which being that the love interest is called Dr Ava London."

"Strewth. He's not subtle."

"Quite. But once you get past where his subconscious desires have spilled onto the page, it is thoroughly enjoyable. I'm up to chapter seven where the dashing pilot, Leonard Miles, is attempting to save their hydroponic harvest."

"He called his hero Leonard? Crikey. I've got to have a read of that when you're finished. I was hunting for breakfast, and then I was going to check in on the team."

"I believe they went to the gym," Toppley said.

"Now I feel even worse for having a lie-in," I said. "Come with me. Let's stretch our old legs together."

With Toppley's help, we found the gym. Still crowded with boxes, it was now packed with Leo, Clyde, Zach, and Nicko.

"You lot having a workout before brekkie?" I asked.

"Breakfast is over," Zach said. "You missed our slot."

"We have a slot?" I asked.

"That's why I never booked a cruise-holiday," Clyde said. "The whole point of a vacation is for your time to be your own."

"Yeah, ships are like prisons," Zach said.

"Not entirely," Toppley said. "Trust me."

"Fine. It's like school," Zach said.

"Sorry, mate, it's actually a lot like work," Clyde said.

"Speaking of which, that's why we're here," Leo added, holding up a clipboard. "Commander Tusitala asked us to catalogue what's in these crates. I think she's hoping we'll find more food."

"It is good to be useful," Toppley said.

"And our task is to determine whether the contents of these boxes are useful, or to be thrown over the side," Leo said.

"They don't know what they brought aboard?" I asked.

"Not the specifics," Leo said. "And they don't have a complete list of what went to the fuel-freighters, or to the convoy."

"Where should I start?" Toppley asked.

"By the bike," Leo said. "Write the contents on the box's lid, and the sides, and then on the clipboard. If it's edible, it'll go to the galley."

"If it's explosive, tell Clyde," Nicko added.

"He's not kidding," Clyde said. "They found a box of C4 in the med-lab, among a crate of single-use syringes."

"How'd that happen?" I asked.

"Commander Tusitala is finding out," Clyde said. "You don't want to be in her way this morning. That's why we're glad to be hiding in here."

"Me, I'm volunteering to clear enough space I can get in a work-out," Nicko said. "It's good to stay trim."

"I told him he should have a kid," Clyde said. "Best all-body work-out you can get."

"You're married," Oakes said. "You can get away with letting yourself go. Bloke in his prime like me has got to maintain his image."

Having a kid is exhausting. I know that from the weekends I'd keep an eye on Bobby for Liu and Scott. But it's not the same as a full-body workout, particularly when snack-time is the cornerstone of maintaining your sanity. A month of irregular rations has kept Clyde lean, if not trim. Nicko, by contrast, is a bloke who buys his t-shirts a size too small. I won't say he's consumed by vanity, but it has been dining on his ego. He's got that self-confidence of a young man who's swiftly risen to the peak of his profession without ever having taken too big a tumble. What I know, and what he'll certainly learn long before he hits thirty, no matter how fast you rise, it's the landing that hurts.

"Did I miss breakfast, then?" I asked.

"We've got some iced tea, Tess," Clyde said. "And there's always some of those oat-bars."

"That'll do," I said, and took the flask to a pair of stacked boxes that would sub for a seat.

"Found it!" Zach said, putting the lid back on a box. He pulled out a pen, and began writing on the lid. "Climbing rope."

"Perfect," Leo said.

"For what?" I asked.

"Doc-Flo wanted some rope," Zach said.

"Again, I'm going to ask, for what?" I said.

"Always good to have a bit of rope handy," Leo said. "She's less distracted when she knows where things are. Throw me a coil, and label the side of the box, too."

Why would *that* scientist aboard *this* ship want a coil of rope? Asking the question a third time wasn't going to get a clearer answer, but it makes me want to keep a closer eye on Avalon.

"Excuse me, Sergeant," the sailor, Sullivan, asked from the doorway. "Colonel Hawker requests your assistance."

"Is there trouble?" I asked.

"No, ma'am," Sullivan said. "The colonel is training some of the new crew in close combat."

"Ah, no worries," Nicko said. "He must want me to show them how it's done."

"He's using the helicopter deck," Sullivan said. "Can you find it? Only I'm supposed to be scrubbing the med-bay."

"I can give you a hand with that," Zach said.

"Um… you're volunteering to help clean?" Sullivan asked.

"You'll finish twice as quick," Zach said. "If that's all right, boss?"

"Permission granted," I said.

"She joined our table for breakfast," Clyde said after the pair, and Nicko, had gone. "To be strictly accurate, Zach joined hers, and we joined him."

"She's something to do with the helicopter crew?" I asked.

"And she's the ship's librarian," Clyde said. "Something of a ship's mascot, too. Saved the commander's life during a fire, then refused a promotion because she was simply doing her duty. She asked permission to take over the library instead."

"Good luck to Zach," I said, and opened an oat-bar. "So how did plastic explosives end up mixed in with syringes?"

"Best I can tell, this was a temporary crew," Clyde said. "The refit was rushed, and the ship was rushed back to sea out of political stupidity. While it was in dock, it was an accounting liability, but if it was at sea, it became an asset. Then came the outbreak. The more experienced hands were sent to command the fuel-freighters. A month on high alert, and standards slipped. But the captain now wants to make space for the injured when we get to Cape Town. She wants to prepare for the worst."

20th March

Chapter 15 - Radio Free England

After three nights aboard, I've begun to fill my days with routine. Breakfast with my team, dinner with the captain. The rest of my time is spent helping move boxes, and in checking up on Dr Avalon. Today, I found her watching videos, though with the sound off.

"Have your headphones broken?" I asked.

"Most of these have no sound," she said, moving the laptop around so I could better see the screen.

"That's a zom attack," I said.

"In Manhattan," she said. "That coffee shop is where I used to wait for Leo. They did a passable croissant loaf."

"Never had one of those. What's it like?"

"As it sounds," she said. "I dislike waiting on others, particularly if I've been summoned from a different continent. I cannot abide an inconsistent application of urgency. That is where I would wait until Leo said it was time." She pressed the space bar with a forceful display of anger. Unusual for her. As was her giving an explanation of her past behaviour. But aboard this ship, we've all found ourselves with time to think and to tally what we've lost.

"Where did you get the video?" I asked as, on-screen, a customer pushed open the doors. She fell to her knees, and was abruptly tugged back inside, out of sight.

"It's one of the clips uploaded before the internet collapsed," Avalon said. "Leo gathered all that he could."

"Watching them isn't good for your mental health," I said.

"I'm watching them to narrow down the location where the outbreak began," she said. "We know it was Manhattan, and it can't be far from the U.N. building. I have a few theories, but those won't be enough when we get there."

"*If* we get there," I said. "I don't know if we'll even get to Colombia."

"If we don't, these videos will be the only evidence we have," she said.

Talking with Dr Avalon is like talking to a drunk witness; it takes a lot of patience, and even more thought, to tease out some sense. But before I could formulate a new plan of verbal attack, a rat-a-tat was knocked on the door.

"Teegan said you'd be here, boss," Zach said, pushing it open a cautious fraction.

"That's nice of her," I said. "Are you looking for me?"

"Not me," he said. "I'm mega-busy, but the captain wants you on the bridge."

"Zachary!" Avalon said, closing the laptop. "Your assignment is overdue."

"You were being serious about that?" Zach asked.

"Of course," Avalon said.

"What assignment?" I asked.

"The first part of his coursework for his degree," Avalon said.

"At which university?" I asked.

"Whichever I decide to teach at when we return to Australia," Avalon said. "I see no reason he can't get ahead of his studies."

"Yeah, actually, maybe you could help, boss," Zach said.

"With your homework? Sorry, but you did say the captain needed to see me," I said.

Life goes on. In weird and odd ways that sometimes seem like nothing more than getting from morning to night. But it does. We find ways of occupying our days, as we search for ways of filling them with joy. Although I'm not sure whether Zach will be getting much joy out of being Avalon's pet student.

Leo was on the bridge, wearing headphones, and scrolling through radio frequencies. The crew were at their screens, but the captain was in her chair.

"Commissioner, thank you. We're between Durban and Port Elizabeth," Captain Adams said. "But I've cut our speed."

"Have we picked up a distress call?" I asked.

"Not as such. These are rough waters, near the Cape. Ships with power, or sails, would have sought calmer waters, while those without would sadly not last long. No, there is a radio signal. It's coming from land, and it's not a distress call. We made good time to Durban. I've taken us out to sea."

The captain has a deliberately split personality. The few times I've been alone with her, she's spoken as a colleague, an equal. It's not surprising. She's only a few years older than me. We're both at a similar level in similar professions, which are dissimilar enough that we're neither rivals or subordinates. But when she's within earshot of her crew, she reminds me a little of Dr Avalon in that she skips a good portion of the explanation, leaving you to fill in the blanks. With Avalon, it's because her mouth can't keep up with her brain. With Captain Adams, it's the self-censorship of command. She's mindful that everything she says will spread through the ship faster than hope, and she doesn't want disappointment clinging to its heels.

"Durban was an evacuation hub for South Africa, wasn't it?" I asked. "After Durban was overwhelmed, some South Africans drove north, crossed the border with Mozambique, and went to Maputo, which was overwhelmed in turn, and so the locals there went up to Inhambane."

"Overwhelmed is an understatement," Captain Adams said. "A liquid gas transport ship exploded in the harbour. We believe it was deliberately targeted. Initial reports suggested a torpedo, though our chief engineer, Mr Dickenson, thinks it could have been a subsurface drone."

"Who would do that?" I asked.

"That's as murky as the Mariana Trench, and nearly as fathomless," Adams said. "At the time, a small military police-fleet was gathering in the harbour. These were coastal protection vessels, cruisers, cutters, and patrol boats from many nations on the African east coast. Lightly armed and lightly armoured. They arrived to refuel, and were then drafted into a new fleet which was supposed to come north and help deal with the piracy problem in the Mozambique Channel. Very few ships escaped the inferno, which has left a floating debris field off the coast, hence our detour. Our next waypoint is Port Elizabeth, on the eastern shores of the Cape. But this radio signal is coming from much further inland."

"From South Africa? It's a distress call?" I asked.

"Not really," Adams said. "They are manually, verbally, repeating reports broadcast elsewhere in the world. The lack of formal radio discipline suggests a civilian, but one with some level of technical skill."

"Can I listen?"

"Do you speak Swahili?" Leo asked. "I don't. But I think that's the language they're currently speaking. We've had English, Arabic, Portuguese, Spanish, and now… ah, maybe it's Zulu. I'm certain it's not Xhosa. There's been no Afrikaans yet, which is an interesting detail. But the place-names repeat, so it's the same message in different languages. It's a recording. Not a live broadcast."

"What are they saying?" I asked.

"That there are pockets of survivors across the world," Leo said. "Survivors with access to a radio transmitter. They mention Israel. Zambia. Tunisia. England. Ukraine. Other than the location, there's no real information. Tel Aviv. The Dnieper River. They're saying there's a station calling itself Radio Free England. No location specified there."

"Do they say what happened in Israel?" I asked. "Or what happened in Ukraine?"

"People survived," Leo said. "That's basically it. They're saying that there are survivors, so if you can hear this, you should look for more. Help each other. Listen to the radio. Help will come."

"From whom?" I asked.

"They don't say," Leo said.

"They don't know," Adams said. "They're broadcasting a message of optimism to keep their own hope alive. There's no mention of the African Union, or of the evacuation to the Pacific."

"What about their location?" I asked.

"They haven't mentioned it yet," Leo said.

"We'll keep listening," Adams said. "But we've got to ask ourselves whether they're really retransmitting radio signals, or are they making up a good-news story to bring hope to anyone listening? I think they mixed up the BBC with Radio Free Europe, and called it Radio Free England by mistake."

"I take it we tried saying hello?" I asked.

"Partially," Adams said. "I broadcast a message asking where they were, saying we were a New Zealand ship, off the coast. Until we know more about them, I didn't want them to know more about us."

"Are we going to look for them?" I asked.

"If they are who they claim, they're a repeater-station run by a handful of survivors," Adams said. "Our priority must always be the largest number of survivors. In this case, the African Union convoy. Once we've secured their position in a coastal refuge, we can arrange a search for this transmitter using soldiers who have local knowledge."

By the time the next watch changed, everyone aboard would know of the signal, and want to know why it wasn't being investigated. Waiting on local knowledge was a believable explanation. But the captain hadn't wanted to explain that to her bridge crew. No, she'd summoned me to the bridge to be her Dr Watson. Why? I pondered that as I watched the waves, uncertain if I was supposed to propose we send the helicopter ashore, or voice agreement for her decision.

"We're back to English," Leo said. "Yep, it's a recording."

"This would be a powerful transmitter, wouldn't it?" I asked. "We can find a list, and map, of large transmitters in South Africa, and narrow down our search area."

"Contact!" Lieutenant Kane said. "It's the sub. Bearing one-four-zero."

"Is it the same submarine, Mr Kane?" Adams asked, her tone instantly becoming clipped, formal, far more precise.

"Yes, ma'am," Kane said. "Royal Navy. Astute-class. Probably the *Adventure*."

"Maintain course and heading," the captain said. "Mr Renton, attempt contact. Same message as before."

"You've spotted this sub before?" I asked.

"This is the second time today, the fifth sighting in total," the captain said. "We picked her up twice over a week ago. As we approached Durban, we caught an echo. She's the newest of the Royal Navy's Astute-class subs. They modified the propulsion system since the first boat in that class was commissioned."

"Does she have nukes?" I asked.

"No, but she is nuclear powered," Adams said. "She's an attack sub, armed with torpedoes and Tomahawk missiles."

I surveyed the seemingly empty ocean. "Shouldn't we go to action stations?"

"If it was our first sighting, yes," Adams said. "She hasn't adopted an aggressive posture. Nor will we. The boat came close to attack range while we were in Inhambane, but then retreated. The next occasion we identified her, she maintained her distance. We picked her up last night just north of Durban. Now here she is to the south. I think she's marking her territory."

"In Durban? I thought you said it was a ruin."

"The harbour is, but some of the city still stands," Adams said. "She doesn't need fuel, but her crew will need provisions. As we can identify her, she'll have identified us, or at least our class, and is aware we were operating in protection of the refugees in Africa. She's decided we're no threat."

"She's gone, ma'am," Kane said.

"Turned back?" I asked.

"We're about to find out," Adams said.

It took me a minute to understand. I held my breath. I wasn't the only one.

"The time, Mr Kane?" Adams finally asked.

"Two minutes, ma'am. No contact."

"Maintain course, increase speed two knots," Adams said.

I said nothing. Not then. Ships have a routine, and so does the captain. She really does set aside time each day for rehab-exercise. Today that involved stripping the motor on one of the ship's fixed-rib boats.

"It's not boxing," she said. "But it does involve my hands."

"And most of your arms, too, judging by the oil," I said. "Need a hand?"

"Start on the starboard bolts. See if you can work them loose."

"Whose boat was this?" I asked.

"The Americans," she said. "Kept ten of their crew alive after their destroyer was blown out of the water by a sub."

"That submarine following us?"

"We don't believe so," Adams said. "But only because it is more comforting to assume that it was someone else."

I picked up a wrench, and attacked the bolts. "If we can't fix it, do we chuck it over the side?" I asked.

"Oh, I'm certain we can fix this," she said.

"But you're making space aboard for the injured, and training the crew in close combat."

"Only because of what I saw in Madagascar," she said. "Not because I know something you don't."

"I reckon there's a lot you know that I don't," I said. "Back on the bridge, you never really answered my question. Is someone going to hunt for the people transmitting the message?"

"I hope so," Adams said. "The general was adamant a foothold be kept in Africa. These broadcasters could confirm whether there is merit in the idea, or whether it will be nigh-on impossible, but our primary mission must be assisting the African Union in securing a coastal redoubt."

"I don't know much about ships except what I've picked up in movies, but your actions seem counterintuitive. We're not trying to contact the sub?"

"We did, and we have," Adams said. "They haven't replied, which is why I believe they are guarding their territory. Britain was an ally, but the old alliances are broken. The British launched their missiles just like everyone else."

"So we don't know if they're hostile or friendly?" I said. "Could it sink us?"

"Yes, and we could sink her if it came to an open battle, but they could run silent, and take advantage of surprise. As no assistance can be summoned, she only has to cripple us and retreat in order to destroy us."

"Then why are we not at action stations?" I said.

"I want them to see we are not hostile even after what they have done."

"Like sinking that U.S. destroyer?" I asked.

"I don't know what specific actions that boat took during the last month," Adams said. "The Royal Navy Trident submarines launched their warheads, following their orders to wreck our planet. This submarine must have had similar orders. Perhaps their target was Durban, or Suez, or shipping in the Mozambique Channel. Did they follow their orders, or disregard them? If they went rogue, they will need a new flag. If they didn't, but if London is gone, they will want a new home. I would prefer it is with us rather than against us."

"You're thinking of the future," I said.

"I'm thinking of the rescue fleet on its way to Cape Town. That submarine doesn't need to refuel. They carry ninety days of supplies, but they can loot more ashore. Munitions are a different matter, but if they had no torpedoes left, why follow us at all? One of the rebroadcast radio signals purported to be from Radio Free England. If this was a genuine broadcast coming from Britain, then England has collapsed. Britain is gone. Your scientists mentioned wanting to collect a sample of their vaccine. That broadcast suggests that vaccine didn't work."

"Dr Avalon was adamant a vaccine was impossible," I said. "We were promised some was on the way, but that promise came from Ian Lignatiev, one of those responsible for the coup. After he was dethroned, we found no trace of communication with Britain among his papers."

"If Britain had a vaccine, wouldn't they have had to know about this virus before the outbreak?" Adams asked.

"Yes," I said. "That assumes the vaccine is real. But why claim to have one if it didn't exist?"

"You said that these cartel sisters were working for, or with, politicians. If they designed this virus, wouldn't they also have designed a vaccine?"

"And given it to Britain?" I asked. "Theoretically. But why only Britain?"

"Exactly," Adams said. "Britain would have been destroyed in the nuclear war. It's an obvious target for Russia. A small target, yes, but impossible to miss."

"But the targeting went rogue," I said.

"No one knew that would happen before the missiles were launched," she said. "I'm correct in assuming that, yes?"

"As far as I know, yes," I said.

"After the outbreak, the traitors would have known the nuclear war was coming. Is that why they made up a story about a vaccine? Because they knew their population was about to die? In which case, those leaders would have fled. How? Aboard a nuclear-powered submarine. Going where? The Southern Hemisphere, to a naval base on some remote island."

"Let's hope it was Diego Garcia," I said.

"It is as likely to be Ascension," she said. "We will not assume the submarine is friendly, but nor are they hostile, and so we shall leave them in peace, and hope they repay the favour. You know what? Forget the wrench. Let's find a drill."

21st March

Chapter 16 - Sherlock Holmes

The surface-level radiation has been rising since we left Inhambane. Slowly. Steadily as radioactive fallout settles from the upper atmosphere. Nuclear winter is a disputed theory, rather than a scientific fact. Something I'd not realised, because, until last month, I'd not given it much thought. Of course, there was only one way of testing this theory, and fortunately, a large portion of the bombs detonated in the ocean. This will present challenges in the medium term, defined by Leo as being from six months to ten years. How insurmountable a challenge is something we'll learn in time. For now, we can only monitor the levels, and they're currently still low. The oceans are vast. I tell myself that over and over. But as we were passing Port Elizabeth, a southerly wind caused the atmospheric sensors to spike. We detoured out to sea, and at maximum speed.

We've passed Cape Agulhas, the most southerly point of the African continent, and so have left the Indian Ocean behind. We are now in the Atlantic, only a hundred and fifty kilometres from Cape Town. Night has fallen, and our speed has been cut. We're as close to shore as the captain dares bring us. Close enough to spot electric lights. Tonight we watch. We listen on the radio. Tomorrow, we should be reunited with Laila and the African Union. What happens next is impossible to predict.

Leo is certain the radiation spike was caused by a crater, inland of Port Elizabeth. So at least one nuclear bomb detonated in South Africa. One from which radiation still plumes into the air, is caught by the wind, and dragged seaward. Leo suggested the plumes were caused by ground-based fires. From his tone, I got the impression that grim explanation was the *best* possible explanation. The wind has changed direction now, meaning that radiation is heading inland, and so across the path of Laila and the African Union, and there is absolutely nothing we can do to help them. It's frustrating. It's not that I long for action, but I hate simply being a spectator. Always have.

Growing up, everyone has a bad year. Sixteen was mine. That was the last time I kept a journal. I tried after Sydney, but the grief was too raw to express with a pen. Age sixteen was when I began to grasp how simultaneously vast, and small, the world was. How repetitive the problems. How reluctant the world was to embrace change. How, even in the far-off places where the grass was evergreen, life was little better.

Did the journal help? Perhaps. It kept me occupied during the long evenings, working in Mum's restaurant, until Mick gave me a copy of *Sherlock Holmes*. Can't have been long after his wife died. Once a week, he'd come in for a meal. Not sure who was looking after Anna. She can't have been more than a few years old. One of her aunts, I suppose. But once a week, Mick came to the restaurant, always with a book for company. He'd sit by the window, eat, and read. I'd stay by the register, occasionally writing. Mostly the same few words over and over. Occasionally synonyms. More often doodles.

One night, a man came in looking for my mum. Except he used her old name. The name she left behind when she crossed the Yalu River. I froze. Mick noticed.

The stranger stood there. Wouldn't leave. Said he was waiting for my mum. Mick told him to go. Bloke ignored him. Mick… By then, he'd already lived a life. He knew how the world was, and he must have known what kind of world Mum had escaped. Mick threw the bloke out into the street.

That was the first time I witnessed *real* violence. Not the schoolyard stuff. Fist and foot. Fast and bloody. Mick had the bloke in the dust in seconds, and kept him there while he called the police. Me? I was frozen with fear.

The stranger wasn't a North Korean agent, just one of the human traffickers who'd smuggled Mum from the North Korean border to the Chinese airport where she'd caught the flight to Seoul. He was on the run from the Chinese authorities who, by then, were cracking down on the trade, and he'd come to shake my mum down.

Afterwards, and after the police had gone, a woman from the South Korean consulate visited. She was young, but wise. Kind as wool, yet hard as diamond. Strikingly beautiful and my instant role-model. Yep, I spent many a night re-doing my hair and wasting make-up trying to copy her look. I always assumed she was a spy. She suggested Mum move to South Korea. I'd get a place at school, and language lessons so I could catch up.

The spy stayed for a week, talking with Mum nearly twelve hours a day, in the kitchen, while they both cooked. I was *not* allowed to listen. Mum never told me what they talked about. After a week, the spy left. Mum announced we weren't leaving. She liked her restaurant. She liked Broken Hill.

I hated her for making us stay in that baking, nowhere city. My misdirected anger should have been aimed at that terrorist government who abused its people to an inhuman degree. But I blamed Mum because she was nearby and I was sixteen, bullied at school, and then punished for fighting back.

Mum had cancer. A result of the forced labour she'd done as a child. That's why she didn't want to leave. She didn't want me to be orphaned and friendless in a country whose language I barely spoke.

She survived it. That time.

You know the weird thing? Afterward, business boomed. There wasn't a single night where I was alone in the restaurant. Mick, or one of his relatives, was in every night. A lot of the older miners, who'd retired close to where they'd lived and worked, but who'd done their national service in the other hemisphere, camped out by the windows. I might have been sixteen, but I knew why.

Had to change the menu a bit. Made it more traditionally Australian. These days, you'd call it Outback-Korean fusion, but it was really just finding a balance between what the customers wanted to eat and what Mum knew how to cook.

Mum got better. She didn't recover. But she was less obviously sick. People kept coming to the restaurant. Ultimately, a few years later, when it was obvious I was on a different path, she was able to sell the business and enjoy a few years of peace.

Meantime, the restaurant was too busy for me to waste the hours doodling in a journal. Mick took to popping in more often. Sometimes with Anna in her pushchair. One night, he left me the book he'd been reading as a tip. I'd have preferred cash. It was *Sherlock Holmes*. Now, if you ask Mick, he'll say it was him giving me that book which is why I became a cop. I won't say it didn't help, even if it did give me an unrealistic view of the importance of trivial clues in solving a case. But that wasn't why I picked up the badge.

That was my bad year. Bullied, and then punished for fighting. Spending my nights working, friendless, alone. Worried that Mum's restaurant was always too empty. Shaken down by a human trafficker. Discovering spies were real. Realising my mum had seen things so dark she could never share them with me. Having my golden ticket away from the desert snatched out of my hands by my selfish mother. Learning she had cancer. Thinking she was going to die.

Yes, it was a bad year, which ended when I pulled my head out of the sand and realised I wasn't the centre of the universe. Other people mattered. Other people cared. Other people were *worth* caring about. Those old miners sat down in our restaurant as a way of standing up to that gallows-joke of a regime. When I realised I was one of *them*, that I *belonged*, I knew I had to find a way of giving back. Of standing up in my own way. That's why I became a cop.

Part 3

Forgotten Lessons from Not So Long Ago

Cape Town, South Africa

22nd March

Chapter 17 - The Cape of Lost Hope

False Bay, Cape Town, South Africa

After she'd watched the helicopter take flight, Commissioner Tess Qwong took a moment to marvel at the view. The captain had parked the ship at the southern edge of False Bay, a massive circular harbour, twenty kilometres deep, twenty wide in the south, and thirty kilometres wide in the north where the city of Cape Town began. To the west of False Bay was the Cape of Good Hope, on which lay Simon's Town and the homeport of the South African Navy. To the north was the city of Cape Town, and Table Mountain. On the eastern edge of the bay was Cape Hangklip, and the rendezvous point with the African Union convoy.

Cape Hangklip was relatively remote and relatively isolated, while still being relatively close to the city, and so to the highways which led north. It was close to perfect as a rendezvous. So where was the convoy?

Tess turned her gaze from the angry ocean and up to the tranquil blue sky in which the helicopter was already a speck, carrying Colonel Hawker, Clyde, and Nicko, in case the search-mission turned into a rescue.

Taking one last deep breath of the wondrously still, gloriously warm, faintly sweet South African air, she went back inside, and up to the bridge.

Leo and Avalon were analysing stills grabbed from the helicopter, while the captain was watching the live feed. The screen showed a rocky shore beset by craggy slopes, windswept shrubs, and a narrow road.

"Is that Cape Hangklip?" Tess asked.

"Yes. The radiation is rising," Adams said, her voice low.

"Technically no," Avalon said. "The *reading* is rising, but at a rate commensurate with the helicopter's ascent and journey inland. Extrapolating, there is an increasing level of airborne particulates."

"Could that be fallout from Port Elizabeth?" Tess asked.

"Yes," Leo said.

"No," Avalon said. "The wind direction is wrong."

"My first captain always said, wait until all the data was hooked before jumping to judgement," Adams said, ostensibly addressing the bridge crew. "These two are a walking example of why."

"Thank you," Avalon said, and sounded sincere.

"Anything on the radio, Mr Kane?" Adams asked.

"Nothing yet, ma'am," Lieutenant Kane said.

"The convoy could have been delayed by a detour around Port Elizabeth," Tess said.

"Indeed," the captain said. "Mr Kane, what of the repeater radio station?"

"As quiet as a kakapo, ma'am."

"Tell the commander to follow the road eastward," Adams said. "The people could be anywhere, but the vehicles would be on the road."

"Movement," Tess said. "Zoms."

On the feed, a trio of walking corpses tumbled down a steep escarpment onto the road, angling towards the helicopter. A fourth zombie was already ahead of them, lurching along the road towards the helicopter, but it was on the wrong side of the crash barrier. After five staggering steps, it toppled down a steep-walled creek.

Tess switched her focus to the screen displaying a digital map. It was a two-and-a-half-thousand-kilometre drive from Inhambane. If the roads were clear, that was a two-day journey.

The Cape of Good Hope was not the most southerly point of Africa, as early European mapmakers had assumed. The city of Cape Town began on the northern shore of False Bay, and sprawled northward, curling around Table Mountain, and along the shores of Table Bay on the far side of the Cape of Good Hope. In Table Bay lay the most famous prison in the world: Robben Island. She remembered that much from the practical lesson in history, equality, and hope as she and her mother had watched apartheid crumble on their restaurant's rabbit-eared TV set: her mother had cried for a week and smiled for a month.

"Mr Renton, ask the commander to make her way along the bay to Simon's Town," Adams said.

"Is that where the naval base is?" Tess asked.

"Yes. It's an obvious place for the convoy to seek refuge if they arrived yesterday," Adams said.

Avalon tapped her screen, which relayed a wide-angle view of the city's southern suburbs. "A selective blaze swept through that suburb. Those shadows suggest more fires half a kilometre north, and a kilometre to the northwest. To the west is smoke. Something is still smouldering."

"A cooking fire?" Tess asked.

"The smoke haze is too large," Avalon said.

"More zombies on the shore," Adams said, watching the live-stream. "But fewer than Inhambane. Fewer shipwrecks, too."

"They're small craft," Tess said. "Are they fishing boats?"

"Pleasure yachts," the captain said. "The shape of the hull gives it away. Larger ships would have been drafted into the evacuation fleet."

"Some zoms, but no barricades on the shore-road," Tess said, looking at the images, trying to piece together a picture of what had happened. Windswept. Storm-rinsed. Sun-baked. Ash-coated. Soot-dusted. Dotted with charred ruins. Filled with walking corpses now following the sound of the copter's rotors. Compact townships. Low-rise apartments. Single-storey homes. Neatly planned subdivisions with scrubby brown gardens. A junction blockaded by cars, ringed by corpses.

"Hold there, Commander," Adams said. "Rotate ten degrees port. Thank you."

Leo pulled up a still of the battlefield. "Over a hundred dead zoms," he said.

"They've fallen in a ring around those vehicles," Tess said. "It's not a last stand, is it? The survivors fought a battle, won, and left. Why fight there? Can you bring up the footage shot before this?"

"I can," Leo said, tapping at the keyboard. "How much do you want?"

"Just that cluster of apartment buildings. Okay, now go back a bit more to the housing development. Lots of low buildings. One-storey, built close together. A township, I think. Yes, there it is! Huh."

"What is it?" the captain asked, coming to look.

"Very few cars," Tess said. "Almost none. It's low-income housing, but there should still be some privately owned vehicles. After those zoms were killed around that junction, no one went to salvage the vehicles from the barricade. The survivors of that battle didn't need the wheels. Where exactly is this?"

"About level with the mid-point of the bay," Leo said.

"Leo, can you find the footage of the road nearer to Cape Hangklip? Yep. Good. Stop. There aren't any cars at all. There's nothing south of here until you reach penguins, so where are all the cars?"

"Which cars?" Leo asked.

"All the cars from Africa," Tess said.

"They went east to join the evacuation," Adams said.

"Not everyone on this continent," Tess said. "Not everyone could have heard of the evacuation. Not everyone would believe it. Some people would have fled south. Not everyone would have had the fuel to reach this far, but surely some would."

"It would be counter-instinctual to leave the security of one's home," Avalon said.

"Human beings are nothing if not counter-instinctual," Tess said. "That's about a thirty-kilometre sweep of road, with no cars at all. Some would have had the fuel to reach this far, but no further. There should be at least one. But there's not."

"They must have stalled on the far side of the city," Leo said.

"Sure, exactly, but why?" Tess said. "I was thinking about Port Elizabeth. If the radiation stopped people from getting this far, did it stop them from leaving, too?"

"That is your answer," Adams said, pointing again at the live-stream. "It's a plane."

Technically, it was an engine and one quarter of a wing, which had torn through a subdivision of beachfront villa-houses.

"Where's the other wing?" Leo asked, tapping at the keyboard, and bringing up a still of the charred engine.

"It wasn't attempting a landing," the captain said. "The plane was shot out of the sky. An A380, I think. Have the commander continue south to the naval base with all haste. I believe the majority of the local population departed here soon after the outbreak. If they used all lanes of the highways, no vehicles would be able to travel in a counter direction. Who would wish to come to a city everyone was fleeing? The roads to the north would become clogged with out-of-fuel cars. That's why there are no cars here."

"The convoy were driving earth-movers," Avalon said. "Stalled traffic would be a temporary impediment to them."

"Wait, there!" Tess said, now watching the live feed. "In the shallows. Another wing. Two engines, jutting out of the water. Two engines on one wing, so it was a different plane."

"You said it yourself, Commissioner," Adams said. "There's nothing south of here but penguins. The planes arrived first, hoping to land, hoping for salvation, but bringing the infection. They were shot from the sky. Ah, but *that* wasn't caused by a crashed plane."

The helicopter had moved on, and was now hovering above three large craters. Offshore, the seawall had been breached in two places. On land, the craters were surrounded by debris and charred ruins.

"That's the naval base," Adams said, checking her charts. "Yes. I'm certain."

"The craters are too small for a nuclear detonation," Leo said. "The diameter is about twenty metres on the smallest, thirty on the largest."

"Eighteen to twenty-six metres, at most," Avalon said.

"Commander Tusitala, return to the ship," Adams said, speaking into the radio herself.

"Are we going ashore?" Tess asked.

"Not here," the captain said. "Do you see the colour of the water around the broken seawall? The way that foam is cresting? Something is submerged just below the waterline. It would be too dangerous to approach. We need to refuel, and it's unlikely the fuel depot survived the impact. We'll try the commercial harbour in the north, around the Cape. The ship will anchor between Robben Island and the mainland. Boats will explore both the island and the harbour, while the helicopter can continue its survey of the ruins, and act as a beacon for the African Union. We'll have it fly back towards Cape Hangklip before dusk, and again after dawn. Commissioner, can you take charge of the search of the city? Find out the level of the threat, and identify how thoroughly the city was looted before it was abandoned. If we can't find fuel or provisions in the harbour, we will have to discuss how long we can wait here for the African Union to arrive."

"I didn't know Africa had mountains," Zach said as they waited for the order to board the fast-boat.

"Haven't you heard about Kilimanjaro?" Pippa Sullivan asked.

"Of course," Zach said a little too quickly. "Is that what it is?"

"That's Table Mountain," Tess said. "Kilimanjaro is in Tanzania."

"Right. Sure. Of course," Zach said. He turned around and pointed at the bulkhead wall. "Behind us, is that the island where President Mandela was imprisoned?"

"Yeah, Robben Island," Sullivan said. "I hope we can go ashore there."

"President Mandela was a gardener," Zach said. "When he was in prison. He kept a vegetable garden. So maybe they kept the garden going. It's a museum now, isn't it? If they kept the garden alive, we could find some fresh food."

"Here's hoping," Tess said.

"How do you know so much about President Mandela?" Sullivan asked.

"Read a book," Zach said with a shrug.

"At school?" Sullivan asked.

"Nah. In the library, of course."

Before Sullivan, or Tess, could ask more, Dr Smilovitz came out of the water-lock door, a bag in each hand, another over his shoulder.

"Take this," Leo said, thrusting a bag at Zach. "And this," he said, dropping another at Sullivan's feet. "Those go on the boat, and stay there until we have time for data collection. Flo isn't coming," he added, turning to Tess. "She's analysing the data the helicopter collected, combining that with prevailing wind patterns."

"What for?" Zach asked.

"That's a question you can ask her when we return," Tess said, who didn't have space in her brain to worry about radiation as well. "You've got the Geiger counter, Leo?"

"Yes, and two spare dosimeters," Leo said. "We should look in the hospital and university for more."

"Tomorrow," Tess said. "Give one dosimeter to Sullivan, and Bruce, you take the other." She looked over her landing team. In addition to her three soldiers, Leo, Toppley, and Zach, four sailors were attached to her team: Sullivan, Mackay, Baxter, and Fairburn. Over their navy blues, they wore body-armour marked with the word *Police* in the hope this would make them appear less like looters to any survivors still in the city. The other two landing parties were similarly labelled.

"Team Stonefish has some new faces, eh, Zach?" Tess said. "Listen up. We're sending three teams ashore. Robben Island, the beach to the north of Cape Town, and we're taking a look at the marina just the other side of that harbour wall. The helicopter's going to be flying back and forth, looking for the convoy, and maybe some survivors. In a city this big, there have to be some. Remember, just because it's got two arms and two legs, doesn't make it a zom. But this is an infected city. The helicopter will lure out the undead, so expect some to come lurching our way. We're looking for food and a base ashore, and for clues as to what happened up in the north that'll explain why the convoy has been delayed. Got it? Got weapons and water? Mackay, you've got the radio? Then let's go for a boat ride."

The small boat sawed through the gently cresting waves. The speed was a shock, the wind refreshing, washing away doubt, and subduing false hopes. As they drew nearer to the shore, she better understood the images the camera had recorded. Cape Town was a dead city, abandoned weeks ago. Everyone on the boat saw it, felt it, understood it, except for Sullivan and Zach who were shouting at each other about sharks.

Inside the seawall, Fairburn cut their speed, following Hawker's direction to take their boat to the nearest pier. Tess turned around, looking for other boats. But by the time they bumped into the tyres slung below the jetty, she'd only seen wrecks, aground on the distant beach.

Before Baxter and Sullivan secured the boat, Oakes and Hawker were on the quay, sprinting towards the shore. By the time Tess clambered onto the concrete jetty, they were at its end.

"Why's the ground moving?" Sullivan muttered.

"Your brain's adapted to the motion of a ship, now it has to reset," Leo said.

"Sea-lubber!" Zach said, bouncing up on his heels.

"Focus," Hawker said. "I want safeties on, and fingers clear of triggers. Tess?"

"The marina's bigger than I thought," Tess said, looking at the neighbouring pier, and the scores of smaller jetties closer to shore. "Baxter, Fairburn, stay with the boat. If we get into trouble, you might have to pick us up from a different pier. Maybe that beach."

"Aye-aye, ma'am," Baxter said.

"Mackay, you've got the radio?" Hawker asked. "Take the rear with Sullivan. Zach, Leo, stick close to Clyde. Teegan, you stick close to the commissioner. Sergeant Oakes, you're on point. There should be people here, but there certainly are zoms."

Chapter 18 - Too Old for Toys
Cape Town, South Africa

At the end of the quay, a concrete concourse was bracketed by a score of small service huts, and secured from the shore by white railings and a heavy gate. Originally, this had been kept closed by a mechanical keypad, but someone had taken a crowbar and sledgehammer to the lock, bending the gatepost far enough to disengage the mechanism. Someone had then secured the gate with a rope, which, in turn, had been cut. Probably with the short-handled axe embedded in the skull of the corpse on the far side of the gate.

"The dents are on this side of the lock," Tess said. "Whoever forced the gate did so from the quay. Probably someone who came, and went, by boat. This is the first quay inside the seawall. I'd guess this was a sailor who was following the coast."

"Plenty of brass among the silt," Hawker said. "About fifteen bodies on the far side. Zoms from the look of them."

"They killed the zoms before opening the gate," Zach said. "I mean, I would."

"They ran out of bullets," Tess said. "Why else use that axe? But they thought this fight was worth the risk, so must have already run out of food. Colonel, take the lead. That looks to be a hotel ahead. We'll make that our first stop."

"A hotel with Table Mountain behind, and the sea in front," Toppley said. "That takes me back."

"You've been here before?" Tess asked as she stepped over the corpses and through the gate.

"Not Cape Town, no," Toppley said. "I was thinking of my first attempt at retirement ten years ago, but I can't see any gun-wielding sentries on any of those balconies. If I were waiting for a ship, that would be a sensible place to station a lookout."

"If they were waiting here, they'll have eaten the food," Tess said. "Pop-quiz, Zach. Where do we look for food now? I should warn you, there's only one correct answer, and failure to guess it will have you swimming a lap of the warship."

"If I guess it right, does that mean *you* have to swim around the ship?" he asked. "You know there are sharks in these waters? Me and Pip saw them. Proper sharks."

"Great whites," Sullivan said.

"Yeah, no fooling," Zach said. "We saw three."

"Two," Sullivan said.

"I saw three," Zach said.

"Fine, no forfeit," Tess said. "But what's the answer? Where do we look for food?"

"Dunno," Zach said. "Supermarkets and groceries would have been looted first so a restaurant, maybe. But not that hotel. It's too obvious."

The architect must have regretted being born a millennium too late, and had constructed the hotel in the style of a tiered desert fortress onto which balconies, columns, and covered colonnades had been reluctantly tacked. Like the road, the hotel's driveway was lined with perfectly trimmed palms. As around the jetty, bodies littered the broken-open gates, though they lay more heavily on the north side, as if at least some of the bodies had been moved out of the way.

"Someone cleared those corpses so they could get a vehicle in, or out," Tess said. "No, hang back here, Zach," she added as he took a step towards the gates, and so after Hawker and Oakes who were jogging to the hotel entrance. "You're right, it's too obvious. We won't find food there."

"So why's the colonel and Nicko—" Zach began, just as the two soldiers, as one, stopped running and jumped back, raising their carbines. Two shots rang out. Another two. A fifth.

Hawker raised a clenched fist, before returning his hand to his gun. The two soldiers prowled forward.

Tess turned her own attention to the road. "Zach, Teegan, watch the hotel. Everyone else, eyes on the road."

"They're coming back, Commish!" Zach said.

The soldiers were running at a quick jog, which wasn't quite a sprint.

"Trouble?" Tess asked.

"Zoms," Oakes said, wiping a long machete with a strip of cloth.

"Where did you get that machete?" Zach asked.

"Zoms," Oakes said again.

"I heard sounds inside the hotel," Hawker said. "They secured the front doors from the inside. But it's not people trapped in there."

"Are they in danger of getting out?" Tess asked.

"They haven't yet," Hawker said. "But give it time."

"Pity," Tess said. "Let's keep going."

"Why's it a pity?" Zach asked, as they moved off, Hawker and Oakes once again in the lead.

"A big hotel right by the waterfront would have been an ideal place for the African Union to wait until the rescue ships arrived," Tess said. "There's even a sign there for a heliport. But if there are still zombies inside… well, either we kill them, or we find a different pier to use."

"What was the correct answer?" Zach asked. "Where do we look for food?"

"You got it," Tess said. "Restaurants, hotels, schools. Not farms or grocery stores or homes, but everywhere in between. Places food was stored, but which would have been closed immediately after the pandemic began. Leo, didn't you say you'd been here before?"

"I didn't make it further than the university," Leo said. "I'd been booked for a trio of lectures on non-proliferation and disarmament. I had a week's vacation planned afterwards, but before I made it onto the stage, I got a call. There'd been another Ebola flare-up in the DRC. The C.I.A. believed it had been engineered. Flo and I got a police escort to the airport, and a fighter escort to the border."

"The Ebola outbreak was engineered?" Tess asked.

"No, but one of the flare-ups was. A local warlord had the idea of getting into the bioweapons business. Fortunately for the world, that guy had skipped the classes on safety precautions. The bunker he built below ground was so badly ventilated, the victims were mostly him and his people."

"Wow. I never knew," Tess said.

"It was never publicised. Didn't want to give other idiots the wrong idea, eh?" Leo said.

"Huh," Tess said. Behind her, Sullivan and Zach were chin-wagging away like the teenagers they were. Mostly about shark movies, from what she could hear. But since she was chatting with Leo, she could hardly complain. "So you were lecturing, but Flo was with you?"

"She's happy working anywhere, but I hoped we might have a few days R&R. Guess which guy thought it was a smart move to book tickets to every activity in advance? Lost three months' salary. Still, could have been worse."

"You mean there could have been another major Ebola outbreak?"

"That, sure, and the government was able to get our hotel and airline tickets refunded."

Every interrogatory fibre of her detective soul wanted to say: *are you sure you two aren't a couple*? But Tess let it go. For now. "How's the radiation reading?"

"Stable," he said, "which is the answer we want."

The road led towards what, once, had been an affluent shopping precinct, built on either side of the road. A road which, now, was blocked to traffic by a charred aircraft engine.

As big as a truck, the engine must have belonged to a mega-jet. The impact had scattered the parts across the road. A rain of burning shrapnel had set the roadside palm trees ablaze. Four cars, which had been mid-commute, had been blown to scrap, their passengers turned to pulp on which flies still buzzed.

"There's a shopping mall ahead," Hawker said. "Stores on the ground floor, covered parking above. Entrance is up that ramp ahead. That upper-floor walkway crossing the road must give access to more stores behind the car park, and on the other side of the road."

“Stores have stockrooms,” Tess said. “We should confirm they’ve been looted.”

“Agreed,” Hawker said. “But we’ll check a selection, then head towards that smoke.”

“Hey, I can see Table Mountain again,” Sullivan said.

“Uluru’s better,” Zach said.

But between them and the plateau-peak, the air was hazy from thin, grey-black plumes.

“Could that be the convoy?” Tess asked.

“You know what they say,” Hawker said. “Seeing is believing.” He held up a hand. “Gunfire! Single shots.”

“North,” Oakes said. “Single-shot rifle. One klick out.”

“Mackay, call it in,” Hawker said. “Everyone keep moving, but be ready to retreat.”

Detouring around the plane wreckage, passing an optician’s with a broken window, a clothing store with charred mannequins, a pet-supply shop where Tess crunched across the glass to look through the window. “Partially looted. Worth checking on the way back.”

“What for?” Zach asked.

“Antibiotics work as well on people as pets,” Clyde said. “Small-arms. Single shots. From the north. It’s over a kilometre away, but the rate of fire is increasing.”

A rasping hiss came from the far side of a wrecked car, abandoned outside the pet shop. A row of three airplane seats had fallen from the sky, leaving a V-shaped crater in the car’s engine before tumbling to the roadway. Three passengers had been buckled in their seats at the time the missile had blown the plane out of the sky. The first had been obliterated on impact with the ground. The second corpse was missing from the chest upward. The third had a thigh bone wedged through her stomach. This didn’t stop her shattered arm from undulating as she limply reached towards them.

“She can’t be alive,” Zach whispered.

Clyde fired. “No.”

Tess brushed the flies away from her face. "Move on. Just to the end of the block, and the end of these stores."

Two small figures jumped through a broken glass window to their left, sprinting across the street.

"Guns down!" Hawker barked. "Hold fire!"

The children, a boy of about thirteen, a girl a year older, stumbled to a halt. Both carried matching hatchets in their hands, and other tools at their belts, all with black-rubber handles, all surely recently looted. On their backs were matching red backpacks, both sagging and empty.

"African Union?" the girl asked.

"Yes," Tess said. "We came by ship."

"The Australian ship?" the boy asked.

"New Zealand," Sullivan said.

"Yes," Tess said quickly, hoping to cut through any further confusion. "We sailed from Mozambique on a warship, here to meet the African Union soldiers. Are you with them?"

"Now, yes," the boy said with a broad smile.

"Monsters!" the girl hissed. "They're following."

Even as she spoke, a clatter came from inside the shop.

"And now they are not!" the boy said with triumph.

"Nicko, Clyde! Clear that store. Mackay, up front!" Hawker said. "Sullivan, watch our six."

"Wait here," Tess said, both to the children and to Toppley, Zach and Leo, and followed Clyde to the store, a jeweller's. Three zombies were tangled in a back-and-forth net of thin chains rigged behind the counter, and in front of a doorway to the stockroom.

"Fishing hooks!" the boy said with pride, having followed them over. "I added fishing hooks! We can crawl underneath, but they do not learn."

The zombies were shredding skin and fingers as they reached and pushed at the hooked chains. Gore dripped to the floor as, inch by peeling inch, they ripped their way through the obstacle.

"Finish them," Tess said.

Clyde fired. Tess turned back to the boy. "Is the African Union convoy that came from Mozambique here, in the city?"

"Yes. But they are hungry," the girl said. "We were getting them food. We can take you to them."

"Can you tell us where they are?" Hawker asked.

"At the airport," the boy said.

"*Near* where the airport *was*," the girl said. "Too many planes exploded."

"The international airport?" Hawker asked.

"You came here to collect food, yes?" Tess asked, forestalling anyone else's questions with a raised hand. "Where from?"

The girl pointed across the road to a toyshop with a window partially barricaded on the inside. "From there. We hid it there weeks ago."

"Clyde, check the toy-store. Bruce, radio the ship," Tess said. "Everyone, keep your eyes open for zombies." She turned to the children. "My name is Tess Qwong. I'm a police commissioner from Australia. That man with the grumpy squint is Colonel Hawker of the Australian SAS."

Oakes sniggered.

"Everyone else is either one of my police officers, a sailor from the ship, or one of the colonel's soldiers," Tess continued. "What are your names?"

"Lesadi," the girl said.

"I'm Thato," the boy said.

"Did you live here?" Tess asked.

"Here?" the boy asked. He laughed.

"In Cape Town, yes," the girl said.

"Store looks clear," Clyde said, pausing by the door. "Did you set up any traps in there?"

"Not in there," the boy said. "Of course not."

"The helicopter's on Robben Island," Hawker said. "They'll return to the ship, grab more sailors, and then head on to the airport. They found hostiles on Robben Island."

"D'you mean zombies or people?" Tess asked.

"Four zoms," Hawker said. "There's no sign of any living survivors, but two yachts had been docked at the pier. Whoever sailed them there, didn't leave. As they didn't deal with the zoms, we're unlikely to find any survivors on the island. How long would it take to walk to the airport?"

"I can run there in ten minutes," Thato said.

"*You* can't," Lesadi said. "But I can."

"Both of you are staying here with me," Tess said. "Bruce, take the radio. Stay in contact with the ship. We'll head back to the boat once we've assessed the food supplies. Clyde, Mackay, go with the colonel. Will that be enough?"

"More than plenty," Bruce said.

"Wait," Leo said, unhooking the Geiger counter. "Take this."

Tess handed her spare ammo to Clyde. "Good luck, Major."

"Luck comes to those who make it," Clyde said. "What's the safest route to the airport?"

Lesadi pointed down the road. "That way. There are plenty of signs."

"I'll show you," Thato said.

"No you don't," Tess said, laying a hand on his shoulder as Hawker and Oakes, Clyde and Mackay, began running. "Everyone get inside the toyshop."

Tess looked back up the street where the four warriors were already out of sight.

"They sure can run," Leo said.

"I feel sorry for Mr Mackay," Tess said.

"Oh, he can keep up, ma'am," Sullivan said. "He once nearly lasted five rounds in the ring with the captain."

Chapter 19 - Rooftop Safari
Cape Town, South Africa

"The waterfront's not the first place I'd expect to find a toy store," Leo said.

"But a toyshop is the last place I'd think to look for a food stash," Tess said. "Very clever."

Blankets and sheets shrouded shoulder-high stacks of canned food. More cardboard trays of shrink-wrapped tins were arrayed on shelves from which the toys had been swept.

"Black beans," Leo said, pulling off a sheet. "Chick peas. Oh, grapefruit! Now that's worth far more than a dollar."

"Sorry, Doc, the African Union soldiers get priority," Tess said. "Since they got here before us, they can't have stopped for supplies, and probably not even to eat."

"It's impressive, yes?" Lesadi asked.

"Very," Tess said. "It's a very clever hiding place. Did this come from a supermarket? A grocery store?"

"From a delivery truck," Lesadi said.

"*Two* delivery trucks," Thato said. "They were parked over there." He waved his hand towards the rear of the store. "The driver was—"

"A zombie," Lesadi said quickly.

"A mother. With her baby," Thato finished.

"Good on ya," Tess said. "You're real heroes for keeping this safe."

"It'll be enough to feed everyone!" Thato said.

"I hope so," Tess said. But she doubted it. "Help Teegan catalogue it."

"Commish! You won't believe it!" Zach said, holding up something which had once been part of a window display.

"Is that a DVD?" she asked.

"Not just any DVD," Zach said. "It's *The Bouncing Dog Sled.* By Dan Blaze!" he added. "I know what I'm watching tonight."

"You want to watch a kids' movie?" Sullivan asked.

"Yeah, because he's the singer back in Canberra," Zach said.

"Put it in your bag," Tess said. "Then go help Teegan." She took a step closer, and lowered her voice. "Chat with the kids. Let them talk, and you listen. Get a feel for what happened in the city during this last month. Find out what happened to everyone else."

She crossed to the other side of the plate-glass window, where Sullivan was watching the street. Leo followed.

"It's about five thousand meals," the scientist said, his voice low.

"It won't be enough to feed the African Union soldiers," Sullivan said.

"But it's a start," Tess said. "We'll have to catch a few fish off the coast. We can, can't we, Leo?"

"You mean with the radiation readings? Sure, in deeper water. This month. Probably next month, too. Ask me again after that. Did you notice there were no boats in the marina, and no cars parked outside here?"

"But if you drove to a store, you'd drive home again, right?" Sullivan said.

"But the people who sailed away from the marina would have driven to the docks," Leo said. "Who took their cars?"

"Plenty of people in this city wouldn't own a car," Tess said. "They walked to the harbour, saw the boats were gone, but that cars had been left with keys in the ignition. The ship reported two boats made it to Robben Island, and the sailors made contact with four zoms. It's unlikely there are any survivors there."

"Where did the other boats go?" Sullivan asked.

"Madagascar," Tess said. "How many people lived in Cape Town before the outbreak, Leo?"

"About five million," he said. "About fifty million in South Africa."

"They were evacuating from Durban," Tess said. "But Durban was overwhelmed, and people went north, to Maputo, and it, too was overwhelmed, and so that teacher we met went to Inhambane. If you lived here, and planes were falling from the sky, and someone said they were evacuating from Durban, wouldn't you go? By boat, or by car, or on foot. It's what they did, and so the evacuation failed. Of course it did. Look at the struggle we had just getting the kids down to Tassie."

"I wonder how the Brits managed it," Leo said. "For years, I've been telling the world that you've got to stay in place, stay home and look after your neighbours. But no one wants to prepare for a blizzard while extinguishing a wildfire."

"Commissioner," Toppley said, coming over. "We might have a problem."

"With the food?" Tess asked.

"In a manner of speaking," Toppley said. "The children gathered this food, but their stockpile, and their base here in this shopping precinct, was seized from them a week ago. They, their entire group, relocated to the airport. The thieves remained. It's they for whom the traps were set. The children had been attempting to lure zombies here to finish the thieves."

"How many thieves?" Tess asked.

"Two or three, all armed with guns," Toppley said.

"Have you made a note of how much food is here?" Tess asked. "Then we'll return to the boat. Send the kids back to the ship, and come back with some more sailors to secure this place. And with another radio."

"And more dosimeters," Leo said.

"And some handcarts for—" Sullivan began, but stopped as the window shattered. Glass fell either side of the up-turned display-table even as they all ducked.

"Rooftop opposite!" Toppley said. "Single sniper."

"Everyone stay down!" Tess said. "Zach, get the kids behind the counter."

A bullet thudded into the floor. A second hit the door.

"Suppressed rifle!" Toppley said, hidden behind a low stack of canned papaya. "Single shots."

"So far," Tess said. "I need a mirror. Teegan? Sullivan? Sullivan!"

Where the others had dropped, Sullivan had fallen, hands clenched to her side. "It's fine," she hissed.

Tess crawling across the broken glass to the injured sailor. "Not too bad," she said as she took out the med-kit. "It'll make a nice scar."

"Pippa?" Zach called.

"Stay there, Zach!" Sullivan said.

"Let me take care of her, eh?" Leo said, taking the med-kit from Tess. "You take care of the sniper."

"Teegan, did you see the target?" Tess asked.

"On the rooftop above the parking garage. Furthest corner from the above-road walkway," she said. "He stood up to take the shot."

A second bullet flew through the broken window and ripped through the soft plastic floor tiles equidistant between Tess and Leo.

"We'll move Pippa back. On three," Tess said, grabbing one of Sullivan's arms as Leo grabbed the other, and Teegan raised her carbine above her head, firing half a magazine blind.

"No!" Tess hissed, even as Teegan shuffled across the glass just as a third bullet slammed into the floor. A second later, a short burst followed, but Topppley was braced behind the pillar supporting the window-frame, and Sullivan was now behind a stack of canned goods.

"The sniper's got a suppressor," Tess said.

"Yes, I told you that," Toppley said.

"No, Teegan, think of the zoms," Tess said.

"Ah, apologies, Commissioner," Toppley said.

"How's Pippa, she okay?" Zach asked.

"You *can* ask me," Sullivan hissed.

"Oh, sorry," Zach said, but he sounded relieved.

"It could be an hour before assistance comes," Toppley said, "but if assistance comes in the form of a helicopter, they could be shot down."

"No worries, we're not waiting," Tess said. "Lesadi you brought this food in from somewhere behind this store, yes? So there's a back door?"

"Through there, yes," the girl said, pointing at the door behind the counter.

"Toppley, watch the front. Zach, safety off, but finger off the trigger, too. Toppley is in command."

"Where are you going?" Leo asked.

"To find us a way out," Tess said, drawing her nine-mil, and attaching her own suppressor.

The Queensland opal mine, the Telstra Tower, the museum: people shooting at her was becoming too regular an occurrence. The difference here was she didn't have to shoot back. The ship's cannon could level that entire building with one shot, assuming she could make contact with the ship. Oh, if only she had a radio. The priority was getting Sullivan somewhere more secure, and if the sniper was protecting this food stash, then absolutely *anywhere* else would suffice.

The door led to the stockroom, and to another door. The lock was broken. It didn't lead outside, but almost into the arms of a zombie. She had her suppressed sidearm in hand, and fired, both shots hitting the zombie's chest, but the impacts didn't slow the back-swung hand which slammed into the side of Tess's head. She rolled with the impact, diving to the floor, firing up even as the zombie turned. Two shots: the first up through the chin, the second through the face, both exiting through the brain. The zombie slumped, and she had to roll again to get out of the way.

It wore a bright red short-sleeved shirt, black multi-pocketed trousers, and designer sneakers which still had the price-and-size sticker on the sole. But the bulletproof vest was almost as interesting as the empty hip-holster. Very new shoes, donned just before he'd been infected, and clean enough they'd done less than a mile of walking. Why wear the vest unless expecting trouble from humans? Hopefully, he was one of the thieves.

She was in a service stairwell. Three steps led down to an exterior door. Not made of glass, but heavily reinforced metal in which were two separate locks. Both locks had keys in them, but both keys had been snapped off. By the thieves, she assumed, leaving only the main-road access point for the toy-store, which could easily be covered by a sniper.

She heard footsteps coming down the stairs, raised her gun, and fired at the zombie even before she saw the shotgun in his hand. One shot to the vest, the second to the face, and he tumbled and fell, onto the corpse of his dead friend. Two thieves dead. One infected. One human. Hopefully only one thief was left, and as far as she could see, only one option was available to her. She paused a heartbeat, tilting her head, listening, before re-opening the stockroom door.

"Zach!" she called.

"Yes, boss?"

"Seal up this door. Remember rule-one? That's our call sign. Counter is rule-two, got it? I think two thieves are dead, leaving only the sniper on the roof. I'll be back in ten."

"Wait," Zach said, but Tess didn't. She pulled the door closed, and ran up the stairs.

At the next landing was another door, and more stairs going up. But the walkway to the garage, and the larger half of the shopping precinct, was on this floor, wasn't it? Hopefully. Gun raised, she pulled the door open. Unlocked. It led into an office. From the logos, it belonged to the toy-store. The office had two other doors, and the one she picked led into a dim hallway: a maintenance corridor with small cubbyhole storage rooms and a pair of nearly windowless doors which had been hacked to splinters. Walking quickly but quietly, she stepped around the debris, gun raised, sweeping wide as she entered the customer-facing part of the shopping centre. Shutters were down everywhere, but with carts, bags, and tools parked outside the broken-open entrances. Ignoring those, she saw what she wanted: the universal P for parking, and an arrow showing her the way.

Another set of fire doors would have sealed the across-road walkway, but again they'd been hacked to splinters. From their partial cover, she leaned forward, looking upward at the rooftop across the road. She heard the distant impact, but not the gunfire, not until someone inside the toy-store returned fire. Bullets sprayed the wall beneath the roof. A second after they finished, she saw the man rise above the edge of the roof, rifle in hand, fire a shot, then disappear again.

Clearly, he was a professional. But he wasn't trying to kill her team, merely keep them pinned while he waited on his comrades to attack from the rear. Tess ran as fast as her hip would allow, across the walkway, and through another set of hacked-apart doors. While the walkway became an upstairs concourse into a broader shopping precinct, to the left was an access door, propped open with a broad machete which, oddly, was attached to a long length of metal wire. Inside, more knives, attached to more lengths of wire, dotted the floor. Broken traps.

The door led to service stairs. The down-flight was partially blocked with wire-grill delivery crates. Below, out of sight but very audible, undead flesh pushed and slapped against metal and concrete. She went up. At the top was another propped-open door leading into a storage area filled with mops, buckets, and cleaning liquid. But steps led up to a door-hatch flush with the sloping roof. Gun close to her chest, she pushed the door open, stepping up and outside.

The roof dropped from a high V at the front to flat at the back, changing from opaque to transparent above the shopping area. She stood on the metal gutter in the dip between two Vs, hidden from the far corner, but the roof was too steep here to climb over, let alone clamber up and shoot.

Unmoving, she waited, listening, until she heard a solitary brass cartridge tinkle to the gutter. Shoes squeaked. A long moment later, a return burst from Toppley tore chunks out of the brickwork.

The thin layer of ash offered a cushion for her feet as she made her way along the gutter, towards the flattened roof. Walking in a half crouch, she kept moving until she reached a nearly flat section where the glass had been reinforced with an internal metal grid. Assuming it could take her weight, she walked, gun raised, quickly, seeing the shooter a second before he heard her.

“Police! Freeze! Drop your weapon!” she called, hoping her accent would do as much as the words to make the man pause. He wore camouflage, but of the safari kind. The same pattern was on his hat and his bulletproof vest. In his hands was a suppressed rifle with a collapsible stock and extended magazine. Right now, it was aimed at ninety-degrees to her, held across the man’s body as he crouched low, close to the wall’s edge.

“Police! We’re with the African Union, and the warship in the harbour,” she said. “This is a misunderstanding. No one else has to die.”

Slowly, without turning around, or rising from his crouch, he released his right hand from the rifle’s grip, raising the hand high. With his left hand, he placed the rifle down on the ground. Without turning around, he stood. But his left hand slipped in front of his body, and so out of sight.

“Both hands,” Tess said. “Let me see both—”

He spun. She fired. One shot, and into his vest. He doubled over, almost into a ball, dropping the compact metal-framed revolver.

She’d attached the suppressor to the pistol in case of zombies, unnecessarily as it had turned out, but that had reduced the bullet’s velocity. The man’s vest should have stopped the bullet from penetrating the skin. And it would have, if the vest hadn’t been made of cloth. It wasn’t bulletproof, just a many-pocketed sleeveless jacket designed for hunting, now dripping with blood from the pulsing exit wound.

Chapter 20 - Nitro Express
V&A Waterfront, Cape Town, South Africa

Tess detached the suppressor, and holstered her pistol. "Clear!" she called, pitching her voice to carry. "Remember rule-one!" she added, before stepping forward, arms raised, hands empty. "Check your boots, Teegan!" she yelled, walking to the roof's edge, and saw the zombies. Three, approaching from the south.

In addition to the rifle and revolver, the dead hunter had a double-barrelled shotgun with a polished chestnut stock. The suppressed rifle had a camouflage-pattern stock, an extended magazine, and almost as long an optical scope. She raised the rifle to her shoulder, searching for the zombies. It was a *very* good scope. She could make out the white bone jutting from the zombie's elbow as the arms loosely swung with each step. Yes, a good scope. Too good. More than good enough to make out the small lamb dangling from the hair-tie on the too-small figure's one remaining pigtail. So good she was nearly blinded when she shifted focus to the third, and the beating sun reflected off the length of steel jutting from its shoulder. A metal-handled carving knife. Too long and ornate to be truly practical, even, evidently, as a weapon. Four shots, less than a minute, and the zombies were down.

Adjusting the sights, she scanned further down the road, hoping to spy the African Union convoy, but she saw five more ghouls instead. Five minutes away, at least. Drifting down the road, and now just passing a large pile of rubble and metal debris from a building destroyed by the falling plane. She lowered the rifle, slung it over her shoulder, and grabbed the hunter's satchel. Inside were pre-loaded magazines for the rifle, and, in neatly stitched loops, dozens of brass cartridges at least ten centimetres in length. She slung the bag, picked up the double-barrelled gun, and made her way back to the roof-door.

When she reached the walkway over the road, she raised the rifle. The rubble around the demolished building had slowed the zombies' approach, but three were now beyond, and still heading this way. Behind, were now another eight. No, nine as a near-naked zombie staggered through the broken frontage of a restaurant. Ten. Fifteen as more appeared from a side road on the other side of the street. She lowered the scope, ran on, and back to the toyshop.

"Rule-one, Zach," she called "It's me."

As the door opened, she pushed her way inside. "The sniper's dead," she said. "So are two men in body-armour who were in the stairwell outside. The sniper was pinning us down, the other two were about to make entry and finish us off, except a zom jumped in on our side of the fight."

"Zombies are helping us?" Zach asked.

"Figure of speech," Tess said. "How's Sullivan?"

"Alive," the sailor whispered.

"Excellent. Can you walk?"

"We've built a stretcher," Leo said. "We can carry her."

"Are we moving?" Toppley asked.

"Zoms are inbound," Tess said. "We've got a few minutes to get upstairs or get out of here. Thato, Lesadi, do you think there could be more than three of these food-thieves?"

"Not here," Thato said.

"Not yet," Lesadi said.

"There *are* more?" Tess asked.

"They camp to the north," Lesadi said. "There's too much food for them to move."

"Good to know. Zoms inbound, zoms in the building, and more thieves could be on their way. We're going back to the boat. Zach, Leo, get Sullivan onto the stretcher. Thato, Lesadi, you help them. Toppley, with me."

"Is that a double-barrelled rifle?" Toppley asked.

"Is it?" Tess asked, taking it off her shoulder, and handing it to the former gun-runner. "I didn't think they still made them."

"By hand, to special order, yes," Toppley said. "Where else would you expect to find an elephant gun, except in a country with elephants?"

Tess handed her the satchel. "There's cartridges in the bag long enough to use as a knife. What kind of range does it have?"

"Sadly, they're not designed for long range," Toppley said. "They are, quite literally, for shooting a charging elephant. The parallel barrels are so you can fire a second shot quickly if your first doesn't finish the job. Against a zom, I would imagine it would have a similar effect as a grenade. It'll be interesting to find out."

"Start with this," Tess said, handing her the suppressed rifle. "You'll watch our backs."

Zach and Leo, and the two children, carried the stretcher outside.

"Zach at the front," Tess said "I've got the back. Everyone else get ready to swap in. Anyone not carrying is watching for zoms. Move. You okay there, Zach?"

"Yeah, no worries," he said.

The stretcher was heavy, and she was tired. Beset by memories of a different rooftop chase, an ocean and decade away.

"How did you make the stretcher?" she asked, focusing on the present to distract herself from the past.

"Backpacks and poles," Leo said.

Two aluminium shelf-support poles held a lattice-work of giraffes. Ten long-necked animals, each belonged to a children's backpack whose straps had been threaded together.

"The bags are from a movie, aren't they?" she said, her eyes on Sullivan. "Do you remember, Pippa? That blockbuster animation released in Feb. Seems so long ago. The release was supposed to be last summer, but one of the voice-actors went off the deep end, nose first, and was arrested with a submachine gun atop a water ride in Florida. A sudden need to recast had led to a quieter, February release date."

"Dunno, maybe," Zach said.

Tess was talking for the sailor's benefit, watching her eyes, looking for a response, but her gaze turned to Zach. For all the violence he'd seen in the last week, he was a month from being a skinny skip-school kid.

"Leo, swap with Zach."

"No, I'm fine," Zach said.

"You'll get a twenty-second breather, and you're swapping with me," Tess said. "We've got five minutes to go, and have to keep up the pace."

The kids were too small to sub in, except in a pinch, but Lesadi carried Sullivan's rifle. Thato had Leo's handgun.

Between their heavy footsteps, and her own laboured breathing, she couldn't hear any shots from the suppressed rifle, but Toppley's occasional satisfied hiss suggested she was hitting a target. Of course, that told her the enemy was now within shooting range.

"Four minutes behind us," Toppley said. "About forty of them."

The airplane engine was just ahead. Beyond were a few buildings, but not many before the massively sprawling, and zombie-infested, hotel. After that was the waterfront. It wasn't far, but they weren't moving fast enough.

"Thato, Lesadi, where can we shelter?"

"Not here," Lesadi said. "Thato made too many traps."

"You didn't say it was too many before," Thato said.

"We need shelter," Tess said. "High up. Now. I'll run to the boat, get the sailors, radio the ship, and arrange a proper extraction."

"Commissioner!" Toppley called. "The extraction is coming to us!"

She heard it. An engine. Loud. Growing louder. She couldn't turn. "Keep going, Leo," she said.

"No, we can stop," Toppley said.

"You sure?" Tess asked.

"One thousand percent," Toppley said.

"Zach, take the stretcher," Tess said.

He grabbed it instantly, clearly wanting to do something more useful than trailing along at the side.

Tess turned around and saw a road-dragon driving towards them. A high-wheeled dumper truck she vaguely recognised from Inhambane. But between it and them were the undead. Far more than she'd realised. Well over forty. Until the truck ploughed into the ghouls. Arm and leg, head and body, bone and blood, guts and skin flew as the zombies exploded with the impact. Others were dragged beneath the monstrous tyres as the truck barrelled on.

"Keep going!" Tess yelled to Leo and Zach, while the approaching truck followed a different instruction. It braked, sudden and loud, both doors opening. Out of the passenger side, Clyde leaped, rifle raised, firing at the partially crushed zombies even before his feet hit tarmac. Out of the driver's side jumped a figure with a blue scarf draped over her head.

"Laila?" Tess asked.

"Good day again," the nurse said, stopping next to the stretcher. "How was she hurt?"

"Shot in the side," Tess said.

"Put her down please, Zach," Laila said. "Can you hear me?"

"Her name's Pippa," Zach said.

"Pippa, can you hear me?" the nurse asked.

The sailor groaned. "Yeah."

"Your ship is nearby, yes?" Laila asked.

"In the harbour, and we've a boat at the quay," Tess said. "It's about a three minute run."

"We should hurry," Laila said. "We need to get her to surgery."

Oakes had followed Laila out the driver's side of the truck, and had added his rifle fire to Clyde's, killing the crawling undead as he and Clyde had backed up, away from the truck, and towards the stretcher.

"Clyde, Nicko, grab the stretcher," Tess said. "Go with Laila. Take the kids. Get to the boat. Send the sailors back here. We'll hold this position."

"I can carry her," Oakes said. "Laila, would that be okay?"

"Haste is most welcome," Laila said.

“I’ll leave you my rifle,” Oakes said, dropping his weapon before scooping up the injured sailor.

“Clyde, cover them. Go!” Tess said.

Sullivan in his arms, Oakes ran at a dead sprint, around the engine, Laila five paces behind.

“Go!” Clyde said, pushing Zach, and then the children after the soldier, leaving Leo, Toppley, and Tess alone, except for a long tail of crawling undead whose legs had been crushed by the dumper-tank’s charging advance.

“The truck,” Tess said, picking up Oakes’s rifle. “We’ll hold that position. Go.”

“We’re not retreating?” Leo asked, as they jogged to the cab, dripping with blood and skin from impact with so many of the undead. Oh-so-many, but not nearly enough.

“We can’t flee,” Tess said. “We need that food.”

On the roof of the cab, she looked behind the lip of the truck bed, filled with blankets, bedding, and even a few chairs. Beyond, she saw the undead.

“Teegan, give me the sniper rifle,” she said. She peered through the scope before lowering the weapon and detaching the suppressor. “About a hundred walking. Can’t say how many crawling. We’ll draw them here. Best we get inside the back of the truck where we’re less liable to fall off when they start thumping the tyres.”

“You want to lure them here?” Leo asked.

“We have to,” Tess said. “The African Union’s stuck inland somewhere. Must have been surrounded by zoms until this vehicle broke out. Now the undead are strung between the airport and waterfront. Oh, what a mess. How much ammo do we have?”

“Not enough,” Toppley said, as she opened the double-barrelled rifle and loaded two hand-length cartridges. “But this is a secure position. A sight more comfortable than the truck in the mine, eh, Commissioner? There are seats here.”

“Looks like they were turning into a bus during their—” Leo began, but the rest of his words were drowned by the explosion from the elephant gun. Toppley staggered back with the recoil, while her target’s head completely disappeared.

“I best sit down for this,” Toppley said.

“Hold your fire, Leo,” Tess said. “We’ve found our way of luring ’em here.”

“This gun can certainly do that,” Toppley said. “I think it could sink that warship.”

“Did you sell many of those?” Tess asked, as she watched the column of broken ghouls crawl and lurch nearer.

“None,” Toppley said. “I’ve seen a few in my travels. They were prized by the type of warlord obsessed with the size of his gun. Watch your ears.” Toppley pulled the trigger, and nearly fell from her seat as the shot reverberated between the metal walls. “I plead age,” she said, holding the rifle out to Leo. “The stock has been sprung to reduce recoil, but my bones aren’t as young as I’d like them to be.”

“The kids said the three thieves had friends,” Tess said.

“Thieves aren’t exactly our primary concern,” Leo said, taking a cartridge from Toppley. Below, the undead drew nearer.

“Hopefully not,” Tess said. “I was thinking about how the locals were fighting over food. Meaning there’s no other obvious or larger cache in this corner of the city, and we’ve got to feed the entire African Union convoy. Oh, we really did walk into a mess.”

Leo raised the rifle. “But Sullivan is alive. The African Union is here. And zombies can’t shoot back.”

After four thunder-quake shots from the elephant gun, it was retired in favour of the less ear-shattering assault rifles. Unspoken, a rhythm developed. Each firing in a separate arc, and ignoring the crawling undead now around and beneath the truck, they methodically mowed down the undead, and were almost out of ammo when Clyde and Oakes returned with one of the sailors who’d been guarding the boat, Baxter.

All three clambered atop the wrecked airplane engine. As Tess, Toppley, and Leo ceased fire, the crawling undead emerged from beneath the truck, squirming towards the gunshots from atop the charred engine. Even as they died, the air filled with a different sound, a second engine, belonging to another bone-crunching earth-mover. Aboard were Hawker, Mackay, and ten African Union soldiers.

Tess righted one of the salvaged chairs, and sat. "It's not over. Not yet, but I reckon we've earned a breather."

Chapter 21 - Never Leave the Living with Regret
V&A Waterfront, Cape Town, South Africa

"Sullivan's dead," Hawker said, holding up the radio. He stood atop the cab of Tess's truck, having climbed down from his when he'd run out of targets to shoot. "She died on the operating table. There was nothing more you could do."

Tess nodded. "That's always what we'd tell the family," she said. "In the outback, at a remote road accident, or at an even more remote cattle station, it always took a while for us to respond. Took a while longer to get the patient back to the hospital. Unless you truly had to give more details, you'd say they died in the operating theatre. Never leave the living with regret, that's one of Mick's rules."

"In this case, it's true," Hawker said.

"Are the kids okay?" she asked.

"They're back on the ship," Hawker said. "Avalon is keeping an eye on Zach. Glenn Mackay knew her much longer," he added, pointing to his own truck. "But this isn't the first death among the crew since the outbreak."

"Probably not the last, either," Tess said. "How many zombies are we dealing with?"

"Immediately? Just under a thousand," Hawker said. "They followed the African Union trucks to the airport."

"The kids said their people were at the airport," Tess said. "How many are there?"

"Locals? About a hundred. Twenty kids, about thirty teens, thirty adults, twenty elderly. Seem to be two groups of families and neighbours who merged together. One from around here, one from a township in the north. Those two kids were the magnet which brought the two communities together."

"They can't be the leaders," Tess said.

"More like the peace-brokers," Hawker said. "As I heard it, they camped out around here, but were chased away a week ago. Relocated to a stadium near the airport. Laila drove right past them yesterday. Zoms followed. They relocated to the ruins of the airport last night."

"The airport's ruined?" Tess asked. "How badly?"

"Unusable," Hawker said. "Couple of large craters on the runway. Fire spread to most of the terminal. Most buildings are unstable."

"Then our priority must be getting everyone out of that airport, and then to make contact with the other locals."

"The airport-evac is underway," Hawker said. "There are two civilian helicopters there. Recent arrivals. The captain's already got mechanics inbound, on the way to repair them. We'll airlift everyone to Robben Island."

"Three helicopters?" Tess asked, reflexively looking skyward. "But that'll take… I don't know how long. Months, probably, to move those thousands of African Union soldiers."

Hawker shook his head. "You don't know? Tess, most of the A.U. aren't here. Only Laila and her advance team have arrived."

"How many?" she asked.

"Twenty-eight."

It took twenty minutes for Clyde to declare the area clear, twenty more to load the toy-store food into the back of the truck, and just as long to drive back to the marina's gate. Leaving Bruce and the African Union soldiers to guard the food, Tess climbed aboard a boat, and returned to the ship.

It was Dr Avalon who met her with a Geiger counter in hand.

"Why the Geiger counter?" Tess asked.

"Do I really need to explain?" Avalon asked, as she swept the ominously clicking detector across Tess's arms and down her body. "You'll have to strip, and go through the decontamination shower. There are clean clothes on the other side. Your old clothes go into this sack, and drop them over the side. I assumed Leo would have noticed."

"Noticed what?" Tess asked. "I thought the radiation readings were fine."

"Laila drove through a hot zone," Avalon said.

"Oh. How bad was it?" she asked.

"You're fine. Or you will be after you change. Rinse. Do *not* scrub. Understand? You're having a shower, not a wash. Do not abrade the skin."

Ten minutes later, and feeling as if she'd never be clean again, she was escorted to the captain's quarters.

"Commissioner, please come in," Adams said.

It was a surprisingly small cabin, though the lack of a bed suggested it came in two parts, with the second concealed behind the concertina-door. This was an office as much as a living space, evidenced by the desk at which Captain Adams had been writing.

Tess crossed to one of the three armchairs. Low to the ground, with thin arms, they screamed a government-issue design, with a government-mandated lack of comfort. But the Geiger counter, as much as the battle, had left her drained.

"I'm sorry about Sullivan," Tess said.

"It's the risk we all take," Adams said. "She wanted to become a librarian."

"In the navy?" Tess asked.

"No. She was good at her job. Diligent. Trusted. Excelled in every task. She had a destiny as a leader. A week into our voyage, an engineer's shortcut created a short circuit. A fire broke out below decks. She was first in, last out, saved two lives, and saved us from having to be ignominiously towed back to port. When I suggested she consider joining the officer-track, she told me no. When her term was up, she wanted to become a librarian because she found the empty ocean terrifying. She did a stellar job at not revealing it. I'd arranged for her to transfer ashore, to my old command in hydrographics. Then came the outbreak. Now I'm trying to write to her mother. Explaining…" She paused and looked at what she'd written before picking up the sheet, and scrunching it into a ball. "I'm trying to justify the cost. But there's no form of words that can salve that pain."

"She was the ship's librarian, wasn't she?"

"A task she begged to be allowed to pursue. How could I say no?"

Tess's eyes had caught the two photographs screwed to the wall. One showed a large family group of at least thirty people enjoying a springtime picnic beneath flowering trees. The other was of the captain, in uniform, though only displaying a commander's rank, standing next to a boy of about fourteen who was wearing her hat.

"Is that your son?" Tess asked.

"My greatest victory," Adams said, glancing around to look at the photograph. "So far his greatest act of rebellion has been a threat to join the army. He's terrified of the sea, too."

"Thanks to Pippa, we saved those kids, and the African Union," Tess said.

"But it is only the convoy's advance guard," Adams said. "Which is a generous description of how many reached Cape Town."

"*Why* are we worried about radiation?" Tess asked. "And how worried should *I* be?"

"Considering the insane number of warheads launched, it's doubtful any precautions will make a significant long-term difference, but it is important to maintain protocols. Important for morale." Adams stood and walked to a cabinet on which stood a flask. "The convoy made good time through Mozambique. A few vehicles disappeared. The occupants took their chances alone, elsewhere. But a few more refugees were collected. When they reached the border, their numbers had swelled by around two hundred. On crossing the border, the general changed their route. The ambassador wished to maintain as straight a course here as possible. The general wished to take a more westerly route, via Mahikeng in the North-West Province."

"Was that where he lived?" Tess asked.

"Laila thinks so," Adams said. She handed Tess a cup. "Iced tea, I'm afraid."

"Thanks. The doc wanted me to cut down on coffee anyway," Tess said. "I guess the general got his way, the convoy went west?"

"They did. The ambassador had only a few dozen people who'd follow her orders over his. She went with the general, in the hope that, after they reached Mahikeng, she could direct the convoy south, to here, and sent Laila ahead to give us the warning."

"So we don't know where the African Union is, or when they might arrive, or if they're still alive?"

"Laila had to drive away in the middle of the night," Adams said. "She'd requested permission to come south and it was refused. She didn't have time to find a Geiger counter."

"That doesn't sound good. She saw craters on her way south?"

"One near Ladysmith. It had completely obliterated the road. They'd been attempting to go south towards Durban, from where they'd follow the coast. Instead, they detoured around Lesotho. They picked up a survivor who'd travelled through Bloemfontein. He died. She's certain it was radiation poisoning."

"I'm trying to recall the map, but would they have travelled anywhere near Port Elizabeth?"

"No, these would be different craters, different bombs. One inland, one near Ladysmith, and at least one on the coast near Port Elizabeth."

"South Africa got a pasting. Why?"

"And from whom?" Adams replied. "They triggered the dosimeter when they boarded the helicopter. We think the contamination was on some ammunition and food they found at a military checkpoint near Middleburg. We're leaving their gear in the airport, and getting them to wash and change when they reach Robben Island. We're decontaminating the Seahawk, and from now on, we'll use the civilian helicopters to ferry them. You know about the civilian helicopters?"

"Two were found at the airport."

"At the stadium. In the middle of the pitch," Adams said. "No sign of the pilots, but it's an obvious location to land if you are unfamiliar with the city."

Tess took a sip of the cold tea. "Radiation isn't an immediate problem for us?"

"No, though it will be for the African Union if they drive due south."

"What kind of range do those civilian helicopters have?" Tess asked. "Is there any way of reaching the ambassador?"

"Not by helicopter. Not by radio. Laila lost contact with them abruptly, an hour into her drive south. It could be they were out of range, or the soldiers switched frequency, or the radio broke, or something equally innocent."

"But maybe they got into trouble. We can't help them. They'll arrive or they won't, so our immediate priority is making contact with the other locals in the city. A hundred survivors were at the stadium?"

"A hundred in that group, another twenty who'd quit the group yesterday, but were thought to be in the vicinity."

"Let's hope they make themselves known when they see the helicopters buzzing back and forth. We've got to consider that group of thieves, too. How many others do the stadium-folk think there are in the city?"

"A few thousand," Adams said. "Two days after the outbreak in Manhattan, the planes were shot out of the sky. That's when people began leaving. All ships were commandeered and formed into a loose fleet. The naval base was attacked. That was day five, before dawn, long before the nuclear attacks. The ships scattered. More people fled. The city, effectively, collapsed. Anything with wheels was driven east, to join in the evacuation to Madagascar. Those who remained had no transport, while the number of infected, of course, grew."

"Sounds grim," Tess said.

"Very. Though the survivors have been getting along until recently. Initially helping, sharing what they had. When supplies ran low, they stopped sharing but they didn't attack one another. Not until this incident with the thieves and the food supplies you found."

"But we're only getting the story of one group of survivors," Tess said. "I better speak to them. They're on Robben Island?"

"It's the safest location. So far, five zombies have been found and neutralised on the island. Two sailing yachts were in the harbour. Seven corpses inland. Four were probably undead. No living survivors have yet been found, but even one person, alone, could deal with five zombies."

"They'd have made themselves known by now if they were hiding," Tess said. "Are there any food supplies on the island?"

"A little. Bulk basics. Rice and milk powder. I understand there is even a little coffee."

"There is?"

Adams smiled. "I abused the full weight of my authority to demand two servings were set aside for you."

"Don't tell the doc," Tess said. "How much food? How many meals?"

"Taken with what you found, and assuming that we can fish offshore using one of those yachts, enough for two weeks with our present numbers. But we hope those numbers will increase tomorrow."

"So we've got to find more food," Tess said.

"Or hope that the survivors have a surplus," Adams said. "There is fuel on the island. Diesel for the ferries. A pipe links it to the mainland tanks. Robben Island will have electricity, and we have enough to return directly back to Perth."

Tess rolled her fingers around the cup. "How much diesel did the African Union have?"

"Enough to reach Cape Town."

"Four tankers, right?" Tess asked. "But if they've gone west, and are now driving around looking for lost relatives, at some point they'll have used up so much, they can't drive south. If we linger here too long, we'll run out of food."

"We'll run out of aviation fuel first," Adams said. "I can't decide how long we can stay here until after tomorrow. After we've searched for more survivors and gathered a more complete picture of what happened here. We'll use the rest of today to collect the ferry the survivors from the airport to the island. Tomorrow, at dawn, we'll bury Pippa Sullivan."

Before she went ashore, Tess went to find Zach. He wasn't in his cabin, but on deck, at the very rear of the ship, watching the waves.

"Seen something interesting?" Tess asked.

"Sharks," Zach said. "There really are sharks down there."

"Big ones, too," she said, peering down. "How are you doing?"

"Tired," he said.

"Me, too. I'm sorry about Pippa."

"I didn't know her," he said. "I mean, all the sailors knew her for longer. She was just fun, that's all."

She nodded. She understood. For the last month, he'd been surrounded by people twice his age. Finally, here, he'd found someone he could relate to as an equal rather than be treated as a mascot. Whether there was more to it, or whether it could have led to anything more, was moot.

"Doc Flo gave me more homework," Zach said. "I mean, that's weird, right? Someone dies, and she hands out homework."

"She's cursed with intelligence," Tess said.

"What d'you mean?"

"She knows she is the smartest person on this ship, maybe even on this planet. Thus she feels like she should know exactly what everyone should do to stay alive, to win, to beat the zoms. As long as everyone does what she says, they'll stay alive."

"And when things go wrong it's because we don't listen," he said.

"Nope, it's because she overlooked something or didn't explain it properly," Tess said. "In that respect, she's no different to anyone else, but she'd never believe you if you told her. No, she's just like the rest of us, consumed by guilt and regret. But there's nothing she could have done to stop the outbreak, and nothing we could have done to stop Pippa from being shot. The guilt lies entirely with that sniper. Those people could have shared the food, or fired a warning shot."

"But if—" he began.

"Nope," she said, cutting him off. "Whatever scenario you're about to concoct, she still would have died. The sniper waited until we were inside the toy-store, and waited until he had a clear shot before pulling the trigger. Sullivan was always going to be put on guard by the door because she had the military training."

"That doesn't make it better," he said.

"No. Only time will do that," she said.

"She was going to open a library," he said. "I was going to help her. We were going to make a fortune."

"How do you make money from a library?" Tess asked.

"Because all the books are digital now, aren't they, but they were all stored on giant computers in America and places. We were going to copy them from e-readers, and then print them out. Or loan out e-readers. We were still working on the details. Not just books, either. Movies. Music. Everything."

"Neat idea. You knew a librarian, didn't you? Ms Godwin?"

"Yeah, I'd go to the library after school. They stayed open late, and she let me stay later."

"We certainly *will* need libraries," Tess said. "I don't know if we can spare the paper to print books out, or the electricity to charge up e-readers. If the copyright was held by a publisher in Manhattan, who gets paid now? It won't be easy, but this sounds like a job for you and Ms Godwin to figure out."

"She's dead," Zach said. "Hit-and-run last December. Only five people went to the funeral. They wouldn't let me stay late in the library after that. Didn't matter. Wasn't like it was that cold at night."

Tess nodded. She'd thought he might be running away from something, though it sounded as if he'd had nothing to run from. No family. No friends. No future. That was why he'd signed up, and why his grief ran so deep.

"Time makes it easier," Tess said. "Each loss is different, so I don't know how long it will take, but we've got to keep going. Keep on fighting for those still alive."

"Yeah, but it's not many, is it? Only twenty-eight made it."

"So far, it's only twenty-eight," Tess said. "Let's go see what they have to say."

23rd March

Chapter 22 - At Sea, On Land
Table Bay, Cape Town, South Africa

As the sun rose, the ship's crew gathered on deck for the funeral and burial of Pippa Sullivan.

Though the words were very different, the formality of the ceremony reminded Tess of a long-ago funeral she'd been unable to attend. She'd watched it on a screen instead. This time, like that other time, the mourners were mostly faces and names, people she knew *of*, but didn't *know*, but in the grief wracking each face, she saw a reflection of her past loss, and her present fears.

Nothing was so loud as the splash as the weighted body sank into the water.

"Our daily struggles have grown so hard, it's increasingly easy to believe we have no future," Captain Adams said. "Behind us lies Robben Island where Nelson Mandela broke limestone rocks with barely more than his hands. For eighteen years he was imprisoned on that island. He never abandoned the struggle. He fought on. Ultimately, he won. He fought on, as did so many others, in so many ways, across all the centuries of our collective past, against horrors as unimaginable to us as our present nightmare would be unimaginable to them. Their friends, brothers, sisters, compatriots, and comrades died, but they fought on. Our friend, our comrade, our sister has died, but the fight is not won. They fought on, she fought on, and so shall we."

The crew were dismissed. Those who were off-duty began forming up to board the boats for compulsory shore leave.

"C'mon, Zach, you can help me with the cameras," Leo said.

"Nah, I was going to catch up on my reading," Zach said, his eyes on the ocean.

"You will not, Zachary," Avalon said. "You will see President Mandela's cell because not all lessons can be learned from books."

"You don't need to tell *me* that," Zach said.

"Then we are in agreement, and so your opposition is pointless," Avalon said.

"So is arguing with her, eh?" Leo said.

"Leo, please, show some respect!" Avalon said. "Poor Zachary is grieving. We all are."

"You didn't know Pippa," Zach said. "*I* didn't know her. Not really."

"We're grieving for everyone we lost," Avalon said. "All of us have lost almost everyone and everything, but we have not had time until now to acknowledge it. A visit to the past will bring a perspective on our future. Come. And do hurry up, Leo. I hate it when you make me late."

Tess returned to her cabin, grabbed her gear, and returned to the helicopter deck, where she found Clyde, Oakes, and Hawker geared up and waiting.

"All set, Commish," Clyde said. "We're just waiting on the boat to bring Toppley and Laila."

Tess had sent Teegan ashore to collect the nurse as a mutually agreed ploy to have her absent during the funeral. Grief and anger were often compatriots, and the old crook was too obvious a target.

"Are you sure about Toppley, boss?" Oakes asked.

"Absolutely," Tess said. "She's probably the most experienced negotiator left in the world. If we stumble across that group of thieves, we'll need someone who can talk them out of revenge."

"Who's going to talk the crew out of revenge for Sullivan?" Oakes asked.

"Can I see your rifle, Commish?" Clyde asked.

She handed him the MARS-L assault rifle, taken from the ship's armoury. In addition to the modular rifle, the armoury carried a number of useful accessories such as the breaching-shotgun beneath the barrel of Clyde's rifle, the grenade launcher on Nicko's, and the suppressors on them all. Once again, they were wearing naval combat fatigues.

Again, the body-armour read *Police*. This time, clipped at the front, were coiled lengths of green rope.

"Why do we have rope?" Tess asked.

"It's the compromise I reached with Dr Avalon," Hawker said. "Dosimeters, spare ration bars, spare water bottles, extra ammo, and rope."

"How is that a compromise?" Tess asked.

"That's what we agreed to take with us," Oakes said. "We'd have needed a cargo plane to carry all the gear we're leaving behind."

"Doc Avalon is that worried?" Tess asked. She turned to look aft, towards where the boats were departing for Robben Island. Instead, she saw Toppley and Laila. The nurse's hijab had been replaced with a red and white scarf of nearly the same hue as the red cross and crescent painted on her body-armour.

"G'day," Tess said. "How's the island?"

"Peaceful," Laila said. "I'm sorry for your loss."

"An experience we've shared too often," Tess said. "While we're waiting on the pilot, let's run through our plan. We've two locations to investigate before the helicopter will have to return to refuel. A hospital and a school."

Hawker gave a reflexive, though brief, glance at the square of map velcroed to his wrist. "The hospital is twenty klicks due east, where the east-west N1 road meets the northbound M16. The school is three klicks north from the hospital, up the M16. Terrain will be urban and hilly. We'll take a looping approach there, surveying the city for smoke and movement, but take a direct path to the ship on our return. That'll indicate to any locals the direction they should come if they're able to make the journey alone. If the helicopter is shot at, or if we're shot at on the ground, we'll retreat."

"Laila, we're acting on your information," Tess said. "What did the locals say about the school and hospital?"

"The information comes from Lesadi and Thato," the nurse said. "The two children roamed this city long after everyone else took to the roofs. The hospital was offering treatment after the outbreak. As conditions worsened, they would trade treatment for food and supplies. The school offered a roof and a meal, but only for one night. It became a place for individuals to gather into groups."

"They became sanctuaries in a lawless city?" Hawker asked.

"In the eyes of Lesadi and Thato, yes," the nurse said. "A week after the outbreak, and after the planes stopped falling out of the sky, a friend of the children's was shot. They took her to the hospital. She died, but the doctors *did* attempt to save her life. Afterward, the children, along with a dozen others, were walked north to a school where they were given food and shelter for the night. The school was overburdened with survivors, and so the children put together a group who went to the waterfront. A week after that, they came back to the hospital to get antibiotics. They were given some. Not enough. But of all the places in the city, all the people, these groups at the hospital and school were the most friendly and helpful."

"There are other groups of survivors beyond these two locations?" Hawker asked.

"Many," Laila said. "At one time, but not as friendly. More recently, most have become defensive, or have disappeared."

"As we saw yesterday, some are hostile," Tess said. "We'll start with those two groups. They should know where the others are."

As the helicopter rose into the air, the recently attached camera-rig broadcast images back to the ship where sailors would hunt for signs of life. Though as they travelled deeper into the city, Tess increasingly doubted any survivors would be found. Up close, from above, the devastation suffered by Cape Town was far worse than she'd realised. Glinting moats of fire-broken glass lay beneath the smoke-blackened tower blocks. Wide daggers of ash and rubble cut through streets and subdivisions. A township had been replaced with a crater. Wood, steel, and cement had become little more than a grey ash cloud, swirling in the rising wind. She wasn't the only passenger who checked the dosimeter, but even if that blast hadn't been nuclear, it had been nearly as devastating.

Smoke still rose from the rubble too frequently to be cooking fires. Figures were everywhere. Moving. In the open. Too slow to be human.

In most cases, it was impossible to identify whether the destruction had been caused by an exploding gas main, static fuel tank, or an unquenched fire, but an occasional tail-wing or giant engine showed how the calamity had begun. Even if this had been an isolated tragedy, unique in the world, the city would have been evacuated. With the undead crawling from the wreckage, clawing their way out of the smoking rubble, with toxic fumes clogging the air, getting away from the city had been the most certain route to survival.

"We're approaching the hospital," Commander Tusitala announced. "Car park is empty. I'm going to circle."

The interchange, where the N1 and M12 met, was expansively empty. Near the roads were two and three-bed starter homes where road noise was less important than affordability. A little further away, squares of brown marked the larger gardens of bigger houses. The smattering of vehicles were in the middle of the road, askew, abandoned if not completely wrecked. But where were the people? From what she could see of the hospital complex, it was desolate and empty.

Modern cities had few fortresses, but in a city with as notoriously high a crime rate as Cape Town, municipal buildings came close. The hospital's six-storey central building certainly fit the part. Built in a T, it had the look of a 1960s build, ringed by the usual sprawl of newer one-and-two-storey buildings housing the medical sciences invented in the decades since.

Now, it was lifeless. No rooftop sentry flagged them down, or warned them off. No vehicles were positioned ready to escape, suggesting everyone who'd sheltered here had already fled.

"I'm setting down in the car park," Commander Tusitala said.

Tess's stomach lurched with the sudden descent, slamming back into place as debris rattled against the underside of the cabin. As soon as the helicopter jolted against the ground, Clyde threw the door open, dropping outside, with Oakes and Hawker bare seconds behind. Head bowed and back bent, Tess slipped outside, waiting for Laila and

Teegan, while the rotors slowed, and then stopped, leaving ash swirling in the otherwise still air.

"Nicko, stay with the copter," Hawker said.

Leaving Clyde at the rear, Tess jogged away from the settling grey cloud, following the colonel across the empty car park.

"It's abandoned," Hawker said, pulling a monocular from his pouch. Still walking, he turned his head, raised the monocular, and lowered it a second later. "There's no one on the roof of the main building, or that smaller tower building to the south. We've been buzzing copters back and forth since yesterday. If they were still here, they'd be waving sheets to get our attention."

"Give them time to climb the stairs," Tess said.

"Why do I always think cities are flat?" Toppley said, as they reached the steep staircase leading up a steeper embankment, and so up to the main building.

On the embankment, and at the top, trees had been planted so the patients in the upper-floor wards had something other than rooftops to look at. But recently, those trees had been felled, and abandoned where they'd fallen, as had the undead who'd been shot.

"Casings," Hawker said, scuffing at the ground. "Noticed some back near the copter. Hold here. Major, with me."

As the two soldiers jogged up the stairs, Tess shifted her grip on the rifle, scanning the fallen bodies for movement.

"The children said there were nurses and doctors at the hospital," Laila said. "A lot of doctors. A lot more patients. They didn't mention soldiers, but there must have been some."

"Clear," Hawker called from top. "More casings. Watch your step."

"There are some human corpses among the undead," Toppley said. "And some animals nearby still seeking food, judging by the bite marks on those bones."

Tess turned to look, but her attention was caught by the thin metal pole embedded in a zombie's skull, by the fire-axe on the gore-flecked grass, and by the hard-shelled med-kit beneath a headless corpse.

"They fought on the high ground, holding the slope," she said. "They fought hand-to-hand. Did they have any vehicles?"

"The children said no. Not when they had to walk to the school," Laila said. "The boats were gone by then. Some nights, they heard engines, but never during the day."

"So if you found a car during the day, you'd wait until night to drive away?" Tess said. "Then people were more worried the car would be jacked than of the risk of fendering a zom. But these hospital-dwellers planned their escape," she added as they reached the top. "They fought their way out."

"Not all of them," Hawker said.

At the top of the stairs, the bodies grew even more numerous, forming a dense ring around the main doors. Above, the windows had been smashed, the shards cleared from the frames to provide a firing position for the defenders. After the bullets ran out, they had improvised, dropping heavy weights onto the heads of the undead. Metal cabinets, trolleys, even beds lay where they'd been dropped near the main doors. Doors which banged open an inch, again, again, again.

"There's no wind," Toppley said.

"Hello!" Hawker called. "African Union! United Nations!"

The door banged again, pushing aside the obstructing cabinet just far enough for a three-fingered hand to curl outside.

"Zoms," Hawker said. "Back to the copter. Careful on the stairs."

He stayed in place, and so did Tess, until Toppley, Laila, and Clyde had retreated back down the steps. Tess stayed just long enough for a second arm to push its way through the ajar door.

Chapter 23 - The Crazy Things We Do for Our Kids
Welgemoed, Cape Town, South Africa

Back in the air, Commander Tusitala circled the hospital again.

"No movement on the roofs," she said. "I'll check again before dusk. If there are survivors inside, they'll head to the roof."

It was a forlorn hope; any survivors of the hospital battleground had fled days ago. The same wasn't true of the school.

Three kilometres north, riding the crest of another hill, were seven long, narrow buildings, built in a row of three, and a row of four, but with sealed walkways linking each.

"Are you sure that's a school?" Clyde asked.

"I can see tennis courts," Toppley said.

"But where's the rugby pitch?" Clyde asked. "There *has* to be a rugby pitch. This *is* South Africa."

"Probably beneath that plane," Toppley said. The wreck was mostly intact. The wings had broken from the fuselage, as had the tail section, but all the pieces were still relatively close together and lying atop fire-ravaged grass. It was an attempted landing gone wrong. Whether it was a school or not, painted onto the roofs of four of the buildings were the words: *Help*, *Hulp*, *Usizo,* and *Msaada*. On the roof of one of the more central buildings was a small cluster of people, one of whom was waving a towel.

"Those look like stretchers," Commander Tusitala said even as the helicopter began to descend. "I won't set down! Don't know if the roof can support me. I'll hover, so make this quick."

"No worries," Hawker said.

"Just like old times," Oakes said, grinning.

Tess took off the headphones, and heard no more except the roar of the rotors. Oakes sat on the edge of the doorway and slipped down. Tess copied his example, staggering on impact, even though it was less than a metre drop. Oakes grabbed her arm, pushing her onward, and towards the survivors, sheltering against the downdraft.

"G'day," Tess said, raising her voice above the ocean-roar of the helicopter. "We're the United Nations. We're here to help."

"African Union!" Laila added, to which the survivors responded with a more visible nod of relief.

Three people lay on stretchers: a pregnant woman with a bandaged leg, a grey-haired man with his eyes closed, a teenage boy with his eyes narrowed in pain, his hands white-knuckled around a bloody cricket bat. Three more children stood around him, all clutching an assortment of tools, though with less determination than the batsman.

Guarding the children and the injured was a bald woman with a very old V-shaped scar running from temple to cheek to crown. She was about thirty. The AK-47 on her back looked twice her age, while her frilled shirt and puffed trousers looked like they'd come from a different age entirely.

"Children and stretchers!" Tess said, unsure if she'd heard that, so bent to pick up the stretcher on which lay the expectant mother. The woman grabbed the stretcher's other end. Nicko and Teegan took either end of the old man's stretcher. Clyde scooped up the injured cricketer, while Bruce led the other children to the helicopter.

"There are more!" the woman with the scar yelled.

"More? More survivors?" Tess asked.

"More children. Downstairs!"

"Commander, more survivors are downstairs!" Tess said as the stretchers were laid in the back of the helicopter. "Take these people back to the ship. Laila, go with them. Come back for us, and for the rest. Go."

As Laila settled the uninjured children inside, Bruce closed the door. Tess grabbed the arm of the woman with the scar, and led her away from the rotors.

"How many survivors?" Tess yelled, as the helicopter took flight.

"Thirteen more children," the woman with the scar said. She waved a hand north, in the direction of the crashed plane. "The music room. They are downstairs, but the zombies are inside the building. Inside and outside, and I am out of bullets."

"No worries," Nicko said, drawing the nine-mil from his vest-holster. "We've got some to spare."

"Are you a teacher?" Tess asked.

"Programming and business," she said, taking the handgun. "Nkechi Nkosi. Rudi is with the children."

"Show us where," Tess said. "Thirteen children and one teacher?"

"Rudi is the gardener, but yes," Nkosi said, leading them across the roof. "We kept buses here, ready to escape. One week ago, that plane crashed. Our supplies were destroyed. We lost our food. Our clothing. It is why I'm dressed as Isaac Newton. The clothes come from the drama school. Mrs Krog said we should leave. She took most people, and our buses, and left."

"But not you?"

"We were the last bus, and it wouldn't start. Rudi got it fixed, but the *dood* came. Zombies, yes? With Ingrid's baby already a week overdue, we thought it too dangerous to leave. More zombies came. We were going to drive to the coast, but as we were moving the children, the dead broke inside. We saw your helicopter, and so came to the roof. But half the children are trapped." She stopped by a large hatch built into the roof, next to which lay ropes, and onto the props of which a winch had been attached. The stairs were fixed, made of metal, and steep. It would have been a monumental challenge getting the stretchers to the roof.

"Which building are they in?" Hawker asked.

"The furthest," Nkosi said, pointing across the rooftops. "There is no roof access. Each block is connected with a ground-level walkway, but the dead are inside. Inside and outside."

"We can get to the adjacent building?" Hawker asked. "Then that's our target. Nicko, you take point."

The steps led into windowless storeroom containing racks of light bulbs and other currently useless supplies. The door led to a corridor, quietly echoing an erratic drumbeat.

On the right were windows, and next to them were barstools and high tables, beanbag chairs, and bookshelves. On the left were the classrooms. Through the window of the nearest, Tess saw bedding, with privacy-sheets hung from the false ceiling. New signs pointed down the hall, towards bathrooms, laundry, and the dining hall. But they also pointed to a barricaded stairwell. The gate was newly installed, bolted to floor and ceiling. The rust on the vertical bars suggested it had come from outside.

Bruce turned the key, already in the lock. Nicko walked through and down the stairwell already resonating to the irregular percussive beat.

As he reached the bottom, Nicko raised a cautioning hand before beckoning them down. The base of the stairwell had three fire doors. One led outside, one to the ground-floor classrooms, and one led to the walkway linking it with the neighbouring school-block. All doors were made of triple-thick plastic and steel, though with transparent panels filling the upper half of the frame. Whether they were made of glass or polymer, the windows were unbreakable, despite the best efforts of the undead on the other side.

Zombies beat against the outside door, and against the interior door that led to the ground-floor classrooms. Beyond, inside, well over thirty zombies milled in the corridor. None were children, but at least three wore uniform. However, the walkway leading to the next building was still empty.

"Turn the key at the top of the frame," Nkosi said.

The emergency key was attached to an O-shaped ring, large enough to fit an entire hand. The lock clunked as it disengaged.

The walkway was four-teachers-wide. Like the doors, the base of the walkway was opaque, the top was transparent. But while the doors were made of lockdown-strength material, the windows of the enclosed walkway were loose at the seams. Only the lack of a sustained assault had kept them from falling inward. The undead who'd been pushing and scrumming near the outer door had seen them, followed, and were already clawing and punching at the panels. The walls shook. The columns supporting the roof shuddered. The bolts creaked, but they held long enough for everyone to get through the corridor, through the door, and into the next building.

Here, the hallway was filled with tables, chairs, and sofas. The doors had first-aid crosses on them. Originally, this must have been one of their temporary refuges, where newcomers like Thato and Lesadi were billeted. But now it was filled with the undead. Seven, clattering into the furniture. Shot dead by a flurry from Clyde and Nicko as Hawker secured the door. But if seven had already got into those ground-level classrooms, so could others.

"We need to get out of here," Tess said.

"Over here," Nkosi said, leading them to the stairwell.

Clyde and Nicko overtook her, but there were no zombies upstairs.

"Is it the next building the kids are trapped in?" Hawker asked. "Nicko, guard the stairwell. Clyde, clear the classrooms. Nkosi, I want a window with a view of the building they're trapped in."

Tess ran ahead, checking alternate classrooms to Clyde, making sure the doors were closed.

"This one, here," Nkosi said, opening a door midway along the corridor.

Stepping over mattresses, pulling down sheets, Tess ran to the window. Outside, below, was a courtyard play-space. To the left was another ground-level walkway linking this block to the one in which the children were trapped. The walkway's roof still held, but was only supported by the far wall. The near wall had collapsed. The walkway, and the playground, was full of the undead.

"Easily a hundred down there," Tess said.

In an upstairs classroom almost immediately opposite, a window popped out of its frame. A grey-bearded man in green dungarees waved a chisel and hammer in their direction.

"Howzit!" he called, his voice muffled by the glass in their classroom, and by the horde of zombies tramping the grass below.

"That's Rudi," Nkosi said.

"Hey, Ms Nkosi, how's this for time-keeping?" the Afrikaner gardener bellowed. "So, you going to get us out of here or what?"

"Did you get all the kids upstairs?" Hawker called.

"You're Australian?" Rudi replied. "You're a long way from home, Mister Kangaroo."

"*Colonel* Kangaroo," Hawker replied. "Are the kids there?"

"They're here, all *lekker*. No problem," Rudi yelled back, his voice loud, but his tone calm. "The door's sealed. We're safer than a chocolate bar at the dentist's. Is your helicopter coming back?"

"Any minute now!" Hawker yelled.

"Ten minutes, yeah?" Rudi called.

"The copter can pick them up from that roof," Hawker said, his voice lower, speaking only to those in this classroom.

"There's no roof door in that building," Nkosi said.

Teegan drew a knife, and began working at the frame of a window on the far left of the room, almost above the walkway.

"What are you doing?" Tess asked.

"Being a solution rather than a burden," Toppley said. "It's blindingly obvious what we must do."

"Clyde, help her," Tess said, uncertain of the gunrunner's plan, but glad someone had one.

"Where's the roof access to this building?" Bruce asked.

"Near the stairwell," Nkosi said as Clyde slammed his shoulder into the window frame. With a pop, the pane burst from the frame, and slammed onto the zombies below, felling one without shattering.

"Saves a bullet," Toppley said.

"You can save the rest of them," Hawker said. "We're going up to the roof."

"Oh, there's no time," Toppley said. She unclipped the rope from the loop on Clyde's vest. "No time, and no need. Major, would you be a dear and hold onto this end?"

"What are you—" Tess began, even as Toppley looped the other end of the rope around her waist. "You're going to climb down?"

"Down to the walkway and then across," Toppley said, dropping bag and rifle. She patted her own rope, still looped on her vest. "I'll climb up the other side, tie this rope to the drainpipe, and pull the children up onto the roof. The soldiers are too heavy, you're too valuable, and this teacher knows her way around the school if we need a plan-B. I can do this, Tess. Trust me. I've done it before."

"You've done *this* before?" Nkosi asked.

"Something very similar," Toppley said, pushing a chair next to the window. She peered down. "Admittedly, I was a lot younger."

Clyde grabbed the loose end of rope, looping it around his own waist. "I've got you."

All the reasons why this was a bad idea lined up too fast to be articulated, but thirteen reasons why they had to try were standing at the long window of the opposite classroom.

"A *lot* younger," Toppley said as she clambered, legs first, out the window. Clyde gripped the rope, bracing his feet against the wall, as Toppley leaned back, letting the rope, and the soldier, take her weight.

"Tess, over here," Hawker said, sheathing his knife, having hacked a second window free from its frame.

Tess ran to the window, and aimed her rifle down, while Hawker worked on the next window frame; there were plenty of targets. If Toppley fell, she'd be torn to pieces. *Please don't fall*, she thought.

Firing, she only caught glimpses of the taut rope, of Toppley's slow but methodical sideways walk. But each step across came with half a step down. The rope needed a pulley. Toppley needed more strength. Nkosi added her own, grabbing hold of the rope, keeping it taut.

Another window popped out, but even as it fell, Hawker ran back to the door. "Contact in the corridor," the colonel called.

Tess ejected her spent magazine, letting her hands reload while she turned her eyes to the door. "Are we in trouble, Bruce?"

"No worries," he said. "Not yet."

The rope was still taut, but Toppley was only above the middle section of the walkway. One foot, then another, she lowered herself down, onto the roof's edge until she was standing spread-eagled, hands braced on the wall, toes on the walkway.

Tess changed her aim, shooting the undead beneath the breached walkway.

"She cut the rope!" Clyde said.

"What?" Tess asked, sparing a second to look.

Toppley was walking in an arms-wide, back-bent crouch along the centre of the walkway's roof. The canopy was sagging under her weight. Below, the zombies were beating against the one remaining wall, and against each other, in unthinking frenzy. But Toppley moved quickly, reaching the far end of the walkway before Tess had fired two more shots.

Toppley spread-eagled herself again, arms flush with the wall, feet almost entirely on the bolts bracketing that walkway to the wall.

"Boss, we've got a problem," Clyde said.

"How is she going to climb up the other side?" Nkosi asked.

Toppley had thought of that. She drew her knife, and reached up towards a narrow-grilled air vent. But she couldn't reach.

"It's too high," Nkosi said. "Give me that." She drew the knife from Clyde's sheath, and tucked it into her costume-trousers. She grabbed the now cut rope. "Hold that rope!" she said, wrapping it around her hands.

"Tess!" Clyde said.

The teacher swung rather than walked, letting go of the rope to land, face first, splayed across the roof. The frame shook with the impact, buckling even as Nkosi crawled onward. Toppley reached down, grabbed the teacher's hand, hauling her up as the walkway on Tess's side collapsed a further three feet. But the brackets on which Toppley and Nkosi stood held.

Toppley didn't have the strength, nor a secure enough perch, to lift the teacher far. But she bent her knee, and crooked her elbow, becoming a human ladder up which Nkosi could climb, high enough to slam the knife between vent and wall. With that as a lever, the teacher swung herself around and up, grabbing a security light's bracket.

"Rope!" Nkosi said. "Throw me the rope!"

Toppley unclipped the coiled rope from her vest and threw it up. Nkosi almost fumbled the catch, but looped it onto her arm before, in a gold-medal move, swinging herself up onto the light-bracket. She stood, and clambered over the gutter and onto the roof. A second later, she dropped the rope to Toppley.

Tess didn't relax until Teegan had both arms atop the roof.

"See, kids!" the Afrikaner gardener yelled from the other building, ostensibly talking to the children, but clearly addressing his colleague. "*That* is why physical education is the most important subject in school."

"How are we doing, Bruce?" Tess asked.

"Nicko's holding his position," Hawker said. "We've got a minute."

Opposite, the two women had hauled up the rope and were already repositioning it above the classroom. Tess picked up Toppley's rifle. "Time for us to get to the roof," she said.

Three of the children had made it to the roof when the helicopter returned. Aboard, from its previous deployment as a U.S. Coast Guard rescue vehicle, were harnesses, a winch, and two sailors who knew how to operate it. Tess leaned back, closing her eyes, not wanting to watch until, far sooner than she'd expected, the helicopter flew northward once more.

Nkosi, Rudi, Toppley, and both of the sailors remained on the rooftop opposite, but they, like Tess, were slumped on the hard floor. The children had been saved.

Tess raised a hand. "That was crazy, Teegan!" she yelled.

The older woman simply nodded, and bowed her head.

"How are we doing, Bruce?" Tess asked.

"We're safe enough," Hawker said. "Lot of zoms down below, and there's more in the classrooms immediately below this roof. Well over a thousand in the grounds. More coming from the northeast."

"Are they following the helicopter?" Tess said.

"They are now," Hawker said. "But zoms are slow. They were heading this way anyway. Maybe following Laila."

"Hmm. It proves one thing," Tess said. "There's no one leaving Cape Town for the zombies to follow northward."

She leaned back, waiting for the helicopter to return, but when she heard an engine it sounded wrong. Larger. Faster. Bigger. Approaching from the north. It was a twin-engine jet with *UN* painted beneath each wing.

Chapter 24 - News From Above
Robben Island, Cape Town, South Africa

Leo was waiting for the helicopter when it set down on Robben Island. Tess grabbed his arm, and dragged him away from the slowing rotors.

"Who was flying that plane?" Tess asked when she was far enough away from the copter that she could hear her own thoughts. "Was it Mick?"

"No, it was Wing Commander O'Bryan," Leo said.

"The pilot running the airport at Perth?" Tess asked.

"She flew out of Rodrigues," Leo said. "The children are there. They're safe. A rescue fleet is on its way."

"On its way to Rodrigues or to us?" Tess asked.

"Both," Leo said.

"Has there been word from the African Union?"

"Not that I know of," he said. "Hold still a moment." He raised the Geiger counter. "You're fine."

"Has anyone not been?" she asked.

"There've been a few cuts, a lot of bruises, and a few concussions. A group made it to the beach. Thirty-nine of them. Zoms followed. Lost two before we got them onto the boat." He held up the Geiger counter. "I've got to check everyone else."

Tess nodded, replaying what he'd said, but kept her finger too long on the mental replay-button, and ended up reliving the last two hours. It was a relief when a voice called her name.

"Commissioner!" Captain Adams waved from a pathway near the museum.

Tess cut across the parched lawn. "I hear there's a fleet on its way," she said.

"Not exactly," Adams said. "A rescue flotilla is on its way to Rodrigues. One ship is being redirected to us. The plane will return overhead in two days, and two days after that, to ascertain whether additional capacity will be required. If the African Union hasn't arrived by then, the convoy will have insufficient fuel to reach Cape Town. Shall we take a walk?"

"That'd be pleasant. Help me shake off the day. I'm guessing the plane didn't see the African Union convoy?"

"No. They followed the coast, assuming that was the road the convoy would travel. No sign. No word. But there are three craters relatively close to Port Elizabeth. One to the southwest, one to the north, one to the north-northeast."

"It sounds like South Africa was plastered," Tess said.

"Was it just *South* Africa?" Adams asked. "But even if we knew, what good would the knowledge do us now? I hear Toppley and a South African teacher swung across the rooftops with knives in their mouths?"

"Almost," Tess said. "It was an impressive stunt. Saved the kids."

"Four helicopter flights and an entire day. I'm not sure how much ammunition you expended, or what other supplies were lost, but it is an unsustainable price."

"But worth it," Tess said.

"Oh, certainly. Your mission absolutely was a success, but I'm considering the future. Thirty-nine survivors made their way to the beach."

"Leo told me."

"We collected them with two boats, and without any of our people firing a shot, partly because those survivors were firing far too many." She tugged at the sleeve of her shirt, which now sported a hole.

"You were shot?"

"Friendly fire," Adams said. "It was a lucky miss. From what Lesadi and Thato told us, and what the pregnant teacher from the school confirmed, the school and the hospital were the most organised and well-equipped redoubts in the city. Speaking to the people we collected by boat, by around a week ago, people had gathered in groups of between a hundred and two hundred. But around a week ago, the food reserves failed, and the groups began splintering. Smaller groups have been moving location on a nearly daily basis as they hunt for food. Wherever people were a week ago, they weren't there yesterday. Who knows where they'll be tomorrow?"

"We've got to find them," Tess said.

"No, we shall let *them* find *us*," Adams said. "We can set up a searchlight at night, and send up a helicopter by day, but we'll use the boats to collect them when they arrive on the beach."

"So we're not looking for them at all?"

"I won't stop volunteers going ashore," Adams said. "But there is a limit to how far they can range before needing to return. We'll need local guides, and very recent knowledge of where to look and where to avoid. However, all of the survivors rescued today saw our helicopters. Everyone in the city will have done the same. It will be more efficient to signal them to come to us, unless they can find a refuge from which to signal us."

"I guess there are worse places to wait," Tess said. "That's a great view of Table Mountain. And to think they turned this island into a prison. When will the rescue ship arrive?"

"In between six and eight days," Adams said. "Food will have to be rationed."

"It doesn't sound like we'll find much more in the city."

"No, and anyone who makes it to the beach will be travelling light. Some might know of a cache somewhere, but can we reach it safely? Whether we stay or leave, we'll be eating into our ship's supplies."

"Leave?" Tess asked. "For Perth?"

"For Panama," Adams said. "We can remain at sea for another month without provisioning. Whatever supplies the relief ship has will be needed for the local survivors, and for their voyage to Perth. There won't be a second ship for you to take west. If we wait until the relief ship arrives, we'll have consumed a week's provisions. Three weeks will remain, and that's not enough to reach South America and return. I say South America, and I hope we could reach Panama, but we will need to refuel in Ascension. If we can't, we'll have to return here."

"If we can refuel, will we go to Colombia?" Tess asked.

"We have to," Adams said. "We are here, and so we have to try. I don't know if we'll find any more survivors along our way, or what help we can offer. We *will* look. We *will* help. And we *will* be the last ship to make such a voyage for many months. There will be other ships, one day. Any information we can gather will help ensure the success of their mission. But yes, we have to go to Colombia. If those terrorists are there, they *must* be destroyed. Any research they have to build this weapon *must* be retrieved. My crew insist on it, now that they know why the scientists are here. I agree with them. Every sailor has a moral duty to help other mariners, and our orders were to protect the refugees. My crew holds tight to that duty, and believe those orders still stand. To protect the refugees in the Pacific, we must end the cartel-terrorists, and end this plague."

"If we can," Tess said.

"We must try," Adams said. "I know you agree, because you're here. The African Union agreed. They volunteered to board a plane to Africa to maintain a foothold they knew it would be near impossible to resupply. After losing Sullivan, after losing so many, no one wants our mission to end here in what seems like a retreat, if not entirely a defeat. The old world is gone. What we thought of as civilisation, as society, as *normal* will never return. We'll build something new, but what will determine whether it's *better* is how soon we can begin. Anything which can wipe out this plague a day sooner *must* be pursued. *This* is the only chance, the last voyage in many months. I know the general wanted to maintain a foothold in Africa, but that's impossible."

"I think he knew it," Tess said. "Canberra certainly does. Before we left Canberra, the prime minister gave a speech saying we had to focus on rebuilding Australia. When we reached Perth, the local commander thought the refugees were gone from Mozambique, and had already redirected every search-and-rescue resource north, up to the Andaman Islands."

"We're in retreat," Adams said. "It was inevitable and it *is* essential so that we can one day come back. It's those scientists who'll determine how close to home that retreat will take us. Small islands might have offered a refuge to some, but India will have fared no better than Africa. Table Bay is a heavy storm away from becoming a toxic swamp. We sailed from Madagascar to Cape Town, found no truly safe anchorage, and lost the African Union convoy on the way. The Northern Hemisphere collapsed before the bombs fell. It will be far worse now."

"Just leaving a question mark over South America," Tess said.

"A question mark is better than *here be dragons*," she said. "I'll leave boats, and pilots for the civilian helicopters, and as much ammunition, medical supplies, and food as we can spare. They only have to wait six days, perhaps eight, until the relief ship arrives. I still can't promise we'll reach Colombia, or even South America, but duty demands we try."

Adams returned to the ship while Tess continued her walk, until, behind one of the houses previously belonging to the museum staff, she saw Toppley, alone, sitting splay-legged on a patch of grass.

"G'day," Tess said, sitting next to her.

"Howzit," Toppley said.

"That was a crazy thing you did back at the school."

"It was ill-conceived and improperly thought through," Toppley said.

"I didn't mean it as a criticism."

"The helicopter, and those sailors with their winch, were already on the way," Toppley said. "The children would have been saved regardless of my foolishness, but I felt old. Useless. Surplus to requirements."

"We didn't know the helicopter was bringing a winch, and none of us came up with a better plan. Something had to be done, and you did it. You're not surplus, and we all feel useless. How can we not? We're savings tens while knowing, just beyond reach, thousands more are dying every day. Even the captain feels it. We're going west tomorrow.

Leaving the boats and those civilian helicopters, and a small crew, but we're going west to look for more survivors."

"Via Colombia?"

"Hopefully. The crew want revenge, and the weapon," Tess said. "The captain wants to save as many people as she can."

"To make up for those she's lost," Toppley said. "She's not the only one who feels like that. A rescue ship is on its way?"

"One. At least one, yes," Tess said. "They should be here in a week."

"After which, we'll be leaving Africa forever," Toppley said.

"For now," Tess said. "But yes, that's what I'll recommend to Anna, but I think she knew it was the most likely outcome before we set out. We have to pull back to Oz, and rebuild before we can rescue."

"Save our people rather than theirs," Toppley said bitterly. "That, at least, hasn't changed since the end of the world."

"We've no choice," Tess said. "We're on the brink of extinction."

"Oh, I know," Toppley said. "But that doesn't make it an easier pill to swallow. Some people will be staying here to look for survivors?"

"To collect any that get to the beach," Tess said.

"I'd like to stay with them," she said. "It's not that I wish to make amends, nor do I seek forgiveness. The past cannot be altered, or forgotten, though so much of it fills me with regret. I would like the future to be different. I'm just ballast aboard that ship. I can be of use here, and I do want to be useful."

"You think this is where you need to be?" Tess asked.

"I'm supposed to be in a cell," she said. "Yet instead, I find myself on this most infamous of prison islands. If that isn't a sign, I don't know what is."

Part 4

The Point of No Return

The Continuing Diaries of Tess Qwong

24th March

Chapter 25 - Other Rooftops

It's two hours since we left Robben Island. As the ship slides into its at-sea rhythm, I'm keeping out of the way. With Teegan still in Cape Town, I'm alone in my cabin. I've got the second book in Leo's trilogy to read, and I salvaged a copy of the Dan Blaze DVD from the toy-store. I don't feel like either. I don't want to sleep, not just because I'll miss mealtimes and end up wandering the ship's gangways and bilges during the middle of the night.

People want there to be patterns. We want there to be connections, and see them in every small coincidence. We ignore the differences and claim the hand of fate, and declare there must be some meaning behind it all. Destiny. A curse. A plot. A plan. Something so far beyond our control we can take comfort that the blame *doesn't* lie with us.

So where does blame lie? Nowhere and everywhere. With Sullivan. With me. With all of us, and with none of us, because blame is different from responsibility. Responsibility is easy to place. A cop, a soldier, we do our duty, and our duty puts us in harm's way. Death is a risk. The responsibility for it can be blamed on our foe. Blame's that little demon which sits on our shoulders, second-guessing our actions, offering a sapping chorus of what-ifs and why-didn't-Is. Blame's the devil targeting our rage outwards and our regrets inward. Blame can help us get through the days after a tragedy, but not the weeks and months and years which follow.

Another city. Another rooftop. Another gut-shot colleague. There isn't really a comparison between Cape Town and Sydney, but ever since the bullet smashed through the toyshop window, my brain's been drawing parallels.

Back then, I was at a crossroads in my life. Is that similar to now? Isn't life always at a crossroads? Things were going well for me, and going better for our investigation. The gang had formed when two dropouts began selling weed and LSD at their old university. Their classmates graduated, and began earning cash, and so did these two as they expanded their client base. They got a taste for money, and wanted more. They wanted *real* money, so they branched into cocaine. They recruited a couple of blokes who worked at the docks. They skipped out the mid-level distribution, and bought direct from the supplier. In five years, they went from small-time dealers to running the import and distribution for half the city.

There was nothing unusual about them. Nothing special. Nothing to warrant more than a footnote in a true-crime podcast. They rose to the top because we'd locked up the people running import before them. After we took them down, someone else moved in. Crims always fill a vacuum: it's a fundamental law.

Like their predecessors, this gang thought they were smarter than the people tracking them. Like their predecessors, we caught them thanks to our hard work and their arrogance. Back then, internet cafes were everywhere. They'd use a different cafe, and a different computer, to arrange drops and shipments. Each time, they shared a password for a single email account, saving the message as a draft rather than sending it. Smart. The messages were going nowhere, so they couldn't be intercepted. We couldn't get a warrant to install key-logging software, or screen-facing cameras, because we didn't know which machine in which cafe they'd use next. But drugs are bought with cash, and you can't email a pill.

The street-dealers were easy to find. Surveillance took us to their supplier. Following her, we found the re-up distributor and his far-too-flash car. A hard brake at some lights when I was trailing the bloke from in front had him ram the rear of my car. That gave me cause to shine a light in his eyes and confirm, like we suspected, he was partaking of his own supply.

The comedown in an interrogation room broke him, and gave us the password to the email account. Forty-eight hours later, we had warrants to arrest twenty-eight people. It was the night of a shipment. We were going to seize the boat, arrest the crew, three customs officers, the harbour-master, two drivers, and the team who'd cut up and repackage the coke. We weren't going to get the boss, but we figured someone would take a deal and turn on him.

My part in the op was to grab the accountant. Lincoln Eisenhower Washington was his name, but he was as Australian as a koala-shaped sunshade. He wasn't one of the original four, but had been recruited soon after they began to expand. He was another university classmate, but he'd actually graduated. He'd worked for a hedge fund, then switched to arranging finance for charities. Except, really, he ran the gang's money-laundering op. It was his name on the launderettes, pizzerias, arcades, and other can't-be-profitable cash businesses.

Every night, he drove his limp-legged squinty-eyed poodle to an old factory for a walk. That was when we were going to pick him up. Me and Sergeant Fredericko Alberto Fermi. To his family, he was Albo. To our team, he was Faffy. To me, he was Fredo, but I was debating renaming him fiancé.

We were in the car, waiting for the go. Washington's car drove up. Stopped. Parked outside the old factory gates. Washington got out, tugging at the dog's lead until it, reluctantly, followed. We called it in. Waited. Got the go.

We got out. Approached. Washington ran.

Even now, I'm not sure why he bolted, leaving his poor poodle limping after him, but he ran so I ran. He drew a gun. Fired two shots. A .38 revolver. Compact. Custom made with a chrome finish and a teak handle, though I didn't get those details until much later. That he carried a gun suggested he was expecting night-time visitors of a very different kind.

"Get the car! Cut him off!" I yelled, and didn't slow, though I did, belatedly, remember to yell, "Police!"

A century ago, the factory had been built to make ceramics. Every few years, it's changed owners and production. Most recently focusing on mid-range clothing, until economies of scale, and the falling cost of shipping, had made local production unprofitable. An application had gone through for conversion to apartments, so we knew it was empty. So did Washington.

He fired another random shot before diving through the metre-high gap in the solid wooden gate. I drew my sidearm, affixing the light, though I left it switched off. I listened until I was certain I heard footsteps running away from the gate, and followed.

It was an ill-lit street at the edge of an expanding residential district. Little illumination made it beyond the wall, leaving the litter of brick, wood, and broken glass a shadowy obstacle course over which I trekked, half-certain I'd lost my suspect. Until I heard metal clang ahead.

Again, I ran.

At the side of the building was a wrought-iron fire escape, complete with a pull-down stair-ladder up which Washington clambered. He used both hands. I could see that much.

"Stop! Washington! Police!" I yelled, but I couldn't shoot. Not when he was clearly unarmed and running away. Or running up. What could I do but follow?

I was twenty seconds behind him when I stepped onto those steep metal stairs. Ten seconds when I clanked my way to the top flight. I thought he'd try for a door. Instead, he jumped, up onto the roof. I yelled for him to stop even as I ran, jumped, and hauled myself after him.

The roof was angled by five degrees, covered in wire-mesh, over which Washington scrabbled until he reached a narrow walkway, close to the ridge. He was a perfect target, brilliantly silhouetted by moonlight. But his hands were empty. I kept on running, gaining ground when I reached the ridge. Slowing when we both neared the end. But he didn't slow. He accelerated. Jumped, off the roof, disappearing from view.

I thought it was suicide, until I got nearer. Between that building and the next was a drop of nearly three metres, and I felt every centimetre when my feet hit the leaf-coated tiles. Another run to the end of the roof. Another jump. Another roof, another jump, and I guessed his plan:

to get to the other side of the factory complex, and the building site beyond, where he stood a chance of losing his pursuit among the construction machines.

I was wrong. One last jump, onto one last roof, this one further away than the last, and when I pulled myself to my feet, he'd vanished. I was atop a two-storey building. A decade old, made of concrete and cement with a scaffolding barrier around the exterior, a boxy glass skylight nearly opaque with dirt, and a hatch built into the floor. An open hatch.

He had to have gone through, so I followed. Down a set of steep wooden steps. At the bottom, I stopped. I knew he was close. I can't say how, but I think it was that I'd stopped hearing him run. I had my gun drawn, but had the light off, and virtually none was making its way through the skylight. Just enough to see that this was one long room, nearly the length of the building, dotted with a few old tables, and some rotting cardboard boxes.

I let my gut take over, and swung my gun, guessing at his position, switching on the light. He had his own weapon raised, but the light threw his aim. His shot missed. Mine didn't.

The knife bit deep into my side. Cold and hot at the same time. Shocking more than anything. Shocking because a second suspect had been lurking in the shadows. The person Washington met when he took his dog for a walk. The whole reason he drove out to the factory. I spun, falling, firing. Three shots, into the dark, collapsing onto a table, wildly aiming light and gun into the shadows, until the beam glistened off blood. I'd hit her. Through the heart.

Who was she? Washington's girlfriend, Kimberly Holne. A nearly honest petty crook, who'd been trying to persuade him they should run away together. He'd acquired false passports. Good ones. He had them both in his pocket. My theory is that they had decided to quit the business and start a new life far away.

What had made him decide to run? Along with the drugs aboard the boat, we seized a crate of machine pistols. The gang had been about to start a drug war. But we stopped them. That's the job.

Had I not chased, Washington and his girl might have run, using those passports. Odds are, because we were closing in, we'd have picked them up at the airport. I'm certain they wouldn't have got far. But he ran, so I chased, because that's the job.

I nearly died there. But I didn't. Lost a lot of blood, and what little I had left had been poisoned by what can only be described as a toxic blade.

Fredo, my partner in every sense of the word, was dead. One of those random shots by Washington had hit him in the neck. He bled out, alone, while I ran after our suspect.

The doctors were adamant there was nothing I could have done to save him. They were trying to be kind, but it made it worse. I could have *tried* to save him. I definitely could have been with him.

No one knew about our relationship, of course. He and I'd talked about it, and decided, once this case was done, we had a big decision to make. Break it off, or make it official. I knew which I wanted, and I'm positive he wanted the same. One of us would transfer. After the big bust we were sure was coming, we were both positive promotions were in our future. But he died, and I was pregnant. I didn't know. Five weeks. Some detective, right? The stress of the case, the twenty-hour days, living on coffee, sugar, and adrenaline, and I didn't realise. I miscarried.

Did I have to run?

We knew all of Washington's addresses. We'd have caught him before dawn. If he'd used that fake passport, we'd probably have picked him up at the airport. But even if he escaped, so what? He was in over his head and looking for an out. He'd have gone straight, near enough. His girlfriend would have given him a reason to stay honest.

A hundred and three arrests resulted from that night's work, though none from my part in it. But I chased because he ran, because that's the job.

How do you go on from that? I nearly didn't. I got a commendation. I got a promotion. Of course I did. They had to call me a hero in order to call the operation a success. I guess it had been successful, just like we'd been successful shutting down the predecessor gang, and how someone else succeeded in shuttering the dealers who took over the territory a few months later. And maybe we had succeeded in stopping a gang war. But me? What had I succeeded in?

He ran, so I chased. If it happened again, I'd do it again. That's the job. My job. Fredo's job. Sullivan's job. Blame will keep you company, but it doesn't help you move on.

But I can't say that to Zach. Not yet. He's still working out whom he's grieving for.

25th March

Chapter 26 - The *Courageous*

Just before breakfast, we sailed into a storm. On balance, the timing was perfect. I was able to fall back into my bunk, barely bumping my head. Each surge threw me in a completely unexpected direction. Couldn't sleep. Couldn't read. Which only left thinking.

I didn't realise how much I relied on my friends until they weren't surrounding me. Back home, almost every day I'd pop in to see Liu for breakfast or dinner. I'd speak to Mick most days, and see him nearly as often, even if it was in conjunction with some remote accident or incident. The co-workers, the people I helped, and many of the crims I cuffed, were neighbours I'd known most of my life. It was a social life, if not always a sociable one.

Now, I miss Teegan. Not her snoring, or the way the first twenty minutes after waking were filled with grumbling, but she was easy to talk with. Bruce Hawker is rigidly professional. He's a good bloke, but he's standoffish. A product of high-risk assignments where he knows at least one of his colleagues will die. Nicko Oakes is fifteen years and more than a generation younger than me. It's not just age, but experience, too; he's not been through the wringer. Clyde still has a wall up around him. Sometimes I can jump high enough to see over, but that's not the same as being invited in. He's focusing on getting through this mission, and getting home to his family.

Captain Adams has her ship and crew to run, among whom I'm very definitely pigeonholed as a passenger. As far as the rest of her crew are concerned, I'm the civilian authority, and a cop to boot. Talking with Avalon requires an aspirin. Leo is busy keeping Zach busy with lessons on… on… actually, I've no idea. Yesterday, it involved a trip down to the engine room. Zach's taken to it like a shark to a swim-class. When we get back to Australia, I'll make it official, assign him to the scientists full-time. I think it'd be safer for him than patrolling a refugee camp. I'm starting to sense that'll be every cop's primary duty for the next couple of years.

I'm not saying I'm lonely; I'm usually quite happy in my own company. And I won't say I'm bored. It's not that I'm a fish out of water, or a camel at sea; I'm a teapot in a pub, or a corkscrew at a christening: I'm waiting to be useful. Which is why I was more than glad when there was a knock at the door.

"Sorry to disturb you, ma'am, but the captain requests your presence," Lieutenant Renton said.

"On the bridge?" I asked.

"No, ma'am. In her cabin. For breakfast."

"During a storm?"

"This is just a swell," he said, far too easily.

"Welcome," the captain said, as Renton closed her cabin door.

"This *is* a storm, yes?" I said, gratefully taking the security of a chair.

"The end of one," the captain said. "We skimmed the edge. Breakfast? It's tea and pancakes."

"Really? Wonderful. Ah, they look like fritters. Made with dried fruit, powdered eggs, and powdered milk. Easy to eat on a rolling deck, and don't taste the worse for being eaten cold, right?"

"Ever the detective. Yes, you're correct, but I like pancakes." She opened a drawer and withdrew a small glass jug. "Syrup? Don't tell the Canadians, and don't tell them it actually comes from Vermont. I traded a crate of Marmite with a U.S. captain a month before the outbreak."

The tea, this time, was hot, and served in a lidded cup. "Where are we?" I asked.

"Twenty-eight hours out of Cape Town, three days from Ascension. It's difficult to be more accurate until we know how far the storm has drawn us from our path."

I took a sip of my tea. "I'm guessing there's a reason we're having a chat in here, rather than on the bridge."

"We picked up a radio signal. It's peculiar and troubling, and I don't wish it known widely." She picked up a tablet, and pressed play.

"*Come in,* Golden Shores. *Come in,* Golden Shores. *This is Counter-Admiral Popolov aboard the* HMS Courageous. *We have received your mayday and are responding.*"

Adams pressed stop. "Well, detective?"

"A Russian accent, and a Russian-sounding name," I said.

"The rank is used by a number of navies," Adams said. "Britain isn't one of them, but Russia is."

"He spoke in English, and was claiming to be aboard a British ship. It's a warship, yes?" I asked.

"The *Courageous* is an Albion-class landing platform dock," Adams said. "Designed for the swift deployment of troops via helicopter, boat, or directly onto a beach."

"Not a rescue vessel?" I asked. "Interesting. He didn't say he was in charge, just that he was aboard. If he wasn't Admiral Popolov, why use that name and rank? If he were speaking Russian, I might understand it. But why is a Russian admiral using the radio aboard a British ship? Why claim to be aboard a British warship if that wasn't his ship? What kind of ship is the *Golden Shores*?"

"We don't know, but we've been unable to pick up any signal from the vessel."

"Where did this signal come from?" I asked.

"The north. The recording was made as the storm began. We haven't heard anything since, nor picked up either vessel on radar."

"If this admiral were attempting to deceive, he'd have someone with a British accent on that radio, claiming to be captain. Or, if he were the only English-speaker aboard, he'd claim to be a general or ambassador from Germany or Latvia, or some other NATO nation. He would *not* identify himself as a Russian. But if he was attempting to reassure, why use his own name, his own rank? Why not just the ship name?"

"Yes, exactly. Any guesses at an answer?"

"There's an obvious one," I said. "It could be that isn't the *Courageous*, he's not an admiral, and his name isn't Popolov, but the

Golden Shores is part of his fleet. This message is a way of proving their identity."

"Proving they weren't a threat," Adams said. "Suggesting there is some threat out here. There's another obvious explanation. He *is* Admiral Popolov, and he seized or salvaged that ship."

"Would that make him hostile?" I asked.

"Old alliances are as meaningless as our pre-war enmities. Before your arrival, around Madagascar, after the ports fell, many ships were low on supplies. We saw them turn pirate simply to feed their crew and fuel their engines."

"If they are hostile, how would we fare in a fight?"

"Victorious," Adams said. "There is no doubt. But only if we recognise the danger before they are close enough to board."

"So we'd have to shoot first?" I asked.

"It is unlikely they'd attempt a direct approach," Adams said. "They would claim to be in difficulty, request assistance, wait until some of our crew were aboard their ship, and they were able to send their crew onto ours."

"Aren't there code words and call signs?" I asked.

"He's not claiming to be the ship's original captain," Adams said. "If they make contact again and claim to have salvaged the ship, should we believe them? Do you see the dilemma? They are to the north, and so between us and Ascension. Between Ascension and Robben Island."

"So if they are a threat, will we have to return to Cape Town?" I asked.

"Possibly, but are they a threat? My inclination, at present, is that they are."

"How so?"

"Because there is one more piece of data. We picked up a submarine again."

"The *Adventure* followed us?"

"We have not confirmed it is that particular boat, but it seems most likely," Adams said. "Why has this British submarine not responded to any of our radio messages? Because the sailors don't have the correct accent. If the *Courageous* is now under Russian command, why not the *Adventure*?"

"But that sub could sink us?"

"Yes, but at a risk, and a cost of irreplaceable torpedoes. I would guess they've identified us as a New Zealand frigate travelling away from home. They would assume we're on some kind of survey mission. If we leave them alone, they will do the same, but they want to claim these waters."

"So we can ignore them," I said. "But will they ignore Robben Island? If they're following us, they're not bothering our people in Cape Town. If we attack the *Courageous*, the sub will sink us. If they both attack us, we're in trouble, and that's assuming they have no other ships."

"Hence the dilemma," Adams said.

"We can't turn around, because it'll still be a few days before the rescue ship reaches Robben Island. Right now, we're the lure. But we can't let them get aboard our ship. So we continue north, and wait?"

"It seems so," Adams said. "I hoped you might have spotted something I'd missed. Yes, I think we'll have to wait, and be ready for whatever's coming."

26th March

Chapter 27 - Brace for Impact

I was woken by the alarm. A blaring siren. Not loud, but pervasive. My first thought was *fire*. But the announcement was a stand-to for action.

Boots on. Belt next. Holster. Ammo. Shoulder bag with its sealed water bottle, and ten of the oat-money-bars I'd plastic-wrapped into a waterproof brick. The un-inflated life-vest came last. Rule-one runs deep, and so I checked the knife was securely buttoned in its sheath in case, in the water, I needed to cut those boots loose. I wasted ten seconds debating the rope: though it might be useful, it would reduce buoyancy, but Avalon would certainly yell at me if I didn't have it. It would be easy to ditch so I attached it anyway.

It didn't take long. Once I was ready, my brain caught up with reality. If the ship went down, and I made it into the freezing ocean, there'd be absolutely no chance at rescue. In the open water, afloat or not, death would take minutes. A lifeboat might drag it out for a few hours, but death was still a certainty. Not wanting to wait for it alone in my cabin, I went to the bridge.

I reached it in time to hear Lieutenant Renton announce, "Torpedo away, ma'am."

"Launch counter-measures," Adams said with an unimaginable measure of calm. "Welcome to the war, Commissioner. Brace for impact."

I grabbed the rail close to the door, just as the ship shook, though not nearly as violently as I'd expected.

"Captain, the torpedo self-destructed after we launched counter-measures."

"Prepare to launch the first torpedo," Adams said. "Ready to alter course, and to launch the second. Hold on, Commissioner."

"Who's shooting at us?" I asked.

"A Russian Akula-II submarine," the captain said. "We think it's the *Vepr*. It's a long way from home, since it should be stationed in the Arctic."

"Second contact, Captain!" Renton said.

"Where?"

"Bearing zero-eight-five," Renton said. "Another submarine. It's the *Adventure*. She's already fired. She's—"

This explosion was more forceful, shuddering the ship's bones.

"The Russian is gone, ma'am," Renton said. "The *Adventure* blew it apart."

"Any other contacts?" Adams asked.

"No ma'am," Renton said.

"Raise the *Adventure*," the captain said.

"No response, ma'am."

"Cut speed to half, but maintain course," Adams said. "Keep trying to reach the *Adventure*."

I stood there, white-knuckled, holding my breath until I saw spots.

"The *Adventure* isn't responding, and she's not following," Renton said.

"Yesterday," Adams said, "we picked up a radio signal from a British ship, the *Courageous*, commanded by a Russian admiral. Tonight, a Russian submarine launched a probing attack and was sunk by a Royal Navy submarine. Maintain heading. Keep trying to raise the *Adventure*."

I'd walked in on the tail end of a battle, but I'd only missed the first few minutes. Ten minutes at most. Probably less. From first contact to the loss of dozens of lives. An entire submarine had been obliterated. Ten minutes. Less. It had almost been us. I looked at my life jacket. I didn't want to ask if we should look for survivors. It seemed unlikely there'd be any, and search-and-rescue clearly wasn't part of the captain's plans.

"Captain, you said that was a probing attack," I said. "They weren't trying to sink us?"

"They destroyed the torpedo after we launched counter-measures," Adams said. "It was fired-by-wire, an umbilical cable linked it back to their boat. They wanted to test us, to gauge our response, our ability, and the level of our munitions. They were assessing the chance of seizing our ship. A frigate makes a better pirate boat than a landing-platform-dock like the *Courageous*. We must assume the pirates control Ascension. If they didn't, they wouldn't operate so close to that old base. The *Adventure* was chased out of harbour. We were the perfect decoy to distract that Russian sub. In which case, the *Adventure* may now ask us for assistance in retaking the *Courageous*, and the island. Mr Renton?"

"No word, ma'am."

"What's our heading?"

"Due north, ma'am."

"Broadly towards Ascension," Adams said. "No, that won't do. Put us on a course to Brazil. If the *Adventure* wants any further assistance from us, they will have to ask. Otherwise, we are leaving this theatre. And plot a course to take us back to Robben Island. A looping course which will travel through waters to the south."

The crew worked. The captain sat. I stood. Everyone waited. For nothing, as it turned out. The *Adventure* changed course by one hundred and eighty degrees and without making contact. No one else did, either, nor was anything picked up on the radar.

After an hour, the captain stood the ship down, though maintained our course towards South America.

"So are we going to Colombia?" Zach asked.

"No talking during the test," Avalon said.

I'd found them both in the scientist's cabin-lab.

"Done," Zach said, closing the book. "Now can I have my oat-bar?"

"Already?" Avalon asked, sounding pleasantly surprised. She handed Zach one of the dollar-ration-bars, which explained how she'd managed to get him to undertake a test, just after a battle.

"Are we going to Colombia, Commish?" Zach asked.

"I don't know. I don't think the captain has decided," I said. "There's something odd going on in these waters. We don't want a hostile ship following us back to Robben Island, but we're not sure who is hostile and who isn't."

"But we're not going to Ascension," Zach said. "So if we don't turn back tomorrow, we'll have to go on."

"We'll know tomorrow," I said.

"Zachary, these are all completely incorrect," Avalon said.

"Yeah, but you didn't say I had to get them right," Zach said. "Only that I had to finish them. You want me to do them right, that'll cost a lot more than one oat-bar."

27th March

Chapter 28 - Axe and Stone

The captain made the announcement at midday: "You all know why the scientists are aboard. In South America, we can serve justice on those responsible for the murder of billions. We could find the key to creating a weapon to restore safety to the living. Or we could find another crater. But if we don't go, someone else will be sent. There's a war being fought in these waters. There's a risk to any ship, and we can't pass that risk on to someone else. We can't return to Robben Island without chancing that risk follows us. There is a danger to us in being unable to refuel in South America, but there are other ways home, and we *will* be home again soon."

Something about the announcement troubled me. Unable to place what, I went looking for Bruce. I found Clyde and Zach first, in the armoury, sharpening axes.

"Aren't you supposed to be helping Dr Avalon?" I asked.

"Yeah, she sent me away. Her and Doc Leo wanted the cabin for private work."

"What kind of work?" I asked, my suspicions rising.

"I don't think they're *really* working," Zach said. "They just wanted me gone."

"Understood," I said. "Anyway, I was looking for Bruce."

"He's running another close-combat session," Clyde said. "But I've been thrown on my face enough times not to need the practice. Is there trouble?"

"I wanted to discuss what we'll do when we get to Colombia," I said.

"Until we've refuelled, it's too soon to plan an attack," Clyde said. "Assuming we *can* refuel."

"Yeah, and no worries if we can't," Zach said. "We're going to fly back from South America, all the way to Auckland. Direct."

"Where did you hear that?" I asked.

"Glenn told me. Glenn Mackay."

"The petty officer? Who told him?"

"Dunno," Zach said. "But it's obvious. All those Americans, I mean North Americans, States-Americans, they'll have flown south, right? So we've just got to find the planes. Airports will have tons of fuel, because there was nowhere for the South Americans to fly. They wouldn't go north, would they? Because that's where the zoms were."

"But they'd have flown to New Zealand if it was within range," I said.

"I bet some did," he said. "But not many, or we'd have known about it in Canberra, right? So that's where the planes are, and that's how we'll get back. It could be like in six days' time."

His logic was cloudy, but I'd let him realise it for himself, and bask in optimism until then. "What's with the axes?" I asked. "Are we that low on ammo?"

"Long-handle, short axe-head," Clyde said, holding his up. "Spike at the top, and another at the base."

"It's for killing zoms," Zach said. "Clyde made them."

"You did?" I asked.

"I designed them," Clyde said. "Mr Dickenson's making them in his machine-shop."

I took the axe from him. With the ship forever lurching back and forth, I wasn't going to risk a practice swing, but it felt well balanced as I tested the weight. "You missed your calling, Clyde," I said.

"Jace wanted me to take up a hobby," he said. "This was after I took the lobbying job. I found wearing a tie suffocating, and was a tad vocal in letting my feelings be known. He suggested restoring clocks, but I didn't want to be stuck indoors, so I bought a couple of rust buckets to repair."

"That was after Somalia, right?" Zach asked.

"What happened in Somalia?" I asked.

"One of my teams was kidnapped," Clyde said. "That's back when I was running in-country field-ops for the charity. We'd agreed on the ransom, but this other bunch of terrorists rushed the exchange. They took the money, and took out the crims' bag-man. The price for the hostages doubled, and the insurance wouldn't cover it."

"Yeah, but he got them out," Zach said. "Tell her how."

Clyde picked up the axe. "The hard way," he said, running a sharpening stone along its rough blade. "There were two of us in-country who'd served, me and Hailey. I'd bumped into a couple of old mates who'd turned merc, and who'd been propping up a bar waiting for work. So I set them up as over-watch. I called in a favour and got sat-coverage of the warehouse. Went in hard and fast, me at the front, Hailey at the side. But inside were rows of crates which reduced visibility. We were one second too slow in taking out their last man. Hailey jumped on the grenade. But we got the aid-workers out. I was down as Hailey's next-of-kin, so me and Jace adopted Hailey's son, Wilbur. That was the last straw for Jace. Now we had a son, he couldn't have me travelling places where it was fifty-fifty I'd come back in a coffin. I took the promotion to Canberra, lobbying for the umbrella group overseeing the charity, trying to squeeze a bit of funding and a lot of policy change out of the parliamentary rock. I got the job because of my medals, and had to go to evening functions wearing them, you see?"

"You were wearing medals and everyone else was in a suit?" I asked.

"Yep. Effective, though I can't undersell how much I hated it. But I loved my workshop, and so does Wilbur. Bought him his own set of wrenches last year. Plastic, but he loves 'em. I bought a few old paddock bashers I was converting into our own little camper. When Wilbur's a bit older, a couple of years from now, I plan to take us on a cross-Oz trip. Still will," he added, putting the axe down.

"You've got to have something to fight for," I said.

"Something to live for," he said.

"But that doesn't explain the axes," I said.

"They're for close combat on a ship," he said.

"Against boarders? I'd prefer my gun."

"Against zoms," Clyde said.

"Because ghost ships will have fuel," Zach said. "That's Mr Dickenson's plan. All those ships they blew up around Madagascar had fuel aboard, so it'll be the same near Brazil. That's how we'll get fuel."

"With axes?" I asked.

"There's thirty sailors we can use for close combat," Clyde said.

"The thirty Bruce is training right now?" I asked.

"Yep. They've been through basic. Some have been in combat. None have ever done anything like this. The danger is ricochets and strays, and it's a *big* danger if we're transferring fuel the old-fashioned way. Boarding axes would reduce the risk."

Clearly, everyone else aboard the ship had been thinking five steps ahead of me, and I didn't like where their thoughts had taken them.

"Bruce wouldn't give these thirty sailors rifles when boarding a ghost-ship?" I asked.

"Oh, they'll have firearms," Clyde said. "But not as a primary weapon. That's assuming the ship is overrun with zoms, and that we've got to fight our way below to access the fuel. Probably won't come to that."

"No, of course not," I said.

Finding a plane which could fly to Auckland sounded unlikely, while seizing a ship sounded dangerous. But neither was at the forefront of my mind. The original mission was to seize notes from the lab in Colombia. If we didn't have enough sailors trained in taking a ship, how were we going to use them to take the sisters' compound?

28th March

Chapter 29 - An Old Type of New Sail

Some people play poker to win. Some play not to lose. Cops play to watch other people. Which is another way of saying I lost every hand we played over breakfast. Rations have been reduced. Eating the meal didn't take long, and the game was a way of passing the time we'd been allotted in the mess hall.

I spoke to the captain yesterday over a mug of tea, which I dreamed was lunch. She confirmed we're keeping our eyes open for a derelict ship we can search for food and fuel. It's unlikely we'll find one. The same is true of a useable runway and working plane. But again, we'll need food, and we'll need aviation fuel to keep the helicopter in the air, so why not look around a coastal airport?

But we've not found a ship yet and we're days away from land. Nothing on the radio. Not as of last night. Nothing on radar. No signs of the sub.

I'd like to spend my time on the bridge, but when there's something we need to know, we all find out immediately. Making a nuisance of myself won't make a ship, or land, appear any sooner. Though the gym is now cleared of boxes, because of the reduced rations, it's off limits. As I was close to learning all of the words to the songs on the Dan Blaze DVD, I went looking for Flo, to borrow the third book in Leo's trilogy.

I found the author himself, in his cabin, watching a tablet.

"On a break?" I asked.

"Working," he said, reaching forward and pressing pause.

"Hang about, is that a movie?"

"Technically, it's a German documentary," he said. "*Die Ursprünge de Landwirtschaft.*"

"They look like actors. And that looks like a very, *very* long time ago."

"We'll split the difference and call it a reconstruction," he said. "The title translates to *The Origins of Agriculture*. It's a best guess at how hunter-gatherers became farmers about ten thousand years ago."

"You think that's how bad things could get?"

"No, I just needed some different stimulus," he said. "The walls, the deck, the sea, the never-changing monotony isn't conducive to planning a new world. How can I help you?"

"How's Zach doing as an assistant?" I asked.

"He seems okay. Adjusting. He's a good kid. Eager. Bright enough. Focused when he wants to be, but what he knows is mostly self-taught, and that's pretty selective. He likes books but hasn't learned how to learn."

"He doesn't like the homework," I said. "Why are you setting it?"

"It's Flo's method of distracting people from grief," Leo said. "Keep them distracted while time does the healing."

"I suppose it's as good a strategy as any, and pretty much the same thing Captain Adams is doing with her crew. Are you stuck, then?"

"Stuck?"

"With your work on the weapon."

"The latest model is compiling," he said, tapping his closed laptop.

"Are you making much progress?" I asked.

"Honestly, that's difficult to quantify," he said.

"Are you getting close to when you'll need a lab?" I asked, attempting to pin him down.

"Perhaps," he said. "Either way, we need to plan for what comes next." He tapped the tablet. "Hence the stimulus."

"After the weapon's been deployed?" I asked.

"After the zoms are dead," he said. "The Pacific needs a plan."

"I'm sure the politicians have a dozen each," I said.

"Their plans will centre around re-creating the old world," he said. "In all our disaster-planning, and I mean *all*, we focused on mitigating the damage and rebuilding what we had before. But the last chance to rebuild went up in a mushroom-shaped cloud of smoke. No one bothers to plan for life after mutually assured destruction because the plan was to ensure there wouldn't be any life left."

"But we are still alive," I said.

"For now. We were saved by the location of those blasts, some in the ocean, most of the rest in the Northern Hemisphere. Radiation levels have yet to reach an equilibrium. Assuming a non-lethal level of atmospheric and oceanic toxicity, we might survive. What then? We don't know what's happened to central Africa, but the southeast African coast has been obliterated. The only ships we've been close enough to contact have been hostile. We can call ourselves the United Nations, or the African Union, or Earth Almighty, but those are just words, and they belong to the old world and force us into old ways of thinking."

"So does watching re-enactments of life a century of centuries ago," I said.

"Fair point," he said. "But take the African Union. The general and the ambassador flew to Mozambique to maintain a foothold in Africa. Do you know why?"

"To assist in the relief and rescue effort," I said. "And to ensure when we did start rebuilding, we put some resources there."

"Exactly. Old thinking. Australia has shipyards and raw materials, and a surplus of labour. We don't need more land. We *do* need more ships because we now live on islands. We need ships to move food and fuel to Papua and Tasmania, but we can't move the supplies to Africa. To transport fuel, you need storage capability in the destination-harbour. Pre-existing fuel tanks are in port-cities and harbour-towns. But cities are living things; without constant maintenance, they die, and become deserts. You saw Cape Town, Inhambane, and as much of Durban as the rest of us. Every city will become like that. Some will be worse. Have I shown you the plot of the radiation levels?"

"I took a glance, and that was enough," I said. "The fuel tanks are still there in the city. We can still use them."

"Purely as a gas station, yes," he said. "But not as the basis of a settlement. Surely the whole point of building these supply ships is to service a community, not simply to service themselves. Within a few years, and for a few decades, there will be no agriculture, no aquaculture, around those old megacities. But if we adopt a policy of rebuilding, of re-adopting the plans of a year ago, we'll try. We'll fail. Everything we build in these early years will have to be retrofitted and redesigned. We'll lose time, and we've little to waste."

"Better we build what we know, and figure out how to best use it later, than to do nothing at all. Unless you've an alternative."

"I do," he said. "For once, we can act without influence from vested interests and lobbyists." He picked up a tablet, and held up a computer-assisted sketch of a four-funnel ship.

"A steam ship?"

"A sailing ship," he said. "Originally designed in 1920. Inside those chimneys are Flettner Rotors. Think of an auger. The pressure differential above and below the edge causes the auger to rotate. Convert that vertical spin to horizontal below decks, and you've got power. In 1925, it was used to sail the *Buckau* across the Atlantic. It took a century for material science to catch up with the concept, but they were finally using this design for short-range ferries and cargo ships."

"That's really a sailing ship?" I asked.

"Yes. With a sailing ship we don't need to send fuel ahead of us. We don't need to build fuel tanks or attempt to sanitise cities. We don't need to drill, refine, and transport the fuel. Think of the labour saved by one ship like this. Just one could take people and goods back and forth between our coastal communities in Indonesia, Malaysia, Chile, anywhere that isn't radioactive. Anywhere that doesn't have a toxic water supply. Anywhere we can build a new city, a new beginning."

"But can we build those ships?" I asked.

"Oh, sure. Easily. Most hulls can be converted."

"But you're still seeking inspiration?"

"Because this ship is barely the start," he said.

"I'll leave you to your thinking," I said, and returned to my cabin.

I'm a pragmatic realist. Or I like to think I am. When we're back in Australia, I'll air my uniform around the outback mines and farming stations. I'll have a hand in rebuilding the justice system from the ground up, but there will be plenty of crime to keep me busy. If Anna wants a sounding board, I'll listen, and offer whatever wisdom I can find, but rebuilding the future? No, that won't be my work; I'll be too busy trying to keep the peace.

Honestly, right now, after being a spectator to war in Africa and on the high seas, I'm glad of that. I'm not looking forward to it. But I'm glad that I don't have Leo's problems.

All of that said, and written, he's hiding something. The copper in me wants to know what.

29th March

Chapter 30 - Simmer and Fizz

A new item appeared on our rationed breakfast menu: a carbonated orange drink crammed with sugar and fizz, originally salvaged in Mozambique, and misplaced among crates of toothpaste and soap. Zero caffeine, sadly. But the coffee found on Robben Island was a brief luxury, now exhausted. Real tea is only available on prescription. We're left with a choice of powdered tea or cold orange. Since Captain Adams has iced-tea running through her veins, and likes to share, I opted for the freezer-cold orange.

"Do you think we can take this onto the deck?" Zach asked, holding up his bottle of fizz.

"Along with a deck chair?" Clyde said. "That's what's missing on this cruise."

"I can think of a few more things to add to that list," Nicko said.

"Trade you an oat-bar for your bottle, Zach," I said.

"No way," he said. "This has got to be worth at least ten."

"I don't have ten," I said.

"Okay, five," he said.

"I don't have five, either," I said. "I was testing the value of food versus a soft drink now our daily cals have been cut."

"I'll swap you one-to-one," Nicko said.

"I don't even have one," I said. "I handed my stash of emergency oat-bars into the purser. But it sounds like the value of food hasn't inflated to contraband-pricing yet."

"Give it a few hours," Nicko said, optimistically scraping his spoon across the empty bowl. "I'm starting to be envious of Elaina, trapped on that island with five thousand kids."

"We've still got catered meals, laundries, and showers," I said. "I could get used to this."

"In my experience, days like this are climbing up to a fall," Clyde said.

"Nah, I'm with Nicko," Zach said. "If I was on the island, I'd be setting homework, not having to do it!"

"You'd still have to mark it," Clyde said.

"What have the Canadians got you on now, mate?" Nicko asked.

"I'm guessing population boom and decline," Zach said. "It's supposed to be a prediction, but how is that not the same as a guess?"

"So you're just guessing the answer?" I asked.

Zach shrugged. "Kinda."

"Doc Flo thinks people are going to have a population boom?" Nicko asked.

"Not people," Zach said. "Animals. Especially fish. They'll boom because no one is fishing them, and then decline because of the radiation."

"So you're counting how many you can see in the water?" Nicko said.

"Reading," he said. "I'm just reading."

"I thought you liked reading," I said.

"I like reading books, but these papers have more numbers than words. That doesn't count as reading."

A tray clattered to the floor on the other side of the mess. Even as I turned to look, one sailor swung at another, missed, and hit Lieutenant Kane in the face. Even as I stood, Mr Mackay jumped in. My heart sank, but the petty officer pushed the sailors apart.

"It's fine," Clyde said, sitting down. "Sit down, Zach. It's all over."

"Has there been much fighting?" I asked.

"Tensions are rising," Clyde said.

"Because of the food?"

"Because we're so far from home," Clyde said.

30th March

Chapter 31 - A Joke of a Ship

Holidays never last forever. Today, mine came to an end. I was losing at cards to Clyde when I was summoned to the bridge. Judging by the sun, it was about an hour shy of midday. The ship had begun to slow.

"A vessel is ahead," Captain Adams said. "Adrift. Travelling across our path. We believe it's the *Southern Star*, or it was before they renamed her."

"The ship that was too long?" I asked.

"You know of her?" Adams asked.

"She's a crime," I said. "And she's the punch-line of a lot of jokes in the outback. Canberra passed a law stating no factory-fishing ships longer than a hundred and thirty metres would be allowed in our waters. So that one was built to be a hundred and twenty-nine. But when our people went aboard, they recorded a length of one hundred and thirty point one, and so they sent her packing. The debate in my branch of the bush comes down to which bunch of fisher-folk were lying about the length."

"I crossed paths with her in my previous command," the captain said. "We escorted her out of Micronesian waters. Twice. Diesel engines, single propeller, capable of fourteen knots. About four thousand cubic metres of storage, if I recall correctly. Built to turn fish into fillets, freeze those, and turn the rest of the animal into fishmeal."

"How many people can four thousand cubic metres feed?" I asked.

"You said there are eight million in Perth? I hope they like fish," Adams said.

"We're going to salvage the ship?" I asked.

"We'll investigate," the captain said. "That vessel is afloat, and adrift, with no obvious sign of damage from weapon or storm. It would absolutely be a boon to our people. There could be fuel aboard. If not, if the engines are operable, we could transfer fuel and a crew and sail her to shore. We're about five hundred kilometres due west of Brazil. That ship could be left at anchor while we search for a diesel-depot. The fuel we transfer does represent a majority of our own reserve, but we would still have our helicopter for a north-south coastal survey. Four thousand cubic metres? On balance, yes, it's worth investigating."

"Movement!" Lieutenant Kane said, pointing at the footage being relayed from the mast-cam. "Captain, it's a person."

"It's a zombie," I said, while on the screen, a figure staggered along the ship's stern-rail.

This was a job for my team. Not the scientists, and not for Zach. Just Bruce, Clyde, Nicko, and me, with Commander Tusitala and Mr Dickenson to inspect the engine room, and Glenn Mackay to crew our boat.

No vests this time. They offer limited protection against zoms, while adding weight. We had the MARS-L assault rifles, with their short barrels and just as short stocks, and the assortment of personal weapons we'd picked up along the way. Clyde offered me one of his new boarding axes, but I'd want to practice before I start impersonating a samurai.

The second warning came as we approached the ship.

"Two more zoms spotted on deck," Mackay said.

"I'm lead," Hawker said. "Nicko, on me. Keep the ladder clear."

He climbed, and I held on to our boat's rail. We had a line attached to the factory ship, but that only added a counter-directional tug to our wave-topping back and forth surge. The fishing ship was nearly twenty metres longer than the frigate, and about the same beam. Looking up, the climb appeared as steep as a mountain. A moving mountain since the ocean was far from calm. Annoyingly, none of the sailors, or the soldiers, were fazed by the roller-coaster lurching, so I kept my face blank, and my thoughts to myself.

Colonel Hawker reached the top, vaulted onto the deck, Sergeant Oakes a second behind.

"Clear!" Oakes called. "Two down. Come on up."

Eight bodies lay on the deck. Only two killed by us, and those were the only two killed recently. The other six had been baked by the tropical sun, but they were each lacking most of their skull. More numerous were the tools, abandoned near the bodies. Wrenches, levers, and long hooks. But no firearms.

"No birds. No insects," I said.

"We're too far from land," Tusitala said.

"Hostile!" Nicko said, firing as he spoke. "Clear. Zom. Definitely a zom because no one else walks around with a cleaver stuck in his chest."

"Nicko, with the commander and Mr Dickenson," Hawker said. "You've got the fuel, we've got the bridge."

The deck of this working ship was full of cover and concealment. Zombies don't hide, of course, and I'd ordinarily stop to listen for their approach, except the entire ship creaked. The frigate has a background noise all of its own. A clatter, clank, whir that goes on day and night. But that's a living ship, ploughing through the waves, and so is a comforting confirmation that all is still well. Here, every squeak and clank sang a clarion warning. So did the stench.

I know the smell of death. The bittersweet rot of a lonely death in the desiccated outback is different to a week-old trip-and-fall in a retirement apartment. A brutal murder, an accidental crash, a longed-for merciful release, they're all similar, but just as similarly different. This was something else. Almost solid. Definitely not human.

The hold was full of the ship's last catch. Possibly post-outbreak, hauled to feed a hastily fortified port. But the zoms had got aboard. From the cluster of corpses close to the ladder, those had been killed while a group had fled to a boat.

An external staircase led to the bridge, adjacent to a water-lock door against which someone, or something, was beating its fists.

"Got to be a zom," Clyde said.

"Tess," the colonel called from the top of the stairs. "Come take a look."

"Watch that door, Clyde. Don't open it yet," I said.

The bridge was a ruin. The windows had been broken from the inside, while shrapnel, some metal, some bone, had shredded the consoles.

"Last stand," Hawker said. "Last grenade, after the last bullet was gone."

"After the boats had gone, too," I said. I took a few photographs as proof, and to give me a little more time to look for a log, a map, anything that would add detail to the hypothesis. "We can't repair this, can we?"

"You're asking the wrong bloke," he said. "They're computers, aren't they? Can we spare some of our own, plug them into the cables?"

"Do we have the software?" I said, putting the camera-phone away. "Maybe we could run the ship from the engine room."

"We'd have to dump the rotten cargo," he said. "The commander's waving, pointing back to the boat."

"I guess that's an answer to whether there's fuel aboard," I said. "So no fuel, no bridge controls, and a hold full of rotten fish. Time is fuel, and we've just wasted a couple of hours and a couple of hundred kilometres finding out there's nothing here."

31st March

Chapter 32 - America

I thought Natal was in South Africa. Shows what I know. Turns out it's a city in Brazil, about thirty kilometres south of Cape São, the most easterly point on the continent. Or it was. Cape São still is. Natal is gone. The steel skeletons of the skyscrapers remain, twisted, shattered, broken, jutting skywards from the tomb of rubble that once was a city of a million people.

We stopped offshore. The helicopter took flight with the intention of buzzing inland to survey the damage, but the captain recalled the bird the moment the cameras captured an image of the crater.

Big. Obvious. Easily identifiable to everyone watching the screens erected in the mess. I went on deck to watch the helicopter return. I stayed there after the ship began to accelerate, heading due north, letting the rising wind kick away the fog. I wasn't the only person who'd come outside for air.

"They'll be dead in a few days," Zach said.

"Who will?" I asked.

"The zombies in the ruins," he said. "Doc Flo says they'll be dead soon. Hundreds were crawling over the rubble. South America's not going to be any better than South Africa, is it?"

"Doesn't look that way," I said.

"I was thinking," he said. "If we could find a plane to fly to Auckland, wouldn't other people already have done that? Wouldn't there be lots of pilots in New Zealand, and no planes left in South America?"

"Maybe," I said. "But we won't know until we look."

"Yeah, but if there are survivors in South America, I bet they've headed for the mountains. That's where we should look for them. It's stupid going up to Panama."

"Someone has to," I said.

"That's what Doc Flo told the captain. Someone had to go, so it should be us."

"*She* told the captain?" I asked, leaning forward. "Water looks oily."

"There's an upturned tanker to the north," Zach said. "The helicopter spotted it. It's mostly submerged."

"An oil tanker?"

"Guess so."

"Kills the view, doesn't it?" I said.

"And the wildlife," Zach said. "With the radiation, this bit of ocean will become another dead-zone. Currents are only going to make it worse."

"Is that what Dr Avalon said?"

"Doc Leo. He said there'll be loads of oceanic dead-zones, and more on land. They'll last for centuries. South Africa, South America, why target those?"

"D'you know why we call in a psychiatrist when dealing with a serial killer? You need a specialist to get inside the mind of someone like that. *You* wouldn't commit genocide. *I* wouldn't commit genocide. Trying to understand someone who willingly would doesn't come naturally. When did Avalon tell the captain we should go to Panama?"

"Back in Mozambique. Just after we arrived and you sent me and them onto the ship."

"Back then?" I said. "Ah, there's nothing to see out here." So I went inside to find Dr Avalon.

I found her, and Leo, in their cabin, reviewing images of Natal.

"It's an interesting crater," Leo said. "From its size, we can determine the size of the blast, and from that, the warhead, and so get a guess at who fired the missile."

"How would knowing that help us?" I asked, closing the door, and leaning against it.

"All information is useful, Commissioner," Avalon said. "Though not always immediately."

"Right. Sure. That's a good answer," I said. "Why are you here?"

"It's quieter than the bridge," Leo said.

"Sorry, my fault. Bad question," I said. "Why are you on this ship? Why did we come west?"

"To find the lab where the virus was made," Leo said.

"You've done this before, right? You've inspected labs where people have been playing around with deadly viruses. Like with Ebola in the DRC?"

"That was a waste of a trip," Avalon said.

"Interesting choice of words," I said. "You know the kind of troops required for seizing a remote compound. A hundred U.S. Rangers, say. Or the sailors and Marines from two U.S. frigates?"

"It's impossible to tell you what we'll need until we know who is there," Avalon said.

"Precisely," I said. "But back in Mozambique, after I packed you two aboard, you told the captain it was important we head to Panama. At that point, you knew that we wouldn't have the military personnel to seize a narco-compound in Colombia."

"We can still destroy it," Leo said.

"I hope so," I said. "But we don't need you two aboard for that. You sold Anna on the idea of heading to Britain and Manhattan for the vaccine and for patient zero, but as part of your work to build a weapon. After we found Sir Malcolm Baker, we compromised on Colombia. Back in Canberra, I was too exhausted to think clearly, and too happy to trust you two and your expert opinions. I didn't begin to understand the technical difficulties of this kind of trip until Captain Adams explained them to me. But you two would have known. It's numbers, isn't it? Distance and range. You would have known both the moment you stepped aboard this ship. Before we left Mozambique you knew we'd never reach the Northern Hemisphere. We'd never get to New York. You told the captain our goal should be Panama. Not Colombia because you also knew we didn't have the people to take that facility. So answer me this. Yes or no. Are you working on a weapon?"

"Yes," Leo said.

"No," Avalon said.

"Leo, quiet," I said, holding up a hand. "Dr Avalon, explain yourself. You aren't working on a weapon?"

"I've finished," she said.

"When did you finish?" I asked.

"That's an impossible—" Leo began.

"Zip it," I said. "Dr Avalon?"

"I had three candidates while we were still in Canada. In Canberra, I gathered most of the data I needed."

"You were done before we departed," I said. "Why aren't you testing it in a lab in the outback?"

"Because that would be utterly insane," Avalon said. "The old world is gone. The old civilisations are history. Do you really want the first great achievement of our new age to be the construction of a weapon of mass destruction?"

"If it would bring a swift end to the horror, yes," I said.

"It won't," she said.

"That's not your decision," I said.

"Whose should it be?" she said.

"The—" I began, and stopped, because this woman doesn't so much walk-the-earth-lightly as tunnel beneath the surface. "Okay, fine, explain to me why you lied to Oswald and parliament, the U.N., to Anna, me, and to everyone aboard this ship."

"I didn't lie," Avalon said. "I can develop a biochemical agent which will destroy the undead. It will also destroy most other living things in its path. Mammals, birds, trees. Probably even the grass. Millions of the uninfected would have been killed as collateral damage. Entire states, entire nations, would become deserts. Including from infection, total loss of life would have stood at two billion. More would die from starvation. But the zombies would be gone. Rivers would still flow. New trees could be planted. Old fields could be ploughed."

"Two billion?" I asked.

"I thought it would be closer to one billion," Leo said. "Depending on what kind of relief effort could be mounted. But this was before the nuclear bombs."

"The nuclear madness made infection-elimination impossible and unnecessary," Avalon said. "Why bother expending resources to turn North America into a desert? There are fewer than fifty million people in secure redoubts in the Pacific, with an estimated further fifty million trapped in day-to-day survival elsewhere in that ocean. At best, three-quarters will be alive next year. It will take a century before the Americas are home to more than scavengers."

"A lot of the land will be irradiated and toxic anyway," Leo said. "Destroying more wouldn't help anyone."

"Okay," I said, doing my best to keep my anger in check. "So why don't you take your idea and develop it, refine it, make something a little less apocalyptic?"

"It's pointless," Avalon said.

"It'd take too long," Leo said. "In six months, the zoms will die."

"No," Avalon said. "In six months, it will become evident that they have been dying all along. The human body is notoriously fragile. The infected can't exist forever. Within six months, this will become obvious to most. Within a year, it will be indisputable."

"That's a nice theory," I said. "It doesn't answer my question. Why aren't you in a lab?"

"The resources required are better deployed developing medicines and delivering them," Avalon said.

"That's not your call to make," I said.

"We've met politicians the world over," Leo said. "If we were given a lab, we'd get given twice the resources we asked for. But it would take about six months to develop something for wide-scale distribution. We'd be given a fleet of aircraft for deployment, and an entire city for manufacture. Six months is the minimum. Then we'd go hunting for some large group of zoms. Such a large group we'd be bound to see some just dropping down dead. But having put a million people to work to build the weapon, it would have to be deployed, because that's how politics works. We'd kill the zoms, and create a desert. The people back home would still be dying from dysentery and easily treatable infections. But as long as Flo and I are working on a weapon, here or in

Australia, everyone else will be focused on rebuilding the technologies that will ensure, a century from now, those abandoned countries will be repopulated."

"You've both missed your calling," I said. "With that kind of fanatical belief in your own abilities, you should have run for office. So we're going to Panama. We won't go any further. Not to New York. Certainly not to Britain. We'll be back in Perth or Auckland in three weeks. What then? Will you refuse to develop the weapon?"

"No one will want it," Avalon said.

"This voyage will dispel all the false hope there are bastion-cities and hold-out ports," Leo said. "The true reality of our situation, of the extent of the radiation, of the scarcity of workable farmland, of the paucity of human life, will be evident to everyone."

"I'm not going to argue the point," I said. "But I still don't see why you're aboard. Why not take the offer of an outback lab and sabotage your own work?"

"There are a few other moderately capable scientists in Australia," Avalon said. "They would have been assigned to us, and they would have noticed."

"Just remember I'm a cop, and you have confessed to treason-level fraud," I said. "A little less of the self-satisfied snark would be advisable."

"If there is a lab in Colombia, we have to make sure it's destroyed," Leo said.

"Bruce could have seen to that," I said.

"No, he would have been given orders to collect as much evidence as he could," Leo said. "Isn't that what our mission officially is? We know politicians. But we know warlords, too. We have to ensure the labs, the notes, and any samples, are completely destroyed."

"The scientists as well," Avalon added. "There can be no Operation Paperclip after this disaster."

"Let me show you the radiation map," Leo said. "I've got a model of the five-year projections for ocean toxicity and its impact on inland desertification."

"No, the images from Natal were enough for one day. So your personal mission is to destroy the research into the undead, and delay any development of a weapon? You've certainly succeeded in the second."

I let myself out, and returned to my cabin; I didn't dare let myself fall into a conversation with anyone. I should really question the scientists in more detail, but there'll be time for that. For now, I don't fully understand why they lied to us, or fully believe they're telling the complete truth.

I assumed we were all playing for the same team, but it turns out we're playing a different game. Their game is the same one they've been playing all their professional lives: keeping WMDs out of the hands of anyone mad enough to use them.

If the HMAS *Adelaide* had been in Mozambique, would we have skipped Cape Town and sailed straight for Colombia and then on to New York? If O.O. had said no to this mission, would those two have spent six months in a lab running into dead ends?

The press would have demanded progress reports, wouldn't they? Everyone in Australia would be listening to each news bulletin in hope of a miracle. Okay, fair dinkum, them being here means there's no false hope. Making it worse for me personally is that I think Anna agrees with them. Since O.O. is the bloke yanking on the levers of power, does it matter what she thinks? If the people have been told a weapon is possible, won't they demand one is developed? Will a few months delay be enough to dampen demand? And what if Smilovitz and Avalon are wrong? What if the zoms aren't all dying?

Who knows? But it doesn't matter. The longer I spend replaying what they said, the more I understand what they were saying. *Not* about the zoms. Six months? I'll believe it when I see it. No, it was what they said about desertification and oceanic dead-zones. The planet is in a worse state than I realised.

Part 5

Two Sisters, One Brother

South America

1st April

Chapter 33 - Bienvenue à la Belle France
Dégrad des Cannes, French Guiana

"Third time's the charm," Tess Qwong said, her words nearly lost beneath the engine's burr as the boat buzzed through the silt-laden Mahury River. Ahead lay the concrete and steel pier of the French military base, just east of the coastal city of Dégrad des Cannes, in French Guiana.

Three times they'd attempted to go ashore on Brazil's northern coast: São Luis, Belem, and Macapa on the estuary of the Amazon River itself. Four, if you counted Natal.

"Welcome to Europe, Zach," Clyde said.

"Yeah, I'm not falling for that. I know this is South America," Zach said, his eyes scanning the treetops.

"French Guiana is part of the European Union, so that makes this Europe," Clyde said.

"Fifty percent correct," Dr Avalon said. "Which is a good grade for a soldier."

"Ex-soldier," Clyde said.

"This is really in the European Union?" Zach asked.

"It really is," Clyde said.

"Was," Avalon said.

"That's just weird," Zach said. He swatted at the swirling cloud of insects that, almost universally among the passengers aboard the boat, had selected him as their appetizer.

The humidity lay so thick, Tess was surprised the boat didn't defy gravity and sail up to the brush-thin clouds. Those were meagre, wispy remains of the sky-slashing storm. Night arrived two hours too early. Rain had hammered the deck, dense enough to swim through. But after ten minutes, the storm grew bored and headed inland, leaving nothing but collar-sponge humidity, and a two-week-forgotten-corpse odour.

Some of that stench was caused by the small boat churning through the surface-layer of silt, washed into the river from either side of the wide river. Mixed in, inescapable, was the smell of death.

"There! Caught one," Avalon said, holding out her hand. On her palm, and nearly as big, was an iridescent green insect with protruding front legs, long body, and bulbous head. "I shall call him… Leonard. Or is it more of a Zachariah?"

"Is it dangerous?" Zach asked.

"It can't be," Avalon said. "The world's ten million most poisonous insects are all found in Australia. This isn't Australia, is it? No, it's Europe, and there are no poisonous insects in Europe."

"Fine, this is Europe, but that was the Amazon River we sailed past this morning, wasn't it?" Zach said. "Aren't there frogs there so poisonous that one lick and you'll cark it?"

"Are you confusing dart frogs and river toads?" Avalon said. "You shouldn't lick them. I wouldn't advocate licking *any* animal. I'm sure Dr Dodson has a rule to that effect."

"Not even the weirdest of anthropologists need to be given that warning," Tess said. "What kind of insect is it?"

"A form of treehopper, a relative of the cicada. It isn't toxic when in the mating stage of its lifecycle, which it is now. Which specific form of treehopper, I'd need a little longer to ascertain."

"Is this really part of the European Union?" Zach asked.

"Yep," Clyde said.

"How many people lived here?" Zach said.

"About a quarter of a million, in a country the size of Tasmania," Clyde said.

"Oh. Wow. Um… how many people live in Tasmania?" Zach asked.

"Half a million," Clyde said. "Before the outbreak."

"Oh."

"There are lakes in Canada bigger than Tasmania," Avalon said.

"There can't be," Zach said.

"I've been nominated for the Nobel Prize twice," Avalon said. "Which of us is more likely to be correct?"

"Didn't know there was a Nobel for geography," Zach said.

To which, Tess couldn't help but laugh.

On being told by Captain Adams that Dégrad des Cannes was a French Navy refuel and resupply base for the Southern Atlantic, she'd pictured a large port with cranes and a dry dock, a shore-battery, and anchorage for a fleet. The reality was an aquatic diesel-stop built on a concrete pier, a hundred metres from shore.

"No movement," Clyde said, as she followed him up the ladder and onto the pier. "I'm going to check the storage buildings. Hold this position."

Tess lingered by the top of the ladder, gun half raised. The refuelling platform was thirty metres long, ten deep, and linked to the shore by a hundred-metre-long pier wide enough for a tank. She doubted any were ever brought ashore here, not somewhere the rainforest grew so dense it had already begun a creeping reclamation. Ringing the platform was a head-height wire fence, except around the ladder, next to which was a steel box, fronting onto the river, with a water-tight conduit linking it to one of the three single-storey huts.

Clyde moved from one hut to the next, throwing open the door, sweeping inside while she watched the corners outside.

"All clear," Clyde called. "Blue door is the pump room."

"Doc, Zach, you check the fuel," Tess said. She turned back to the boat, in which Petty Officer Glenn Mackay waited by the controls. "Call the captain. All good so far."

Oakes and Hawker were aboard the helicopter, heading for the civilian city and harbour a kilometre up-river. Their secondary destination was the airport in the city of Cayenne, ten kilometres north and on the other shore of this bulbous peninsula.

She joined Clyde by the gate sealing the refuelling platform from the shore.

"The gate's been blown," Clyde said, untying the loop of rope currently holding the gate closed. The newly exposed steel on the jagged-edged lock plate was already rusting in the humid air. "Shape charge. Someone knew what they were doing, but they were in a hurry."

"Probably had food or medical supplies as their priority," Tess said. "Looks to be a mechanical lock, originally. Not digital. Because of the humidity, I suppose. Plenty of security cameras here."

"Sat-uplink back to a base in France is cheaper than soldiers," Clyde said. "But not nearly as useful in a crisis. The garrison left the keys in the pump-room controls. That small hut is a tool room. The other's a sentry post. They've been searched and looted. We're not the first people to come here looking for fuel. But I'd say the garrison left with the first lot of ships."

"Returned to France?" Tess asked.

"Could be," Clyde said, looping the now loose rope over the lock. "About two hundred personnel were stationed here. On shore, the other end of the pier, that'd be their base. Terrorism was a risk. Theft, not so much."

"What I know about French Guiana comes from having read *Papillon* just after I learned Australia used to be a penal colony," she said.

"Devil's Island," he said. "That's further up the coast."

"You've been?" Tess asked.

"Not even close," he said. "Jace stuck this place on our one-day-maybe list, mostly because of that book."

"You've a weird idea of holiday-research if you learned about the military bases."

"Nah, last year we were approached to help clean up the Colombia-Venezuela border," Clyde said. "Politically, it was expedient to use French Guiana as a staging ground, and get the European Union to cover some of the costs. We were still negotiating access come February."

"We've struck oil!" Zach called out, as he and Avalon came out of the pump-room.

"Diesel," Avalon said. "A scientific mind prizes precision, Zachary. But that is not what will be of most interest to our detective. There is a log of all the ships refuelling here since the outbreak." She held up a transparent plastic envelope.

"A single piece of paper?" Tess asked, taking the sheet out of the envelope. "I count twelve ships. Lists their names. And… okay, some writing in French, some in Spanish, and some in Portuguese. Can you translate?"

"It's twelve entries, but only eleven vessels," Avalon said. "Nine went north. One returned and went south. The other two only went south. The second entry claims to be from the *Aconit*, a French warship, though it is distinctly unmartial in its phrasing. *La France est morte. L'Europe est morte. Le nord est radioactif.* Would you like me to translate?"

"I get the gist," Tess said. "What's the most recent note say?"

"It's from a ship called *Isabella la Bella*," Avalon said. "The captain writes that Natal was destroyed. Their vessel was going north, despite the warning left by the French warship."

"Zach, photograph the note. Return it to its envelope, and to where you found it. We'll ask Captain Adams if she wants to write an entry from us."

"Saying what?" Zach asked.

"That'll be up to the captain," Tess said. She glanced down at the dosimeter. "Doc, go back to the boat, and radio the ship. Tell the captain there's fuel, and it seems safe enough to bring the *Te Taiki* in to dock. Tell her about the log, too. We'll take a look ashore."

"There's a croc!" Zach called, peering over the rail close to the gate. "There's a croc in the water!"

"Nonsense," Avalon said, following him over.

"Its eye just opened," Zach said. "Don't you tell me that's a log."

"It's a caiman, not a crocodile," Avalon said.

"What's a caiman?" Zach asked.

"A type of alligator," Clyde said.

"We'll take a look at the military base," Tess said. "Clyde, watch for zoms. Zach, watch for crocs. Flo, go call the captain, and tell Mr Mackay he better come up onto the platform."

"What are we looking for?" Zach asked as Clyde pushed open the gate.

"Supplies, survivors, and the story of what happened," Tess said, as they walked side-by-side down the perforated metal planking covering the pier. "But if eleven boats have already docked here, we'll be salvaging the dregs of the dregs."

The military camp was more clearly visible now. Ringed by the same type of fence as the pier, and that fence seemed to be all that was keeping the rainforest at bay. Single-storey huts, a few vehicles, and a radio antenna dotted with CCTV cameras so it could double as a watchtower.

"No smoke. No lights. No greeting," she said. "No one's here."

"What if we find people?" Zach asked. "We'll help, right?"

"Always," Tess said. "Don't ask me how. Not until we find them."

"Because not many people lived here, but Brazil was huge, wasn't it? Loads of people lived there, and it's not that far away."

"Suriname is immediately to the northeast," Clyde said. "Brazil is to the south and east. To the north, across the sea, are the Caribbean islands. Rainforest and rivers are everywhere except where it's water. But someone targeted the coastal cities in Brazil. You saw the images the helicopter brought back? Belem wasn't nuked. It was shelled."

"Why do you think they did that?" Zach asked.

"Orders," Clyde said. "Because that's what soldiers are trained to do."

"Yeah, okay, but why were those orders given?" Zach asked.

"Debate it later," Tess said. "Focus on the present. On what you can see, and whether that means danger for our ship."

"I can see jungle," Zach said.

"I think this is rainforest," Tess said.

"What's the difference?" Zach asked.

"Taller trees," Tess said.

"There's more crocs down there," Zach said as they neared the shore. "A lot more." He stopped. "Boss?"

"I see them," Tess said. "Don't worry, they're no threat to us up here."

The shore-side of the pier was blocked with another high gate, again with a lock, which had been professionally destroyed and then re-secured with a length of chain held in place by a half-metre-long steel road-tie.

"Someone left a note here, Commish," Clyde said, pointing at a corner of paper still taped to the broken lock.

"Probably a message warning people not to go any further," Zach said.

"Probably," Tess said. Beyond the gate were bones. Five femurs, a few smaller bones. No skulls. While the bones danced with insects, barely any muscle and flesh remained. Beyond the bones, the fence continued for another ten metres. At a sentry-post checkpoint, the fence branched left and right, following the shore. Beyond the sentry post was a battered military four-by-four, and a bullet-flecked civilian bus. On either side of the road were regimented rows of military prefabs, tall lampposts, and scraps of bone-filled clothing. But Tess was drawn to the figure in the lurid flower-patterned shirt. Definitely the kind of shirt someone would buy for an equatorial holiday. Probably after they arrived. Had it been someone from France, visiting Cayenne? Or had they taken their vacation on an island but made it to the mainland before the infection had found them? The feet and hands had been chewed, but not eaten, whereas the bones by the gate had been gnawed.

"Zom!" Clyde said. "The left."

It wore military green, though without any boots, and walked the monsoon-soaked embankment path between the fence and the river. Until it slipped, splashing into the water. The river rippled as dozens of semi-submerged crocs sped towards the floundering prey. The water churned, bubbled, and foamed black as the zombie was tugged underneath. But the zom kept on fighting. So did the croc. Finally, the zombie resurfaced. Not swimming, not even floating, just thrashing until it disappeared beneath the churn as another caiman took its turn.

"Let's go through," Tess said.

"What, in there?" Zach asked.

"Someone has to, and we're the ones here," she said. "The fence keeps the crocs outside."

"Tell that to the bones," Zach said.

"More zoms coming," Clyde said. "Two, on the embankment side of the fence."

Tess pulled the gate open, kicking the bones out of her path. "Two more in front of us," she said.

"Got them," Clyde said, raising his rifle. They fell, thudding into the dirt, causing a flock of iridescent birds to scatter from within the trees' broad branches.

"Hold," Tess said. The birds circled, landed on a distant hut's roof, only to dart skywards again before disappearing into the forest canopy. From behind the hut the birds had rejected as a roost, a zombie staggered out. A second followed. A third.

"Hold fire," Tess said, but only until she counted to ten. "Take them, Clyde. Zach, radio the ship. We need sailors, ammo, and something better than a broken chain to secure this gate. Same for the gate at the far end of the pier. Go."

Clyde kept firing, shifting aim from one rotting head to the next, but they came on faster than he could fire.

"Rivers and rainforest," he said. "Stops people leaving as much as arriving, doesn't it?"

She'd come ashore with a carbine, and without a suppressor, but silence wouldn't help them now. She raised her weapon, firing five shots before stepping back, and nearly losing her footing on a bone.

"Back through the gate," she said, taking up a position on the far side. At least two hundred zombies were heading towards them now, with more still emerging from around the buildings on the western side of the camp. "If we close the gate, can you fire through that fence?" she asked when her carbine clicked empty. The nearest zombies were now at the sentry post.

"No worries," Clyde said.

They slammed the gate shut, rethreading the chain. Clyde drew a bayonet, forcing it through two links, before replacing the original metal pin.

"That won't hold them for long," Tess said.

"No worries," Clyde said, balancing his barrel on a diagonal of chain-link. "The crocs aren't massing by the shore," he added as he fired. "Did you notice that? The caimans are survivors, too. Chased here by the zoms."

"Rescuing a bunch of gators is definitely beyond our remit," Tess said. "Can we blow up the pier?"

"Fuel tanks must be inland," Clyde said. "Pipe runs underneath. Just down there. We'd be blowing up the fuel-pipe."

Feet pounded the metal walkway behind them. Mackay, Zach, and Avalon all sprinted to a halt by the gate.

"Mackay, my left," Clyde said. "Doc, you're on the Commish's right. Zach, you get ready to sub in when I say. Count about five hundred so far."

"Where'd they all come from?" Zach asked.

"Nowhere," Avalon said. "They were here all along. In the trees, I suspect, and ventured further into the rainforest when our helicopter flew inland."

Conversation ceased as the zombies staggered nearer. Some wore uniform. Some wore civilian garb. Many wore unidentifiable rags, coated in oily mud.

Above, the helicopter buzzed low, returning from its inshore survey mission. Behind, feet clanged on the pier's metal planking as the captain led twenty sailors to their relief. Half were armed with rifles, the rest carried tools.

"Mr Renton, form a firing line," the captain said.

Tess stepped back, surveying the still approaching foe. The dead lay knee-deep, but even more walking corpses staggered out of the rainforest and around the huts, pressing up around the perimeter fence.

"Captain, how long will it take to refuel?" Tess asked.

"Which time?" she asked. "Because we'll need to refuel on our return. Unless we make Robben Island our next destination, we *must* hold this position."

"But how much weight can this bridge take?" Tess looked around for inspiration, and found her gaze caught by the V-shaped waves rippling across the river. "Can we dismantle the fence there, at the side of the pier, and build a new wall further back? Give the zoms somewhere else to go but straight on. Let them fall into the river."

Adams looked from the approaching undead to the caimans below. "Feed them to the crocs? Major Brook, hold this position. Mr Renton, your team with me. We're dismantling the causeway."

Four sailors began unbolting the metal plates that formed the pier's roadway. Two more detached a long section of chain-link, and then the horizontal support bars. Adams, with the rest, began bolting the plates into place. Tess returned to the firing line. The dead zombies had created a trip-hazard. In turn, that spoiled her aim. Every other bullet was wasted as the lurching column fell into a crawling mass now pushing against the gate.

"Fall back!" the captain called.

"Zach, get the doc to safety," Tess said. But she waited with Clyde. "Time for us," she said when everyone else had retreated.

"You go," Clyde said, not lowering his carbine.

"You first," Tess said.

Clyde lowered his weapon. "We need to pull that pin, and the bayonet, from the chain," he said.

"Exactly. You've got a son to get home to," she said. "You've got that rope, haven't you? Seal off the causeway. Tie the rope to the open gap, and tie it short. I'll jump off the gap and swing back to safety on the other side of the wall. Go on, before we run out of time. Go!" She pushed him back, and raised her carbine, firing into the nearest walking corpse. One shot, then the next. One target, then the next, until her magazine was spent.

"Commish!" Clyde called. "Ready."

Tess used the butt of her carbine to knock the pin loose, grabbed it, and pulled it free. That left only the bayonet. She gripped the knife's handle, took a breath. The gate creaked as another two undead pushed against it, while five behind pushed against them. Along the bridge, drills whirred as the new wall was still being built.

"Now!" Adams yelled.

The creaking was growing louder. The sound didn't come from the gate, but from below, from the pier itself. She tugged the bayonet free, and ran, looking for the rope. Behind her, the gates swung open. Flesh smacked into the metal road-plates as the undead fell forward. Bones cracked as more pushed forward, falling over that first rank. She saw the rope. One end was looped around the edge of a support post where the fencing had been removed. She wrapped it around her left hand, turned, and saw the horde approaching. Teeth snapping, hands grasping, hundreds, with more coming from the shore, and now only metres away.

She'd intended to walk-climb-haul herself around the outside of the fence, but with death approaching so fast, she jumped. Fell. The rope went taut, sending a jolt through her shoulders, and down her spine. Her feet entered the water, nearly ankle-deep. Bending her legs at ninety degrees, she raised them up as V-shaped ripples dashed towards her. A metre-long croc rose out of the water, mouth open, snapping closed on air a whisker shy of her heel.

Behind came a splash as the first zombie hit the water. Another. But her rope was being pulled upwards, and to a gap behind the new wall.

"Lost your bayonet," Tess said. "Sorry, mate."

"No worries," Clyde said.

"You didn't lose the rope," Avalon said. "So no harm done."

"Fall back!" Adams called. "We'll build another wall here."

"There!" Zach said, pointing upriver. "Look up there at the river bank. The crocs are crawling away."

"Says it all, really," Clyde said. "It really does."

2nd April

Chapter 34 - Evidence at Sea
Guyana

"Croc. Croc. Bug. Croc," Zach said, swiping left through the photographs downloaded onto the tablet. "Croc attacking a zom. Bug. Croc. Doc Flo took a lot of photos of animals."

"Check them all, and check them again," Tess said. "Right there is perfect for the desk, Clyde."

"I'll bolt it down," he said, and picked up the drill.

With the gym off-limits, Tess had requested permission to claim it as a temporary investigation centre. In practical terms, that involved bringing in a desk and a couple of whiteboards from the galley.

"If we're not moving any of the workout machines, does that mean we can use them?" Zach asked.

"Absolutely not," Tess said. "If coppers don't obey the law, you can't expect anyone else to. Back to those photos."

"Yeah, but what am I looking for?" Zach asked.

"You *won't* know it when you see it," Tess said. "Not at first. There *won't* be a perfectly timed eureka moment where everything slots into place. You have to build up a mental picture of what the scene was like before, and what happened next. From that, eventually, you'll work out who committed the crime."

"But there wasn't a crime at that French refuelling base," Zach said.

"Not that we know of," Tess said. "But it's still part of the wider crime which brought about the end of the world. When we return to Australia, there will be an inquiry with questions from parliament, and the U.N. Probably televised. Definitely published. Everyone will want to know what we've seen."

"Beats doing homework, right?" Clyde said.

"I guess," Zach said, and sounded unsure.

Tess picked up a pen, and began copying the names of the ships listed in the refuelling log onto the board.

It always took a while for the clues to slot into place. On this occasion, it had taken about thirty hours. There was a certain kind of copper, the worst kind of copper, for whom the first rule of policing was: *everyone can be charged with something*. That kind of rule belonged in the world her mother had escaped, and it was not going to be the foundation of the new world they were trying to create.

Avalon and Smilovitz had deliberately lied to the prime minister. That wasn't a crime, or else every session of parliament would be held behind bars. As the Canadians' avowed goal was to avoid production being diverted from essential logistics and medicine production, it would be ridiculous to charge them with wasting governmental resources. Treason was a possibility, though it would set a dangerous precedent if refusal to rush to production a WMD were to become an offence.

Not that she was in a position to arrest them. Not while aboard ship, when the captain and crew would ask why. She'd destroyed every entry in her diary mentioning the weapon, and was debating disposing of the rest, too. Not to cover up the crime, but to avoid any of the sailors learning the truth. The crew believed the mission was vital to constructing a weapon to end the undead, and so they'd given up a chance to head for home. Revealing the lie probably wouldn't lead to a lynching, or even to the scientists being stranded on the first stretch of rocky shore, but it would dent cohesion when they were sailing through very troubled waters.

When they returned to Canberra, she'd have to tell Anna. The Canadians didn't want their new society to begin with the deployment of another WMD, but she didn't want it to begin with a conspiracy and cover-up, so she'd have to tell O.O. too. It was difficult to predict what would happen afterwards. Probably, publicly, nothing.

The outcome depended on just how dire the situation in the Pacific had become, but the scientists were too valuable not to be put to work. They had still lied. There would be consequences. Someone would be blamed. She wouldn't let it be Zach, so she'd reassigned him, away from the scientists.

"France is gone, Europe's gone. The north is radioactive," Clyde said, reading from a tablet. "That was the message from the French warship, the *Aconit*. It's a grim start to the report, but it sets the tone. And there's that sub. Did it recently come south, or has it been in these waters for weeks?"

"Which sub d'you mean?" Zach asked.

"Both," Tess said.

"Speaking of those subs," Clyde said, "why did the *Adventure* want to sink the *Vepr*? How many ships did either submarine sink since the outbreak?"

"Write the questions up on that board," Tess said. "We won't answer all of them, but it'll help keep us focused on what answers we're looking for. Ah, this could be something. The first ship to travel through Dégrad des Cannes wrote its name, and the direction it was travelling. The others who came through copied that. So we know the *Viaje Segura* was going north. We don't know where they sailed from, or when. But it's a Spanish name."

"It means safe journey," Clyde said.

"I hope, for them, their journey was," Tess said. "But a Spanish name suggests they were from a Spanish-speaking country. So not Brazil. Potentially, then, they came from Uruguay or Argentina."

"We don't know the ship's range," Clyde said. "Or where else they might have refuelled."

"No, but we do know the coastal areas of Brazil were devastated during the nuclear war if not before," Tess said. "We can't draw a conclusion, not yet, but most of these ships were sailing north. We're not likely to find a refuge in the south, but there could be another fuel supply."

"But why didn't they go south around the Cape?" Clyde asked.

"That's another question to go up on our board," Tess said.

"What does the rest of the message say?" Zach asked.

"My Spanish isn't great," Tess said. "But I think this means: *we cannot go home, so we'll look for a harbour in the north.*"

"So if we know where they came from, we know where to avoid," Zach said. "We could ask Doc Leo for help with the translation."

"No, we should let the two scientists work," Tess said.

"The message from that French warship is weird," Zach said. "It's not very naval. Bet their captain was dead."

"Rule-seven in policing: leave the jumping to the kangaroos," Tess said. "All we can say is the message probably wasn't written by the captain. When we return this way to refuel, if the zoms are gone, we can take a look in the barracks."

"Or search the city of Cayenne," Clyde said. "We'd be more likely to find food there."

"Oh, yeah, good idea," Zach said. "Is it lunch yet?"

"Not even close," Clyde said. "Let's take a look at those photos of the zoms."

"The coolest one is… here," Zach said. "You can see two crocs each going for a different leg."

"Strewth, mate, no," Clyde said. "I want to look at the uniforms. See if we can piece together where they came from."

Tess returned to the photograph of the note left by the ships' captains. The notes were brief. Six in Spanish, four in Portuguese, and two, both from the warship, in French. She walked over to the whiteboard, and added another question: *Where did the French ship go*?

When she'd invented this make-work exercise, she'd expected it to be little more than a distraction for her and for the crew. Questions would produce theories they couldn't possibly confirm, but the more she stared at the map, at the list they'd found at the French harbour, and the summary of their recent voyage, one of those theories was beginning to solidify.

One line had been repeated three times by three different crews though with a slight variation: the Atlantic was dangerous.

"This photo's interesting," Clyde said. "I count three uniform jackets here."

"Do you know whose they are?" Zach asked.

"No, but someone in the crew might," Clyde said.

"Clyde, would a sub commander have orders for what to do if satellites went down?" Zach asked.

"Yep," Clyde said.

"So someone gave them an order to plaster South Africa and Brazil?"

"Yep," Clyde said. "South Africa is in the Southern Hemisphere. Relatively safe from fallout. Situated at the confluence of two oceans, it's a logical hub for regrouping and re-organising."

"But why attack it?" Zach asked.

"Because the purpose of nuclear weapons was to wipe out the species," Clyde said. "That's what it comes down to. Probably worth asking Leo for the details on that."

"Not at the moment," Tess said. "Three ships wrote that that the Atlantic was dangerous. Twice in Portuguese. Those would be ships from Brazil. If you were a ship sailing out of Natal, wouldn't you consider going east? The *Aconit* was a French stealth frigate. Not quite new-out-of-the-box, but still a piece of top-ranked military hardware. They didn't stay in Dégrad des Cannes, on either occasion, and they didn't go east, either."

"Do you think it was because of the subs?" Zach asked.

"Could be," Tess said.

The alarm rang for battle stations, even as the background engine thrum changed. "This is the captain. A wreckage field lies dead ahead, the result of a recent battle. We will look for survivors."

"Can we go to the deck and help?" Zach asked.

"Once you've secured everything here," Tess said. "But I'm going to take advantage of rank and go up to the bridge."

The captain stood by the bridge window, surveying the wreckage. The sea's surface was rainbow-slick from spilled oil, dotted with strips of sailcloth, split masts, and fractured fibreglass. A more intact hull was ringed by a pool of greenish-white foam.

"Was there a battle?" Tess asked.

"A massacre," Adams said. "Those were yachts. Sailing boats. Travelling together. At least twenty so far, but likely to be around ten times that number. They were deliberately sunk, and within the last week. Probably within the last seventy-two hours. Possibly even more recently than that. I've sent crews to the deck to look for survivors."

"Who would do this?" Tess asked. "Sorry, that's the wrong question. How was it done?"

"Heavy machine gun and explosives," Adams said. "It's too early to be certain, but I would think a torpedo."

"From a submarine?"

"Or from a ship," Adams said.

Tess crossed to a console, where Mr Kane was analysing images from the ship's cameras.

"Wait," she said. "No, can you go back a couple of seconds?"

"Where to?" the lieutenant asked.

"I thought I saw… yes, there's a life jacket, but without anyone inside. Captain, life jackets are marked with the name of the ship, aren't they? Can we pick some up?"

"We can certainly get images of them."

It took an hour to travel through the debris field. They were able to put names to fourteen different vessels either from life jackets, upturned hulls, or other floating wreckage. One of those ships was the *Isabella la Bella*, the last vessel to have recorded its name at Dégrad des Cannes.

3rd April

Chapter 35 - Tomorrow's Battle
Venezuela

At midday, the appointed hour for the planning meeting, Tess stepped into the wardroom, and was surprised to find it almost empty. Only Captain Adams and Colonel Hawker were present.

"Am I early?" she asked.

"After discovering the wreckage yesterday, I decided to limit who was involved in this decision," Adams said. "I can offer you water. We're out of tea, even the powdered kind. We're so low on supplies we might be forced to eat those dollar-bars you brought from Australia, though we're not so desperate yet."

"How does the wreckage of those yachts change our plans?" Tess asked.

"It clarifies them," Hawker said.

"That's an apt description," Adams said. "When you first pitched this mission of yours, I thought we might get as far as Ascension, and find it a flooded graveyard. On deciding to cross the Atlantic, I wasn't sure what we'd find. I didn't expect South America to be worse than Africa. By now, I thought we'd have met some local survivors with local knowledge of what happened here. We've only found ghosts and echoes, without a single piece of actionable intel."

"Does this change our destination?" Tess asked. "Are we skipping Colombia?"

"No," Adams said. "We will still aim for the cartel's redoubt."

"The lack of information limits our options," Hawker said. "I've been staring at this map for a week. Trying to think like these Herrera sisters. They knew what none of the rest of us did. They knew a nuclear war was coming."

"They knew about the zombies, too," Tess said.

"Proof if we needed it that we're not dealing with a rational mind," Hawker said. "We're planning with severely limited data. We know there's a coal mine and a runway, and there must be a water source, but the region is mostly desert." He pointed at the regional map displayed on the wall. "Our target is Puerto Bolivar, fifty kilometres west-southwest of Punta Gallinas, the most northerly point on the continent. It's a peninsula on a peninsula down which the border with Venezuela runs. The nearest major city is Maracaibo in Venezuela. Beyond the desert are mountains and jungle-rainforest. It's relatively untouched, and relatively uninhabited. But across the sea is the tourist-island of Aruba. If we ignore the mountains, it's not that far from the Venezuelan oil fields. This is not where you'd rebuild civilisation, but it's a great place to wait for the fallout to settle."

"The jungle, the mountains, and then the desert all create a barrier to refugees arriving by land," Adams said. "So does the sea, of course, and the wreckage we saw yesterday tells us what happens to unarmed ships sailing through these waters."

"You think they were attacked by the sisters?" Tess asked.

"The wreckage was too recent to have been caused by the *Vepr*," Adams said. "Either it was the sisters, or there is another hostile ship in these waters."

"The cartel had a coal mine," Bruce said. "I'd guess that was a cover for smuggling. But a mine requires miners, and they require food. That flotilla would have contained a lot of hungry mouths. Easier to sink them than persuade them to turn around."

"A coal mine and a water source," Tess said. "They must have a coal turbine."

"Probably, but they would have diesel for the ships," Adams said. "At least one of which was capable of destroying that flotilla of refugees. Don't think of the locals as miners. Not anymore. Think of them as conscripted soldiers. If they want to eat, they have to fight."

"They used the coal mine as cover for shipping narcotics," Tess said. "The limitation is you can only ship to countries which still imported coal."

"But the narcotics are cover, too," Hawker said. "Cover for the laboratory where they made compound-zom. But what about imports? They knew the apocalypse was coming. They'll have brought in weapons and food to keep that army fed."

"Weapons to sink a ship," Tess said. "You could install a deck-mounted torpedo-system on a fishing trawler, couldn't you? Wouldn't buying some of those be less conspicuous than buying a warship?"

"The captain on my first posting said you should always assume the worst," Adams said. "It isn't always the best advice. But here it holds. Natal is the most easterly cape. Punta Gallinas is the most northerly. Let us assume the sisters fed false intel to their associates, and the destruction of Natal was an attempt to wipe out the cartel. In which case, the sisters knew that a submarine might be sent to hunt them. Yes, they would have been prepared to try to sink a sub. A fishing trawler with a torpedo might be inconspicuous enough to manage it. But we must also assume they sank that flotilla we saw yesterday."

"That's not the worst case," Hawker said. "The worst case is that they're in command of the *Courageous* and the *Vepr*, or possibly even the *Adventure*."

"We've had no contact from that submarine since it sank the Russian boat," Adams said. "We should assume the worst, but not weigh ourselves down with fear."

"So what do we do?" Tess asked. "You said our choices are limited."

"They are pirates," Adams said. "They have to be destroyed. I'd hoped we'd find this place lightly defended, perhaps overrun with the undead, and we could gather the data the scientists needed. I dreamed we might even make use of the lab to construct a working prototype we could test locally. That recent wreckage suggests otherwise. Colonel?"

"We've no satellite data," he said, walking over to the screen, "so we've got to make a few guesses. We know the runway and pier are on the western side of this bay. Between the harbour and the northern cape are many small bays and inlets in which a boat might shelter. The cartel rule by fear, so wouldn't want to let even a fishing boat get too far beyond sight. They'll keep their fleet in the bay. It'll consist of captured yachts and sailing ships, but with a few large diesel-powered cargo vessels. Probably the coal-haulers. Plus at least one vessel equipped with torpedoes."

"We'll assume they have a few fast-boats," Adams said. "The entrance to the bay is about two kilometres wide, but we have no charts listing depth. We can't stopper the entrance."

"If this were me," Hawker said, "I'd place artillery positions on either wing of the bay. These women might have engineered the end of the world, but they were still narco-barons. They'd be limited to what could be smuggled in disguised as mining machinery. Forget artillery. But they could have portable missiles. I'm assuming Russian-made Igla anti-air, with a range of five kilometres."

"They have a runway," Tess said. "They could have a fighter plane or an attack-copter."

"They could," Adams said. "But how quickly can they launch it? We've installed a missile strut on the Seahawk. At fifty kilometres distance, the helicopter will launch. Commander Tusitala will approach the bay from the east, identifying any battle-capable vessels they have, but with the primary goal of launching a missile at the runway. A second strike will take out the airport fuel tanks. By which time, we will have entered firing range. Our first target will be smoke from their coal power station. The helicopter will draw fire from any portable artillery guarding the bay, and perhaps the warship. That will provide us with our next targets."

"We're using the helicopter as bait?" Tess asked.

"Nicko and I'll be aboard," Hawker said. "Worst case, if we have to ditch, we'll hike back to the coast, and paddle our way to New Zealand."

"Why can't we pick you up?" Tess asked.

"Because that'd mean the ship had to wait off the coast, within range of their surviving boats," Hawker said.

"I hope we can take out their ships, the runway, any above-ground fuel storage, and their power station," Adams said. "But we won't neutralise any shipping outside of that bay. I'm not concerned about speedboats chasing us away, but any larger vessel patrolling nearby. If our initial strike is unsuccessful, if the helicopter is downed, we will have to retreat, south, to French Guiana where we shall refuel before our enemy has a chance of destroying those fuel tanks. If we wait for Commander Tusitala, they could beat us to French Guiana."

"Let me be aboard the helicopter," Tess said.

"Not a chance," Hawker said. "This is what we trained for. We'll set an ambush, grab some wheels, and put the desert between us and them. We'll reach the Pacific long before you."

"I guarantee we'll destroy any coal power station," Adams said. "I can predict, with near certainty, we'll neutralise their runway and the majority of the shipping anchored in the bay. After which, the future becomes murky. I'd have a go reading some tea leaves, but we're out of even the powdered kind. There'll be no negotiations, no warnings, no attempt to take prisoners. We won't wait for them to fire at us, or to wait for a radioed call-and-response. That's why I didn't want anyone else here. We're acting on your intel, Commissioner. This is a coalmine, surrounded by desert. It's unlikely the undead have reached this far. Perhaps these sisters didn't, either. We are about to perpetrate a massacre. Is it justified?"

"Are there no alternatives?" Tess asked.

"The alternative was coming in with a hundred U.S. Rangers," Hawker said. "Without them, what we have is a warship capable of obliterating the target."

"We'll destroy their lab," Adams said. "And we can't let the scientists go ashore. You understand, I hope." She sounded genuinely apologetic, and more than a little disappointed.

“I do,” Tess said, a flash of guilt rushing through her bones. She looked at the map. They’d come this far. They couldn’t simply turn back. But until now, she’d not truly considered what would happen when they arrived. Her primary source was Sir Malcolm Baker, who’d never let the truth get in the way of a great headline. Toppley had confirmed some of it. But not enough for a shoot-first policy. Not in the old world. But this was a new and terrible era where police officers planned wars. An era when absolutely no one would ever condemn her for taking the more violent path.

“So our warship will appear from nowhere, and shell the shore,” she said. “It won’t be the first time that’s happened since the outbreak.”

4th April

Chapter 36 - A Desert Rose
Puerto Bolivar, Colombia

Before dawn arrived, everyone was at their station, counting the seconds during the stultifyingly tense period of inactive expectation preceding the battle. For Tess, Zach, and Clyde, their place was on the helicopter deck with Nicko and Bruce. Zach and Nicko were playing poker so badly they seemed to have invented an entirely new game. Clyde was either asleep, or pretending to be. Bruce was reading a pocket-size volume of poetry, though he'd not changed the page for ten minutes.

The previous evening, Captain Adams had explained the plan to the crew, giving more detail than Tess had expected, though not nearly as much as she'd have liked. The *Te Taiki* would be used as bait to draw the large ships out of the harbour and into the bay's entrance. There, those vessels would be sunk, blocking access or egress to all but the smallest ships. To make the warship appear a tantalising prize, the fast-boats would be allowed to approach close, and even board. That should deter portable artillery fire from the shore until said artillery could be neutralised.

Pirates weren't zombies; they could shoot back. She didn't know who the enemy really was. Farmers? Miners? Street-level dealers? Professional mercenaries like Kelly and her crew? What were they armed with? Shotguns, rifles, RPGs? How many were there? What if they were just local survivors, taking shelter on a desolate swathe of coast, hoping a rescue ship might arrive? What if they took prisoners? What if—

But her musings were cut short by Commander Tusitala sliding down the ladder.

"Are we a go?" Hawker asked.

"Cap'n thinks they're gone," Tusitala said. "We're ten kilometres out, and there's not a squeak on the radar or puff from their power station. We're going up, but for a recce."

"That's me, kid," Oakes said. "You can pay up when I get back."

"I thought I was winning," Zach said.

As the helicopter took off, Tess headed to the bridge.

"Deserting your post, Commissioner?" Adams said, relief evident in both voice and words. "I'll have to make you walk the plank."

"There's nothing on radar?" Tess asked.

"Or radio. Nothing on the horizon."

"Radiation?" Tess asked.

"Lower than Natal," Adams said.

Which was an inexact answer loaded with implications.

"Negative visual on the bay," Hawker's voice came amplified through the bridge speaker. "No ships. Repeat, no ships in the bay. Negative on artillery. Pier on the western spit. No ships at the pier. Scratch that. Two sunken vessels. Fifty metres long. Steel hull. Cargo ships."

Tess turned her attention to the images being relayed from the helicopter, still showing the view of the empty bay. The sea became the shore. The shallow beach morphed into desert, except in the south where it rose into grey-shadowed mountains. The image lurched as the helicopter pivoted, and she saw a long and battered pier. Ashore, the beach and desert were stained black with a pitch-trail of carbon leading to a towering mountain of coal.

"Is that the coal bunker?" Tess asked. "Assuming those railway freight cars are a standard size, that's got to be two hundred metres by five hundred long. That's a lot of coal."

"It is," Adams said.

The freight-railway tracks disappeared into the desert, in turn giving a hint as to where the mines themselves lay, but the helicopter had already moved on, buzzing high over a ramshackle company town where a handful of large villas were encircled by at least a hundred concrete block-houses. Metal roofs. Stubby trees. A basketball court. A stalled car. Onshore fuel tanks. A mansion with a high wall. It was a confused snapshot as the helicopter flew low and fast, but one constant was the bodies.

"They're all dead," Tess said, and then corrected herself. "They're not moving."

"There's a desalination plant," Adams said. "That type of pipe-work is unmistakable. That could be a large diesel turbine next to it."

"Where?" Tess asked, reflexively turning away from the screen.

"Near the onshore fuel tanks," Adams said.

"They weren't burning coal," Tess said. "Can you ask the commander to turn around?"

"Not until they've reached the airport. I want confirmation there's no aerial threat," Adams said. "That's it! There! That's the runway."

Three twin-engine civilian island hoppers were parked next to the runway, but there were no helicopters or fighter planes.

"No cooking fires. No smoke. No people," Tess said. "Just bodies."

They lay clustered near the runway's edge. A pile of ten, then twelve, then six, almost as if they'd been waiting for a plane. More likely, the survivors killed some zoms, retreated a few paces, killed some more, retreated again, and again, until they'd died.

"There's no threat here," Tess said. "I don't know what we've found, but it's not a danger to us. Look at this place. It's nearly perfect for a refuge. Remote. Desolate. With enough coal for a year. But there's a splash of green beneath those mountains on the southern shore of the bay. There's water here at the edge of the desert. Oh, it's perfect, and there's no one here. Sir Malcolm lied, and sent me to the other side of the world."

"Commander Tusitala, return to the ship," the captain said. "Mr Renton, I want a shore party. Take the boat up to the pier. Commissioner, would you care to assist them?"

"Could I borrow the helicopter?" Tess asked. "Send Bruce to the airport. See if there's anything aboard the planes indicating where they've come from. But I'd like the helicopter to drop me off near the houses. That's where we'll find food, and where we might find the reason Sir Malcolm sent us here."

The helicopter's rotors whipped up a thick black cloud of carbon-stained sand as it slowed its descent to a hover, a metre above the cleared and empty ground adjacent to the coal bunkers.

"Stay frosty, Zach!" Oakes said.

"In this heat, the electricity bill would bankrupt him," Clyde yelled back. "On three, Zach, but don't jump."

Which was when Oakes pushed Zach out of the helicopter. Clyde slid downward, carbine raised.

Head bowed, Tess dropped off the edge, and the helicopter ascended, even as Zach stood up.

"What the hell, Nicko!" Zach yelled up into the swirling black cloud.

"The sarge didn't want you doing a slice-and-splat impression of a boiled egg," Clyde said.

The swirling mist of orange grit and black soot, given flight by the rotors' updraft, slowly settled, revealing a landscape that had been apocalyptic long before the outbreak.

"Who'd want to live here?" Zach said.

"I was just thinking it reminds me of home," Tess said. "Except for the bodies."

"Weapon up, Zach," Clyde said. "Eyes ahead, gate and fence, road and alleys, doors and corners. We're walking abreast. Those are dead zoms," he added. "Headshot."

"Head *stab*," Zach said. "That bloke's still got the knife in his eye."

"Five shot, four stabbed, one bludgeoned, three uncertain," Tess said. "That's just those between here and the road. Gate is down, but so is the fence. Looks like it was for keeping dogs out, rather than thieves."

"Who'd steal coal?" Zach asked, wiping the sooty dust from his forehead.

"Anyone who wants to boil their billy," Clyde said. "Rail tracks."

"There's a train here?" Zach asked.

"To bring the coal from the mine," Tess said. "That other set runs to the harbour where the coal would be loaded aboard a ship."

"Freight cars at four o'clock," Clyde said. "Single loco. Looks to be diesel."

"Coal goes out by ship, so the tracks run to the mine, but not back to civilisation," Tess said. "Ships need diesel, so they'd ship in extra for the people. This place is remote. Very remote. More remote than it appeared on the map, so you know what we should ask? Where'd the zoms come from?"

"Where are we heading, boss?" Clyde asked.

"The houses," Tess said. "Food's a priority, and if there's none here, we'll be gone before nightfall. Sir Malcolm lied to us, or he was misled. I think this is just a remote coal mine."

"Zom," Zach said, pausing by the body. "Or was she? She's got a shovel next to her. But she was shot in the head. I guess people can get shot in the head, too."

"First rule of policing, don't jump to conclusions," Tess said as they picked their way around the bodies and over to the broken fence.

"You said the first rule was check your boots, and that it was universal," Zach said.

"Fine. Call that rule-six," Tess said.

"Nah, you said rule-six was listen more than you talk."

"That one's universal, too," Clyde said. "Bodies here. Guns next to them. Kalashnikovs. No magazines. Skulls intact. Think this one was shot."

"Died at least a week ago," Tess said. "Could be two weeks. Hard to tell in this climate."

"Zoms don't shoot people," Zach said.

"No, they don't," Tess said.

More bodies lined the road. Mostly zombies. Mostly shot in the head. So many it was easy to overlook the dismembered limbs, the torn flesh, and the clawed corpses of the defenders.

"Was this a fighting retreat?" Tess asked.

"Can't tell," Clyde said.

"AK-47," Tess said, as she pointed at a Kalashnikov. "Old model, but a new stock. The magazine is missing."

"Let me check that house," Clyde said and walked up the pair of wooden steps to the broken-open door surrounded by bullet-flecked plaster.

"We'll wait down that alley," Tess said. "Cover your mouth, Zach. You don't want any of these flies hitching a ride."

"Miners lived in there," Clyde said, coming out of the back door. "Kitchen is meagre, but it's been looted. They took the food, left everything else."

"Someone survived the battle," Tess said. "After they killed the zoms, they came back for the food and ammo."

Not everyone living in this working town had been a miner, evidenced by the sun-bleached trike at the alley's end.

The larger houses were easy to find. A low terracotta-coloured wall ran around the entire block. Just inside the wall, on either side of the road, were two small, but neat, houses, both with squares of front-garden-patio, a shade-covered porch, two storeys, and a flattened roof on which was another sunshade, and where the snipers had stood. On the road, the pavement, the lawn, the low wall, the porch, the doorway, and inside, lay bodies of the undead. Shot, stabbed, bludgeoned; there had been hundreds here. Not because of these two small houses, but what lay beyond: a villa that was ringed with a high wooden palisade, which blocked from view everything inside. The tall gate was open, and filled with more corpses.

"About five hundred," Tess said.

"Six," Clyde said. "They spill over behind the watchtowers."

"What watchtowers?" Zach asked.

"Those two houses by the road," Clyde said. "The flat roofs are so someone could stand guard."

"Keeping those trees watered would have cost a fortune," Tess said.

Four trimmed palms lined either side of the pavement, leading to the mansion. Or was it a compound? Who had wooden walls somewhere without forests? Someone who wanted to display their wealth.

"Whoa!" Zach said as he slipped on a pile of spent brass.

"Got you, mate," Clyde said, grabbing his arm.

"Rule-one," Tess said, as she picked her way through the bodies and to the wide-open gates.

The clothes worn by the dead were familiar from the outback. Denim bleached by the sun rather than in the factory, criss-crossed with stitches from where rips had been repaired rather than cherished. They were work-clothes because living in these harsh conditions *was* labour. Home-tailored to fit rather than some designer's aesthetically tight and baggy. Practical rather than modest. Affordable rather than cheap. Faded, but not drab. With a scrub, they'd be found in any arid mine or farming town in either hemisphere. Except for the priest, identifiable from dog collar and crucifix, though he still gripped the barrel of an assault rifle in his hands.

"You notice what's missing?" Tess asked.

"Not the guns," Zach said.

"Missing from the bodies. What the dead aren't wearing," she said. "Very few are wearing hats."

"I've not seen many zoms in hats," Zach said.

"The dead without a head wound must be the immune," Tess said. "Some of these would be locals, infected here, and I can't see many hats lying in the dirt, so they left their home after dark. That's when the zoms came. The locals threw up what barriers they could, and rushed here. To this compound because it had walls."

"I'll tell you something else that's missing," Clyde said. "There are no dead kids."

"You spoke too soon," Zach said.

Just inside the courtyard, lay the body of a boy, shot in the head, but with an AK-47 lying partially beneath his body.

The courtyard was large enough for a dozen cars to be parked, though none were there now. Another row of desiccated jungle-palms separated the car park from the house, a squat two-storey with small windows and white-painted walls. A marble colonnade supported an upper-floor balcony, which had an awning above and flowerpots beneath. The house was big enough for perhaps ten bedrooms, depending on their size. A large house, but not a huge one. The main entrance had wide wooden double doors, which were closed. All of the windows had frosted glass; an odd feature for any room that wasn't a bathroom. But most noticeable of all were the bodies.

"You okay, Zach?" she asked.

"Mmm," he said.

"Get on the radio," she said. "Tell…" She paused, uncertain how to finish the sentence.

At the edge of the courtyard, close to the house, were three bodies. Their eyes had been plucked from their skulls, but that could have been the work of birds. The rest was the work of evil incarnate. Each victim was pinned to a table by a kitchen knife embedded in ankle, thigh, wrist, and forearm. That had only been the beginning of their torment.

The body of the man nearest the house was etched with a root-work of cuts: thin, long, unbroken lines running from scalp downward. Some made it to chest, to groin, to fingers, but only five incisions made it all the way to the toes. It was as if the killer had been attempting the longest unbroken incision.

The second victim had been partially skinned. Squares of skin hung loose from her abdomen and thighs, exposing the muscle beneath. The side of each square measured ten centimetres in length. Tess could tell because the killer had marked the woman's entire body before they'd begun, using a ruler and marker pen, both of which lay in the blood-soaked sand.

The third victim, by contrast, was nearly unmarked. In addition to the blades wedged in ankle and wrist, more had been hammered into her left arm, but one must have nicked an artery, mercifully ending the terminal ordeal.

"Tell the captain we've found three bodies, executed in the fashion favoured by the cartel," Tess said.

"Empty ammo crates over on those tables," Clyde said. "A few weapons, too. Assault rifles, RPGs, a few shotguns. No ammo, but there's a lot of ammo boxes. A lot of spent cartridges. They fought a real battle here."

"The locals," Tess said. "After the outbreak, when the zoms came, they retreated here and used the cartel's arsenal to hold back the undead. At some point, they turned their defence into an attack. Killed the zoms. *All* the zoms, because we've seen none. They gathered the food from the houses and stripped the ammo from the dead." She turned back to the mutilated corpses. "Then the sisters returned home."

"You think this was them?" Clyde asked.

"Captain said they're coming ashore," Zach said. "We're not to touch anything. Whoever did that's sick," he added.

"They are," Tess said. "It's just like we saw in the bunker in Canberra, like I saw in Broken Hill. It's the work of the cartel's assassins. Take a look around, Clyde. Don't touch anything."

"Understood," he said.

"I don't," Zach said.

"This is a message," Tess said. "So whom was it left for? The wooden walls are there to make a statement, but this place isn't really built for a siege. Defence would come from its remoteness, but every luxury would have to be imported, and few could make up for the coal floating thick in the air. The sisters might have come here, but they didn't *live* here. Sir Malcolm wasn't lying. He was brought here, but because the sisters didn't care if he reported the location, and we came looking. These three victims were left here as a message, and I think that message is intended for people like us."

"Commish, over here!" Clyde called.

On a trestle table in the shade of the courtyard's wall was a laptop plugged into a satellite dish transmitter, next to a very old-fashioned, solid stone, domed cake-stand.

"Power cable runs to a generator in that hut," Clyde said, pointing to a room built into the walls of the palisade.

“What’s under—” Zach began, his hand reaching for the cake stand even as he spoke.

“Don’t!” Clyde said, even as Tess grabbed Zach’s arm.

“What?” the young man said.

“People who skin people alive are the kind who leave traps,” Tess said.

“Oh. Like a bomb or something,” Zach said. “I thought it was going to be someone’s head under there.”

“The termites aren’t interested,” Clyde said, pointing to the industrious column of insects marching from beneath the wood-fronted palisade to the trio of crucified corpses. “So whatever is under there isn’t something they’d call food. Step back,” he said. “Far side of the building. Out of the line of sight.”

“Do you know what you’re doing?” Tess asked.

“This is the work I’ve been doing for a decade,” Clyde said.

“Bomb disposal?” she asked.

“War zone clear-up, because no farmer ever asked for a battle to be fought in their field. Go on.”

Tess took Zach’s arm and pulled him around the corner.

“Clear!” Clyde called a scant few seconds later.

Beneath the pottery dome was a digital camcorder.

“It’s just a camera?” Zach said. “Is there a video?”

Clyde held up the memory card. “Yep. But I’m more interested in why the generator has another power-cable running towards the rear of the house.”

The back of the house had even larger doors than the front, with a clear route to a similarly large rear gate. A massive table suggested the owners might have dined outdoors, while a roofless cube-frame of concrete and steel might have once held an awning. Hanging from it now were three large pulleys, through which a rope had been threaded. From one end hung a hook and chain. The other was attached to an electric winch into which the generator’s power cable ran.

"Hold," Clyde said, walking up to the door. His right hand on his gun, he ran his left around the ajar entrance. "Clear," he said, and pulled the door open. "Do you see this tripwire? It's been disconnected."

"It's a trap?" Tess asked.

"Think so," Clyde said. "Wait here, let me take a look."

"Winch, pulley, rope," Tess said. "How long do you think that rope is, Zach? A hundred metres?"

"You'll want to see this," Clyde called, pushing the door open wide.

They entered a large hall, in which the furniture had been pushed apart and the rugs pulled back. To the left, through a door-less alcove, lay the kitchen with a restaurant-sized range, two double-wide refrigerators, and an industrial dishwasher. The cupboards above were flat-pack. So was the table, and the sofa and chairs in the sitting room at the front of the house. The paintings, rugs, and the empty flower vases were similarly European, though they imitated a Mediterranean style. She wasn't sure what style the wainscoting was, except that it had been used as camouflage.

Clyde knelt next to where the cream-painted wood panelling had been removed from the wall.

"It's C4," Clyde said. "Did you see where the panelling had been removed in the other rooms?"

"I only went as far as the front doors," Tess said. "The detonators have been removed, yes?"

"The trigger as well," Clyde said. "There's a tripwire rigged to the rear door, another at the front. That should have set off a timer. But it's all been disconnected."

Tess turned to Zach who was staring down into the hole taking up half of the rear hall.

The hole was three metres wide, two long, and had another pulley hanging above, attached to a steel pin. When the hole was covered with the floorboards and a rug, a chandelier would hang from the pin. That pulley was in the perfect position for a rope running through the doors and to the winch outside. Tess joined Zach by the hole's edge.

"Shine your light down there, Zach," she said. "About thirty metres deep, maybe a bit less."

"The walls are mostly concrete," Clyde said. "The C4 is positioned to level the property."

"Bringing it down on top of this hatch," Tess said. "A hatch which leads to a tunnel. The whole property is a front. We were supposed to see those bodies outside, then force our way in, trigger the bombs, and level the house, hiding this tunnel from view."

"The stone cake stand would have kept the camera and memory card safe," Clyde said.

"Are we going to watch whatever's on the memory card?" Zach asked. "Or are we going down?"

"Clyde, what do you think?" Tess asked.

He shone his flashlight downwards. "There's a ladder at the side. Looks like a cage-elevator at the bottom." He stepped back, and shone his light up at the pulley and hook hanging from the ceiling. "No coal power station, so why set up at a coal mine? Has to be for the mining machinery, so they can excavate long tunnels."

"It's for their lab, isn't it?" Zach said. "This *is* where they made the zoms! We're going to look, right?"

"Sooner or later, *I* am," Clyde said, picking up a length of rope. "I say now. I'll belay down, check for bodies, or movement, or more traps."

"We'll pull you back up if there are," Zach said.

"I'll jump up that ladder if there are," Clyde said. "Boss?"

"Sooner or later we've got to look, and I'd like to get out of here as soon as possible."

Holding the rope, Clyde stepped into air, and began quickly descending.

"Yeah, nah, it's not for me," Zach said.

"What isn't?" Tess asked.

"Soldiering," Zach said.

"I'm with you there," Tess said.

"Clear!" Clyde called up. "Safe to come down. It's a staging post. Supplies gathered to be taken top-side."

"I'm going down," Tess said. "It's up to you whether you want to wait here for the captain, Zach."

"Wait here with the crucified bodies and the explosives?" Zach asked. "Yeah, nah, I'm going down. You want me to get a rope?"

"Rule-nine, stick with what you know," Tess said. "So we'll take the ladder. Hang on. Let me see your gear. Safety on. Lights on. And the camera. Might as well record everything." She turned his cap back to front. "Eyes open. Ears, too. If you think you hear something, or see something, say so. Overly cautious has never been listed as a cause of death."

Chapter 37 - Solar Panels Underground
Puerto Bolivar, Colombia

It took Tess and Zach longer to descend than it had for Clyde, giving the soldier time to finish surveying the antechamber.

"Four metres by five," Clyde said, when they reached the bottom. "Just over head-height tall, with a horizontal tunnel leading due west. That tunnel's laid with railway tracks on the right-hand-side, and storage on the left. Two handcars over there, with a generator, rope, winch, and hook at the front of each. Anchor the other end of the rope, and the handcar becomes a crude train."

Tess shone her light on the fuel gauge of the first handcar's generator, then on the rubber tube wedged into the fuel-cap of the second. "No fuel," she said.

"There are guns in these boxes," Zach said.

"AKMs," Clyde said. "Couple of hundred in those crates lining the side of the tunnel, but they're unloaded and factory fresh."

"No crates of ammo here," Tess said, shining her light around the space, stopping the beam on the long tunnel leading west. "But you wouldn't stockpile guns without the ammo. Those crates don't have any factory markings." Something beyond the rifle crates reflected the light. "What's that?"

Zach darted forward before either Tess or Clyde could stop him. "It's a bike!" he said. "They brought bicycles down here. I guess after they ran out of fuel for the handcars. Nice bikes, too. Brand-new, they look."

"Let me take point," Clyde said, skipping ahead of him. "Ten bikes. Brand-new."

"Ten?" Tess said, following them both. "And more crates beyond. We'll take a brief look, then head back to the surface."

"Safety on, Zach, but stay next to the Commish," Clyde said. "Be ready to run back to the ladder."

"I don't think any zoms are down here," Tess said, shining her light on the loot stashed on the left-hand-side of the tunnel.

"Maybe it's Zach's influence," Clyde said. "Maybe it's Mick Dodson's, but I'm reminded of every horror movie I've ever seen. This tunnel must have another entrance."

"No horror movie has solar panels," Zach said. "They're still in the box. More solar panels here. Hang on… yeah. Like, twenty boxes. For camping, I guess, from the picture. For a family holiday in a camper van. Cool."

"You could buy those in a store," Tess said. "Same with the bikes."

"Not the AKs," Clyde said.

"Should I take some photos for evidence?" Zach asked.

"I'm recording video," Tess said. "That'll do for now."

"Are you recording sound too?" Zach asked. "You should have said."

"Insulated cables," Clyde said. "More ahead. I think they're heavy-duty electrical transmission lines."

"Keep going," Tess said.

"Boxes of walkie-talkies," Zach said. "Bet you could buy those in a shop, too."

"Or online," Tess said.

Next were empty water barrels. Then three more compact generators, five crates of emergency blankets, ten crates of industrial laundry detergent, and five of luxury hand soap. A stack of portable stoves, ten microwaves, still in their boxes, five beer-fridges, and ten portable camping toilets.

"Canoes," Clyde said. "Three self-assembly canoes."

"This is totally weird," Zach said.

"Tunnel widens ahead," Clyde said. "Another antechamber. It's… it's not a lab."

The chamber was ten metres by eight, with wooden props regularly spaced two metres apart, supporting a wood-plank ceiling. The tunnel, and tracks, curved almost ninety degrees, and continued nearly due south.

"They excavated this chamber so they could make that turning," Tess said, shining her light at the wooden ceiling, looking for a hatch. "They wanted the exit beneath that mansion, and must have misjudged their digging. The mansion must have been built first. Interesting."

"Maybe it's a bunker," Clyde said.

"It's a treasure cave!" Zach declared, making a beeline for the furthest corner. "There's a fridge. A lot of beer inside. Just beer. No food. There *is* a microwave, and canned food. Chilli. Lots of it."

"Is the beer cold?" Tess asked.

"Nah," Zach said. "Do you want one?"

"Never when on duty," Tess said. "Check inside the microwave, and nearby for hot food, and for any half-finished bottles. Anything to indicate someone was here within the last day or so."

Her torch settled on the sofa, heaped with blankets, but with only one pillow. Facing the sofa, propped on the fridge, was a small TV and DVD player. A cable ran from that, and from the fridge and microwave, to a silent generator.

"Is the generator petrol or diesel?" Tess asked, picking her way around the waist-high maze of boxes and crates.

"It's petrol," Zach said.

"Same as the portable generators we saw further up the tunnel," Tess said. "Diesel would be brought in for the ships. Petrol wouldn't be a priority."

"So why buy petrol generators?" Zach asked.

"They didn't think it through," Tess said. "They didn't know what they needed, so bought whatever they could think of, which could be sent to wherever the coal-ships sailed to, or those small planes flew from. There's an air of desperation in this stash. Too much for one person. Not enough for a group."

"You mean like they had a credit card and went online to buy everything they could?" Zach said.

"Exactly that," Tess said. "So perhaps these supplies weren't laid in by the sisters, but by whoever was guarding this place for them. Bought after this guard was told precisely what was about to happen to the world."

"There's a dunny here," Zach said, pulling aside the sheets hanging in the furthest corner.

"A portable toilet. A sofa brought from upstairs," Tess said. "A microwave, a fridge. One pillow. One sofa. One person."

"But why hang sheets in front of the loo if there's no one else to see?" Zach asked.

"Standards and routine," Clyde said, bending to open a crate. "Important to maintain both when you're living like this."

"Okay, fine, sure," Zach said. "But there's a mansion upstairs. Why not live there?"

"With those bodies outside, would you want to live up there?" Clyde asked. "There's enough food for a year here as long as you didn't mind eating chilli. Here's a box of first-aid kits. Contains twelve. Box has been opened. One kit's been used for dressings and sutures."

"Zoms," Zach said.

"Since when do zombies bandage themselves up?" Clyde asked.

"Nah, I mean someone was bitten, and stuck on a bandage before they turned," Zach said, aiming his light towards the other tunnel.

"No wrappers, no waste," Clyde said. "That was dumped somewhere else. Toilet would have been emptied there, too."

"I bet that tunnel, ultimately, links with the coal mine," Tess said. "Looks to be a bit wider, and just as full of stashed supplies. A coal mine is a dry, stable temperature environment, making it a better place to store things than above ground in a desert."

"But the petrol generator was bought by someone who didn't get to order what fuel was brought in," Zach said. "So was this all bought by the tunnel-guard?"

"Canoes," Tess said. "He bought canoes. You know what that tells me? No one ever audited what he bought. After the tunnels were dug, and the crates of rifles were brought down, there was a lot of unfilled space. He asked his bosses, the sisters, if he could fill it with things he thought would be useful, and he went overboard. But no one checked.

No one stopped him. No one more important than him looked. Or cared."

"It's not just rifles," Clyde said, having stopped next to a stack of military transport-cases next to a pillar-prop.

"What's that?" Zach asked. "Strewth, that's a bazooka."

"It's a Swedish-made AT4," Clyde said. "A single-use, anti-tank missile. Do not press the trigger," he added as Zach picked it up.

"Six crates?" Tess asked, shining her light on the ground. "They were moved here recently. So the main supply, the important supplies, must all be further down that other tunnel. AKMs with no factory markings, and Swedish anti-tank missiles."

"Whose tanks were they going to blow up?" Zach asked, raising the AT4 to his shoulder.

"That thing has a range of five kilometres," Clyde said. "You could take out a building, or a ship, if you knew how to aim. You could definitely take out this mine, so keep your finger away from the trigger."

"Why Swedish?" Tess asked. She shone her light around the boxes until the beam fell on the railway tracks. With the beam, she followed the rails into the tunnel, just far enough to catch the edge of a moving shadow.

"Hello!" she called. "*Hola*!"

A woman stepped out from behind the stacked boxes just inside the second tunnel. The boxes were wooden, similar in style and size to the AKM crates near the tunnel exit, and stacked to head-height, providing a perfect spot for eavesdropping on the conversation.

"My name's Tess Qwong, from Australia," she said. "Who are you?"

"*La cura*," the woman said, bringing her hand up fast. Something flew from it, too fast for Tess to see, thumping and rolling across the loose-packed dirt.

"Grenade!" Clyde yelled, and dove on top of the thrown explosive.

Tess reached for her slung rifle even as she dropped to a kneeling crouch, but she'd only raised the weapon to forty degrees before the detonation.

The mine quaked. Dirt rained from between the wooden roof panels. Dust fountained from the tunnel while rock pattered from the ceiling.

"Zach?" Tess asked. "You okay?"

"Sorry, boss," Zach said.

She turned towards him, and saw his face covered in blood and dust.

"Zach! Are you hit?"

"It's not my blood," he said.

She turned towards Clyde, except he was standing up, gun levelled towards the second tunnel.

"Dud," Clyde whispered, his voice hoarse. "Grenade was a dud."

"So what just happened?" Tess asked, shining her light on the rock-fall covering the second tunnel.

"Sorry, boss," Zach said again. "That was me."

"The—" Clyde began, coughed, and cleared his throat. "The AT4, right?"

"Yeah, I just… yeah, sorry," Zach said.

The ringing in Tess's ears dropped in volume, freeing more of her neurons to process the last ten seconds. Zach had fired the missile into the tunnel, well beyond the woman who'd thrown the grenade. The explosion had knocked them all from their feet, but where the antechamber had pillars supporting the roof, the tunnel's mouth had none. The roof had fallen, blocking the tunnel, and crushing the woman.

"Back to the exit," Tess said. "Zach, help Clyde. Clyde, help Zach."

But she staggered her way over to the crushed corpse. The woman was dead. Only about thirty, so not one of the sisters. Dressed in beige cargo-shorts and shirt, with a long knife at her belt, and a bag around her neck from which another grenade had fallen. A river of dust fell from the ceiling, directly into the dead woman's open eyes. Tess shone her light on the woman's arm, and on the old tattoo: a three-leafed branch.

"Boss, you coming?" Clyde asked. "Because that roof's about to come down."

"She's cartel," Tess said, following them to the exit-tunnel. "Clyde, that C4 upstairs. Is there any chance the detonators were duds?"

"Like the grenade?" he asked. "Could be. I'll check upstairs."

"She was in the cartel?" Zach asked.

"That's right. Someone senior. Had the tattoo, and had it for about a decade."

Tess wasn't sure of the last, but the certainty brought comfort, and not just to Zach.

"So I did okay?" Zach asked, just as a loud crash shook the tunnel, causing more dust to cascade onto the railway tracks.

"Next time, try a bullet rather than a bomb," Clyde said. A growling creak came from behind them, as much a sensation beneath their feet as a sound in the air. "This time, I say we run."

"The detonator looks real," Clyde said, when they'd finally climbed back up and into the house. "There's an obvious way to test it."

"Not around here," Tess said. "We shouldn't stay, not when the ground is liable to collapse. Call the ship, Zach. Warn them about the tunnels."

"Yeah, there's no need to radio them," Zach said, standing in the open door. "They're outside."

Four figures, all in hazmat-orange suits with transparent helmets, walked slowly across the courtyard execution ground. Two carried rifles: Oakes and Hawker. Avalon was recording video. Leo was almost swimming in sweat behind his transparent visor, hauling two bright-blue rigid holdalls, one over each shoulder.

"What did you do, where did you go, and what did you touch?" Avalon demanded, her voice muffled by the protective face covering.

"Why are you dressed like that?" Zach asked.

"You disappeared off radio," Avalon said. "Who does that?"

"They deployed VX gas," Hawker said. "We found about a hundred bodies by the harbour. Locals. They were poisoned on the waterfront."

"It wasn't gas," Avalon said. "It would have been an aerosol."

"VX, seriously?" Tess asked.

"Oh, don't worry," Avalon said. "If you'd touched it, you'd be dead already."

"The captain's recalled everyone to the ship," Hawker said.

"What's VX?" Zach asked.

"A nerve agent," Oakes said. "One drop on your skin, and you'll be dead in minutes."

"Is there a cure?" Zach asked.

"Atropine," Leo said, holding up one of the two bags. "But it's not really a cure, so let's get out of here."

"Yeah, big needle, straight to the heart," Oakes said.

"He's kidding," Clyde said.

"He is? Oh, good," Zach said.

"The needle goes into your thigh," Clyde said.

"You can continue winding him up when we're back aboard," Tess said, looking down at her hands. Assuming they lived that long.

Chapter 38 - Atropine for the Soul
Puerto Bolivar, Colombia

They had to catch a boat back to the ship, and not from the pier, but from a sandy stretch of shore four hundred metres to the east. Zach spent the walk exaggerating what they'd found in the tunnel, talking out of the same fear that kept her quiet. At the boat, they had to strip, with most of their gear left on the shore. Clothing and weapons could be replaced, though they kept the memory card, and the phone on which she'd been recording video since the helicopter had dropped them off. At the ship, they had to go through a decontamination scrub, after which she was exhausted.

"You're clear," Avalon said, handing her a towel.

"Are you sure?"

"You'd be dead if you weren't," she said, returning the atropine back to the case. "There are clothes here, and the captain wants to see you on the bridge."

"Are you certain it was VX?" Tess asked.

"Either that, or something with very similar effects," Avalon said without a trace of her usual logical stubbornness. "I'll have a report for you and the captain within the hour."

The shower-damp helped hide the fear-sweat as she made her way to the bridge. Leo and Bruce were already there, as were a full watch of sailors.

"I apologise, Commissioner," the captain said. "Had we flown the helicopter over the pier first, we would have seen the dead flamingos among the bodies of the people."

"Dead flamingos?" Tess asked.

"They must have arrived after the nerve agent was deployed," Adams said.

"Probably an air-burst missile rather than artillery," Leo said, "but I think it was deployed from the east. Doctor Avalon will provide a more definitive answer in a few hours."

"Are you sure it was VX?" Tess asked.

"Yes. From the position of the bodies, how quickly they died, how mothers were shielding their children," Leo said. "There are other indicators, too."

"We'll get to that," Adams said. "Tell her about the recording on the memory card."

"Did you watch it?" Tess asked.

"Yes, but I've seen the first half of the footage before," Leo said. "The second half is the torture and execution of the three people crucified in the courtyard. The first half was uploaded online before the internet finally collapsed. Back in Canberra, I was collecting all the footage people had grabbed before the net went down, and found dozens of copies of this file. Thirty-six people all took it in turns to speak to the camera, to say a few words of encouragement. Not to each other, but to the world. The gist being that if we all stood together, forgot past differences, past enmities, we could defeat the horror. The clip ends with a priest giving a blessing, telling the camera, as much as his flock, that if they don't give into fear, they can still restore this Garden of Eden. That's when they opened the gates and attacked."

"The defenders opened the gates?" Tess asked. "They wanted to die?"

"They wanted repentance," Adams said. "They knew for whom they worked. I understand you found supplies in the tunnels. Assault rifles, medicine, and food. These locals dug those tunnels. They knew what was down there. Knew who had hidden it. I suspect they knew why, too."

"There were more than thirty-six bodies at the pier," Leo said. "A lot of them were kids. I think the message, and their intent, was as the captain said, but these people had a more immediate need to rescue their families who were trapped nearby. That's why they attacked rather than fought a defence."

"That's the first half of the video?" Tess asked. "And the second half is the torture and execution of those three?"

"Yes, I've got it cued up here if you want to watch," Leo said, pointing at a screen.

"No, I've seen the end result," Tess said, though she reflexively turned to look. "Hang about. That's the woman from the tunnel. Her, in the blue shirt. She's… she's not armed. But she's watching the camera."

"Watching the audience," Leo said. "I'm certain there was one. I've not yet determined whether it was locals, or guards."

"I'll take a look at that later," Tess said. In the still, a man in an immaculate white suit, with an equally immaculate goatee, held a long, thin, flensing knife above his head. With his arm raised, she could see the belt and holster, made of reptile-skin, which matched the boots on his feet. "Yes, I'll take another look at this later. But was that blue-shirt woman in any of the earlier footage?"

"Not that I remember," Leo said. "I'd have to look again."

"Later," Tess said. "We found crates of AKMs in the tunnels. Some medical supplies and food, but we only saw a small fraction of their total stash. The tunnel must run from the house all the way to the coal mine, and must have been excavated from that direction. I don't know precisely how many rifles were down there, but we saw no ammunition. They'd stashed a few AT4 anti-tank missiles, so there could be other military supplies down there. Most of what we saw was off-the-shelf survivalist supplies. Solar panels, lights, compact generators, bikes, even a few self-assembly canoes. From the quantity, and almost random nature of it all, I reckon it was bought in panic by someone for whom money was no object, but who'd just learned the world was about to end. Say a senior member of a drug gang with a box of fake credit cards, or a suitcase of laundered cash. It could have been bought online, or in a big-box store. Bought, I think, by that woman we found down in the tunnel."

"She was a member of the cartel?" Adams asked.

"Yes, she was," Tess said. "What I don't know, and what we need to work out, is whether she was left there to guard the place against when the sisters came back, or whether she was abandoned there to die. In either case, she seemed to be living below ground."

"Because of the VX above," Leo said.

"The grenade she threw was a dud," Tess said. "I have my doubts about the detonators attached to the C4 built into the walls of the house, but we left the detonator on the shore with our gear. Would it be safe to return to collect more evidence?"

"Let's put a pin in that question for now," Adams said. "What do you think happened here?"

"The zoms arrived after dark," Tess said. "The locals didn't have much time to throw up defences. They, or some of them, fought a fighting retreat back to that big house. They must have raided the tunnels for weapons. They recorded that apology and exhortation, and uploaded it to the net, and then the locals attacked. Some survived. And if Leo saw that video before, then this all happened near the beginning of the outbreak. The locals didn't clear away the bodies, so they made camp somewhere else, but close by. They gathered food from their own houses and ate that before raiding the underground stash."

"They were terrified of the cartel, even after the outbreak," Adams said. "Terrified for good reason, judging by that video. There are two large shipwrecks in the bay. It's possible those brought the infection here. The ships were sunk with portable artillery in an attempt to stop the undead. With the ships sunk, there was no escape by sea. But why didn't they flee by land?"

"Because they hoped the sisters were dead," Tess said. "And if they had been, then here was a remote bastion with enough supplies to last until the world began to recover. After the nuclear war began, maybe they thought they really were safe. Except the sisters did come."

"There are no sixty-year-old women in that footage," Adams said.

"That doesn't mean they didn't come here themselves," Tess said. "They'd know never to be caught on camera at a crime scene. I saw murders like that in Canberra, and in Broken Hill. People skinned alive. They employed torturers, each of whom was trained to use the same M.O. Back before the outbreak, we thought it was work of an international serial killer, and I think that was the point. It threw us off the scent, while instilling fear in the gangsters who were in the know. You said they used VX?"

"Or a new nerve agent with very similar effects," Leo said. "But it's probably VX."

"Where did it come from?" Tess asked.

"Originally, Porton Down in England in the 1950s," Leo said. "But it was banned back in 1993. North Korea never signed the Chemical Weapons Treaty, and instead kept a crazy-huge stockpile ready to be deployed in the event of an invasion from the south. VX has a low volatility. It lingers, making it an ideal defensive area-denial weapon. That you aren't dead suggests a low-altitude dispersal. I'd say they gathered the locals at the pier, together, and clearly packed for travel. It could mean they only had a very limited supply, rather than enough to drench the entire bay."

"Sir Malcolm Baker mentioned North Korea had a link to the sisters," Tess said. "But would that living-crime of a government have been insane enough to give a pair of narco-queens a WMD?"

"The Russians poured money into biochemical R&D," Adams said. "What was the name of their lab? The Kamera. Could it have come from there?"

"It could have come from anywhere," Leo said. "But it's most likely to have come from the same lab-network that developed compound-zom."

"You mean the zombie virus?" Tess asked. "Is there anyway of nailing down some of these theories?"

"Not without risk and time," Leo said.

"We've run out of time," Adams said. "Commissioner, what is your assessment of the supplies down in those tunnels?"

"The tunnels are extensive," Tess said. "I didn't see enough of the contents to form a conclusion. It's reasonable to assume the sisters laid in enough rifles and food to turn those miners into an army. Say, enough food to keep a thousand alive for a year."

"Dr Smilovitz, how long before it would be safe to use that pier again?" Adams asked.

"I'd prefer to wait a year," he said. "A month is probably sufficient. It's possible that it's safe now, but I'd want to send in a canary first. Or a flamingo."

"Let me rephrase the question," Adams said. "Could the sisters return tomorrow to claim what is down in the tunnels?"

"Sure. They'd have no qualms about using a person to test the pier," Leo said.

"Ashore, there is a vast quantity of coal, and of mining machines, and of diesel for the machines and the ships," Adams said. "They alone are reasons for the sisters to return. Commissioner, was there any sign of the laboratory?"

"Not beneath the house," Tess said. "And not in the town, but I can't begin to guess how extensive those tunnels are."

"Dr Smilovitz, if we return to shore, it would be to search for the laboratory. You understand the risks, and the potential benefits. Is it worth it?"

Leo looked down at the screen, still displaying the frozen image of the torturer about to begin work. He turned to the bridge window. Tess watched, as did everyone else on the bridge.

"No," he finally said. "The lab *could* be here. If the locals believed their work had helped make Hell a reality, it would better explain the video they uploaded. But if they dug one tunnel, why not two? There could be more guards, more gas, and maybe more zoms. But if this was where the sisters developed it, when they came back, they would have destroyed the lab, and taken the research with them."

"Commissioner? It was your investigation which brought us here." Adams left the question half asked.

"I'd love to search it properly," Tess said. "I want to know where the sisters went. But the risk is too great. You're thinking of blowing the place up?"

"They have mining machines, they could excavate the tunnels," Adams said. "We'll destroy the runway, the pier, the above-ground fuel storage, and the mansion. They left that recording as a message to whoever came looking for them. It was a message to instil fear. Let them experience that feeling. Let them know we came. Let them *think* we are looking for them still. But we shall make for the canal and then return home. Let them live in fear, and let them die that way, too."

It was a nice line, Tess thought, as she left the bridge. But it was a message for the crew. A way of making failure seem like a victory. They *had* failed. They hadn't found, or destroyed, the lab. The cartel had escaped. Though they might destroy this supply cache, the sisters clearly had some other lair that was surely better equipped.

Her feet took her to the deck, where she went looking for shade, and found Zach, lurking near the stern.

"If you're going to hang around out here, you'll need a hat," she said. "The sun's fit to boil the ocean. You all right?"

"I've got logs for legs," he said, bracing hands and feet against the rail, rocking back, stretching. "Yeah, that was intense."

"It was a bit," Tess said. "How are you doing with it all?"

"You mean after atomising a lady with a missile? Yeah, nah, I'm cool. I mean, you're asking if it bothers me? She was trying to kill us, and she was one of the people who tried to take over Oz, right?"

"Defo," Tess said. "We've got her on video. On that memory card. She was one of the torturers."

"Cool. Cool," Zach said, with an air of relief. "I didn't mean to fire. I just had the bazooka in my hands. It was automatic, I guess."

"You've got good instincts," Tess said.

"Yeah, well, I don't want to do it again. I can't believe Clyde jumped on a grenade. I didn't think people did that in real life. I mean, I don't think I'd ever do that."

"Nor me," Tess said.

"Is that something they train you for in the army?"

"I think that's instinct, too," Tess said.

"That woman, she was evil, right?"

"Absolutely. You saved me and Clyde, and probably the ship, too. One of those missiles could have done some serious damage."

"Cool," he said. He sighed. "Is it always like this?"

"Policing or war?"

"Both. I dunno. Yeah, I'm gonna be a librarian. Definitely. That stuff in the tunnel was weird, right? It's like… it's like what I would have bought if I'd been prepping for the end of the world."

"Yeah, some of it would have been useful," Tess said. "Not sure about the canoes, though."

"No, like it's not what you'd buy if you were super-rich."

"The super-rich all bought bunkers in New Zealand," Tess said. "Pretty sure none of them made it down there after the airspace was shut down."

"Commander Tusitala says they had a plan to nationalise all the bunkers anyway," Zach said. "She said it was a mega-bucks stealth-tax to cover the Kiwi disaster planning. All those places with solar panels and wind farms are perfect for refugee camps. She says you've got to be a particular kind of stupid to think money would help after a nuclear war."

"A particular kind of arrogant," Tess said.

"But the sisters weren't," Zach said. "They weren't stupid. That woman, she bought canoes and bikes. Lots of them. But no petrol for her generator. Was she going to paddle through the desert? Or cycle? But the sisters bought guns. Lots of guns, and missiles, and explosives, because we found those in the house, too. No, they weren't stupid."

"They were scared," Tess said.

"Seriously? Them?"

"They left that video. Not just the bodies, but the video, too, to make sure whoever came here knew exactly why those people were tortured."

"That doesn't sound like scared," Zach said.

"Think about it. They struck deals with politicians who, later, started a nuclear war. The sisters knew those politicians would come after them, but that they'd send their armies. Or perhaps just their submarines."

"Like that Russian one?"

"Yep. Or the British sub. Or they thought someone like Malcolm Baker would tell someone like Lignatiev, and they'd send a navy to destroy the evidence. That's who the message was for, the Sir Malcolm Bakers of the world. Ultimately, that's whom the sisters were terrified of. Nemesis. Destiny. And it's who they'll be thinking of every night until they die."

"Yeah, well, I'm still terrified of them," he said. "The tunnels would have been expensive, right? The tunnels and all the stuff stashed in them?"

"Very. They required running an entire mining town as cover. Probably blackmailed their way into getting it for free, but the workers would need wages and supplies."

"So there won't be another underground base somewhere?" Zach asked. "Because there's lots of mines in Australia."

"I'd say no, not in Australia," Tess said. "I'm still piecing together what they considered a best-case scenario. Essentially, they got in so deep their only way out was to destroy civilisation. I'm not so blind as to say it's impossible for them to have bought a lair in Australia, but buying a mine anywhere would attract attention, either from locals, from the regulators, or from protestors. And, of course, from the politicians they were in league with. No, I think there was only one mine."

"But probably more supplies somewhere else," Zach said.

"Probably," Tess said. "But the guns were for an army. The miners are dead. No way will they find another."

"There you are, Zach," Clyde said, clambering out the water-lock door. "I was looking for you."

"You were?" Zach said.

Clyde held out a bottle of the fizzy orange soda. "Thanks for saving my life, mate."

"Me? You were the one who jumped on the grenade."

"I was bloody lucky it was a dud. Wouldn't have stopped her from flinging another our way. Good on ya. I'd give you a medal, but this is better."

"No worries," Zach said, taking the bottle. "You want to share?"

Clyde pulled another two bottles from his bag. "I snaffled a couple more when the purser wasn't looking. We better destroy the evidence."

"You worked with explosives in the army, didn't you?" Zach asked.

"I don't know if I'm allowed to talk about it," Clyde said. "I do know I don't *want* to. Afterward, I wanted to help rebuild. But there's not much point beating a bloke's sword into a plough if a forgotten bomblet will take out his tractor. So I got a job clearing up the land."

"You can't talk about it?" Zach asked. "So it's like a national secret or something?"

"It's classified," Clyde said.

"Still?" Zach asked.

"I guess so," Clyde said. "So talking about it would be a breach of the law we're out here trying to uphold. Never could abide hypocrisy. Came across far too much of it during my service. At home. Abroad. I'm not saying I'm not occasionally guilty of it myself, but we must strive to be better."

"That's like the complete opposite of Toppley," Zach said.

"Not the complete opposite," Clyde said. "I was talking with her. We've a few friends in common. At the edge, where life and death walk hand in hand, right and wrong are hard to tell apart, but you can always tell good from evil."

"That's a—" Tess began, and was cut short by the alarm.

"They're about to fire," Clyde said.

"We should get inside?" Zach asked.

"Nah, we'll be okay out here. You just wouldn't want to be on shore," Clyde said.

The shot was loud, but not nearly as loud as the explosion as the harbour-side fuel tanks detonated in a haze of orange flame.

"Now that's what I'm—" Zach began.

The ground erupted. The shore vanished, replaced by a burning cloud of sand and oil. Dust and flame mushroomed upwards, while a wall of noise and heat shot outward. The ship rocked. Tess dropped to a knee. She could hear yelling, but couldn't place from whom.

Clyde pushed Zach inside the water-lock. Tess staggered in after them. With the door closed, she realised the screaming was the ship's alarm. By the time she reached the bridge, the ship was underway, slowly lumbering northwest, picking up speed, the cameras aimed at the shore.

"What just happened?" Tess asked.

"There must have been a fuel store below ground," Adams said. "A *very* large one. I'm sure the scientists can calculate the size, but the answer will be in the millions of litres."

"That's why they didn't bother with a coal power station," Tess said. "They had all the diesel they needed until they could pump some more of their own."

"The main blast triggered a string of tertiary explosions further inland," Adams said. "These were smaller than that initial blast, but there were at least four, and in an almost straight line. I think that was the tunnel, and it makes me wonder what else was stored down there."

"Captain, the fire has spread to the coal bunker," Lieutenant Renton said.

"That settles the fate of this place," Adams said. "The coal will burn for weeks. Nothing usable remains there. The mission *has* been a success. We've destroyed the sisters' supplies, and what had to be their principal fuel depot in this ocean. Take us north, Lieutenant, and plot us a course for the Panama Canal."

5th April

Chapter 39 - Two Out of Thirty Minutes
The Caribbean Sea

Tess pressed the spacebar to pause the video playing on the laptop. To conserve energy, and so fuel, the internal temperature was being kept only a few degrees below outside. And outside, it was a furnace as a weather front followed them west. But inside the cabin shared by the two scientists, with its doors closed for privacy, it was a stuffy oven.

"This video was shot in New York, two days after the outbreak?" Tess asked.

"You just watched a zombie die," Leo said. "My theory is that the pre-infection health of the host correlates with the re-animate's life expectancy."

"A theory which is almost completely wrong," Avalon said.

"In what respect is it correct?" Tess asked.

"That from the moment a host is reanimated, the zombie is dying," Avalon said. "Within six to twelve months, it will become numerically obvious."

"Does that mean we'll start to see it?"

"Notice it," Avalon said. "We'll see it all the time, but how will we know how a corpse died? Thus, we're calculating a timeframe when anecdotal data will become irrefutable."

"There's no way we'll get to New York," Tess said. "After Panama, we'll return to Dégrad des Cannes, and head back to Robben Island, and then home."

"Home for you," Leo said.

"Yes, fine, sure," Tess said. "I want it to be clear that there is no way at all we'll get to New York. But if we had a sample of that zombie, would you be able to prove they could die?"

"Why would we need to, when we have that video?" Avalon asked.

"I mean could you develop some kind of lab test that would produce graphs and charts that we could stick in a newspaper or describe on the radio news?" Tess said. "Something definitive."

"Nothing can be definitive," Avalon said.

"Leo?"

"Yes," he said. "But that's not what you want, and not why we want to get to that particular specimen. You saw the bodies in Inhambane and Cape Town, and in Colombia. Some would have been zoms which simply died."

"Calling them zombies is bad enough," Avalon said. "Please don't abbreviate. It's a short route from there to copying the crew and calling it compound-zom."

"Go on, Leo," Tess said.

"We can take samples," Leo said, "but we don't know what happened to the… to the subject before it died. An intact skull doesn't preclude brain injury. Weeks of decay turn a diagnosis into a mere hypothesis. In Colombia, the nerve agent could have had an effect of some kind. But here, in New York, we have these three videos. The woman is running. She's infected. She turns, and then the zombie dies, all within thirty minutes."

"Only two minutes of which are on camera," Tess said. "The rest is conjecture."

"The videos are time-stamped," Leo said.

"It wouldn't stand up in court," Tess said.

"But it would in the court of public opinion," Avalon said.

"Fair dinkum," Tess said. "But, by now, that corpse has been rotting in that doorway for months. Assuming New York wasn't nuked or flooded, how reliable would any samples be?"

"Priceless," Leo said.

"I concur," Avalon said. "It is highly improbable we will find more video footage, or identify a similar subject from any of the footage we've gathered. Thus, the only way to find a similar test subject would be to infect people until we replicate that same effect."

"We're not doing that," Tess said. "And we're not going to New York. Assuming it hasn't been destroyed. No, we're going home." She closed the laptop-lid and handed it back to Leo. "Where was home for you? Was it New York?"

"Vancouver," Avalon said.

"For two months of the year if we were lucky," Leo said. "We spent more time travelling than at home."

"Vancouver was hit by a bomb," Tess said. "I'm sorry for your loss, for *all* you've lost. But these videos will have to suffice. It's a good theory, though. People will want to hear it. Maybe that's better than proof."

"That is never the case," Avalon said.

"We've got to think of the future," Tess said. "We came here following a lead given us by Sir Malcolm Baker. A lead that proved reliable. The cartel's depot was blown up. Considering the size of that explosion, it must have been their central fuel store. For all we know, the lab could have been there. I don't know if the sisters are still alive, but I don't see them as a threat to the Pacific. As far I'm concerned, we came out here to find a lab, and we failed. You want to go on to New York, but it is a logistical impossibility. That conversation we had a week ago can be forgotten. When we get back, when you're asked to make a weapon, what you do and say is entirely up to you."

"Any weapon we make would be more potent than VX," Leo said.

"I figured as much," Tess said. "But it's not my call. You told Oswald Owen you could make one. When we get back, he'll ask you to manufacture it. You can say no, but that'll come with consequences."

"So would deploying a chemical weapon," Leo said. "Oceanic radiation levels will continue to rise until they reach a new equilibrium. The aquatic population will boom this year, but crash next year to fifty percent of pre-outbreak levels. It could be as low as ten percent, and continue to drop. Entire eco-systems have already been destroyed, but we could be looking at the utter destruction of the marine environment. This won't only impact our food stocks, but the oxygen cycle. Half the planet's O2 comes from plankton, yes? The entire planet could suffocate."

"That's going to happen anyway, right?" Tess said. "So there's nothing I can do about it. Nothing Canberra can do. What you do and say when we get back to Australia is *your* affair. Do we understand each other?"

"We do," Leo said.

"Good." She stood up. "Do you really think they might be dying?"

"Everything is, from the moment it's born," Avalon said.

"We're positive," Leo said.

"Maybe there's hope, then," Tess said.

A fist thumped into the door, which was thrown open by a sweating Zach.

"There you are," Zach said. "You missed the plane!"

"What plane?" Tess asked.

Two minutes later she was on the bridge, looking at a still image of an aircraft.

"A twin-engine jet," Tess said. "Is that the best picture we have?"

"Unfortunately, yes," Adams said. "Commander Tusitala thinks it's a Cessna Citation with a range of around five thousand kilometres. It approached from the east, and was following the South American coast. It didn't change course when it saw us, nor did it make contact. It must have seen the smoke in Colombia, and then it saw a warship. After which, it turned north."

"Was it heading towards Mexico?" Tess asked.

"Yes, but will they land there, or when beyond radar range, will they change course again?" Adams said. "There are many islands in the Caribbean Sea. Many tax havens. Many runways and many private planes."

"So that could be where they came from," Tess said. "But where were they going? They didn't respond to a radio call?"

“It’s the *Adventure* all over again,” Adams said. “At present, all we can be sure of is that there is at least one working runway, with a fuel supply, somewhere in the Caribbean.”

6th April

Chapter 40 - A Ship, a Plan, a Canal: Panama?
The Panama Canal

"I wish they'd stop telling us what the radiation levels are," Zach said.

"You and me both, mate," Clyde said. "Have you got a spare mag for your sidearm?"

"I mean, I wish they'd just say whether a bomb had been dropped nearby or not."

Tess found herself looking south, watching the helicopter disappear. Aboard were the two scientists, and Hawker, Oakes, and Commander Tusitala. As far as Tess understood it, while the radiation readings had increased, that was to be expected here, ten kilometres north of Panama, where the Caribbean Sea reached a dead end.

A quite literal dead end. The surface was littered with unidentifiable flotsam, a floating carpet of wood and plastic which had grown increasingly dense as they neared the isthmus. But that wasn't why the captain had brought the ship to a halt. Ahead floated a luxury ghost-yacht, dead in the water, its sails furled.

About fifty metres in length with a white hull, low bridge, aft sundeck, and small pool. Forward of the bridge was enough deck-space to land a helicopter if the mast hadn't been in the way. A second mast rose from inside the cockpit. According to the hull, the vessel was the *Fortunate Son*, and it wasn't on the list they'd found in Dégrad des Cannes. Though the vessel had engines as well as sails, they were three and a half thousand kilometres from French Guiana, and those sails would have allowed it to travel from anywhere.

The sails were furled, rather than left to be ripped ragged by the storms, but the only things alive on the ship were the quartet of gulls perched atop the giant masts.

"Leave the carbine, Zach," Clyde said. "It's a small ship with very narrow corridors. Take an extra bag instead."

"What for?"

"Booty," Clyde said. "This is the Caribbean, mate. Time for you to learn how to be a pirate."

Aboard the yacht, as Clyde went below, Tess headed up to the cockpit.

"Clear," she said, holstering her sidearm. "Come on in, Zach."

"Three captain's chairs," Zach said. "That's cool. They've got more screens than the warship."

"Look around for a journal or ship's log," Tess said.

"Bet it's on the computer," Zach said. "I could try turning them back on."

"Rule-eleven," Tess said. "Never turn something on unless you're certain you can turn it off. Otherwise we could go shooting off towards Mexico before we find the brake."

"Nah, there's no books here," Zach said. "Can we go below?"

She drew a crowbar. "Keep your gun holstered. The interior walls will be thin. Accidentally shooting Clyde would be a seriously bad way to end the day."

The spiral staircase led down into a space the same size as the bridge, but with a single flat screen dominating the aft wall. Four armchairs were bolted to the deck, but with additional seating provided by the cushioned bench ringing two walls.

"Four armchairs down here," she said. "Not a sofa. But there's only three chairs on the bridge."

"They swivel!" Zach said, falling into one, and giving it a spin. "Cool. But weird."

"The ship must be custom built," Tess said, crossing to the aft doors. "Four seats, I'd say that means a family of four."

"Or four kids," Zach said. "Or one guy who had three friends."

"Fair point," Tess said. "Galley and toilets through here. Have you got your bag?"

"Yeah, hang on, wait. There's a book wedged down here. It's a journal."

"Chuck me the bag while you take a read," Tess said.

The galley cupboards were half stocked with a mix of the ultra-expensive and solidly sugar. Bright pink marshmallows shared a shelf with jars of stuffed lychees. Caviar kept company with peanut butter. Goji berries neighboured jellybeans. All together, it was almost enough to fill the bag.

"Anything in that diary?" she asked.

"Yeah, they came from Louisiana. That's in the U.S., isn't it?"

"Yep. In the south. On the Gulf of Mexico."

"They found the boat after the outbreak. It wasn't theirs. They claimed it."

"Pause the reading for a moment," she said. "Take this bag onto the deck, and tell the ship we're cool."

A clunk marked the sound of the room's other door opening.

"She's empty," Clyde said. "The engine's been partially dismantled."

"I guess they didn't know how to use the sails," Tess said.

"Let me see if they wrote about that," Zach said, flipping through the book.

"No, take the bag onto the deck, and get Mr Dickenson to come aboard to check the engines," Tess said. "Then come help me loot. I've grabbed everything from the snack-galley, but from the amount of food in there, there must be more below."

There was, but it was all the same odd mix of adult-luxury and kid-marketed junk foods.

While the engineer inspected the engine, Tess carried the loot back to the deck, where Zach was working his way through marshmallows and the book.

"Share and share alike," she said, taking the candy from him. "What've you found?"

"A girl wrote this," he said.

"Does she have a name?"

"Not yet, but the handwriting is readable, plus she dots her I's with hearts. Bet it's a girl. Like fourteen, fifteen years old, I think, because she mentions how all her high-school friends must be dead."

"So maybe a bit older than fifteen," Tess said. "Did she escape Louisiana alone?"

"No, she was with her dad. No mention of a mum. She started writing after they found this boat, but they first went to Atlanta."

"That's in Georgia," Tess said. "The city has one of the world's largest airports."

"Does it? Okay, so here, near the beginning, she writes: *Savannah was barricaded. Wouldn't let us in. Told us about Toronto and Ottawa and Boston. Met Santiago at Blackbeard Creek. He'd been hiding. Waiting for things to calm until he went north. We told him about the northeast, how there's nowhere left. We'll have to go south with him.*"

"So was this Santiago's boat?" Tess asked.

"Think so," Zach said. "The next bit is about her old life. Her friends. How they must be dead. So I guess she wasn't in immediate danger when she wrote that. Must have been at sea."

"Could be," Tess said. "Savannah and Atlanta are both in Georgia, but I'd have to look at a map to know how far from Louisiana they are. People in Savannah warned them about Toronto, Ottawa, and Boston, and they warned Santiago about the northeast. Let's assume it was the same warning that they were passing on."

"Does that mean nukes?" Zach asked.

"You've got the book, mate, you tell me," she said.

He skimmed ahead. "Havana was nuked. That's in Cuba, isn't it?"

"It is. Did they go there?"

"No. She says: *We picked up radio reports from Miami. So many people ashore need help. Dad says we can't help them all. We'd be swamped. Lose the ship. A Cuban ship came alongside. A navy ship. I thought we were dead, but they gave us food and fuel, and told us to avoid Havana. It was bombed. They were going north, to Greenland. There's supposed to be a refuge there. We told them how Canada was nuked. They still went north. We went south.*"

"Havana, too?" Tess asked.

"Was there a refuge in Greenland?" Zach asked.

"I don't think so," Tess said. "General Yoon was setting up a redoubt in the northeast of Canada. Sounds like it was targeted. The other Canadian refuge was in Vancouver, and we know that was bombed."

"Deliberately, right?" Zach said. "Like South Africa and Brazil, to stop us rebuilding?"

"I expect so," Tess said. "Go on, what else does she say?"

"It's a bit… well, personal," he said.

"Skip ahead," she said. "How did they end up here?"

"Well, first…" He turned a page, and then turned back. "Yeah, first they went to Mexico. A place called Puerto Morelos. Santiago went ashore and bought more fuel with gold."

"He paid with gold?" Tess asked.

"That's what it says," Zach said. "They found it in the safe."

"What safe?"

"Oh, that was at the beginning. There's a safe somewhere on the ship. They spent days figuring out how to get it open. But it was just full of gold."

"Right, so this wasn't Santiago's boat originally?" Tess said.

"Guess not," Zach said. "Does it matter?"

"Guess not," Tess said. "What happened in… where was the place they bought fuel?"

"Puerto Morelos," Zach said. "All it says is they traded gold for diesel. She was surprised people were still accepting gold as money. The next day, it says Santiago took their boat ashore. He came back with a woman called Maria. I think that's where she joined the ship. There was no mention of her before, but the next day it says she made corn pancakes."

"Why did they go ashore when they found Maria? Was it to look for food, or because the woman was signalling?"

"Doesn't say," Zach said. "Next day they found food on a small freighter. Lots of zoms aboard. Her dad got bit and… no! He survived!"

"Cool. So where are they now?"

"Um…" He skimmed a page, and another. "Dunno. It says they're out of ammo. The engine's broken. Only got the junk food left. Hang on." He turned back to the beginning. "But they have a small boat. Dunno how small, but they tied it up on the deck. It was the same boat they used right at the beginning to come aboard in Blackbeard Creek. Bet that's why they're not here. They took their small boat ashore."

"But where, Zach?" Tess asked. "It can't have been long ago or far away. Keep reading. See if there's any more clues."

But he'd found no answers before Captain Adams and Lieutenant Kane came aboard.

"Mr Dickenson has repaired the engine," Adams said. "Mr Kane has volunteered to take the ship back to the Pacific as a prize."

"This ship?" Tess asked. "Can you make it?"

"Aye, ma'am," Kane said with a grin. "Been sailing boats since before I could walk."

"Let me rephrase that, is it wise?" Tess asked.

"The Pacific needs ships," Adams said. "Vessels independent of fuel will be vital in the months ahead. Mr Kane will make for Dégrad des Cannes, and can wait for us. We'll only be two or three days behind."

"We're not going south, too?" Tess asked.

"I'd like to scout some of the islands first," Adams said. "We're more likely to find survivors, and more likely to find food."

"Captain, I should get my people aboard," Kane said.

"Thank you, *Captain* Kane," Adams said.

Tess watched the young man jog back to the small group of sailors who'd come aboard with him. "Taking prize ships at sea?" Tess asked. "It sounds like something from a different era."

"I know," Adams said. "But we do need ships like this. There is little chance its like will be built again."

"Isn't there a danger he might sail into the sisters?" Tess asked. "We know they have a ship, and someone sank those vessels northwest of French Guiana."

"Yes, it's a risk," Adams said. "But oceans are vast, and the sisters have now lost their fuel reserve. It *is* a risk, but one we should take because this vessel can sail all the way home. Perhaps Mr Kane can answer the question of what lies south beyond French Guiana."

"He's sailing down to the Cape?"

"Possibly. Sailing boats have managed it before, Commissioner. It will depend on how the ship performs on its way to Dégrad des Cannes. I might ask the colonel to accompany him, but before I do that, and before I ask Mr Kane to take that additional risk, I would like more information on what he might find deep below the equator."

"Zach found a diary left by one of the ship's previous passengers," Tess said. "Boston, Ottawa, and Toronto were nuked. It sounds as if the entire American northeast was targeted."

"Which is to have been expected," Adams said.

"Havana was bombed, too," Tess said. "They met a Cuban warship going north, hoping to reach a redoubt in Greenland. They traded gold for fuel in Mexico, at a place called Puerto Morelos. But previously, they'd found people in Savannah. A redoubt of some kind who wouldn't allow them entry."

"We'll have photographs taken of the diary, and send those with Mr Kane. *Captain* Kane. What can you tell me about the ship's crew?"

"There were probably four of them," Tess said. "A father and daughter from Atlanta, a man who'd found this boat off the Georgia coast, and a woman they picked up in Mexico. There's no sign of them aboard, or of violence. A small boat is missing, and we think they took it ashore after they dismantled the engine. I heard the helicopter return. What's the canal like? Could the survivors have gone ashore here?"

"The canal was the target of multiple missile strikes," Adams said. "Conventional warheads, which did as much damage to the cities as to the canal. The waterway is clogged with debris. Returning it to operational status isn't a matter of maintenance but of repair, and will require dredgers and tugs. Manageable, but time-consuming. Delaying the work for six months will make it no more difficult."

"Assuming it's such a priority we can divert the resources within six months," Tess said.

“Commish!” Zach called, running up the steps, and nearly slipping on the deck.

“Steady,” Adams said, catching his arm. “Why the rush?”

He held up the book. “It was right at the beginning. I nearly missed it because it was right at the start. They left Atlanta *after* the bombs! Someone was running an airlift to Canada from the airport in Atlanta. Hundreds of planes. But not everyone went. A plane was supposed to come back if there was somewhere to land. But everywhere in the north was bombed. That’s why they went to Savannah.”

“Everything that happened in that diary was after the bombs?” Tess said. “How long after they found this ship did they meet the Cubans?”

“Dunno. Weeks,” Zach said. “That means they were aboard *really* recently. Like within the last few days. We could still find them.”

“I’m sorry, Zach,” Adams said. “That’s very unlikely. We could search the nearby shore for their boat, but they wouldn’t still be on the beach.”

“Oh. Yeah, I guess not.”

“People in Savannah survived the nuclear bombs,” Tess said. “Some might have survived in Miami, but they certainly survived in Puerto Morelos, trading fuel for gold, and only a few days ago. You wanted information, Captain. We’ll find it in Puerto Morelos.”

7th April

Chapter 41 - Pirates of the Caribbean
Corn Island, Nicaragua

"But I can't have drunk all the fizzy orange?" Zach said, his plaintive cry directed at the sailor behind the mess-counter.

"No tea. No coffee. No fizz," the sailor said. "Some of the soda appears to have gone missing. Bit of a mystery. Don't suppose you'd know anything about it?"

"If water's good enough for the fish, it's good enough for us," Clyde said. "Come on, you." He pushed Zach away before the young man incriminated himself.

"Iced water?" Tess asked.

"Yes ma'am," the sailor said. "I can add some essence if you like. Vanilla, almond, or lemon?"

"No worries, that would only make me dream of lattes and pastries," Tess said, and took her glass over to their table.

"We gave too much food to Mr Kane," Zach said, looking forlornly at his already-empty breakfast bowl.

"He's got a longer voyage ahead of him than we do," Tess said.

"We're travelling further," Zach said.

"He's travelling slower," Tess said. "If the wind is blowing south, they might attempt to circumnavigate Cape Horn."

"Fair dinkum," Zach said. "But he didn't have to take all the *good* food."

"Those multi-coloured calories wrapped in additives cannot be described as food," Avalon said. She had ended her voluntary exile and returned to the team's mess-table.

"There was *popcorn*," Zach said. "It's been ages since I had popcorn."

"Good news for you," Tess said. "We're going ashore in the Corn Islands to look for fuel for the helicopter. With a name like that, we might get lucky finding some corn growing in a field. Or maybe even some food in a store cupboard."

"Afterwards we're going to Puerto Morelos, right?" Zach asked.

"It's the island of Cozumel first," Tess said. "There are a lot of islands north of Puerto Morelos, and more north of Cancun. But those islands could have been swamped by post-bomb refugees from Cuba."

"Or zoms," Zach said.

"I thought Florida was the closest landfall to Cuba," Nicko said.

"It would depend upon which part of Cuba you're travelling from," Avalon said. "If you have a pen, I'll draw you a map."

"I'm happy in my ignorance," Nicko said. "Cancun is a tourist city, isn't it?"

"Famously," Avalon said.

"Famous enough for me to have heard of it," Tess said.

"So it has an airport?" Nicko asked. "That plane had to have come from somewhere."

"It's under fifteen hundred kilometres from where we sighted the plane," Avalon said. "So yes, we are within range of a Cessna Citation."

"But so are any of the tax-haven islands south of Cuba," Tess said. "Plus there's all of Central America. That's a lot of countries, a lot of islands, and so a lot of runways. It's unlikely we'll find that plane, but the best place to look is Puerto Morelos."

"Are you not hungry, boss?" Zach asked. "Because if you don't want your breakfast, I could finish it."

"Not a chance," she said.

It didn't take long to finish their meagre repast. Afterwards, as Avalon began a lecture on the domestication of corn, Tess went to the bridge. Captain Adams was nearing the end of a rant partially directed at Commander Tusitala.

"Do you know the *most* frustrating thing?" Adams asked. "There *is* coffee galore on the mainland. Ah, Commissioner. Good morning."

"G'day. Are you thinking of an excursion to a farm?" Tess asked.

"No, I was bemoaning the existence of the undead," Adams said. "We're only seventy kilometres east of Nicaragua. If we had fuel for the helicopter, there'd be nothing to stop us flying to Nicaragua, finding a farm, and harvesting coffee beans for breakfast."

"Even *if* the zoms really are dying like the scientists think," Commander Tusitala said, "dying's not the same as dead."

"Ah. Right. That," Tess said. "I want to believe them, but it sounds like a theory with little evidence to back it up."

"We'll get the evidence when we get back to Auckland," Commander Tusitala said. "Someone over there must have seen it, too. Next trip, we'll pick up the coffee, Cap'n."

"Next voyage, we'll be heading for the tea plantations of Sri Lanka," Adams said. "But perhaps we'll find some supplies on Corn Island."

"Will we arrive there today?" Tess asked.

"Within the hour," Adams said. "We're ten kilometres south of the Corn Islands. There are two, Big Corn, and Little Corn. Another hundred and fifty kilometres west-northwest is the island of San Andres, but I think we'll investigate there on our return."

"How far to Puerto Morelos?" Tess asked.

"Another thousand kilometres," Tusitala said.

"We're low on aviation fuel," Adams said. "The helicopter is essential to an effective survey of the Mexican mainland. Tourist-cities are the last place I'd want to seek refuge in a disaster. I doubt we'll find many survivors near the coast, but those that are there could have sought refuge at the top of tall hotels."

"Hopefully hotels with a helipad," Tusitala said.

"Exactly," Adams said. "We might find a few survivors hiding on the rooftops, but I doubt we'll find supplies. No, this whole region was too popular with tourists, and too close to Cuba. It's been too long since the outbreak. Survivors will have moved inland, towards a source of fresh water. We'll need time to find them. Time, and food, and fuel for the Seahawk."

"Are we changing our priority from reaching Puerto Morelos to finding survivors?" Tess said.

"The two are the same," Adams said. "Puerto Morelos is a coastal overspill for Cancun. There's no refinery, no large harbour. It's barely more than a port on our charts. I'd guess it's for people who want a quieter holiday than you'd find further up the Yucatan Peninsula. My theory is that this group were selling the fuel contained within a diesel-tanker originally servicing the remote tourist-harbours of the Caribbean. The Mexican Gulf, and the states and nations bordering it, ooze with oil. If these survivors had been workers at a refinery, who'd just refuelled a fuel-freighter when the outbreak hit, what better vessel to seize?"

"Have you a map of the Gulf?" Tess asked.

"You want to look at this one," Tusitala said. "It marks the major refineries, and the off-shore platforms."

"But there are smaller refineries which aren't on our charts," Adams said. "If this group of survivors were protecting a fuel supply in a small harbour town, why didn't they barter passage aboard any of the ships travelling through there?"

"If it were me, I'd have taken the first ship," Tusitala said. "Unless I had something to protect."

"Like a family too large to fit in something like that yacht," Tess said.

"I was thinking of something far bigger than that," Tusitala said. "Why trade fuel for gold with ships that will never return? If they had so much food and ammunition they didn't require more, why trade fuel at all? If this is such a large group, so confident in their position, they can effectively give diesel away, why didn't that yacht stay with them? If they controlled an airport, too, wouldn't we have seen more than one plane, and wouldn't that plane have radioed us, selling us a pitch to come bring our gold to Mexico?"

"I bet you have an answer," Tess said.

"We both do," Adams said. "*Different* answers."

"I think they've got an oil platform, and a refinery," Tusitala said.

"There's a refinery in Puerto Morelos?" Tess asked.

"Not one listed on our charts," Adams said. "One point we both agree on is that Puerto Morelos might not be precisely where that yacht bought the fuel, but a guess by that young diarist as to where they were nearest when they met these traders. I believe they had a diesel-transport vessel, and the plane we saw is looking for them. The commander believes that plane is looking for land."

"Farmland," Tusitala said. "That's what they'll want now. Farmland within sailing distance of the refinery."

"Oil platforms in the Indian Ocean were targets for pirates even before the first bomb fell," Adams said. "It's less likely they will have survived here. It is unbelievable that the roughnecks, on reaching the mainland, would not have gone looking for their families."

"They came back," Tusitala said. "Or the traders are the workers from the refinery whose families live nearby."

"A ship, or a refinery?" Tess asked. "Why not both? Diesel is valuable. Too valuable to swap for shiny yellow rocks. But you don't want people coming to your refinery, so you use a tanker-ship as a decoy. The traders would want information, wouldn't they? I would, if I were there with my family. Information on where to look for farmland, and where had been bombed or overrun. That's what they were really trading diesel for. Information on where the yacht, and other ships, had been, what they'd seen. Where not to go. Where does this leave us? Are we looking for the plane, or the refinery, or the ship?"

"All three," Adams said. "Though first we need aviation fuel. However, we only have three days to search. Taking into account the speed differential between our ship and his yacht, if we don't turn south in seventy-two hours, Captain Kane will depart Dégrad des Cannes before we arrive. In which case, his orders are to sail for Robben Island. But if we arrive before he departs, and if we can provision him, he can sail south down to the Cape. As much as we need a fuel transport vessel, or a refinery and oilrig, we're more likely to find survivors deeper into the Southern Hemisphere. From home, we'll find it easier to mount a rescue of any groups in Argentina. It is even possible, if they've survived this long, we could find a sustainable enclave we can resupply. First, we'll need aviation fuel for the helicopter, and provisions for us and Captain Kane. We'll look on Corn Island."

"Is it a large island?" Tess asked.

"Barely bigger than the runway," Adams said. She tapped at the screen, and brought up the digital chart. "The largest of the two islands is about ten square kilometres, and has one runway. It's another tourist hub, and about seventy kilometres from the Nicaraguan mainland, well within sailing range."

"Well within fly-and-crash range for an infected pilot," Tusitala said.

"True," Adams said. "The nearest alternative candidate is San Andres, an island a hundred and fifty kilometres west, but if we change course now, we'll never reach Puerto Morelos. I'll set aside two hours to confirm whether there is fuel on the island, or whether it has been overrun."

"I'll get my team together," Tess said.

Barely had she gathered her crew on deck when she was summoned back to the bridge along with Colonel Hawker.

"Take a look at the screen," Adams said.

"That's a lot of ships," Tess said. "Is that Corn Island?"

"We're now within visual range of Big Corn, and under two kilometres from shore. There is one large ship docked at that pier, but around thirty boats. An even mix of working craft and pleasure yachts."

"No fuel tankers, though," Tess said.

"What kind of vessel is that larger ship?" Hawker asked. About a hundred metres in length, it had a raised bridge and large deck-crane, with a red hull and white super-structure.

"An icebreaker," Adams said. "They have very large fuel tanks, and the capability to refuel other vessels at sea."

"She's a bit lost for us to find her here," Hawker said.

"Now take a look at this," Adams said. She brought up a different image.

"That bloke's fishing," Hawker said.

A man sat at the end of a long pier, amid the shadow of the sailing ships, next to three fishing rods braced in a stand. He wore a green long-sleeved shirt, a brown, very wide-brimmed hat, and off-white slacks. Next to him were a trio of coolers. He opened one, extracted a bottle, and raised it as if towards the camera.

"He can see us, can't he?" Tess said.

"Easily," Adams said. "There are no other craft at sea. Only one person ashore. Lieutenant Renton?"

"Nothing on any radio frequency, Captain," Renton said.

"Any smoke?" Tess asked.

"None, but they could have syphoned fuel from those boats for a generator," Adams said. "Or he could be sleeping aboard his boat."

"Let's go say hello," Tess said.

"No, hang on," Hawker said.

"What is it?" Tess asked.

"This is the most normal thing I've seen in two months," Hawker said. "I don't like it. Take a small team. Not the scientists. Nicko and I'll be in the helicopter. If there's trouble, we can rope down. Do we have enough fuel?"

"For a rescue, certainly," Adams said.

"What's the signal?" Tess asked.

"You'll draw a gun," Hawker said.

"Mr Mackay, take the commissioner ashore," Adams said. "Commander Tusitala, prep the helicopter."

Chapter 42 - Catching a Shark
Corn Island, Nicaragua

"Where are the crew for those boats?" Clyde asked as their own small boat skimmed the waves, approaching the fisher, who was still enjoying his beer at the end of the pier.

"Want to place a bet on where they all went?" Zach asked.

"Not here, not now," Clyde said. "Keep focused."

"Back at Robben Island, the boats' crews got themselves infected," Glenn Mackay called out as he slowed the boat's speed to half. "Here, one person survived. A lone angler with a sea to himself. Looks like paradise."

Tess looked for signs of other survivors, but there were too many places for them to hide. Over thirty boats, and the giant ship, were tied up at the single long concrete pier. To east and west, a few wrecks dotted the orange-sand beach, but again, they were small yachts. Behind those, nestled amid a forest of palm trees, were waterfront buildings that could be houses, or bars, but they all had sea-facing decks. Those decks were as empty as the boats. Other than at the end of the pier, the only life was among the trees. From a cluster of palms at the pier's end, an iridescent blue flock took wing, merging with the near cloudless sky as they flew north.

"Oh, yes, paradise," Mackay said. "If only it were closer to home."

"There could be zoms inland," Tess said.

"Paradise lost," Clyde said. "If it were me, I'd camp out in the icebreaker. A ship designed for long missions in the Antarctic would have the most comfort."

"But maybe not air conditioning," Zach said. "So I'd go for that two-master with the mermaid painted on the bow."

"It was a warning, not a guess," Clyde said. "Watch that icebreaker for snipers."

Tess watched the trees, looking for more birds taking flight, until she caught movement, far closer. Ten metres from the pier, the angler put down his bottle and raised his hand, but only briefly, before returning it to his reel.

Mackay had brought them in obliquely, away from the man's fishing line, and to an empty mooring space on the western end of the long pier. Their boat bumped against the rubber tyres slung against the pier's side. Zach grabbed a rope, while Clyde grabbed the ladder, throwing himself up to the quayside before the boat was secured.

"We're police, we're friendly," Tess said, as she followed Clyde ashore.

The angler, some ten metres away, still hadn't taken his attention from his rods.

"G'day," Tess said. "*Kia ora.*"

And one of those, or both together, seemed to do the trick. The man stood, turned, removed his hat, raising it in front of his face, blocking out more of the sun.

"*Hola,*" he said. "You're police?"

The word was stencilled on their body-armour, though they wore naval fatigues beneath, and were each carrying a rifle as well as the usual armoury of weapons at their belts.

"Commissioner Tess Qwong," she said. "Australian Federal Police. We're here under a mandate from the United Nations, the African Union, and the Pacific Alliance, looking for survivors."

"The United Nations. Ha! A zombie organisation in a zombie world." He laughed. "Call me Mikael," he said.

Hearing his name, she pinned down his accent. It wasn't South American or Spanish, but something Slavic. What she could see of his chest beneath his half-open shirt was tanned to a crisp. But the top of his bald head was pale, his eyes were sapphire-blue, and the tattoo on his left forearm consisted of nine characters written in Cyrillic. About sixty, a facelift had tried to subtract a few decades, but the equatorial sun had only added them back on. Except for a long knife strapped to his lower leg, he wasn't visibly armed, nor were there any obvious firearms next to the chair or coolers.

"Good to meet you, Mikael," Tess said. "Are there many survivors here?"

"There are few anywhere," he replied. A frantic ringing erupted from a bell attached to the middle of his fishing rod. "Ah, lunch!" he said, grabbing the rod. "You, boy, you can help."

"M'name's Zach."

"You have two hands? Make them useful," Mikael said. "Here. Here. Hold!" As Zach held on, Mikael began working the reel.

With the year they'd been having, Tess was ninety percent certain a zom was on the other end of the line, but until it was hauled up, or the line broke, there'd be no more conversation from the angler. She looked north, instead, up the pier, and towards land. Palm trees dominated the view, but only partially obscured a cluster of buildings at the pier's end. A blue pick-up truck had been driven onto the jetty, and must belong to Mikael. There was no one else by the vehicle, nor were there any gates or barricades at the end of the pier. That the vehicle had been driven onto the pier suggested the angler didn't call any of the shore-side buildings his home. To the east of the pier were a cluster of concrete service buildings for the small cruise ships, tourist boats, and fishing hires that generated the islanders' income. The large timber-and-plank one-storey on the western side of the pier was a bar-restaurant with a wrap-around sundeck jutting out and above the beach.

"Ah-ha!" Mikael yelled. "Hold! Pull! Lunch!"

Tess turned around to see a metre-long shark flapping at the end of the wire-line.

"Over the pier! Over the pier!" Mikael said, grabbing the rod and turning it so the giant fish was over the jetty. Droplets of seawater splattered as the aquatic monster flapped and thrashed. Mikael dropped, his knee slamming onto the shark's belly as he dragged the knife from his ankle-sheath. One stab, and one last thrash of the tail, and the shark was still.

"A reef shark," Mikael said. "But it is young, like you, boy. Have you eaten shark? You shall, and then you shall be a man! You came here to arrest the zombies?"

"To look for survivors," Tess said, watching the blood pulse from the shark, pool in the gutter, and drip over the side of the quay.

"How many have you found?" Mikael asked as he crossed to his two iceboxes. He picked up a towel, wiping his knife clean, and then his hands.

"You're the first in South America," Tess said.

"I did wonder," he said. "We all did."

"There are more of you here?" Tess asked.

"I wouldn't need three rods if it was only me," he said, waving a hand at the boats.

"Are there zombies on the island?" Tess asked.

"Not anymore," Mikael said. "But there aren't many of us, either."

"Do you know what happened in the north? To the mainland?" Tess asked,

"Nothing good," Mikael said. "But it will take time to tell you what we know, so we will talk over lunch. We will share food and learn we are all friends. Do you want to radio your ship? Hmm." He looked down at his two coolers. "Boy, help," he said, wheeling the larger of the two coolers over to the still-bleeding shark.

Balancing the shark on the cooler, and with Zach pushing on one side, he began wheeling his catch towards the shore, leaving a blood trail behind.

"Glenn, use the radio on the boat. Call the captain," Tess said.

"Aye-aye, ma'am," Glenn said.

Clyde took his hand from the radio on his vest, and placed it on his gun.

"How many are you?" Tess asked.

"Fifty of us, now," Mikael said. "Some died. Some left. So it goes. You came from the south? You say there is no one there?"

"Not that we found," Tess said. "But we found nuclear craters in Brazil."

"Ah. I thought of going south, but my travelling days are done."

"You retired here?" Tess asked. Her ears pricked. An engine approached, and from inland.

"I retired to Miami," Mikael said. "Years ago, for my health."

"What was Florida like?" Tess asked.

"Beautiful. Once. But everywhere changes," he said. "Ah. Hernando is here! Good. Leave the shark, boy. Hernando will carry it."

It was obvious he was talking about the truck that had appeared from among the trees. It had approached from the north and parked at the end of the pier on a square of weather-beaten asphalt that was as much a car park for the bar-restaurant as for the pier.

Three people jumped out of the truck. Two men, one woman. All mid-twenties, athletic and lean, wearing bright shirts and pastel slacks, but carrying submachine guns as well as holstered pistols and sheathed knives. But it wasn't the weapons which rang a warning bell.

"Hernando! Come. Get our lunch!" Mikael called, raising a hand, waving to the trio.

"Who are you?" one of the men replied, and he wasn't addressing Mikael. His accent was Spanish-American. A cream-coloured straw hat shadowed most of his face, but beneath was a fussily neat goatee trimmed so as to accentuate his cheekbones. Seeing his companion's crumpled trousers and shirt better emphasised that Hernando's were pressed as, indeed, were Mikael's. Pressed, but not a good fit. Hernando's short sleeves were a centimetre too long, and an inch too baggy. His beard was so precise it hadn't just been shaved but plucked. His reptile-skin belt, holster, and long belt-sheath matched his boots.

"Telstra Tower," Clyde said, his voice low.

"The Canberra bunker," Tess replied, and then raised her voice. "We're from Canberra."

"They are Australian police," Mikael said. He'd stopped now, halfway along the pier, level with the anchored icebreaker.

Tess looked up. She could see no one up on the icebreaker's deck. She looked back at Hernando, and knew exactly where she'd seen him before. The clothes were pressed, but that just required electricity.

Laundry required water as well. No, these clothes had been looted. Salvaged. But not the reptile-skin boots. Not the belt and holster. No, those were his pride and joy. He'd wear them everywhere. He'd worn them in Colombia in front of that video camera. Weeks ago, when he'd wielded that knife. Yes, she recognised him, but so did Zach.

"You're the torturer!" Zach said.

Tess's hand dropped to her holster. Mikael raised his knee, drawing his knife. The gun's grip was oddly warm in her hand as Tess dragged her weapon up. Mikael grabbed Zach's wrist with his left hand, twisting his arm up behind his back while his right hand brought his knife to the young man's throat before Tess had a bead on his forehead. It took less than a second. Clyde had his carbine raised, and each of the two goons had their own weapons levelled. Not Hernando, though. He'd not moved at all.

"No!" Mikael called. "This is not polite. You police are disinvited to lunch. Leave your weapons. Get on your boat. Go. Or I throw the boy into the water. Lots of sharks there now."

"It's okay, Zach," Tess said, keeping her weapon aimed just above Zach's ear. She almost had a line on Mikael's forehead. "Let Zach go and we'll leave, too," she said.

"*No dispares*," Hernando said. His two guards lowered their weapons. "No shooting. Let him go, Mikael. Let them leave."

And that was most worrying of all.

She let her gun drop a fraction. "Clyde, we're leaving."

"I've a question," Zach said.

"Later, Zach," Tess said.

"Nah, it's important," Zach said. "What do sharks and police have in common?" he asked, and slammed his head back and into Mikael's face while stamping his heel down on the old man's foot. From her left came a triple rat-a-tat-tat as Clyde opened fire. Zach's free hand grabbed for Mikael's knife hand as the young man attempted one of the break-and-throw moves Nicko had taught him during the voyage. But Zach didn't have the timing that only came with experience. Tess did. Even as

Mikael leaned back, she fired, once, her bullet clipping the man's skull, spraying blood against the icebreaker's hull.

"Clear!" Clyde said, even before Tess had turned. Hernando and his two guards were down.

"Are you okay, Zach?" Tess asked, running past him.

"Yeah, no worries," he said.

Clyde overtook her, sweeping his gun from one corpse to the next, and then to the treeline.

"That was dumb, Zach," Tess said.

"Nah, because I know him. I know Hernando. He's that bloke from the video in Colombia. He's the torturer."

"I know," she said, "but shouting it out wasn't smart."

"Yeah, but it's over now," Zach said. "We won."

"We haven't," Clyde said. "That was all wrong. That's not how you go about hijacking a warship."

"What d'you mean?" Zach asked.

"Back to the boat," Tess said. "We need to warn the captain."

But it was too late. The helicopter buzzed low over the sea, not heading towards the pier, but looping low above the beach. Mackay ran along the pier, rifle raised.

"It's the cartel," Tess said as she walked over to Hernando's body. On his wrist was a tattoo she'd seen before: a branch with three leaves. "It's the bloody cartel. Glenn, warn the captain. Clyde, are these ships empty?"

"If they weren't, we'd be dead," Clyde said. "Some bullet holes in that yacht. Old ones."

"Soldiers are being deployed inland," Mackay said.

"I think we found the sisters," Tess said. "Zach, behind me. Clyde, eyes on the road. Mackay, watch the trees."

She led them down the pier, around Mikael's truck, and took cover behind Hernando's vehicle. To her left was the restaurant and bar, festooned with signs offering boat hire as prominently as drinks. To her right was the harbour master's office, and behind that were the port's service buildings. All small. All dark. Not a single electric bulb was on, but it was a blue-sky midday.

"They drove here from somewhere," she said. "Mackay—"

The ground shook, and the roar of the ship's cannon was lost beneath the earthquake detonation. Dust and smoke plumed upward, inland.

"That was the runway," Mackay said, half-listening to the radio. "Captain says— ugh." He fell, clutching his leg.

"Sniper!" Clyde said, pushing Zach from his feet. "East. The trees. Stay behind the truck. Zach, take my carbine. Keep your head down, and empty the entire magazine into the trees on the count of three. Three. No more, no less. Start counting."

And before Tess could stop him, Clyde ran from behind the truck, and towards the palms. A single shot strummed through the broad leaves as he disappeared from sight.

"Now, Zach," Tess said. She grabbed Mackay's vest-straps, hauling him closer to the vehicle. Behind, and above, lead tore through the air with a machine-rattle bark that was over almost as soon as it began.

"I'm out," Zach said. "Should I fire another magazine?"

"No. Grab the radio. Call the ship," she said, pulling out her emergency med-kit. "You'll be okay, Glenn. The bullet missed the artery. Zach, tell the ship we're taking fire and want to know what the captain's plan is."

"Sorry, ma'am," Mackay hissed. "Ducked when I should've jumped."

"No worries. We'll get you out of here," Tess said.

"They're the cartel, aren't they?" Mackay asked.

"Seems so. That should stop the bleeding," Tess said, securing the dressing. "Zach, we're commandeering that blue pick-up. We'll chuck Glenn in the back, drive to our boat, and kick our way back to the ship."

"We're not," Zach said, lowering the radio. "The helicopter saw boats leaving from the north of the island. The warship is chasing them. That explosion we heard, that was us shooting at a plane trying to take off. We blew it up!"

"Are the cartel fleeing the island?" Tess asked.

"I guess," Zach said. "The captain's chasing them."

"Clear!" Clyde called from the trees. "Coming out. Hold your fire."

Tess slowly leaned around the car, only standing when she saw Clyde jog from between the palms.

"Only one sniper," he said. "Atop a generator-shed."

"The cartel are fleeing the island," Tess said. "Taking boats from the north. The *Te Taiki* is in pursuit, but she blew up a plane trying to take off."

"Understood," Clyde said, and without explaining, sprinted off to the bar, pushed open the door, ran in, and ran out again a moment later. "Zach, help the commish with Mackay. We're getting him inside there until our ride returns."

She and Zach carried a barely protesting Mackay inside, and onto a bench seat near the door. Clyde followed, but stayed in the doorway.

"If the enemy are fleeing, some might come here for those boats," Clyde said. "We don't want to be on the water halfway between a cannon and its target."

"So we'll wait here and ambush anyone fleeing," Tess said.

"Your call, Commish," Clyde said.

"You mean you wouldn't?" she asked. "We're in your world now. Tell me what to do."

"They're on the run, so let's keep them running," he said. "Drive north, and drive them before us, in that truck, before they can dig in or get organised."

"Agreed," Tess said.

"I'll radio in what we're doing, then we'll move," Clyde said.

"Zach, find the back door," Tess said, though she glanced back to Mackay before returning to the window, watching the approach road to the harbour. They'd stumbled into a war, so she'd trust to Clyde's judgement. Besides, floating atop shark-infested waters wasn't the best place for a bleeding man to wait for safety.

A plane had been destroyed attempting to take off. Was it the same plane they'd seen a few days ago, closer to the smoking mass grave in Colombia? Maybe. The cartel had been waiting for the warship, and hoping it would sail elsewhere. When it approached, Mikael had been sent to the pier. That didn't entirely explain the three-sided nature of the quayside confrontation, but they had killed the torturer. Hopefully those two who'd accompanied him were his best people.

"Helicopter's out of fuel," Clyde said. "Nicko and Bruce are on the ground, west of the runway. There's a third pier on the island's western shores. Our boys just neutralised a group trying to escape. We'll drive north, meeting them at a junction with a west-bound road."

"Zach, stay here," Tess said.

"What? No way," he said.

"Your mission is to keep Glenn alive," Tess said. "If they try to come into this bar, shoot them. But if they go for a boat, let them, and let the *Te Taiki* send them straight to Hell."

Chapter 43 - Pursue and Ye Shall Find
Corn Island, Nicaragua

In a crouch, Tess ran from the bar and across the empty car park. From the north came the crackle of gunfire, a small explosion, then a larger though more distant one. The battle wasn't close, but nor was it close to being over.

"I'm driving," she said, as Clyde ran to the driver's side of the green pick-up.

Barely slowing, he jumped over the hood.

"Show-off," she said. "This car's nearer to retirement than me. But it's old enough not to have any electronics, so why is the interior newly refurbed?"

The keys were in the ignition, and the truck started on the first go.

"No guns, or gun rack," Clyde said.

"Yep, I noticed that," she said, spinning the truck back, and around Hernando's bullet-flecked truck. "Mikael wasn't armed, and wasn't entirely in command."

"Do you think he was the local warlord," Clyde said, "but Hernando was the sisters' lieutenant?"

"That would explain the quayside confusion," she said.

"According to the copter, this road should run parallel to the runway," Clyde said. "Down there. Halfway, there's the turning to the western pier. That's the R.P."

"They kept boats in the north, south, and the west, plus a plane ready to go on the runway. Mikael said there were fifty people here. If he wasn't lying, how many are left?"

"Not many," Clyde said. "So we'll keep 'em running."

She drove past houses, a shop, a small hotel. The managed palm-wilderness suddenly gave way to the rigidly cleared runway from which dusty smoke plumed from a crater and poured from a broken plane. The jet lay on its belly with its nose on the road, but other than cloying smoke flowing from its port engine, it appeared intact. So did the pair of people helping each other into the back of a red taxi which had stopped on the road a hundred metres ahead.

"Slow!" Clyde said, rearing out of the window, firing at the car. But Tess had to swerve around the debris the plane had left on the road. Clyde missed his shot.

Tess drove them up onto the kerb, shattering a quartet of terracotta pots, two on either side of a sun-bleached front door. The fleeing plane-passengers were all aboard the taxi, which was reversing at speed. Tess brought the truck back onto the road, beyond the smoking plane, and the taxi was now directly ahead of them. But the enemy was driving backwards, and she was catching up.

The taxi reversed into a courtyard-driveway shared by three two-storey villas, and stopped. The two passengers ran to the steps leading up to the middle of the three houses while the driver jumped out, and sheltered behind the car as he levelled an assault rifle.

"Slow!" Clyde said, firing blind out of the window. He missed. Their enemy didn't. Bullets shattered the wing mirror, ripping paint from the bodywork, and pierced the windscreen, tearing a hole through the padded roof.

"Brace!" Tess yelled, as spider web cracks frosted the windscreen. She ducked low, and ducked lower as another burst from the assault rifle shattered the glass in front. Screaming in key with the engine, she stamped her foot on the accelerator, ramming her truck into the taxi. Momentum slammed her back against the seat, while physics shunted the taxi forward, crushing the shooter sheltering behind.

Clyde threw open his door, falling outside, staggering to his feet, bringing his rifle to bear on the villa's partially open door. Tess eased outside.

"You okay, Commish?" Clyde asked.

"No worries," she said, wincing, testing her limbs. Bruised, but not broken.

Shots rang out inside the house. Tess drew her sidearm, and trained it on the curtained windows while Clyde aimed his weapon at the door.

"Going in?" he asked.

"Have to," she said.

"Who's there?" someone called from inside, a woman with a U.S. accent.

"Australian Federal Police, acting on a U.N. warrant to find survivors. Your mob shot at us."

"Australia?" the woman called back. "You're not with the cartel?"

"No," Tess called. "Are you?

There was a whispered back-and-forth on the other side of the closed door, of which the only words Tess could clearly discern were: "*well, of course they'd say that*." It was a man who'd spoken, again with a U.S. accent.

"We've got a warship in the harbour," Tess called. "If you don't open the door, we'll have them drop a shell right on your head."

"Hang on," the man said.

"Seriously?" Clyde said. But he lowered his carbine a fraction. "Don't think they're hostile, Commish."

To the left of the door, a net curtain moved. A face appeared, but vanished too quickly for her to see more than a shadow.

"No way," came a half-hissed comment from inside.

"I'm losing my patience out here," Tess called.

"What do you want me to do, boss?" Clyde asked.

"Is that Inspector Tess Qwong?" the woman called from inside the villa.

"Who's there?" Tess said.

The door opened. A woman stepped out. Her hands were cuffed in front of her, though they were holding a bloody machete. More blood covered her jeans and shirt, while exhaustion covered her face. Far paler than when Tess had seen her last. Far older, though it was only two months. But she wouldn't forget the face of the hermit-woman hiding from her past up by the dingo-fence in the outback.

"Corrie Guinn? How did you end up here?" Tess asked.

Corrie wasn't alone. The man who stepped out of the shadows was her brother, Pete. The third-degree sunburn from when she'd first met him had faded into a tan, over which was laid a week of sweaty grime, and beneath which were bruises. Like his sister, the signs of a crash diet were visible around his eyes and neck, though his cheeks were covered in a youthfully eccentric beard. Like her, he wore a tourist's left-behinds: cream slacks that barely reached his ankles, but with material to spare for the waist; a lurid shirt in such a violent purple hue it was nearly a crime; no socks, no shoes. His hands were cuffed, and awkwardly holding a revolver.

"Inspector Qwong!" Pete said. "You can't believe how good it is to see you. To see anyone."

"No worries, Pete. Good to see you, too. We're out here hunting down the sisters. The cartel terrorists."

"You've found them," Corrie said. "Not the sisters. They're not here. But these are their people. They caught us in the States, and flew us down here to wait for their bosses."

"Hands, Pete!" a different woman said. Short, barely topping one-point-six metres tall, with equally short hair, hacked rather than cut. Her figure hard to discern in the baggy tourist-reject shirt and shorts, cinched around her waist with a belt, but in her hand was a key.

"This is Olivia. Livy, this is Tess Qwong. Remember me telling you about her and Liu Higson from Broken Hill?"

"Hands, Pete," Olivia said briskly. "Nice to meet you, Ms Qwong."

"How many hostiles are here?" Tess asked.

"Forty-three, yesterday," Corrie said instantly. "There are five other prisoners. Locals. I don't know where they're keeping them, but last time we saw them, they were in a really bad way."

These three, by contrast, were not. They were dirty, bruised, exhausted, but had no obvious cuts or broken bones.

"Commish!" Clyde called.

Tess spun, and saw Clyde pointing north, but with his hand rather than a gun. Two figures sprinted towards them: Hawker and Oakes.

"There are five more prisoners, plus you three?" Tess asked. "Is anyone else on this island friendly?"

"Not even a little," Corrie said.

"Bruce, there's forty-three hostiles," Tess said as the colonel ran into earshot.

"Not now there's not," Hawker said.

"You own the battleship, right?" Pete asked.

"A couple of days ago, their plane spotted a navy warship to the south, near their Colombian fuel-base," Corrie explained. "They had some weapon in the hangar they were going to use to kill you."

"Bruce, that's probably the VX," Tess said.

"They won't fly anything out of here now," Hawker said.

"But it might be rigged to blow," Clyde said. "That'd be a good way to ensure we wouldn't follow them. You said it was in the hangar over there? I'll go check it out."

"Nicko, time to earn our pay," Hawker said. "Tess, hold this house. If there's an explosion, get inside, close the windows and doors, and stay inside until the dust has settled."

While the three soldiers jogged across the road, to the runway and toward the hangar beyond, Tess leaned against the car, taking a moment to allow her brain to catch up with events. "Pete and Corrie Guinn. Of all the places in the world, of all the people, I find you here. And you found Olivia, Pete. Good on ya, but how?"

"Accident," Pete said.

"Destiny," Corrie said.

"A little of both," Olivia said. "How is it you're here, Inspector?"

"Essentially, we've been hunting the cartel," she said. "I'm a commissioner now. Corrie, do you remember Anna Dodson? She's the deputy prime minister in Canberra. We've had a..." She trailed off, turning towards a mosquito-whine rising in volume to diamond-drill. An engine. Two engines: a lime-green Kawasaki speed-bike that could have outraced a plane during take-off, and a bright red Ferrari-convertible as old as Mick.

The biker raised a pistol. The first shot was a close one, whistling past her ear and slamming into a wooden window shutter, but the recoil threw off the biker's balance. The bike weaved. The biker's second two shots went wide. So did Tess's first, but not her second. The bullet clipped the man's shoulder, sending up a haze of blood which hovered in the air as the bike tumbled to the verge. The rider rolled across the road, and into the path of the old Ferrari. The rider hit the splitter, rolled up the bumper, and onto the hood, before the car swerved, shaking the corpse off, and ruining the aim of the woman with the submachine gun in the back. Bullets sprayed everywhere, but mostly at the sky. Tess fired back, but though the car was trailing sparks as well as dust, it kept on speeding south. Towards the pier. Towards Zach and Mackay.

"Hold this position!" she yelled, running to the fallen motorbike. Holstering her gun, she pulled the bike upright.

So this is war, she thought as she rode off, *it's just another chase*.

The bike wanted to race. She didn't let it, keeping her speed low as she followed the settling cloud back to the pier. Above the engine's burr, it was hard to hear anything, until she heard gunfire. Growing in volume.

At the pier, the Ferrari had to slow to drive around the stalled truck, but it didn't stop. Zach was shooting from inside the bar. The car's rear-passenger emptied her submachine gun's magazine. But the car was weaving, and Tess was nearing.

The convertible burst onto the concrete pier, accelerating, then braking just as swiftly, stopping by the icebreaker.

Tess braked, stopping by Hernando's increasingly battered truck, waving at the bar in the hope for recognition more than as a signal. She drew her pistol as someone by the stopped convertible opened fire. Single shots, and so ill-aimed, Tess couldn't tell if the woman was shooting at her or at the bar. Using the truck as cover, Tess returned fire, emptying her magazine before ducking down, moving to the other end of the truck as she reloaded. She heard two cracking retorts, but only a single thud of a bullet slamming into the vehicle's bodywork.

The situation wasn't ideal: three hostiles, armed, boarding an icebreaker which had a hull as thick as armour. It wouldn't be as fast as the warship, but the warship was engaged with boats in the north. Plane, boats, icebreaker, all departing from different directions. Scattering. Making it impossible for everyone to be captured. But this icebreaker had been kept until last. It was Hernando's boat. Mikael's boat. The leaders' boat. A shot hit her truck. A burst hit the bar.

She sprang up and fired at the man climbing up the ship's side. He made for an easy target. Her bullet took him in the side. As he fell, he twisted, turned, so he hit the jetty head-first. It was a high enough fall to knock him out, but probably not to kill him, except that the ship had drifted half a metre from the pier. The man's legs and waist were over the edge. Slowly, he slid down into the water, already foaming as the engines increased their tempo. The ship was already prepped for departure. That was why Hernando, if not Mikael, had come to the pier. Another burst, poorly aimed, ripped through the vegetation behind her.

She sprang from cover again, but couldn't see any targets on the pier. They'd made it aboard. Gun raised, expecting to see a shooter at the stern, she ran, sprinting for the side of the boat. Ropes had been holding the vessel in place, but those fell, severed from the deck. The icebreaker was manoeuvring slowly, and was over a metre from the jetty when she jumped for the ladder. Her left hand caught the rung, but her gun-hand slammed against metal. The pistol fell from her grip as her elbows, and then her knees, slammed into the ship, but her feet found the rungs. Below, the sea frothed, and not just from the engines. A fin cut through the waves, speaking of a horror below as visceral as that on deck.

A familiar pain rose from her hip, joined by newer aches from shoulder and knees, but one rung at a time, she hauled herself up, pausing only when a distant explosion rocked the island. Hoping it was just a cannon shell, she gripped the top rung. Leaning back, she brought her feet up further, then launched herself over the side, rolling into a crouch as she landed on the deck.

An axe was running towards her, its wielder barely a metre behind. The axe swung up while the gangster pounded down the gangway. Experience told her there wasn't time to draw her knife, so she dived, tackling the man at the knees, pushing up and off, and throwing him over her shoulder, over the side of the ship into the shark-infested waters below.

Barely had she time to regret the guilty flash of satisfaction when an anvil slammed into her chest. She fell back to the deck, rolling again, and beneath the shadow of the deck-crane even as she gasped for air. Shot. She'd been shot. Right in the vest. And someone was shooting still. Bullets pinged off the deck-crane around which she sheltered. A large crane made of thick steel, with even thicker steel panelling running around the base, but with a control unit close to her head.

She pulled herself upward, every breath an agony. The shooting had ceased, so the shooter was approaching, wanting to confirm the kill. This ship was ready to depart. How ready? The crane controls had a shed of levers and a star-scape of lights, but one of the recessed red buttons was marked *emergency release*. She slammed her hand down. The lock disconnected, the cable unspooled, and the hook slammed into the deck. Not as hard as she was expecting, but if she'd not been holding herself upright, she'd have fallen. The shooter *hadn't* been expecting it. The shooter *had* fallen.

As Tess swung herself around the crane, and while the uncoiling cable lashed around the deck, she saw her enemy, the woman who'd been in the back of the convertible. She was prone, on all fours, at the base of the ladder, but already pulling herself back up. Tess staggered onward, drawing her knife, while the woman wasted time looking for her fallen gun.

The shooter bent to pick up a dropped revolver. Tess lunged, just as the ship rocked, adding its motion to her weight, as the blade plunged into the terrorist's side. Hot blood washed over Tess as she pulled the blade out. The woman grabbed Tess's arm, but her grip was weak, and growing weaker. Tess pushed her away, down to the deck. It was easier than killing a zombie. Far easier. Tess grabbed the dying gangster's revolver, and hauled herself up the steps towards the bridge. Behind her, the clack of the winch was replaced by a slithering groan as the loose cable slid across the deck.

Not her problem. No, hers was on the bridge, because someone must have been aboard the icebreaker, getting this ship ready for departure. But the bridge was empty.

Tess staggered to a halt against the console. Through the window, she saw empty ocean as the boat churned through the waves, still picking up speed.

Her eyes tracked from one control console to the next until they settled on the familiar sight of a radio.

"*Te Taiki*, this is Tess Qwong on the icebreaker. Can someone tell me what a ship's handbrake looks like?"

Chapter 44 - A Long Way from the Outback
Corn Island, Nicaragua

With a wrenching effort, Tess removed her vest, in which two slugs were still embedded. She didn't remember the second shot. Her ribs were bruised, but probably not broken, and she was, remarkably, alive.

It took twenty minutes for the helicopter to arrive overhead. By then, following Captain Adams's radioed instructions, Tess had cut power to the engines. Three sailors jumped from the helicopter, which took flight almost immediately, returning to shore. Leaving Lt Renton to turn the ship around, she began the search for the last terrorist.

He was easy to find, as he'd taken refuge in the captain's cabin which he'd then secured from the inside. She put a sailor on guard, and limped back to the bridge, only pausing to examine the bullet marks in the bulkhead and bloodstains on the deck.

By the time they reached the shore, the battle was over. Clyde was waiting on the jetty. She waved him up to the deck.

"There's one last cartel killer in the captain's cabin," she said. "Can you find some cutting gear?"

"I'll try talking first," Clyde said. "Can I offer him a deal?"

"No, but you can tell him we want to know what happened here. If he wants to pretend he's a victim, that's fine, so don't mention any prisoners we've freed. What's happened ashore?"

"We won," Clyde said.

"Good to know, but are there any specifics I should be aware of?"

"They stuck two bricks of C4 with a timer beneath the runway's fuel tanks," Clyde said. "Found it before we refuelled the helicopter."

"That's good," Tess said. "And it's good there's fuel for the helicopter. And that it didn't blow up."

"I think the device was supposed to be another diversion, because they didn't rig the bomb to the VX."

"You found more nerve agent?" Tess asked.

"Two canisters so far. First was in the hangar. In a transportation-container. It's military grade, and custom-built, but unmarked."

"It's a WMD," Tess said. "Which nation would want to sign their name on that crime?"

"It's a deeper tragedy than that," Clyde said. "I found the second canister beneath the plane."

"Do you mean the crashed plane?"

"It doesn't appear to have leaked. The scientists aren't taking any chances. They're geared up, and dismantling it. The canisters slot into a dispersal device built beneath the plane's wing. That's a commercial jet, and it's a military-grade dispersal device. The design would have been trialled. Tested. It's a wing-mounted delivery system that looks remarkably similar to a spare, external fuel tank."

"Trialled it? But not with VX or surely we'd have known about it," Tess said.

"You'd like to think so," Clyde said. "But the evening news had a limited number of spots for faraway tragedies."

"Can you guess who designed it?"

"Not yet, but there aren't many suspects. This is the work of a national government, and a military-grade factory."

"Then every possible suspect is dead," Tess said. She took a deep breath, and stalled halfway through, wincing as she rubbed her ribs. "D'you know, I'll be glad when we're out of this sea. So the explosive at the fuel tanks would have been a diversion. But so were the boats, leaving from different piers. How many got away?"

"Four were sunk. Two fast-boats, two yachts. There's no way to know how many people were aboard."

"Could a ship have evaded detection?"

"Possibly," he said. "It's possible there are some cartel-terrorists still hiding on the island. Give me a team of ten, and thermal imaging, and a week, and I'll find them."

"What could they tell us that the man in the cabin couldn't?" Tess asked. "You get him out, I'll speak to the former captives, and then to the captain."

With a weary sigh, followed by a clenching wince, she climbed over the side of the ship.

She reached the shore-side bar at the same time as a white pick-up, marked harbour-master, and driven by Captain Adams. Two sailors with a stretcher jumped out of the back, and hurried to the bar.

"We're collecting Mr Mackay," Adams said. "We're docked in the north."

"Were there many fatalities?" Tess asked.

"None yet, but there were casualties," Adams said. "The enemy was trying to flee rather than fight."

The two sailors came out of the bar with Glenn Mackay strapped to a stretcher, and with Zach a step behind.

"The cartel were keeping prisoners on the island," Tess said. "Five were reported to require medical assistance."

"We've found eight," Adams said. "Three from the U.S. who seem to know you, and five South Americans. Two are in a bad way. Three are worse. They've been transferred to the ship. Your friends are still in the crossroads house."

"An enemy combatant's locked himself into the captain's cabin on the icebreaker," Tess said. "Clyde's fishing him out."

"Was that ship our diesel trader?" Adams asked.

"Couldn't say," Tess said. "Not yet. But a battle was fought on that icebreaker long before we arrived. There are bloodstains and bullet holes in the corridors. I'll need more time to inspect it."

"Perhaps your old friends will be able to tell us," Adams said.

"Are you coming, Zach?" Tess asked.

"Well, I'm not staying here," he said.

They drove slowly until they reached the crashed plane, where a pair of yellow-clad figures were huddled near the wing.

When they stopped at the house, Tess jumped down. Adams got out, too.

"Zach, stay with Glenn," Tess said, and looked back towards the crashed plane while the truck sped away. "If you'd not stopped the escaping boats, how far could they have reached?"

"The mainland, easily," Adams said. "It's only seventy kilometres away. The island of Little Corn is much closer."

"They must have had a destination in mind," Tess said. "Clyde said an explosive had been rigged at the runway-fuel tanks, so that plane wasn't going to land here again."

"It was a lucky shot that took out the plane," Adams said. "A life at sea breeds superstition. It's a habit I tried to avoid, but it's a notion that seeps into one's thinking. The shell hit the runway in front of the plane, and from sufficient distance the pilot, instinctively, turned. The plane careened off the runway, and so broke its landing gear. A second earlier, the plane might have made it into the air. A second later, and we'd have scattered the plane's contents across the island. There's VX aboard."

"Clyde told me. In a military-grade dispersal system."

"They might have constructed it to survive a crash, but not a direct impact," Adams said.

"During the confrontation on the pier, the bloke I think was their leader wanted us to get back in the boat and return to the ship," Tess said. "That plane is why. They were going to strafe the warship."

"I imagine so," Adams said. "Would we have shot down a civilian plane flying low overhead? Probably not. These sisters knew the politicians they'd been bedding down with would want to obliterate all witnesses. An attack sub, or even a destroyer, would be too noticeable an acquisition for two drug-dealing gangsters, so they purchased a nerve agent, and a system with which to deploy it against enemy ships. After the end of the world, to them, every ship became an enemy."

"So they're not likely to be the fuel-traders," Tess said. "Though I'm not ruling it out. But it does make me wonder, among other questions, why they came to this particular island."

"Let's see if your friends know the answer," Adams said.

When the truck had pulled in, the three Americans had been sitting on the stoop of the central villa. Corrie and Olivia had stood up, though Pete hadn't. He sat, head bowed over a food-can whose contents he was shovelling into his mouth. Olivia rested a hand on his shoulder. Corrie had taken a few steps towards them, but then stopped, waiting, clearly anxious while the two professionals conducted their private conversation.

"Hey Corrie," Tess said with a broad smile. "I can't believe you're here."

"We're guarding the food," Corrie said, coming over to meet them.

"There's food here?" Adams asked.

"This is their stash-house," Corrie said. "They kept the food upstairs. They kept us in the cellar. You'll want to know everything, Inspector— sorry, Commissioner, but can we talk alone?" She nodded towards Olivia and Pete. "I know everything you need to know, and they don't need to relive it."

"Sure," Tess said. "Can you walk, Pete?"

"Mmm," he said, his mouth full of pineapple.

"Take that road, and you'll find my ship and crew," Adams said. "Tell them there's food here, and I want it aboard."

"This is Captain Adams," Tess said, as the couple walked away. "Corrie used to live in my patch of the bush, keeping an eye on the dingo-fence. She's a mate of mine, and of Mick Dodson's."

Corrie nodded. "Hey. Thanks for saving us."

"How did you come to be here?" Adams asked.

"After we flew to Canada, me and Pete went to find Olivia in South Bend. That's where she and Pete lived before. Afterward, we linked up with General Yoon's army. We were at the rear when the bombs fell, but the front was close to the Saint Lawrence. Ground zero for the nuclear strikes. The general's army was wiped out. Judge Benton took command and was organising a retreat, but the three of us went west to see if we could make contact with you, with the Pacific Alliance. We didn't get very far. But we found Lisa Kempton. She was being held prisoner by these cartel people."

"Kempton? Do you mean that eccentric billionaire?" Adams asked.

"Oh, you don't know?" Corrie asked. "Lisa's been trying to stop these people for decades. The cartel and their pet politicians. Well, she failed, obviously. She went east to finish them off. We went west to try to reach you guys, but we didn't get far before we learned Vancouver had been bombed and people were fleeing inland. It was a real mess. Zombies and refugees don't mix well. People were hungry and scared. So were we. The three of us drove south, and crossed the border. Kempton had set up supply stashes for her people, for after the apocalypse. That's where they caught us."

"Who's they?" Tess asked. "Do you mean the cartel?"

"They were waiting for Kempton but we turned up instead."

"How did they get you here?" Adams asked.

"By jet-plane," Corrie said. "We stopped once. I overheard them talking while we changed plane, and I think they said we were in West Virginia. We were blindfolded the whole time, and drugged when we changed aircraft, but it can't have been more than two days between them grabbing us and bringing us down here."

"They found you at a stash house in the U.S., near the Canadian border, and flew you here?" Adams asked. "Why not kill you?"

"Because I persuaded them I knew stuff," Corrie said. "Things about Kempton, like where her other safe houses were. Where she might be. How she'd stayed ahead of the sisters all these years. I exaggerated a lot, and lied about the rest, but they believed me. Except the sisters were supposed to be here, so it was stupid."

"It kept you alive," Tess said.

"No," Corrie said. "Because afterwards, Hernando explained what the sisters were going to do with Kempton when they caught her. They wanted to torture her for years. Literally. He was trained as a doctor. He even knew her blood type so he could set up transfusions. It was… even in a year where we've seen zombies and nuclear bombs, it was sickening. It would have been better if they'd killed us up north, because when the sisters got here, he made it clear he was going to practice on us."

"But the sisters didn't arrive?" Adams asked.

"No, so we were treated… not like guests, but we weren't really harmed. Not except when we almost escaped. We made it to the docks, but they had a sentry watching the boats. We had some food with us, so they… they skinned the woman who was in charge of the kitchen. In front of us. It was like back in that golf club in Broken Hill."

"We saw it in Colombia, too," Tess said. "They even left a video of Hernando torturing some of the locals."

"Right, you went to their mine, didn't you?" Corrie said.

"You know about that?" Tess asked.

"*They* knew about that," Corrie said. "The plane flew around looking for ships, looking for the sisters. Any ship that wasn't cartel was lured here. Except, a few days ago, the plane returned reporting the mine was now just a smoking crater, and a warship was seen sailing northwest."

"That was us," Adams said. "What happened to the other locals, and the ships' passengers?"

"The passengers were killed and dumped in the sea. Fed to the sharks. Usually after they were dead. Usually. But it was worse for the locals. Um…" She looked back at the house, and up to an upstairs window. "After we tried to escape, they beat Pete up. They were going to start on Olivia, but I got Mikael to stop them."

"The old man? About sixty?" Tess asked.

"Yeah, him," Corrie said. "He's their brother."

"Whose brother?" Tess asked.

"The sisters," Corrie said. "He's their younger brother."

"He's dead," Tess said. "The sisters had a brother?"

"He's dead? Good. He was a disappointment to them. Wasn't evil enough, you see? He had a son, and the son, the sisters' nephew, is the heir to their underworld. The sisters went to collect this nephew from somewhere up north. In North America. Mikael was brought here from Miami where he was sort of under house arrest in a mansion. The sisters, and the nephew, were supposed to come here, but they never arrived."

"Was Mikael a prisoner, too?" Tess asked.

"Not exactly. Hernando was in charge, but Mikael was obviously way more important to the sisters than anyone else here. He was no saint, but he was also a lonely old man. He wanted company, and I thought maybe that was a way to keep Pete and Olivia alive."

"I understand," Tess said. "So Hernando was in charge, but Mikael was the V.I.P. The sisters were supposed to come here with the nephew, but never arrived."

"What happened to the rest of the locals?" Adams asked.

"Poisoned," Corrie said. "They were given an injection of what they were told was the British vaccine. The cartel had their supplies stashed in Colombia. Food and medicine mostly. But the plan wasn't to come here specifically. It was to take over an island. Any island. But not to decide on which one in advance. Find an island, kill everyone, and then wait. They thought they would be betrayed. Their original plan was to seize the Panama Canal and charge all the world's governments for access. It was a route to legitimacy and empire. The sisters didn't think the apocalypse would get so bad. But they never came here, and you destroyed their supplies in Colombia."

"We did," Adams said.

"After the plane spotted the smoke, Hernando decided he'd done enough waiting. If your warship came this way, he was going to drop poison on it. All the boats were going to scatter, but he was going to take the icebreaker and go look for the sisters. He was that scared of them. Even now, he was going to look for them. Mikael was certain they were dead, though. He wanted to stay here. Start a new life in paradise."

"The sisters bought the VX for Panama," Tess said. "That's why they had a base in Colombia, in the desert. Within range of the canal, but nowhere near enough they would need to worry about poison carried by the wind. Drop the VX, kill the survivors, and any new survivors who turn up, and then move in a month or two later."

“That’s more or less what Mikael thought,” Corrie said. “But he didn’t know about the VX until we came here.”

“You said Mikael was brought here because they thought they’d been betrayed,” Tess said. “Was this suspected betrayal before or after the outbreak?”

“Before, I think, but I’m not sure,” Corrie said.

“Perhaps one of our two prisoners know,” Adams said. “Am I right that Lisa Kempton went looking for the sisters and this nephew?”

“I think so,” Corrie said. “Lisa was hunting the politicians, too.”

“As the sisters never arrived, perhaps she found them,” Adams said.

“What about the lab?” Tess asked.

“What lab?” Corrie asked.

“Back in Australia, we caught one of their conspirators. He told us the lab which developed the zom-virus was in Colombia. That’s why we came to this sea. But if Hernando picked this island at random, the lab can’t be here. Do you know where it is?”

“Sorry, Mikael didn’t know anything about it, or the zombies. I don’t think Hernando did, either. But I can’t be certain. He was less like a leader and more like a courier. A caretaker. He returned to Miami a day before the outbreak, with orders to get ready to move Mikael. Someone else was supposed to arrive and take charge. Maybe it was the sisters, but I don’t think it was supposed to be Hernando. More than half his people were just street-dealers. After the outbreak hit Manhattan, he grabbed everyone he could as quickly as he could, and fled south.”

“If he could only recruit amateurs, let’s hope that means the professionals are all dead,” Tess said. “Do you know where they were fleeing to from here?”

“Sorry, no,” Corrie said. “Before you destroyed their depot in Colombia, that was their rendezvous. They must have picked somewhere new, but they didn’t tell Mikael. Or he didn’t tell me.”

“We think they had some kind of attack ship,” Adams said. “Something sank a flotilla of sailing ships on the southern shore of the Caribbean Sea, but there’s nothing on this island with that capability.”

"I wasn't allowed out much," Corrie said. "The cellar, Mikael's rooms, and sometimes we'd sit out on the veranda behind the house, but that was it. The only time we made it to the shore was when we failed to escape."

"Do you know where Hernando slept?" Tess asked. "I'd like to search his things."

"It was one of the big houses on the other side of the junction," Corrie said.

"You won't have long, Tess," Adams said. "We can't guarantee we've caught or killed all the enemy. I want to be gone before nightfall, when a sniper might come looking for revenge."

The sound of an approaching engine had them turn to look north. The truck was returning, with Zach behind the wheel.

"We'll talk again later, and in more detail," Tess said. "Sorry, it's vital, but it can wait until we're aboard the ship and sailing for home. You should go there now. See the doc."

"I'm fine," Corrie said. "I'll help them move the food. I'd prefer to keep busy, you know?"

Tess nodded, walking back across the courtyard, Captain Adams at her side.

"What's your view of her story?" Adams asked.

"Officially, or personally?" Tess asked.

"Are they different?" Adams asked.

"Officially, the sisters didn't come here. They should have. As this is where their brother was, they surely must have intended to. They didn't, so they're dead. Probably killed trying to find this nephew. Possibly killed by Lisa Kempton. Officially, we will assume they are missing, presumed dead. The lab *could* have been in Colombia. I'll look at Hernando's possessions for clues, but if he was that scared of the sisters, I doubt he'd even dare write it down. If he was just a go-between, he wouldn't have been told. No, considering the resources we have, and the effort in getting here, finding the lab would be next to impossible. So, officially, I'm going to say that the sisters are dead, the cartel's principal supply-stash has been destroyed, and they no longer present a threat."

"And personally?"

"These people are fanatics," Tess said. "I'm certain a few of their agents escaped capture in Australia, but the sisters ran a global empire. Even if they're gone, a new underworld will emerge, headed up by people who think nothing of skinning victims alive. Ideally, I'd take a few days to gather any intel left here by Hernando and Mikael. Specifically, I'd want the address of the mansion in Miami. There we might find other addresses, hopefully in the Pacific. We'd go there, and follow every other lead, building a dossier on any missing terrorists. The first time we found a hint of their activity in home-territory, we'd open the file, and check the photos. I'd run them in the papers. I'd run them on the TV. I'd make a big show of the hunt. Remind people that justice might sometimes be slow, but it's inescapable. Except, sadly, that's impossible."

"For me, it's the Russians and the British," Adams said. "Were those submarines hunting for the sisters? Who sank the flotilla of yachts? What kind of threat will they be in the months to come? Those are the questions I want answered."

"That's it," Tess said. "It's the months to come. But in the years after that, the real danger to our future is radiation. We've not avoided extinction yet, so we must put aside the personal, and take back an official report that'll reassure our citizens."

"We can hope it will prompt any stray gangsters to reform," Adams said.

"The best we can hope for is they'll keep their heads down," Tess said. "But I'll take a look at Hernando's place, anyway. See if he was kind enough to leave us a signed confession."

"Before you do, there's one other issue to settle," Adams said. "The two prisoners. Our options are limited. In fact, realistically, there's only one thing we can do."

"I know," Tess said.

"Excuse me, Captain, Commissioner?" Pete Guinn called. He and Olivia walked over.

"Pete, hi," Tess said. "Everything okay?"

"Kinda," Pete said.

"Not really," Olivia said. "Corrie says you're returning to the Pacific?"

"Via a few fuel stops," Adams said. "We should be back in Perth in two weeks."

"Could you drop us off on the mainland?" Pete asked.

"The mainland? Why?" Tess asked.

"Over to you, Pete," Olivia said.

"Judge Benton sent us to make contact with the Pacific," Pete said. "And we did. So now we've got to go tell her."

"Who's Judge Benton?" Adams asked.

"General Yoon's deputy," Pete said. "She took over the Canadian army after the bombs fell."

"What was left of it," Olivia said.

"Do you know where she is?" Adams asked.

"Not exactly," Pete said.

"But it would be in Canada?" Adams asked. "So closer to the pole than the equator? You want to walk a quarter way around the planet."

"Hopefully we can drive," Pete said.

"You won't make it," Tess said. "Even if you had a specific destination in mind, you probably wouldn't make it. When we left Canberra, we thought we could reach New York. Here we are, about to turn around, and I had a warship and no need to worry about zoms on the open sea."

"I know it's a long shot," Pete said. "That doesn't mean we shouldn't try."

"If you found her, what would you say?" Adams asked.

Olivia folded her arms. "Yeah, Pete, what would you say?"

"Um… head for the Pacific, I guess," Pete said.

"No," Adams said. "It will be a minimum of two weeks before we're back in Perth. At least another week before we, or another ship, could sail north. Two more weeks before we reached the northern coast of northwest America, and we still might get there before you. But *where* should we go? We don't know where's safe, and nor do you. It's spring in the Northern Hemisphere. Anyone who's survived this long will be thinking about planting. By the time you find them, they'll have a crop in the ground, and a secure farm from which to watch it. You can't ask them to give up that to trek west in the hope a ship might be there. And what if there are more people than we can fit on one ship?"

"You see, Pete?" Olivia said. "A rescue is impossible." She turned back to the captain. "But as much as I hate to admit it, Pete's right, we still have to go ashore."

"You do? Why?" Adams asked.

"If not us, who?" Olivia said. "There are people who need help. Maybe we can find a safe route to the Pacific, and somewhere we can keep them safe until a ship comes. Or maybe we find somewhere to wait until you find us. But Pete found Corrie, and they found me. I don't know who is out there who needs finding, but if we don't look, they'll die. It's the right thing to do. The *only* thing."

"A noble sentiment," Adams said. "But I've got to think of my crew, and the people in the Pacific in desperate need of a ship which can carry medical supplies to the millions of refugees."

"Right, exactly," Pete said. "So if you just drop us off on the mainland, and maybe with some gas, we'll drive north."

Tess laughed. "Strewth, mate. Talk about sticking me in a corner. How can I go back to Canberra and announce to the world that I let you three trek off alone? Again! Captain, that icebreaker works. What kind of range does it have?"

"Twenty to thirty thousand kilometres," Adams said.

"Loan it to me," Tess said.

"You'd need a crew," Adams said. "I won't give you one if you intend to go to Canada. Not when we know so many bombs were dropped there."

"Agreed," Tess said. "Puerto Morelos would still be worth investigating. It's too close to here for me to hold out much hope of finding people, or a tanker, but we should still look. Same with Savannah. From there, would we have the range to return to Robben Island?"

"You should, but I'll ask Mr Dickenson to examine the engines and confirm it."

"Or maybe we return to Dégrad des Cannes and go south, and around the Cape," Tess said. "But first, we'll go as far north as we can, and then we'll turn back. All of us. Including you three. Would that satisfy your conscience?"

Pete opened his mouth, but Olivia beat him to it. "Absolutely," she said. "But there is one final favour to ask, Captain."

Epilogue - Do You?
Corn Island

The two cartel-terrorist prisoners had been brought inside the shore-side bar-restaurant. They were seated two metres apart, with their hands cuffed behind their backs, and with three sailors on guard.

"That's Felipe," Corrie said, indicating the thirty-year-old with the broken glasses, receding hairline, and mouse-muscle physique. "He had something to do with import and export before the outbreak. It sounded like accounting work, but only in the U.S. I think Mikael knew him in Miami, but they'd met infrequently. I got the impression Felipe would sometimes come to Mikael's house, but not to meet him."

"Was he meeting Hernando, or the sisters?" Tess asked.

"I'm not sure," Corrie said.

"What do you know about her?" Tess asked.

The other prisoner had been knocked unconscious by an explosion at the western dock. She was in her early twenties with the well-defined musculature of someone who'd devoted time to her physique. The placement of her tattoos suggested some of that time had been in prison. Both sides of her scalp were shaved, revealing the ink beneath. On the right was a death's head. On the left was a single branch from which three roses grew. A cartel tattoo which could be hidden as quickly as it took for the hair to grow out.

"That's L.C.," Corrie said. "Lucia Catalina. She was the one who grabbed us up in America. But I think she came from south of the equator. She didn't like taking orders from Hernando, and really, *really* didn't like Mikael."

"Do either of you want to talk?" Tess asked.

L.C. glared at Tess. Felipe glanced at her, then bowed his head.

"He knows stuff, sure," Corrie said. "But it's all about drugs and import and sales. She knows a bit more about the sisters' plans, but not where they are now. I think she's just muscle. Another assassin."

"So he knows where the bodies are buried, and she knows how they died?"

"Pretty much," Corrie said.

"Do they speak English?"

"Absolutely," Corrie said.

Tess turned around, checking Zach was pointing the camera the right way. This had to be recorded for posterity, and for public broadcast back in Canberra.

"My name is Commissioner Tess Qwong, and I speak with the authority of the Australian Government and the United Nations. You are being charged with war crimes. Specifically, complicity in genocide and the use of a banned chemical weapon, a substance we believe is VX nerve agent." She paused, looking between the two prisoners, watching for any reaction. "And you are being charged with crimes against humanity for your involvement in the development and distribution of the virus which caused the outbreak, and for involvement in orchestrating the nuclear war which followed." Again she paused.

Felipe had hung his head, but L.C. had lifted hers, and was now watching Tess. She appeared calm. Puzzled, perhaps. Amused. But not scared.

"Do either of you have anything you wish to say?" Tess asked. "No? Zach, stop recording. Take the camera outside."

Felipe looked up. L.C. looked across to Felipe, but she still said nothing, nor did Felipe.

"That was your chance," Tess said. "Reflect on that in what little time you have left. Take them away."

Felipe began struggling as the sailors stood him up. L.C. spat at Tess's feet.

As they were led away, Corrie crossed to the bar, leaning against it. "That wasn't as satisfying as I'd hoped for."

"It never is," Tess said.

"I was hoping for some weeping or pleading, or something," Corrie said.

"I hoped for some solid information," Tess said. "I gathered what I could from Hernando's place. But I don't think it will help us, nor would anything those two have to say. The impression I've gathered is that they ran the operations in the Caribbean and the Mexican Gulf, yes?"

"Hernando did. But I don't think even he ran it. He was more of an overseer, or a messenger. He'd take messages from the sisters to the local gang-leaders, and then check in on Mikael, and then go back to the sisters. He was trusted to know their secrets, but not critical to their operation."

"Since he wouldn't have had the answers we want, those two certainly won't," Tess said. She walked over to the bar, looking at the rows of empty shelves. "Times like this call for a drink."

"Champagne is traditional," Corrie said.

"Nicko found a couple of bottles of rum," Tess said. "That will have to do, but it's aboard the ship, and we should be getting aboard ourselves."

Corrie looked at the door through which the two prisoners had left. "It feels so… so unsatisfactory."

"What would you rather we do?" Tess asked. "What alternative is there? Laws have existed for longer than coppers. The concept of justice has been around since the beginning of recorded history. You don't need a badge to do what needs to be done. You don't need a judge to decree what is just."

"Theoretically, I can see how this is the just thing to do," Corrie said. "But it still doesn't feel right."

"Because you *deserve* revenge," Tess said. "You deserve a more specific and personal vengeance from those two than anyone else, but everyone alive today are their victims. Stringing them up won't bring back the dead. It'll only further tarnish our souls. They'll sail back to Australia aboard the *Te Taiki*. There will be a trial. There probably *will* be an execution. But everyone at home deserves justice, too. Whether any trial, with its inevitable verdict, can be called just is a question for the philosophers. For us, if we are trying to build a better world, we can say that we began with mercy, not murder. That's about the only thing that can make your sacrifice, our sacrifices, worthwhile."

But though there would be no execution, the captain had a different, but as equally old-fashioned, duty to perform on the deck of the icebreaker. Six members of the prize-crew formed an honour guard. The others, and the newly promoted Captain Renton, were busy familiarising themselves with the ship's controls and engines before the icebreaker and the *Te Taiki* sailed off in separate directions. Otherwise, of the New Zealand sailors, only Captain Adams and Commander Tusitala were present: the captain to say the words, and the commander to fly her back to the warship at the ceremony's conclusion.

Tess found a place next to Clyde, at the rear of the small crowd, gathered at the aft of the ship. Nicko and Bruce, Avalon and Smilovitz, Zach and Corrie, forming a ring more than the usual two columns, behind the bride and groom.

"For something new to begin, something old must end," Adams said. "So a marriage is not a beginning, but an affirmation of intent. A public acknowledgement to the world, as represented by those here present, of the love and devotion that you both have demonstrated to each other, and pledge to continue demonstrating in the years ahead. It is traditional, now, to talk of the future, of the trials and troubles ahead of you. Of the compromises and concessions you'll have to make. Of the sacrifices. But that tradition is a few months out of date. While each of our futures are uncertain, you two can enjoy the certainty of spending the rest of yours together. So, I'll ask you, Olivia Preston, do you take Pete Guinn—"

"Parsley," Corrie called out. "His real name is Parsley."

"Sis!" Pete said.

"You want to do it properly, don't you?" Corrie said.

"She's right, Pete," Olivia said. "Sorry, Captain."

"No worries," Adams said. "Do you, *Parsley* Guinn, wish you'd legally changed your name before the outbreak?"

"I do," he said.

"Too late now," Adams said. "Olivia Preston, do you take Parsley Guinn for your husband."

"I do."

"And do you, Parsley Guinn, take Olivia Preston for your wife?"

"I do."

"Then I pronounce you both married. Congratulations."

An hour later, Tess was standing in the metal-sided shelter at the ship's stern. It might originally have been built as a bad-weather observatory, but from the yellow nicotine stains on the walls, the previous crew had mostly used it as a smoking room.

"There you are, Commish," Clyde said. "I was looking for you."

"Is there trouble?" Tess asked.

"Not even a hint," Clyde said. He held up a bottle, and two glasses. "But you missed the toast."

"I wanted to see the captain off," Tess said. "She's a link with home."

"We'll be seeing her again in a couple of weeks," Clyde said.

"I said the exact same thing to Anna back in Australia," Tess said. "How is Captain Renton?"

"Getting a feel for his new command," Clyde said. "He's a good bloke, and the colonel will keep an eye on him. Nicko's asleep. Zach's helping Corrie in the galley. The scientists are going through the documents we grabbed from Corn Island. The happy couple are below. The crew are getting familiar with their new home, but I think we've earned a few hours rest." He split the last of the bottle between the two glasses. "What shall we drink to?"

"Happiness," she said. "May it always find us, especially when we're not looking."

"I'll drink to that."

She took a sip. "Not bad. How was the island off for supplies? That bar was practically empty when we arrived."

"They were running low. I got the impression one reason they killed off so many locals was so as not to share the food. We'll need to look for more around Puerto Morelos."

"I don't think this ship was being used to trade fuel," Tess said. "But there's no way the cartel would let a prize like a fuel-transporter remain unclaimed. I think the captain was correct, the fuel's aboard a ship, but it was sailing north, and kept on sailing north. We won't find it off Puerto Morelos."

"Maybe we'll find a helicopter. Bruce wants to try flying one."

"He's got a licence?"

"Not exactly," Clyde said. "But he's done three take-offs and six landings. That's nearly as many as Captain Renton."

"Bruce landed twice more than he took off? Now there's a yarn I want to hear. But finding a helicopter isn't a priority. Not now, anyway."

"You're not sure where we'll end up, then?" Clyde asked.

"How could anyone be?" Tess said.

"Ah, but if you're not certain, then you can get in on the pool. We're taking bets on how far north we'll get before we turn around. Nicko's got Cancun. I've got Savannah, and Zach took Washington, D.C."

"Washington? We're not going that far."

"It's not that far from Georgia," Clyde said. "We might even go a little further, all the way to New York. Captain Renton says it's a theoretical possibility. The scientists showed him a video of some zom they say died just after infection. They've convinced him some samples from that corpse could prove the zoms are dying, and give a timeframe on the rest."

"I doubt it," Tess said. "But then I'm not the captain."

"Renton made it clear he wouldn't go north of New York, and wouldn't attempt Savannah unless we can resupply before then. That's why I placed my bet on us turning around when we reach Savannah."

"How much is riding on this bet?"

"Twenty dollar-bars," Clyde said. "Bruce put his money on the big U.S. navy base."

"Which one?" Tess asked.

"Whichever we reach that hasn't been destroyed," Clyde said. "Because if it's not been destroyed, we're guaranteed to find some survivors there. When we find more than a few survivors, we'll have to turn back to organise a rescue fleet. But he overlooked that the biggest U.S. naval base is in Norfolk, Virginia, and it's not that far from Washington, D.C. Zach might win the bet yet."

"Where do the scientists think we'll get to?" she asked.

"New York," Clyde said. "And if I were allowed to change my bet, that's where I'd switch it to. That's why they're here, isn't it, rather than being on the warship heading back to Oz to work on their weapon?"

"I don't know," Tess said. "They were useful in Colombia, and on Corn Island. Dr Avalon can double up as a ship's medic, and Leo's a decent engineer. But this is where they said they needed to be."

"People like that, you've got to trust they know what they're doing," Clyde said.

"I keep telling myself that," Tess said. "I do hope it's true." She finished her glass. "We're not certain we found all the cartel on that island, but I don't think they had a large ship capable of sinking that flotilla of yachts near French Guiana. If they did, they would have tried sinking us before we reached their island."

"So maybe there's some other group of pirates in these waters," Clyde said. "But don't worry about them. We've got thick armour, and the weapons systems we brought aboard can make any small ship change its mind."

"And if it's a large ship?"

"Large ships don't need to play pirate," Clyde said.

"I hope that's true, too," she said. "Okay, I won't worry about pirates. I'm still worried about the sisters. I'm not convinced they're dead. More importantly, nor do their followers. Look at what happened on Corn Island. Those people followed orders even after they must have thought, even hoped, their bosses were dead."

"I've seen that level of devotion before," Clyde said. "Usually hidden behind a false veneer of religion."

"It's more than that," Tess said. "The sisters organised a trap for Lisa Kempton after the outbreak, and after the bombs fell, and flew a jet plane a quarter-way around the world. With prisoners. They kept those prisoners alive, and healthy, just so their bosses could better enjoy their revenge. These people won't just give up or fade into the crowd."

"We've done all that we can to stop them."

"Have we?" she asked. "Are we? Let's say the sisters' plan was to seize control of the Panama Canal, and trade access for legitimacy to their empire. The sisters also suspected a betrayal from inside their organisation. What if that was why the canal was destroyed? The *Vepr* or the *Adventure*, or someone else, made sure this particular dream of the sisters would never come true. That's why they never came south. What chance would some misguided billionaire have against those kind of people? The reason they didn't come south is that they're building a new empire up north."

"Do you want to go look for them?" Clyde asked.

"Yes. But we don't know where to begin," Tess said. "I'm not being a gloom-monger. I'm thinking of what will happen after we get back to Australia. What people will talk about after my report is published. They will assume the sisters are alive."

"You can't change that," he said.

"We can give them something else to think about," Tess said. "This really will be the last voyage into the Atlantic for a long time. Nothing we've seen gives us a reason to survey the damage to the canal, let alone build the machines needed to repair it. No, this is the last voyage, so we *should* go to New York. We should find that corpse the scientists think died. Forget a weapon. What use would it be in South America or

South Africa? We don't need hope that the worst is over. We don't need proof the sisters are dead. We need the certainty that the zombies will die. We should confirm the Northern Hemisphere is as lost as the evidence suggests. We should return to the Pacific with the news that the zombies are dying, that we are the last bastion of the old civilisation, and that our species' future is entirely in *our* hands."

"If not us, then who?" Clyde said.

"No one," Tess said. "If not us, there is no one else."

To be continued...

Printed in Great Britain
by Amazon

62776934R00220